Bella Fortuna

Bella Fortuna

ROSANNA CHIOFALO

KENSINGTON BOOKS
www.kensingtonbooks.com

KENSINGTON BOOKS are published by

Kensington Publishing Corp.
119 West 40th Street
New York, NY 10018

All Kensington titles, imprints, and distributed lines are available at special quantity discounts for bulk purchases for sales promotion, premiums, fund-raising, educational or institutional use.

Special book excerpts or customized printings can also be created to fit specific needs. For details, write or phone the office of the Kensington Special Sales Manager: Attn. Special Sales Department. Kensington Publishing Corp., 119 West 40th Street, New York, NY 10018. Phone: 1-800-221-2647.

ISBN-13: 978-0-7582-6653-8
ISBN-10: 0-7582-6653-7

First Kensington Trade Paperback Printing: September 2012
10 9 8 7 6 5 4 3 2 1

Printed in the United States of America

For my parents,
Francesca & Giuseppe Chiofalo
I vostri sacrifici non furono vani.

And for my husband,
Ed Aponte
Your love is my *bella fortuna.*

ACKNOWLEDGMENTS

There are so many people to thank for this book becoming a reality. First, I'd like to thank my editor, John Scognamiglio. John, you are not only an editor extraordinaire, but also a dream maker. For you made my childhood dream of becoming a published novelist come true. Thank you for believing in me and in my novel. I'd like to thank Steve Zacharius, President and CEO of Kensington Publishing, and Laurie Parkin, Vice President and Publisher of Kensington Publishing, for not only publishing my novel, but also for all the efforts you have put forth behind a first-time author. The entire team at Kensington Publishing has gone above and beyond, especially Kris Noble, who designed the gorgeous book cover for *Bella Fortuna*. Kris, you captured the very essence and special beauty of Venice perfectly. And a cover would not be a cover without clever copy. Thank you to Tracy Marx, Copy Chief at Kensington Publishing, and especially to Lorraine Freeney, who wrote the beautiful jacket copy on *Bella Fortuna*. For the entire Kensington marketing department, especially Lesleigh Irish-Underwood, Shannon Gray, Michele Santelices Dragon, Katie Chan, Sakina Williams, Alex Nicolajsen, thank you for the outstanding marketing/promotional efforts on my behalf. They will never be forgotten. A special thanks goes to John Masiello, Creative Director of Advertising/Promotion. Thank you for the gorgeous designs you created on my ads and promotional pieces. Thank you to the entire production department, especially my production editor, Paula Reedy, who treated this book as if it were hers by ensuring all of the production on *Bella Fortuna* went smoothly. A book's backbone is without a doubt a strong copyeditor. Thank you to Monique Vescia for copyediting my novel and for being so thorough. I truly valued your suggestions and comments. I'd like to thank the entire publicity department at Kensington, especially Karen Auerbach and my publicist, Vida Engstrand. Vida, your name is synonymous with brilliant. Thank you so much for all of your hard work and for your creative publicity ideas. A very warm thank you to the entire sales team at Kensington, especially David Lappin, Helen Dressner, Doug Mendini, Darla Freeman, and all of the outside sales force. A special shout-out goes to Meryl Earl, Director of Sub Rights, and Jackie Dinas, Foreign Rights Associate: Your enthusiasm for my book and diligent work to secure foreign rights for *Bella Fortuna* were greatly appreciated.

Thank you to my family for your unconditional love and support. As you will see when you read the pages of *Bella Fortuna*, many of the characters are named in honor of you. And for those of you who do not see your names, I promise they'll make an appearance in the second and third novels. To my parents, Francesca and Giuseppe Chiofalo, this book is as much yours as it is mine. If it weren't for my mother and all of the sacrifices she has made in her life, this novel would never have happened. *Ti voglio bene, Ma. Non ti dimenticare mai.* And if it weren't for my father instilling in my siblings and me a love for education, none of us would have received the success we have in our careers. Nothing was more important to my father than receiving a good education. Though sadly, he did not receive the same encouragement in his own academic pursuits that he gave to us, he had the wisdom to know how important education is and to fully bolster our academic careers. *Grazie, Baba.* I'd like to thank my brother Anthony Chiofalo for nurturing my early love of reading by buying books that many considered "too difficult" for a child my age to read. I always proved this theory wrong by not only finishing the lengthy books, but reading them in a record amount of time. To my brother Mike Chiofalo, thank you for introducing me to the power of music and lyrics that have influenced my writing. And thanks for letting me hang out with you in your room when I was a kid just so that I could listen to my favorite Blondie albums over and over again! To my sister, Angela Chiofalo Mansfield, thank you for being a friend in addition to being a big sister. Your friendship and company were two of the things I missed most when I lived in Austin. To my nephews and nieces whom I'm so proud of: Joseph Chiofalo, Nicholas Chiofalo,

Michael Mansfield, Brandon Mansfield, Kyle Mansfield, Olivia Mansfield, Samantha Prosser, Gregory Prosser, Megan Prosser, Melanie Prosser, Brandon Aponte, Colin Aponte, Rebecca Aponte, and Ben Jacquez. To my mother-in-law, Raquel Aponte-Carroll, thank you for all the love, friendship, and support you have given me these past eight years. A woman could not ask for a better mother-in-law. To my father-in-law, Juan Aponte, thank you for your love and for all the laughs you have given me. To Ralph Carroll, my stepfather-in-law, I've taken your advice and words of wisdom to heart. Thank you to all of my sisters-in-law and brothers-in-law, Raquel Aponte, Tania Prosser, Louise Aponte, Susan Cardenas, Juan Aponte, Greg Prosser, and Bill Mansfield.

A special thanks to all of my friends, especially Tiziana D'Angelo, the little sister I never had but had in you; Maria Colletti, who's cheered me on 100 percent; Ingrid Yardeny, whose unwavering friendship has stood the test of time and with whom I've shared so many special memories as we grew up together (You always knew I'd be a writer someday. Thank you for having faith in me.); "Bensonhurst," who's been so loyal to me in the fifteen years we've known each other (You are my brother in addition to my friend, and as you always say to me, "Astoria, we're cut from the same cloth." I'll never forget everything you've done for me and will always cherish our friendship.).

There are a few people who never lost faith in me and my writing—even at times when I'd lost the faith. To the amazing and hugely talented Libba Bray, thank you for always believing in my writing; you've been a huge inspiration to me. To Charlee Ganny, thank you for always reminding me that "We could do it too!" To Paul "Gramps" Dinas, thank you for the words of advice you gave me on writing that took me years to fully grasp, but I eventually did. To my high school writing teacher, Ms. Davies, thank you for setting such high standards in your class and for giving me the courage to pursue creative writing by expressing how much you liked my writing. To my college creative writing teacher, Carolyn McGrath, thank you for believing without a doubt that I would become a published author someday.

And to my husband, Edgardo "Ed" Aponte, thank you for your

insights as I was working on the novel. Thank you for one of the best author websites that's out there, the phenomenal author photo you took, and all of the promotional work you've done for me. Most of all, thank you for being my #1 fan, my best friend, and my soul mate. I couldn't have done this without you. I love you!

❧ 1 ❧

Unlucky 13

I've never considered myself very lucky. Maybe it has something to do with my being born on Friday the 13th and one day shy of Valentine's Day. For a long time, I've been convinced that my birth date is the reason why I've been so cursed in love. And my being named after the patron saint of love, St. Valentine, when I've had nothing but *agita* in romance just makes it more painfully ironic. *Agita* is what Italians call grief of the worst kind. To top it off, my mother is very superstitious and believes in the dreaded *malocchio*, or evil eye, even though it's 2010. *Malocchio* is when someone puts a curse on you. And many Italians are fervent believers in the mighty power of the *malocchio*. But none of that matters anymore since I've finally met "the one."

Thinking about this and how my luck has changed, on this cold Sunday morning, I walk out of church. January in New York City is definitely not one of my favorite months. But as every New Yorker knows, the frigid temps don't stop you. The streets are the quietest on Sunday mornings, my favorite time to be walking through Astoria, the Queens neighborhood where I grew up and still live.

The attendance at the eight a.m. Mass at Immaculate Conception is usually low—too early for most people to get up on the weekend. Even though it's a drag to get myself out of bed, I still go through this weekly ritual. It's meditative for me. It's not often one can go somewhere in New York City without running into a crowd so you have to grab your quiet moments when you can. Sunday mornings are when I can hear myself think best. Even though it's just slightly above the freezing mark, I take my time walking home.

The shops that do open on Sundays are slowly coming to life. Several joggers pass me on their way to Astoria Park. Dogs are trotting along, immune to the nip in the air.

Anyone who knows me will tell you that I love to people-watch, and New York City is a great place to do it. Probably nowhere else in the world will you encounter as many people from different ethnic, socioeconomic, and religious backgrounds—well, except for at an airport!

The aroma of fresh baked bread from the Italian bakeries reaches my nose. Through the windows, I spy a few old men already sitting at the bakeries' tables, sipping their *cappuccinos* and reading *La Corriere della Sera* newspaper. As I step through the doors of Antoniella's Bakery, I spot Paulie Parlatone's S-shaped receding hairline behind his newspaper.

Paulie is known as "the Mayor of 35th Street" or *"Il Sindaco"* for his meddling in everyone's affairs on my block. He has no idea he'd been christened with this nickname, just as he has no idea that he talks too much. The irony isn't lost on everyone that his last name, "Parlatone," means "big talker" in Italian. Paulie will stop you in the street and grill you to the point where you finally surrender and tell him your personal business just so you can end the conversation more quickly.

The worst is when he shows up at your house unannounced. He often comes to my home right after dinner, asks my mother for a toothpick, and makes himself just as comfortable as if he's sitting in his own house. While he talks to us, he picks his teeth with the toothpick. And no matter how well you hide your dirty laundry, nothing gets past Paulie.

I quickly walk by Paulie's table at Antoniella's, praying not to be noticed.

"Valentina!"

I keep walking, pretending I can't hear amid the din in the

crowded bakery. Already there's a line of customers, waiting to get their Sunday Danish, croissants, and *biscotti*. I try to hide behind the Shaquille O'Neal dead ringer who stands in front of me on line. But not even the man's tall figure disguises me. A finger taps me on the shoulder.

"Valentina! Didn't you hear me?"

"Ohhh, Paulie. I'm sorry. I'm a bit preoccupied, and with the noise in here, I guess I didn't hear you." I give him a faint smile.

"Always thinking! That's been you since you were a little girl. Remember the time you almost hit me while you were riding your bike? You were staring right up at the clouds. I had to whistle to get your attention."

Of course I remember that day. It's true, I did like to daydream a lot as a kid. Sometimes, I wish I had hit him—nothing too serious—just enough to shut him up for even a second.

"Well, enjoy your day, Paulie." I return my attention to the pastry display case, pretending I still haven't made up my mind as to what I'm ordering.

Paulie doesn't seem to notice or care.

"So where are you off to?"

"I'm going to the shop."

"You're open today? Sposa Rosa's never been open on a Sunday. Are you losing money?"

I picture myself on my childhood bike, hitting him head on—again and again.

"No, business has actually never been better, especially after the feature *Brides* magazine did on us a few months ago. I have to finish my wedding dress, and with the store being as busy as it is, the only time I get to work on it is late at night or on Sundays."

"Of course! Of course!" Paulie slaps his forehead. "How could I forget? Our little Valentina is finally getting married. You know I was beginning to get a little worried for you."

Oh, how I wish I were on that bike right now—no, make that a car instead.

"Paulie!" I laugh through gritted teeth. "I'm not the only woman in New York to have waited to get engaged until she was in her thirties!"

"I know. I know. But I just couldn't understand why no one had snagged you sooner. You're such a pretty girl with a good head on your shoulders."

Apparently, Paulie's definition of shoulders is different from mine since his eyes rest on my breasts. I forgot to mention that Paulie is also a perv. He rarely misses a chance to ogle a woman's boobs.

"I was just picky. There aren't enough good men out there."

"May I take your order, miss?"

The salesgirl saves me.

"It was nice talking to you, Paulie. 'Bye!"

I place my order for *Palline di Limone biscotti* and even throw in a few assorted mini Danish so I can talk to her longer, hoping Paulie will leave me alone.

" 'Bye, Valentina."

It works! Paulie walks away.

"Hey, Valentina!" He stops, returning to my side.

"Have I told you I can't wait to spin you around the dance floor at your wedding? Oh, wait! You're getting married in Venice. That's too far. I won't be there."

Thank you, God, Mary, and all the blessed saints in heaven! I nod sadly, belying my true thoughts of elation. Then I look down into my purse as I search for my wallet. I know I'm being rude, but I don't care. Paulie has been rude toward my family countless times. He finally leaves the bakery, picking up one of the complimentary toothpicks on the counter.

I breathe a sigh of relief. Choosing to get married in Venice was the best decision I ever made. I put Paulie as far away from my thoughts as possible, and focus on returning to the meditative, blissful state I was in before I ran into him.

After leaving the bakery, I pass Anthony's Salumeria. My mouth waters as I spot Anthony slicing *prosciutto*—my favorite Italian cold cut. Unable to resist, I walk into the deli and order half a pound of the salty meat along with a block of sharp provolone.

"Good morning, Valentina!"

"Hi, Anthony! How are you?"

"Can't complain. I'll be out of here by noon. The Giants are playing so I've got that to look forward to."

Anthony always gives me the first slice of meat to sample even though I know he carries nothing but the freshest products.

"Hmmm! Still the best!"

Anthony smiles. Sometimes, I think he goes through this ritual more for his own sake than mine. He just can't resist hearing his cold cuts praised.

Although I am used to the sights and sounds of the neighborhood that has been my home since I was a child, they seem more vibrant today. The bread at Antoniella's Bakery smells particularly heavenly. The froth threatening to spill over from the patrons' *cappuccinos* looks thicker, and the *prosciutto* at Anthony's is the sweetest ever. Even my three-carat emerald-cut diamond engagement ring sparkles brighter today.

Yes, it's the start of a new year, and finally I feel like this is going to be my year. After designing and sewing wedding dresses for other lucky brides-to-be for so long, it will now be my turn to shine in the spotlight. In just five months, on June 14th to be precise, I'll be marrying Michael Carello in my favorite city in the world— Venice.

I had secretly admired Michael since I was ten years old. Michael was thirteen, but even though he was three years older than me, he always said hi and tried to make me laugh. Popular at school and in our neighborhood, Michael and his family lived around the block from me, so I often saw him playing football or hockey with his friends on my street.

He has blond hair and blue eyes, defying the dark southern Italian stereotype. He takes after his mother. Iva Carello is beautiful even now that she's in her late fifties and is often told she resembles the deceased Princess Grace of Monaco in her twilight years. His father, Joseph Carello, also poses a striking figure, with intense black eyes and a full head of hair at sixty. He always wears a suit, and on his days off from work, he still wears trousers with a button-down shirt, minus the tie and jacket.

Michael has definitely inherited his parents' sense of style. Even as a kid when he wore jeans or got dirty playing sports, he always looked good. It's hard not to notice Michael. But what really branded my devotion to him was when he had come to my defense at Li's Grocery Store when I was a kid.

I passed Li's Grocery Store every day on my way to school. My mother sometimes bought a few groceries there. It wasn't a real supermarket in the sense that you could get your week's worth of shopping. Mr. Li, a Taiwanese immigrant, owned the store and never had a smile for his patrons. Maybe that, along with its limited stock, was why hardly anyone frequented the store. But Li's did have an aisle full of cool school supplies like pretty binders with flower or fairy patterns, spiral notebooks with sparkly glitter covers, Hello Kitty pencil cases, and my favorite—Strawberry Shortcake erasers that smelled like strawberries, of course.

Every afternoon when I walked home from school for lunch, I would stop by Mr. Li's to eye the stationery I couldn't afford. I always politely greeted Mr. Li, who acknowledged me even if it was just a stern "Hello." So I was shocked when one day he yelled at me as I was leaving the store.

"You! Yes, I talk to you. What you have in pocket?"

I froze as if he had a gun cocked right at my head.

"I say what in pocket? Take hand out."

I took my hands out of my powder-blue, faux-fur-trimmed coat, holding my palms up to show him they were empty as I whispered, "Nothing."

"You come every day. No buy anyteeng. Why?"

"I was just looking."

My heart was beating as fast as my cat Gigi's after my mother had thrown her heavy clog at him for stealing food off our table when we weren't looking.

"Hey! Leave her alone! She didn't take anything!"

I hadn't even seen Michael and his best friend, Sal, standing at the register. Utter humiliation washed over me as my face flushed, resembling the color of the half-rotten pomegranates that lay in the boxes at the front of the store.

"She here every day. Hide in back. Teenk I no see. I no idi-uht. She never buy anyteeng. She steal."

"I know her. She would never steal a penny. It's a free country. She can come in here and look without buying anything. Just because she doesn't buy your crummy stuff doesn't mean she's stealing."

Mr. Li frowned and glanced at me again. I lowered my eyes to the floor.

"It's okay, Valentina. Come on, let's get out of here."

Michael placed his arm around my shoulders, leading me out. I could feel Mr. Li's gaze burning a hole through the back of my head as if he was trying to read my mind, still questioning if I'd somehow stolen something and had cleverly hidden it.

Once outside, Michael turned to Sal. "Give us a minute. I'll catch up with you in a second." Sal nodded his head and walked toward school.

Michael removed his arm from my shoulder and bent his head lower so his eyes met mine. I stared at the ground, wishing I could shrink to the size of the ants that were crawling around the broken pieces of bread that someone had thrown to the pigeons.

"Are you okay?"

I nodded my head. "Thanks," I managed to mutter in a tiny voice.

Michael patted my arm. "Don't feel bad. You hear me? You didn't do anything wrong. You're a good girl, Valentina. Mr. Li's a stingy jerk. He once wouldn't let an old lady who was short a quarter walk out of there with a loaf of bread. I gave him the quarter. What a creep."

I just nodded my head again and continued to look down at the cracks in the sidewalk.

"Well, I gotta get back to school. My lunch break is almost over. But if you want, I'll walk you home."

I shook my head. "No. That's okay. Thank you."

"Don't sweat it!"

I turned and began walking home.

"Hey, Valentina!"

I stopped and looked over my shoulder, still not meeting Michael's worried gaze.

"If anyone ever treats you like that again, just tell me. I'll take care of them for you."

I finally managed to smile at him. He winked at me and then turned around, running to catch up with Sal.

That wink was all it took to make me fall completely in love with Michael. After that day, every time I saw Michael he always winked at me after he said hello. It was as if he knew its power. For with that one wink, I felt myself soar high above the sky, dancing in midair with the birds. Now my childhood fantasies of wedding my prince someday were replaced with dreams of marrying Michael.

And that was how my crush on Michael began. But I had to watch helplessly over the years as he dated one girl after another. When I turned fourteen and puberty finally decided to pay me a visit, filling in my flat chest and narrow hips, Michael still seemed to look at me as if I were that ten-year-old kid whom he'd rescued. I'd noticed his friends staring at me a few times when they thought I wasn't looking, but not Michael. Unlike his friends, his gaze always met mine rather than my boobs, which were already a C-cup at that point. But something had changed in how he treated me. He no longer winked at me after he said hello. In fact, he didn't even try to make me laugh, as he'd loved to do when I was younger. I didn't get it.

So I started dating, having one miserable relationship after another or not having a boyfriend when important occasions arose like a friend's Sweet Sixteen party or my sophomore-year dance. My best friend, Aldo, had gone with me to the dance. I could always count on Aldo when I needed a date. So I'd put on my best poker face and pretended I was having a blast with him when all I could think about was, *Why can't I have a boyfriend for longer than two months? Why can't I have a boyfriend here with me instead of my best friend?*

Of course, Michael still wound his way into my thoughts, but not as much since he'd left for Cornell University. I only saw him when he came home for breaks. I was beginning to accept the fact that he'd never have any interest in me as anything more than a childhood friend. I was the little sister he never had, nothing more. Yet from time to time, my mind still wandered to him, wondering what he was doing.

"Swaying room as the music starts . . . strangers making the most of the dark."

Madonna's "Crazy for You" was playing. I loved this song. I felt a hand on my shoulder and turned around.

"Wanna dance?"

Michael!

"Hey! What are you doing here?"

"I heard the music from outside. I couldn't resist coming in and catching up with some old friends and teachers."

"They let you in?"

"Of course! Why not?" He winked at me.

Oh my God! He hadn't winked at me in years. It still had the same bone-melting effect on me.

"Come on. Let's dance." Michael took my hand, leading me to the dance floor. My heart was racing so fast, I was convinced he could see it. He pulled me close to him as we slowly danced to the music. He rested his chin on my shoulder. I swallowed hard. I should probably make some conversation. But all I wanted to do was close my eyes and listen to the words of Madonna's "Crazy for You."

"Isn't this such a great song?" Michael pulled his head back and looked into my eyes, smiling.

"You like this song, too?" I asked incredulously.

"Yeah, it's one of my all-time eighties favorites, right up there with The Cure's 'Just Like Heaven.' "

"Oh my God! I *love* that song!"

"No way!"

"Yeah, *way!*"

We laughed together. He put his chin back on my shoulder.

Again, my insecurities were telling me I should make more of an attempt at conversation. Why couldn't I just relax and enjoy this moment? It would probably never happen again.

"So how's Cornell?" I managed to get out.

"Stuffy and dull!"

"Oh, come on! I can't believe it's all that dull! I can only imagine all the fun you must be having at those parties and all those interesting classes. I can't wait to go away to college."

"Really?"

"What's so surprising about that? You think I want to stay in Astoria and commute to school? Get real!"

"I don't know. I just thought you'd be like the other Italian girls in the neighborhood and stick close to home. Besides, will your parents let you go away for college?"

"Probably not, but I don't care. I'm going to do it anyway!"

Michael laughed. "You've got spunk! I like that. You *are* different from a lot of the girls around the neighborhood. Promise me you'll stay that way." Michael pulled his face away and stared into my eyes again, waiting for my promise.

I shrugged my shoulders.

"Promise me!"

His face came closer to mine. My heart started pounding again.

"Okay." I blushed and looked away. He was staring at me in the most peculiar way.

"Good!" He winked at me again and pulled me close to him. I could smell his cologne. Drakkar Noir. Every guy wore Drakkar Noir back then. It just occurred to me that Michael wasn't dressed for a dance. After all, he wasn't planning on coming. I didn't care. He was the sexiest guy here tonight. His dark-wash denim jeans and black V-neck sweater made him look like one of those male models I'd seen on the covers of *Maxim* magazine or *GQ*.

"So you like The Cure, huh?"

"Yeah, they're one of my favorite eighties bands."

"I might be able to score some tickets to one of their concerts at the Meadowlands this summer. Would you be interested?"

I looked up into Michael's eyes.

"You know. For you and a friend."

"Oh. Sure. That would be nice." Just as soon as my hopes had soared, they immediately took a nosedive.

The song was over. We looked at each other a bit uncertainly.

"Thanks for the dance," I said.

"Hey! No sweat. I'll let you know about the tickets when I'm back in town for the summer. They're supposed to go on sale next Monday, but there's someone at school who scalps them. He said he'd hook me up."

"Okay. Sounds good. Thanks."

"I'll catch you later. I want to say hi to Mr. C."

"Sure. Go ahead." Boy, I sounded lame! Like he needed my permission to leave.

Michael smiled and looked at me as if he wanted to say something else. Then he walked away.

I made my way to the refreshments table and asked for a Coke. My mouth felt so dry, and my hands still felt shaky. Part of me was elated that Michael had asked me to dance, but another part was disappointed, too. For a second, I thought he was going to ask me to go to The Cure concert with him.

"Hey, Vee! You guys looked amazing! Give me all the juicy details!"

"There are no details to give, Aldo."

I crossed my arms and searched the room for Michael. Mr. C., the American History teacher at St. John's Prep, was talking to Ms. Vicelli, my English Literature teacher. It looked like Mr. C. was flirting with her, touching her shoulder regularly as he talked animatedly with his hands. He must be bragging about something. Mr. C. often told the most outlandish stories from his days when he was young, as he liked to put it. I couldn't help feeling he had chosen the wrong career path. He loved attention and should've gone into politics or acting. Ms. Vicelli was pretty with light golden brown hair and highlights that framed just her front bangs. It seemed like every male teacher at St. John's Prep was in love with her. She was one of the nicest teachers at school.

Michael approached them and shook Mr. C.'s hand. Ms. Vicelli gave him a hug. Suddenly, I felt jealous. I knew it was crazy to be jealous of Ms. Vicelli. She was, what? A dozen years older than Michael? But still. I wanted it to be me hugging him, *not* her.

Aldo broke in on my thoughts.

"I saw the way Michael was holding you while you guys danced. And the look on his face! He has the hots for you big-time! Trust your big bro Aldo. He always knows best."

"Well, you couldn't be farther from the truth."

"Aldo's eyes and instincts have never failed him!"

"Okay, I admit. I thought I was getting a few vibes from him, especially a couple of times when he looked at me extra long."

"I knew it!"

"Control yourself! There's nothing to it. We talked a little about music, and he's also an eighties music nut like we are."

"This is getting better and better. And the man has good taste!" I wanted to smack Aldo.

"Well, he told me he might be able to get tickets for The Cure this summer. He asked me if I was interested."

"Ahhhhh!!!!" Aldo grabbed my shoulders and shook me back and forth. A few people standing near us looked at him and frowned.

"He then added, 'For you and a friend.'"

"Oh my God! You *have* to take me! You *have* to take me! I'll never talk to you again if you don't." Aldo jumped up and down. Then he suddenly stopped.

"Wait. This is *not* good. I'm so sorry."

"I was beginning to wonder how long it would take for your brain to register what I said."

"Oh, Vee! I'm so sorry. I'm such an idiot. Here you are thinking Michael is finally going to ask you out on a date, only to have him say he'll get you a pair of tickets to go with someone else, and I'm thinking about myself."

"It's okay. I know how much you love Robert Smith. If it were someone else, I wouldn't have forgiven you." I smiled, letting Aldo know we were good.

"Vee, I think it's the jail-bait thing. I really do. He's just waiting for you to turn eighteen, and once you do, he's going to ask you out. I'm sure of it."

Michael was now eighteen years old compared to my fifteen, hence, the jail-bait issue.

"I wish I could share your optimism, Aldo. But I'm too realistic. You're also forgetting that he was dating Danielle Santucci in the fall. She's just seventeen."

"But you're different. He respects you. Danielle has no class. Everyone knows she lost her virginity when she was in sixth grade, for crying out loud."

"You don't know if that's true. It's just a rumor! And I can't see Michael dating someone who would have a rep like that."

"I'm sure he heard about it and that's *exactly* why he dated her."

"He's not like that, Aldo."

"Excuse me, Miss DeLuca. Does Michael have a penis?"

I shook my head.

"No, he doesn't? You are holding out on me. How long have you been sleeping with him?"

"That's not why I'm shaking my head, and you know it."

I couldn't help laughing at what he'd said.

"Aldo, stop being so sarcastic all the time! You know the closest I've ever gotten to him is this dance we shared tonight."

"But you do agree that he is a man?"

"This is stupid, Aldo."

"Just humor me, for once, please!"

"I'm always humoring you. I know where you're going with this. Just because he's a man doesn't mean he thinks like every other man out there."

"Vee, you're being naive. I know Michael is a nice guy, but a guy nonetheless. Men can't turn off their sexual needs as easily as women can."

"Hey, watch it! That sounds sexist. I thought you were on our side anyway!"

"Of course, I'm always on the woman's side. But as you like to say, 'I'm being realistic.'" Aldo smirked. "I just think you're placing Michael on this high pedestal that no human—man or woman—could ever live up to. He's going to fall off it if you expect so much from him and keep thinking he's perfect."

"I know he's not perfect."

"Right." Aldo grabbed a lemon from the cups that were on the refreshment table next to the iced tea. He sucked on the lemon wedge, scrunching up his face. Aldo loved lemons and ate them all the time. One concoction he was especially fond of was cutting a lemon into wedges and then sprinkling lots of salt, olive oil, and vinegar over them.

"Oh, the rush this gives me!" he'd say with a scrunched-up face, reveling in the salty and sour taste of the wedges.

It was a Sicilian dish that I'd seen my mother prepare many times. But after trying it once as a kid, I rinsed my mouth out under the kitchen faucet for almost half an hour to rid myself of the sour taste.

"Enough about Michael." I wanted to change the subject and fast.

"All I was trying to say, Vee, is that he respects you, and that's probably why he won't date you now while you're jail bait. I've seen the way he looks at you, and not just tonight. He's been looking at you that way ever since your curves paid you a visit."

"Well, I've never seen him look at me below my eyes."

"Of course not. He's too smart. He's not like those blockheads he hangs out with who make it so obvious. Geez! You'd think they were starving or something. I've caught him looking at you when your back was turned, and he thought no one was looking. But I see everything! That's my job. I'm your spy."

I laughed. "Aldo, you're too much!"

"I'm just looking out for my girl."

"And I love you for it!" I hugged Aldo. "I see what you're trying to do. But you don't have to make me feel better."

"Are you implying that I'm lying? You know I'd never do that to you."

"No, I'm not saying that. But maybe, like me, you're seeing something you want to see or hope to see because you care about me so much. That's all."

"Look, Vee. I would tell you if I thought you were wasting your time chasing this particular tail."

I couldn't help laughing silently. No matter how many times I'd told Aldo that "chasing tail" was what one said when referring to girls, he still insisted on using it for girls who chased guys or even guys who chased guys. Aldo had come out of the closet to his family last year. And just as I confided in him about Michael, he told me about his crushes and whose "tail" he was chasing at the moment.

"I would totally tell you to look for other 'tail' if I thought Michael wasn't attracted to you. And I'm glad you haven't been sitting around, waiting for when he's ready to ask you out. I can't stand anything more than girls who are loyal to guys who they just have crushes on. They're not boyfriend/girlfriend, for crying out loud! It's insane! Anyway, I really do think there's more to it with Michael."

"We'll see. I'm not holding my breath. I'm not even holding my breath that he'll remember to get me those Cure tickets."

"So, who are you going to take if he does give you two tickets?"

"Ohhhh, I don't know. I owe my little sister Connie a favor, and she still hasn't even been to a concert. This would be a treat for her."

Aldo was looking down at the floor. "Oh, sure. I bet."

I kicked his combat boots. He insisted on wearing nothing but his combats even when he attended formal occasions like this dance or a wedding. At least, he had worn a suit with a super-thin tie, harking back to his favorite era of music, the eighties, and the New Wave bands who had made the look popular. He slicked back his dark brown, shoulder-length hair. Except for his piercing black eyes, he could've passed for U2's Bono from their *Joshua Tree* album days.

"You know I wouldn't dream of taking anyone else to the concert! Why are you even playing this stupid game?"

"Yes! You're the best! I knew you wouldn't let me down! Oh my God! We're going to see The Cure! The Cure!" He grabbed my hands and twirled me around.

I was excited about the possibility of seeing The Cure in concert, too. But I would've been more thrilled if Michael had asked me to go with him. I looked toward where he'd been standing earlier with Mr. C. and Ms. Vicelli, but Michael was no longer talking to them. I searched the room, but couldn't spot him. Maybe he'd left. I felt my heart sink a little that I wouldn't see him again. I was secretly hoping he'd ask me for a second dance.

Aldo and I hopped into a cab after the dance was over. I lived within walking distance of school, but Aldo lived on Upper Ditmars Boulevard and was too tired to walk all the way back home.

The cab let me out at the corner of my street instead of making the turn, saving Aldo some money in cab fare.

" 'Bye, Vee! I'll call you in the morning for brunch."

"Forget it, Aldo! It's almost midnight. I'm not waking up before noon!"

"That's why it's called brunch! Noon is actually early. Later!"

"Whatever!" I stuck my tongue out at him. He stuck his out, too. We both laughed. Aldo waved one last time and rolled up the window as the cab pulled away.

Aldo had a way of making me feel good when I needed it. I knew I hadn't fooled him tonight with my act, and he'd sensed I was blue.

Although my neighborhood was extremely safe and you always saw people walking late at night on Ditmars, I still decided to walk fast in my three-inch pumps. My feet were absolutely throbbing from all the dancing Aldo and I had done. I stopped suddenly. A couple was leaning against the wall of a driveway, making out. I tip-toed past them, trying to get closer while stealing a glance. The light from the street lamp shone on the girl's backside. She was leaning into the boy, whose back was up against the wall. They were kissing. The girl was wearing a super-tight mango-colored cocktail dress, which was bunched up around her waist. The boy's hands were running up and down the back of her exposed thighs. There was something familiar about that dress. I looked away and kept walking when it hit me where I'd seen that dress. Tracy was wearing it at the dance! How could I forget? Every guy's head was spinning in her direction. Her dress pushed her cleavage way out of its bodice, and every curve in her butt showed. I was afraid the seam on the back was going to burst open.

Though Tracy Santana was my best friend since grade school, we were very different. Unlike me, school didn't come easily for Tracy. She tried very hard and studied, but the best grade her efforts produced was a C. Her mother hit her with a belt when she brought home poor grades. She often showed me and our other friends the pink welts that stood out on her paper-white skin. Her super-straight, thick hair was jet black and hung down to her hips.

Tracy's mother was always on her case about cutting her hair short, whereas my mother encouraged me to keep mine long.

With her very fair complexion and raven-colored hair, Tracy reminded me of Snow White. But instead of having an evil stepmother, Tracy's own mother was the witch. My parents, on the other hand, never laid a hand on me. Sometimes, I felt as if Tracy envied me for my good grades and for having parents who didn't punish me with a belt.

We became best friends when we were in first grade. After that, we spoke every night on the phone, sometimes for as long as two hours. She only called me after her mother left for her night job and after Tracy had prepared dinner for her father and brother. I cringed when I called her house and her mother answered.

Now that we were in high school, the differences only seemed to be growing between us. She had no problem showing off her figure to the point where she might as well have been walking around in her underwear. I didn't mind looking sexy, but I also believed in the old adage, "Leave something to the imagination."

Tracy wasn't as afraid of her mother anymore and seemed to rebel more with each passing day. She flirted heavily with the boys, whereas my shyness prevented me from even talking to the boys unless they approached me first. Tracy was a size zero and wore a super-padded bra to amplify her A-cup breasts. Her green eyes, which stood out in stark contrast to her dark hair, were her best feature. And Tracy used them to full advantage when talking to boys, squinting her gaze to give herself an extra sexy allure. I'd seen the less-confident boys quickly look away when she stared at them, but the more cocky guys stared back, looking completely mesmerized.

Tracy was more outgoing than I was. Her good sense of humor attracted everyone to her, but her lies always caught up with her and would eventually alienate all the friends she'd made. Throughout grade school, she often lied to mutual friends of ours and told them I'd said things about them when I hadn't. I always forgave her. I don't know why, I just did.

A stray cat darted into my line of vision, bringing me back to the present. Who was Tracy kissing? Amazingly, she didn't have a boyfriend at the moment either. It seemed that she went from guy to guy within a day after one relationship ended. It was as if the boys were on a waiting list to date her. Tracy's last boyfriend had broken up with her just three days before the dance. But this time, she bravely chose to go alone. You wouldn't have known it, though, since she'd managed to find a guy to dance with her to almost every song.

My curiosity was getting the better of me. I knew I shouldn't be snooping, but I had to see who was with her. I quietly walked up the front steps of the house whose driveway they were in. I crouched down behind a rosebush, hoping it would be enough to conceal me. Suddenly, the guy spun Tracy around so that her back was now up against the driveway's wall. The light shone on his profile.

Michael!

My hand flew to my mouth as I gasped. Luckily for me, they were too caught up in themselves to have heard me. No! Not *my* Michael. It was dark. I must not be seeing right. I stood up higher to get a better look. It was definitely Michael. He removed his mouth from Tracy's and began kissing her neck. At this point, I was standing to my full height, forgetting that I wasn't concealed anymore. I just kept staring at Michael. Aldo was right! He was acting just like every other guy would. I felt so stupid. Tears stung my eyes as they spilled down onto my face. I finally glanced over at Tracy, and my heart stopped. Her eyes met mine dead-on. Her lips turned up into the most wicked smile. She then lowered her head and kissed Michael. Her eyes shot open again while she was kissing him, staring right at me. I turned my head away and ran down the steps, not caring if Michael heard me. If he did, he didn't care, since I didn't hear my name and no one was chasing me.

How could she? She knew how I felt about Michael. Besides Aldo, she was the only other person I'd confided in about my crush on Michael. She'd listened to me tell her how I hoped, some day in the future, we'd end up together. She had sympathized with me and even told me, "Don't worry, Vee. He'll be yours someday. He just needs to sow his wild oats before he comes to you."

Apparently, she was helping him sow those oats.

I ran as fast as I could down the block to my house. All I could think of was Tracy's twisted little smile as she stared at me. She looked happy that I'd caught them. She didn't care that she'd just stuck a knife right into my heart. I could feel the pain pressing against my chest. I couldn't stop crying. Why would my best friend do this to me? How *could* she?

I got to my house. My mother was probably waiting up for me. I searched frantically in my purse for a tissue. Not finding one, I wiped my eyes with the back of my hands. I unlocked the door. There was a box of tissues on the foyer table. Pulling a few out, I patted my eyes. My reflection stared back at me in the hallway mirror. Pools of mascara swirled around my red eyes.

"Valentina! *Tu sei?*"

"*Si*, Ma."

I ran into the bathroom down the hall, just as my mother entered the hallway.

"*Sta bene?*"

Behind the bathroom door, the tears started racing down my face again. I knew if I answered right away, she'd hear the sobs.

"Valentina? You okay?"

I flushed the toilet, trying to buy some more time. I quickly swallowed and turned on the sink.

"Yeah, Ma. I'm okay. Just had to use the bathroom really bad."

"You have a good time?"

Ugghhhh!!! No matter how many times I told my mother I couldn't hear her well while I was in the bathroom with the water running, she always continued to have a conversation with me.

"Yeah, it was nice. I'll tell you about it in the morning. I'm going to get ready for bed. I'm really tired. Did Baba go to sleep already?"

"*Si, si*. He knew you were in good hands with Aldo. I did, too, but you know me. I still worry when one of you girls is out late. Ahhh! *Va bene. Buona notte, fighita!*"

Fighita had been my mother's endearment for me since I was a kid. It meant "dear one" or "sweet one." I started crying even more.

I washed my face with cold water. Making sure my mother really had gone up to bed, I listened behind the bathroom door. Deathly still. I cracked the door open an inch. Only the nightlight was on near the stairs leading to our bedrooms. I took the stairs two at a time, which was hard to do in my snug dress, though not as snug as that tramp's who was kissing the love of my life. As I passed my parents' bedroom, light streamed from underneath their door. I could hear Ma's low whispers as she prayed. Pausing for a moment behind her door, I tried to hear what she was praying about but was unable to. I began to raise my hand to knock but dropped my hand back to my side and tiptoed to my room. No matter how much I wanted her to help me feel better, I just couldn't bear to see the hurt in her eyes when she'd see how pained I was. Besides, she didn't know about my feelings for Michael.

I took off my dress. When I had put it on earlier in the night, I was so proud of it. My mother had made it for me. It was a deep emerald green with black tulle and lace trim throughout the dress. It had a square neckline with a V-cut in the center, giving a tiny peek to my cleavage. I had worn one of my minimizer bras out of fear of showing off too much cleavage.

When my sister Rita saw me, she said, "What a shame to hide those magnificent tits!" I scowled at her. You'd think she was years older than me and more experienced, the way she talked.

Before taking off my dress, I stared at myself in the full-length mirror that hung on my closet door and remembered how earlier in the night I'd wished that somehow Michael could've seen me in it. My wish was granted when he showed up at the dance. But my hopes that the sight of me in this dress was all it would take to convince him I wasn't a little girl anymore were crushed—first with his mention of getting the concert tickets for a friend and me, and then seeing him making out with my girlfriend, who was quickly becoming the town tramp.

I threw the dress onto the floor. Stupid! How stupid could I have been? Aldo had nailed it exactly when he said that I saw Michael as this perfect guy and above the lousy frat-boy behavior his peers often exhibited. What did I know about him anyway? Not much. I was basing my knowledge of Michael's worth just from that day he'd saved me at Li's Grocery Store. I was still that same kid looking up to her idol, who could do no wrong in her eyes.

I sank into bed with a heavy weariness. Pulling the sheets close to my chin, I promised myself that night I would forget Michael Carello once and for all. But keeping that promise would prove to be much more difficult than I ever could've imagined. For over the summer, my world was about to shatter. And Michael would prove to be my knight in shining armor once again.

The snow that is now falling shakes me back to the present. I fight back the memories from that summer and take a deep breath of cold air, letting it cleanse my lungs and spirits. I quicken my steps along Ditmars Boulevard.

New York City is having a record amount of snowfall this winter. We've had three major snowstorms already, and it's only mid-January. February often packs the biggest wallop of the season where the cold and snow are involved.

The pink sign of Sposa Rosa soon comes into view as I round the corner of Ditmars and 38th Street. I can still feel that thorn pricking my side whenever I look at the shop's name. Leave it to my mother to choose "pink bride" as the name of the bridal boutique that she'd opened ten years ago. I still remember the battle I had with my mother as if it were yesterday.

"But, Ma, hardly any bride wears pink unless you've been married five times, and even then some people still prefer to wear white!"

"*Basta,* Valentina! The name is going to be Sposa Rosa, and that's that. It's memorable. It rhymes. And it's different. When I die, you can call it "Always White" or some other unoriginal, boring name. But right now this is Olivia DeLuca's shop, so the name stays. *Finito!*"

My sisters Rita and Connie giggled in the background. They knew Ma was teasing my traditional tastes. When we were kids, Rita had nicknamed me "Plain Jane." I guess I couldn't blame her. I ate my pancakes without maple syrup and my hot dogs and burgers without ketchup or mustard. I liked more classic styles when it came to my clothes. But that didn't mean I always chose to be conservative. My mother and sisters were in for a shock later today when I would unveil my wedding dress to them.

Sposa Rosa was famous for copying couture designer dresses but offering the dresses at a significantly reduced rate. As I was telling Paulie Parlatone, *Brides* magazine recently did a story on our—I mean, Ma's boutique. Although the shop was in Ma's name, we all thought of it as ours, and we knew it would be our mother's legacy to us after she died. Anyway, the article in *Brides* mentioned the store's custom of featuring a different couture designer dress every month. *Brides* had also paid us the highest compliment by stating, "Attention to detail is flawless, and the dresses are made so well that even the designer might not be able to tell which is the original and which is the knockoff."

Ever since the article was published, more customers were swinging through Sposa Rosa's doors. We were all thrilled even though we were exhausted by the time Sunday rolled around.

With fewer than six months to go until my wedding, I'd been fretting over completing my dress. After all, everyone knows the dress is the most important detail of the wedding. With the shop being so busy, it was hard to devote more time to my dress and overall wedding planning. My family helped any way they could, but I admit it, I was guilty of wanting to micromanage my wedding.

I'll also be the first to acknowledge that I can be guilty of a few Bridezilla moments, but my temper tantrums have been mild compared to some of Sposa Rosa's clients. From witnessing so many monsters, I made a promise to myself a long time ago that I would never resort to being one when it was my turn to get married. It's been annoying having to put Sposa Rosa's clients' dresses before my own, especially when it's for a Bridezilla. But this is my career and passion; it comes with the territory. Whenever I remember how lucky I am to have the skills to be able to design and sew my own wedding dress—the dress of my dreams that no one else will have—my frustration lifts. And today, I would finally have my first fitting!

I decided to model my wedding dress after one of our featured dresses of the month from last spring. It was an Amy Michelson design that sported a lace bodice and halter neckline. One of my favorite features of the dress was its plunging back. A champagne-colored sash wrapped around the waist and tied into a loose bow just above my derriere. But I put my own mark on the gown by adding pearl beads to the lace-covered bodice. Another twist was the detachable organza skirt that gave the appearance of a full ball gown skirt, but once removed, the dress was transformed into a body-hugging, sexy sheath with a daring shorter hem that fell just below the knee. The shorter front hem of the dress was visible even when the detachable organza skirt was attached to the gown. But no one would be able to detect there were two separate pieces. The skirt of the dress was bare and did not feature any of the lace or beading that was on the bodice.

The suspense of showing the dress to my mother and sisters was giving me heart palpitations. I just couldn't wait to see their faces. They knew I had chosen the Amy Michelson design, but they had no idea I'd altered it. Although beautiful in its original, more simple design, the Amy Michelson dress was now a bold gown that screamed, "Look at me!" I didn't want a dress that so many others would have. I wanted my own unique dress.

The thought of the dress makes me even more anxious to get to the shop. Arriving finally at Sposa Rosa, I unlock the doors and turn on the lights. Even after being in business for ten years, I am still in awe every time I walk in. Ask any girl, and she'll tell you there's something magical about a bridal boutique. It all starts with the glittering, beautiful dresses in the storefront window, which catch your eye and lure you to step inside. Then there's the excitement in the air when customers are trying on their dresses, and teary-eyed family and friends are looking at the bride-to-be as if she's the Madonna. Okay, I know that's a stretch for our times, but you know what I mean.

The marble floors, imported straight from Italy, shine immaculately. My mother mops them every night before we lock the store. The walls are shades of celestial blue and creamy eggshell. Sketches of our bridal designs hang on the walls, along with black-and-white photographs of brides, some of whom have bought their dresses over the years at Sposa Rosa.

My youngest sister, Connie, always makes sure to light scented candles when she arrives in the morning. "Ambience is key to selling," is one of her favorite quotes. Connie is a New Age guru. She does yoga every morning at the crack of dawn, meditates before she goes to bed every night, and has recently become vegetarian—a fact that drives Ma absolutely insane since she can't understand how anyone would give up her *ragù*, *bracciole* on skewers, or her famous sausage and peppers.

Connie had fought with us over adding bubbling fountains with rocks. But she was right. Several clients commented how much they liked them and how they added to the Zen-like atmosphere of the shop. Connie had downloaded her favorite New Age tunes onto a CD to play at Sposa Rosa. Of course, the irony didn't escape any of us that we were aiming for serenity in a place that was fraught with loads of tension!

My job can be very rewarding, especially when I see the light flash in a customer's eyes that this dress is "the one." Almost always, the girls look to me as if to say, "How did you know?" Of course, it makes me feel special. And we're all good at being able to tell which is the right dress for most of our clients. My mother and sisters have begun recently taking bets on how long it'll take them to find the dress that the brides will say is "the one." Of course, my mother with her seasoned skills beats us all. But last week, one of my clients chose the first design I'd sketched. She didn't even want to look at the samples of dresses we'd created for other brides in the past or our portfolio. She wanted a custom dress that did not look like any of the other designers' dresses that were currently on the market. A bride being satisfied with the first sketch we design *never* happens!

My mother was miffed about it. I'm sure she was scared I would usurp her place. Connie comes third at finding the right gown for clients. Rita takes being last in stride, saying, "What's important is that I find the right dress for our client even if it takes a little longer. After all, we don't want them walking out of here without leaving a deposit."

Making my way to the back of the store, I place my cold cuts in the refrigerator we keep in the kitchen where we take our lunches and breaks. I leave the boxes with the Danish and *biscotti* on the square wooden table, which has been passed down the generations dating back to my great-grandmother. Then, I walk over to the alterations room. Taking the muslin off a mannequin, I stare at my dream come true—my perfect wedding dress. Tears come into my eyes. I still can't believe that after ten years of making gowns for other brides-to-be, I'm finally the lucky girl.

With the wedding date fast approaching, I'm also anxious to finish the dress because I've been neglecting Michael. But after today, I can relax a bit and see Michael twice a week and the entire weekend, just as we'd been doing before I began working on my dress. Of course, Michael has been understanding, especially since he's had to work late himself.

To make it up to me, Michael surprised me last night by taking me to Water's Edge, a four-star restaurant in Long Island City with stunning views of Manhattan. Ever since I'd first heard of Water's Edge in high school, I had fantasized about going there with someone special. As we dined and watched the lights around New York City go on one by one, I couldn't help thinking how serene the whole night was. There was never any doubt in my mind of Michael's love as he continually looked into my eyes.

"How do you do it?"

"Do what?"

"How do you always manage to look like a star? No matter what you're wearing—a dress or jeans—there's a certain glamour about you."

I could feel my cheeks warming up. "Oh, Michael. You're too good to me."

Michael took my hand in his and stroked it. "It's true, Vee. And you know what makes you more beautiful? You don't even know it. That's why I love you so much."

"I love you, too, Michael."

After dinner, Michael had a limo waiting for us outside. We crossed the 59th Street Bridge into Manhattan and went to a heliport, where we took a helicopter for a spectacular aerial view of the Big Apple at night. It was the most romantic night.

Buzz! Buzzzzzz!

I'm jolted from my thoughts by the sound of Sposa Rosa's

buzzer, signaling a customer. What's the matter with me today? I can't stop daydreaming.

"Valentina!"

My mother! I spring into action, quickly draping the muslin over my gown.

"I'll be right out, Ma!"

"When are you going to let your sisters and me see that dress—the wedding day? You girls are all so secretive nowadays. I remember in my day a daughter shared everything with her mother."

I've heard this lecture countless times. Having grown up poor in Sicily during World War II, Ma doesn't understand the concept of privacy. Her feelings are instantly hurt if she discovers that one of the DeLuca girls has been keeping something from her. Rita had hidden the fact that she had a boyfriend when she was thirteen.

One day, Ma was sitting on a bench in Astoria Park, taking in the view of the magnificent Manhattan skyline as the sun set over the East River. She noticed a very young boy and girl standing by the water and hugging. When the girl turned around and kissed the boy full on the lips, Ma dropped the vanilla ice cream cone she'd just bought from Mister Softee right on her lap.

"Rita!" she screamed. *"Che stai facendo? Disgraziata! Disgraziata!"*

Of course, there was no need for Ma to ask Rita what she was doing. It was plain to everyone at the park. She kept cursing at Rita until she caught up to her. Rita hadn't even heard Ma until she was about five feet away from her. Ma grabbed Rita by the arm and pulled her away. But she stopped after taking two steps and turned around, looking menacingly at the boy Rita was with.

"You come near my daughter again, I kill you!" And then she made the famous Italian gesture of moving her hand across her throat as if she were slicing it.

On the way home, after Ma lectured Rita about being too young to have a boyfriend and her famous, "What if the neighbors had seen you?" line, which was uttered on a weekly basis to one of us, she said, "How could you have not told me you had a boyfriend? I'm your mother. You don't keep secrets from your mother."

Rita blurted, "Because I knew you'd act like the crazy lady I just saw in the park."

"Crazy lady, huh? I show you crazy lady. You can't go out with your friends for a year."

Then there was the time Connie got a tattoo of a small angel on her lower back. That was only a year ago, and though Connie was in her twenties and shouldn't have been afraid of my mother's disapproval, she was. The only time she exposed her tattoo was when she was out with friends. And if the whole family was at the beach together, she wore a one-piece bathing suit instead of her usual teeny string bikinis to hide the tattoo from Ma. But the secret only lasted six months.

Connie had fainted while she was steaming a wedding dress on what was the hottest day in July last year. Our air conditioner was on the fritz and though we had fans blowing until the repairman could come, the heat was stifling. Connie fell face forward, knocking down the enormous tulle ball gown she was steaming. The dress's super-poofy skirt seemed to swallow whole Connie's petite figure. At least she had a good buffer to cushion her fall. Her shirt had ridden up her back, and she was wearing low-waisted jeans. When Ma ran over to help her, she immediately saw the tattoo. At first she thought it was a bug on Connie, especially since she'd left her reading glasses on the sewing machine. She swatted at it. But when it didn't move, she took a step back to get a better view and spotted the little angel.

"Disgraziata!"

She then turned to me. "Did you know about this?"

My face colored, but I ignored her. "Ma, we have to revive Connie."

We hoisted her up into a chair. Rita ran to the kitchen for vinegar. Connie came to after getting a whiff of the vinegar. Ma barely gave her time to recuperate from her fainting spell as she tore into her.

"What does the Bible say about marking the body? Eh? Eh? How many times I tell you and your sisters tattoos are not for ladies. Only *puttanas* have tattoos!"

Connie was too disoriented to try and lie. "You saw my angel?"

"*Si, si*. I saw your angel. *Stupida! Stupida!* You ruin yourself. What boy is going to want to marry you someday? Eh?"

I tried to defend poor Connie. "Ma, everyone has tattoos now. They're not just for whores and men. Haven't you noticed all the tattoo shops opening on Ditmars and Steinway Street? Even movie stars get them now."

"Movie stars, they're one step away from *puttanas!* On Monday, I make an appointment to have that tattoo removed from you."

"But, Ma, I'm not a kid anymore! I'm in my twenties, for crying out loud! You can't make me do something I don't want to do!" Connie was screaming at the top of her lungs.

"If you don't get that tattoo removed, I am taking your name off the will."

"Go ahead! I don't care!"

The two of them went at it for another fifteen minutes. Then Connie stormed out of the shop.

"Secrets. That's all you girls know how to do. What about you, Valentina? What are you hiding from me?"

"Nothing." I lowered my head.

Ma stared at me for what felt like an hour. Then she let out a long sigh and walked away, whispering to herself in Sicilian and shaking her head.

"Valentina! What is taking you so long to come out?"

My mother's voice snaps me back to the present. I make my way to the front of the store and kiss her on the cheek.

"I have good news, Ma."

"Oh no! You're not pregnant already, are you? With just a few months to go before the wedding that would be the death of me!"

"I said *good* news, Ma. Why do you always have to think the worst?"

"I just like to be prepared for the worst so that when it happens I'm not so shocked."

"Gloom and doom . . . gloom and doom. I should start calling you that!"

"Don't be smart with your mother! Remember, I . . ."

". . . know best. I've heard that since forever." I roll my eyes.

"So what's your good news?"

"I'll wait until Rita and Connie get here."

"Oh, now you're going to make your mother wait. I'm your mother. You can tell me first. They'll understand."

I bite back a retort. She's right. She does deserve priority. Ma has been my number one fan and my best friend. True, sometimes we get into horrible arguments. But no one can take the place of my mother.

"Okay. I'll tell you. But let's keep it a secret between you and me. I wouldn't want to hurt my sisters' feelings."

Ma smiles. "*Si, si.* Now, out with it."

"I finished the dress, and I'm ready to show it."

"What are you waiting for? Let me see it!"

"I can't. I know you'll start crying once you see it, and then Rita and Connie will know something's up."

"Ahhhh!!! You are the death of me. Okay, okay. I'll be patient. They should be getting here soon anyway. I'll go make some *espresso.*" She pats my cheek as she walks by. "Have I ever told you . . ."

". . . I'm a good daughter. Yes, Ma, you have. You're a . . ."

". . . wonderful mama. I know, *fighita.* I know."

She winks at me and begins singing her favorite song, *"Maledetta Primavera,"* which means "Cursed Spring." Even her choice in music and movies leans toward the cruel twists of fate life can have. But that's Olivia DeLuca, and I learned a long time ago Ma is set in her ways.

2

Gloom and Doom

Olivia DeLuca opened a fresh pack of Café Bustelo. She loved everything about *espresso,* from the special *espresso* coffeepots, to the doll-like cups and teaspoons, to the aroma it gave off as it brewed. The only way to make *espresso* was in her *espresso* pot that she'd received as a gift for her wedding forty years ago. She'd already had a pot imported from Italy for Valentina's bridal shower. She'd rather be struck dead than have her daughter use one of those modern dual coffee/*espresso* machines young brides today fancied. The *espresso* was as good as water when made in those bastardized American contraptions. And forget about getting a nice foamy froth when making a *cappuccino* in one of those. *Merda!* Total crap is what those coffeemakers were.

Olivia cut the twine off of the bakery box that held Valentina's favorite *Palline di Limone biscotti.* She took a bite out of a lemon ball, savoring the intense citrus flavor. She still couldn't get Hunchback, or bakery owner Antoniella, to reveal the secret of her lemon ball *biscotti.* Olivia had tried various recipes from Italian dessert cookbooks for years, hoping to replicate Antoniella's or even to beat them, but none had come close. She'd tried in vain to convince the Hunchback that she'd still buy her *biscotti.* She just liked to experiment in the kitchen every now and then. If she ever did figure it out, she'd stop buying them from the Hunchback even though she'd assured her she wouldn't. It would serve her right, after all the money Olivia had spent in that bakery. She shrugged her shoulders. Someday she'd get that recipe. As she chewed on another lemon ball, her thoughts turned to her daughter.

"Hmmm . . . gloom and doom."

Valentina's words stung a bit. Could she help it that she was a realist, after all she'd been through? Although Olivia knew she was her usual self, preaching about the realities of life, the truth was that the past few months had been some of the happiest in her life. Her oldest daughter, Valentina, had found a good man and would finally be getting married. She'd worried about her daughter for a long time. Ever since she was a young girl, Valentina had been a bit of a loner. She'd been too sweet and innocent for the tougher kids in their Queens neighborhood. Like wolves circling a lamb, the kids had sensed Valentina was easy to prey on. It was hard for her to make friends, and the one she had ended up backstabbing her. Thank God for Aldo, her best friend.

Valentina met Aldo her freshman year of high school. With a similar love of fashion and gabbing about celebrity gossip, Aldo was like a brother to Valentina. Aldo's parents were from Naples, so he understood the DeLucas' Italian culture. Olivia loved Aldo, but it hurt her that Valentina didn't have a female best friend after all these years. She angrily shook her head. It was the fault of that *puttana* Tracy, who betrayed her when she needed friendship the most.

Olivia had often warned Valentina about Tracy, even when they first became friends at six years old. There was something about the girl Olivia did not trust. She knew it was crazy to be suspicious of a six-year-old child, but it was a feeling more than anything the girl did. And Olivia always trusted her feelings. Their friendship was strange, too. They spoke for hours on the phone every night and saw each other at school, but it wasn't until junior high school that Mrs. Santana, Tracy's mother, finally allowed her daughter to visit Valentina's home.

Valentina always commented on how strict Mrs. Santana was. Olivia felt sorry for the girl after she learned that Tracy cooked her family's dinner every night after her mother went to her night job. Tracy's mother was from Argentina. Italian mothers could be strict, too, and Olivia remembered how harsh her own parents had been with her and her siblings when she was growing up in Sicily. But this was America. Things were different here, and it was a different time.

But Valentina would not listen and still chose to be friends with Tracy. Even Aldo had once told Olivia that Tracy often caused trouble for Valentina by lying to others about things she'd never said. Then, Olivia had heard from some of the other neighbors about Tracy's reputation. The Mayor of 35th Street was the first one, of course, to inform Olivia of how popular Tracy was with the boys in town.

"If I were you, Signora DeLuca, I'd keep my daughter away from the likes of that girl. There's nothing but trouble waiting around the corner where she's involved."

Olivia didn't want to believe Paulie, since she knew how he ex-aggerated. But then, some of the other neighbors had also com-mented about Tracy's questionable moral character.

"Puttana! Puttana!" the Italian neighbors whispered to Olivia as if Tracy were hanging around and could hear them. "Save your daughter! Before it's too late!"

When Olivia told Valentina what the neighbors were saying, she didn't say anything. Her silence proved to Olivia that Valentina was aware of the gossip swirling around her best friend.

"You don't have to worry about me, Ma. I don't do what the other kids do. I know what's right and wrong."

That had consoled Olivia, but only briefly. She knew her daughter was a good girl. But she still worried about her hanging out with Tracy. And then when that *puttana* betrayed her daughter, Olivia wanted to kill her.

"Dio mio!" she whispered, making the sign of the cross several times. "Forgive me, God. I did not mean that. Well, maybe a little bit. But I'm sorry."

Olivia had tried to forgive Tracy. She had to remind herself that Tracy was still a child with a polar bear of a mother who had beat her and never shown her much love. But when she thought of how her Valentina had looked on that day when her best friend betrayed her, all she felt was rage. How could Tracy and those other kids have been so cruel? Didn't their parents teach them anything about treating others kindly? No wonder her daughter couldn't trust again after what they did to her. It's a good thing Nicola was too sick to know what had happened. He couldn't stand his daughters to be in pain of any kind.

Olivia sighed. Even though it had been fourteen years since Nicola had passed away, she still missed him terribly. She wiped the tears that were forming in her eyes with the back of her hand. That was the past. But she could not forget about that girl who had hurt her daughter so much. Olivia was also convinced Tracy had given Valentina the *malocchio*. Even if she hadn't actually placed a curse on Valentina, just her jealousy would be enough to cast the mighty *malocchio*. For fourteen years, she lit candles and prayed to the Black Madonna of Tindari—her Sicilian hometown—begging her to lift the curse off Valentina. Her prayers were answered once Michael proposed to Valentina. Lord knows Valentina had had such a hard time finding the right man. But none of that mattered anymore. She would live a happy life with Michael. Her daughter couldn't have chosen a finer young man.

Michael was the son of Joseph and Iva Carello, owners of Carello Accounting. The Italians in the neighborhood only trusted Joseph Carello to prepare their taxes and handle their other accounting matters. Like an obedient son of Italian parents, Michael worked in his father's office in high school and during his breaks from college. But these kids of today have bigger dreams. After graduating, he became a stockbroker for Smith Barney. Olivia couldn't complain too much. At least he'd be able to provide her daughter with a good income. And not only did Michael have impeccable manners, he had impeccable taste in fashion! He'd asked Olivia to make him a few custom-made suits. In fact, Olivia's gift to her future son-in-law would be a custom-made tuxedo. She'd been afraid he would've preferred to buy a ready-made tux, but Michael was thrilled and accepted Olivia's generous gift, much to her pleasure. The boy knew how to warm up to his future mother-in-law! And he never failed to compliment her cooking whenever he came over for dinner. But even Signora DeLuca knew no one was perfect. If Michael's parents were Sicilian, instead of Venetian, then he would've been perfect.

Olivia's nerves had been ruffled a bit that her daughter didn't insist on getting married in Sicily, but she had to be grateful for what God had given her. Michael was a good man from a respectable family. They'd known him since he was a young boy. She had always secretly hoped that one day he would take a liking to Valentina. She could tell her daughter had harbored a crush on him since she was a little girl. Olivia had also noticed how Michael stared at Valentina once she became a beautiful young woman. And the way he'd checked in on her after Nicola had died. He'd taken off from school to attend the funeral, and he'd come to the wake every one of the three nights of the viewing.

But for some reason, they didn't start dating until only two years ago. Valentina was twenty-eight and Michael was thirty-one. Olivia couldn't understand what had made him wait so long to finally ask her daughter out on a date. Hmmm! In her day, when a man liked a woman, he didn't waste any time. Now all anyone did was wait. Wait to get married . . . wait to have children . . . wait to buy a house.

Yes, Michael was a good choice for a husband. And Olivia was still thanking God that Valentina hadn't done the unthinkable by marrying a Calabrese! Even though Calabria neighbors Sicily where it sits at the point of Italy's boot, Olivia would rather have a Venetian as a son-in-law than a Calabrese. They're too pigheaded and *cafone!* All one had to do was take a look at the Mayor of 35th Street, Paulie Parlatone—a Calabrese himself—to see *cafone* defined. The steam whistled through the *espresso* pot.

"*Vieni,* Valentina! *L'espresso è pronto!*"

Putting her thoughts out of her mind for another day, Olivia sat down for her favorite ritual of the day—*espresso* and *biscotti.*

~~~ 3 ~~~

Evil Eye

I have to stop eating so many sweets if I hope to fit into my dress on my wedding day. It doesn't help that Antoniella's Bakery is so close to the shop. As Ma and I are finishing up our *espresso* and *biscotti,* my sisters finally stroll through the door.

Rita, the talker and complainer of the family, is twenty-six years old. Connie is twenty-four. Though they look nothing alike and have a two-year age gap, our neighbors call them the DeLuca Twins because they are rarely seen apart.

Rita resembles my mother with her fair complexion, onyx-colored eyes, and rich chocolate brown, thick, curly hair, which she wears long, way past her shoulders. She takes great pride in her crowning glory and rarely ties it back or puts it up, even in the sweltering heat of the summer. Of the three of us, she's the tallest at 5'9", taking after our paternal grandfather. As a size twelve, she has a full figure compared to the more petite frames Connie and I have. We attribute Rita's curvier figure to her sweet tooth, which is worse than mine. Every afternoon, she walks into Antoniella's Bakery for a *cannoli* and a *café latte. Cannolis* are her favorite. Some days, she even has two *cannolis!* She also loves to bake on her days off from work. Her *Torta della Nonna* is the best I've ever had—not even

Antoniella's can beat Rita's recipe. And that says a lot, considering Antoniella has the best bakery in all of Astoria.

Rita is known for her bluntness. Sometimes her candid remarks cut far closer to the truth than any of us like, but you can never accuse her of being phony. She's full of life and loves to party and can't understand how I often find pleasure just with a good book to keep me company. She loves to dance and frequently goes out to the latest trendy nightclub in Manhattan with Connie and her friends.

In contrast to my classic fashion sense, Rita loves embellishment. Her clothes often sport beading or flashy sequins. You never catch her in anything understated. She doesn't even own any neutral or solid-colored lingerie. Her bras and panties all have patterns—animal prints, polka dots, flowers. She shudders when I come home with a shopping bag from Ann Taylor and says, "B-O-R-R-R-I-N-G!"

"The more the better" is her motto. She's a slave to fashion and wears all the latest trends. Right now she's wearing a purple studded Marc Jacobs empire-waist tunic with black lace leggings. She loves the elaborate bridal designs of Oscar de la Renta and Pnina Tornai. I know when she gets married someday she'll probably go all out with a full ballroom gown, heavy on the tulle, lace, and crystal beading. Of course, her dress will have a sweeping cathedral train with matching cathedral-length veil. Although she often makes cracks about brides and their "deluded princess fantasies," as she puts it, I see the way her eyes light up whenever she tries on one of the dresses we've completed to see how it fits. And she often wastes no time in volunteering first to try on ball gowns that scream "princess bride." Rita just won't admit to us that, deep down, she has the same dreams most women have had since they were little girls of being a princess on their wedding day. So underneath her Teflon exterior lies a Cinderella waiting for her Prince Charming.

Rita had chosen to follow in my footsteps and had gone to New York's famous Fashion Institute of Technology (FIT). She'd graduated with a degree in accessory design. When she isn't baking on her days off, she's designing and creating handbags, which she sells online. She even designs and makes a few clutch purses for the bridal shop, which are a huge hit. Ma keeps asking her when is she going to introduce more designs. But Rita's true passion is designing non-bridal purses.

"It's my escape from this warped world we work in," she said to me once.

I think it's a shame that Rita doesn't take more interest in the shop, since she is very talented as both a wedding dress designer/ seamstress and purse designer. Sposa Rosa is, after all, our mother's legacy to us, and as such, we need to take it seriously.

Rita's toughness comes through in her relationships with men as well. She really makes them work for her approval and love. But once they earn it, she showers them with affection while constantly reminding them she's the boss in the relationship.

At 4'11", Connie matches my mother's height and is the shortest. But that's all she's inherited from my mother. She takes after my father with her olive complexion and short chestnut brown hair. Her hair is also much straighter and finer than any of the DeLuca women's hair. She usually wears it spiky or slicked back—a sexy look that plays up her large hazel-colored eyes. She accentuates her sultriness by lining her eyes in thick, smoky gray liner.

Connie is obsessed with her complexion, which leans toward the oilier side. She never goes anywhere without her compact, and throughout the day, she checks her face and powders it. She became fixated with her complexion after taking the bus home from school one day. Connie and Rita had chosen to go to Bryant High School instead of St. John's Prep. My mother had warned them that the kids tended to be meaner at the public schools. But Connie and Rita reminded Ma how nasty some of the kids at Immaculate Conception were, where we'd all attended elementary school. Christine Murphy, who hated Connie for no reason, yelled out at Connie just as she was getting off the bus, "That's right! Get off the bus, you grease monkey!" Connie couldn't help glancing toward the voice, as she was about to step off the bus. Christine yelled, "Yeah, I'm talking to you, you shiny grease monkey!"

Christine and her friends were howling with laughter. Connie came home crying. Maybe Christine hated Connie because she was jealous of her perfect hourglass figure that looked good even when she wore tattered jeans (her favorite) and a sweatshirt. Christine, on the other hand, was pudgy and looked as if she'd never grown. She must've been 4'8" even though she was fifteen. Rita said Christine could get a job at Ringling Bros. Circus as a midget, since she was certain she'd be a high school dropout.

Connie's weakness is expensive shoes, and when she loves a particular style, she buys them in every shade of the color spectrum. Her most recent splurge was a pair of Christian Louboutin stiletto pumps in what she loves to call Barbie pink—a cross between fuchsia and light pink.

But Connie also goes crazy for jewelry, whether it's real or fake. She has a degree in jewelry design from Parsons. And just like Rita, Connie sells her designs online. As a gift, she's going to make the jewelry I'll be wearing on my wedding day. To show her my appreciation, I decide to fully place my trust in her skills and let her come up with the design. She hasn't begun designing the jewels yet since she needs to see my dress first.

Connie has more of a rebellious, avant-garde style. Her favorite fashion designer is Betsey Johnson. Of course, she thinks Sposa Rosa is the perfect name for the boutique.

"If it were up to me, I would've called it Loca Esposa."

"We're Italian, not Spanish," Rita reminded her.

"In the Sicilian dialect, *loca* means 'crazy,' just as in Spanish," Connie informed Rita.

"Whatever!" Rita rolled her eyes, hating it when her little sister bested her at anything.

Yes, that's just like Connie, calling a bridal salon the crazy bride. She loves the bridal couture designs of Badgley Mischska and Matthew Christopher. Our more rebellious and daring clients go wild for Connie's designs. On her wedding day, I can see Connie wearing a basque-waist mermaid dress with a sheer lace corset bodice or even a daring short dress. Then again, I can also see my youngest sister foregoing marriage completely.

Connie never has a problem making friends. She doesn't let things get to her the way my mother or I do—well, except for Christine teasing her about her oily complexion. She's always smiling or telling a joke. It's no wonder that people flock to her and that she embraces as much as possible the serene New Age lifestyle.

Connie is a hopeless romantic and falls in love with every guy she dates. Unlike Rita, she doesn't believe in ever dating casually. Her favorite movies to watch are romantic comedies. At the moment, neither she nor Rita are seeing anyone. Usually, I'm the one not involved with anyone while both of them are either dating or have boyfriends. Now, here I am engaged, while my two bubbly, popular sisters don't have prospects for a serious boyfriend anytime soon. Secretly, I'm relieved since I am the oldest, and as the oldest, I feel I should be the first one getting married. I always thought Rita would be first, even with her tough brand of love. Two of her relationships had lasted three or more years, and she almost got engaged to her last boyfriend. But she said something just didn't feel right, and like Ma, she's learned to always trust her gut instincts.

Because of their ages, it's natural that Rita and Connie are closer to each other than they are to me. I know they love me, but I also realize that as the big sister, I represent an authority figure to them. Still, I can't help wishing I were more a part of their inner circle. Yes, I'm jealous of my sisters' bond with each other. No one knows this—well, maybe Ma—nothing gets past those eagle eyes.

Ever since grade school, I've always longed for that one special girlfriend with whom I can share secrets and do everything with, as so many other girls have. Though Tracy had been my best friend growing up, I only saw her at school. Her mother wouldn't let her come over to my house while we were in elementary school. And then when high school came, she'd come over, but there was something lacking. I guess it was because at that point I didn't fully trust her anymore with all the lying she'd done. She was also hanging out with other kids, who got drunk a lot and sometimes even snorted coke. She still called me almost every day, though. And I knew there were certain things she told me that she didn't tell her new friends.

"Hey, Vee! Hey, Ma!" Rita and Connie sing out in unison, as they swing through Sposa Rosa's doors. It had started out as a joke between them, since everyone calls them "the DeLuca Twins." But after the third time in a row of their announcing themselves in this ridiculous way, I told them how incredibly stupid they sounded. Instead of stopping, they just continued with it. I love my sisters even though they can be a huge pain in my butt. I've decided my best course of action is to ignore their antics as much as I can.

"Hey! What took you guys so long?"

"We got stopped along the way by the Mayor of Thirty-fifth Street. What else?" Rita elbows Connie, and then they break out into laughter. Rita almost drops the cake platter wrapped in foil that she's carrying. No doubt she'd been baking last night.

"Why is that especially funny today? He's been chewing our ears off since we were kids."

"Well, there is more to it." Connie gives Rita a sly smile.

"Okay, quit it. What's going on?"

"He told us that he ran into you this morning, and your upcoming nuptials in Venice came up. He said that it would be a shame if he missed out on your wedding, and even though it's so far, maybe he will be able to go."

"You're lying, Rita. Wipe that smug grin off your face. Paulie Parlatone is not about to part with his money. When have you known him to take a vacation? Hmmm? *Never!* You expect me to believe he's going to take a trip?"

"He did say he was long overdue for a vacation, especially since he never took one before he retired." Connie says this while looking at her complexion in one of the shop's many mirrors. She continues looking at her face while she quickly whips out her compact, which she keeps in the front pocket of her purse for easy access. She pats feverishly the shine on her nose and forehead.

"Your face looks fine, Connie. If you put any more powder on, I'm going to have a hard time telling if you're alive or dead!"

Connie scowls at me. "With your dry skin, you have no idea what I go through! I never see a bead of grease on your face."

"I'd rather have your skin. Mine will start cracking soon from how dry it is. At fifty, you'll probably still look like you're twenty. So take it easy on the powder."

"Yeah, I keep telling her that all the supermodels go for that glow over their nose and cheeks now. It's in. But does she listen? She's still hearing that midget Christine's taunts in her head!" Rita tries to grab the compact from Connie, who jumps away in time.

"We're getting off the subject. So we were saying that Paulie is going to fly all the way to Venice just for you and your wedding!" Connie is always a master at taking the attention away from Rita.

"So you're not putting one over on me?"

"Vee, would we do that?"

If they are lying, they're doing a great job of it.

"Uggghhhh!!! Now I have to suffer the Mayor of Thirty-fifth Street at my own wedding! Why me? I must've been a bitch in a former life."

"Do you want to come with me to my yoga studio next Monday night? They're having a workshop on past lives." Connie looks at Rita, trying to keep a straight face.

"Ha! Ha! Really funny." Squinting my eyes narrowly, I give her my most dirty look.

"He said he was heading over to Kyle's Travel to book his trip before all the flights were sold out. You know how anxious he gets!" Rita laughs.

"Girls, you know I always book my trips to Italy at least six to nine months in advance. It's better to play safe than sorry. Paulie has a point, even though I hate to admit he's right about anything," Ma chimes in.

"I can't believe this! He's going to be so crass at the reception with his usual obnoxious questions and picking his teeth."

I sink down on the office chair behind the receptionist's desk.

"Psych!" Rita and Connie scream out in unison, giving each other a high five as they laugh hysterically.

I throw two fat spools of thread at them, missing Connie, but hitting Rita on the arm. "I'm going to kill you both!"

"Oh, Vee, the look of desperation on your face when you thought he was flying to Venice! Priceless!" Connie looks at Rita, nodding her head to gain her sidekick's approval.

"Yeah, you looked so tortured. I almost broke and told you we were kidding almost as soon as we announced he was going. But you know us, Vee, we can't miss a good laugh."

Rita lifts her curls on top of her head with one hand and fans her face with the other. She always does this when she gets excited. Like me, she flushes easily.

"Or the chance to tease your older sister. It's a good thing I have a soft spot for you guys or else. And, Connie, isn't lying against your Buddhist ways?"

"I never said I was a Buddhist just because I practice yoga and meditate."

"If I ever catch you changing your religion, you'll be out of this family!" Ma looks up from the hem she's stitching on one of the bridal gowns and waves her index finger, which is covered with a thimble, at Connie.

"I know. I know. Catholic till I die." Connie makes the sign of an X over her chest. Rita and I laugh.

"So what's up, Vee? Why did you want us to come in on our day off? Dare I ask?" Rita's lips turn up in her trademark crooked smile that matches Ma's smile. She hates it, but I love it.

"Yes, you may ask."

"It's finished! I knew it!" Connie claps her hands together.

"Enough for a first fitting!"

"Yay!" Rita jumps up and down, followed by Connie. They embrace me, and I have no choice but to hop up and down along with them. I enjoy this rare moment where I feel like one of the girls and included.

"Have my daughters gone mad? I haven't seen you jump like this since you used to play Ring Around the Rosie."

"Ma! It's finished! Valentina's dress is finished, and she's showing it to us today!"

I quickly look at my mother, raising my eyebrow to remind her of our secret pact.

"Valentina! At last!" Ma holds her hands up to the ceiling as if she's thanking God for ending a centuries-long drought. Leave it to her to overact when she's lying.

"Well, what are we waiting for? Don't keep us in suspense any longer, Vee!" Rita takes me by the arm and leads me to the back where my dress awaits its debut.

Nothing beats the feeling of slipping on your wedding dress for the first time, knowing *this* will be the gown your future husband will see you in. I want to savor every moment. As I carefully step into the fluffy pools of organza that swirl around my feet, I bask in the whisper-light feel of the fabric brushing against my skin. Since the gown features a halter neckline, I don't have to worry about my family seeing the dress from the back first so that they can help me with the zipper. I can just place the halter around my neck and hold the dress against my waist to give it a more fitted look. Taking a deep breath, I look in the mirror.

The pale ivory of the dress complements my fair-to-medium complexion, and my shoulder-length chestnut brown hair gleams in contrast. My hair is a blend of my parents'. It is thick like my mother's and Rita's, but unlike their tight curls, I only have waves. My hair is closer to Connie's and my father's shade, but not as light. Even my skin tone is a blend of my parents' coloring.

I admire how the halter straps of my gown show off my high neck and toned arms, thanks to the Pilates sessions I've been taking since I got engaged. It has been hard squeezing the three sessions a week into my already-packed schedule, but I know it's important to look my best on my wedding day.

The A-line of the skirt doesn't overpower my petite frame. Though I'm not as short as Connie, I am still only 5'3".

I keep staring at myself in the mirror. Spinning around, I look at myself from all angles and whisper, "I never want to take you off. You're perfect!"

"What are you doing in there, Valentina?" Rita screams out.

"We're giving you to the count of three, or else—Whoa!"

I open the fitting room door.

"It's beyond beautiful. It's brilliant!" Rita gently lifts the hem of the dress, closely inspecting my stitch work.

"I almost forgot. Can someone zip me up?" I turn dramatically around and hear Rita and Connie gasp.

"Oh my God, look at the back! Vee, you sexy siren, you! Who would've ever thought?" Connie has her hand over her mouth. With her taste for sexy clothes, I can tell she definitely approves. "Are you sure this dress is for you and not me with that racy back?"

I laugh.

"This isn't the Plain Jane we grew up with. What happened to safe and classic? What did you do with my sister? You're her clone." Rita shakes her head, but I see the look of awe in her eyes.

I look at my mother. She's been terribly silent. She's just standing there with her arms across her waist.

"Ma, what's the matter? Don't you like it?"

My heart starts to drop, but then my mother's eyes fill with tears, and I'm quickly reassured.

"You're so beautiful! The dress is absolutely stunning! Yes, it's very different from your usual fashion tastes. But it's perfect, and it looks perfect on you! You look like Venus coming out of the sea. It's a masterpiece! I can't believe I'm standing here, watching my oldest daughter in her wedding dress at last! I never thought I'd see the day."

"Oh, Ma! Stop with the hysterics!" Rita laughs.

"Shush! You're ruining the moment for me. Come here, Valentina."

Ma opens her arms wide. I pick up the skirt of my dress and walk over to her, letting her embrace me.

"I'm so proud of you. Look at the gorgeous work you've done on this dress. Your seamstress skills are impeccable. But of course, you learned from the best."

Ma winks at me.

"I'm glad you like the dress, Ma. Your opinion means the world to me."

"Let's get some shots! You'll need them to show the stylist when you go for your hair rehearsals." Wasting no time, Connie grabs her iPhone and clicks away.

Suddenly, the sounds of Madonna's "Vogue" come streaming through the shop's stereo system.

"This is a Madonna moment!" Rita exclaims. Though it's 2010, Madonna remains her idol.

"Oh God! You guys are cheesy!"

But I decide to indulge my sisters for once, and begin striking poses.

"That's it! You show it off, girl! Whoo-hoo!" Connie shouts as she continues taking pictures.

I pick up my hair and pout my lips, giving them my best sultry pose.

"Now, you're talking! Where have you been hiding all these years, Vee?" Rita asks me.

"I'm the big sister. I have to be a role model. Just because I don't flaunt my wild side doesn't mean I don't have one!"

"Whoa!!!!!" Rita and Connie yell out.

"You girls are crazy!"

Ma is blushing, but she's also laughing. And tears are still streaming down her face.

"Valentina?"

I whirl around.

"Michael?"

He's standing still, gaping at me, much like he did the first time we made love and he saw me naked.

And then it hits me.

"Oh my God, Michael! Get out of here!" I scream, ducking for cover behind Rita.

All hell breaks loose. Ma yells like I've never heard her yell before, "*Malocchio! Malocchio!* Go, go! Get out! You'll give her *malocchio!* It's bad luck forever!"

But Michael is still just standing there, staring at me, even though by now my sisters are doing their best to use their bodies to shield my dress from view. It reminds me of when we used to play Twister as kids. Then, Connie quickly leaves my side. I crouch lower behind Rita's back, incredulous that Connie has abandoned me. But just as soon as this thought pops into my mind, a fabric is dropped over my head.

"Stay there! Don't move!" Connie orders me.

She drapes muslin over me. Rita moves away from my crouching figure and adjusts the fabric. I drop to all fours, making it easier for Rita and Connie to cover me. I feel like a dog after it's been shampooed against its will and is seeking refuge by rolling up in a towel. But I'm not doing any rolling. I'm just frozen in place like a squirrel, too petrified to move. How ridiculous must I look now to Michael!

I hear Ma's heavy wooden Dr. Scholl's clogs as she scurries over to Michael.

"Please! Go now!" I hear the bell of the door and the sounds from the street once it's opened.

"Okay, okay. I'm going." Michael is laughing. "Don't worry, Signora DeLuca. There's no such thing as bad luck."

"Don't tell a woman what she knows. I've got forty years over you, hot shot. Now go and don't come back in here until after the wedding! You never know when Valentina will be trying her dress on for alterations."

"'Bye, Vee, I'll see you later, if you ever get out from underneath that cloth."

I can still hear him laughing as my mother shuts the door behind him. The lock turns in the door. She's not taking any more chances.

I pull the muslin off me and almost lose my balance as I try to stand up. Rita helps me.

Ma crosses herself as she exclaims, *"O, Dio, aiuto. malocchio . . . malocchio."*

Snow is falling again as I glance out Sposa Rosa's windows. The forecast is only predicting light showers. Lately, I've been closing up the shop every night since I'm working on my dress. The Michael Fiasco, as Connie likes to call it, has stirred things up. After my mother ushered him out yesterday morning, she kept telling me I had to make some alterations to the dress so it would be different from the dress Michael had seen.

"You can't start a marriage out like that, Valentina. It's bad luck."

"Oh, Ma. We're living in the twenty-first century, and you still believe in the mighty evil eye. Give it a rest. I like the dress the way it is. I'm not changing it. *Basta!*"

"*Basta?* Don't *basta* your mother. I say when enough is enough. I won't be able to get a night's rest forever if you leave that dress as it is."

I knew I wouldn't get a night's rest either if I didn't compromise.

"Okay, okay. I'll figure something out."

As soon as my mother left the shop, I consulted with Rita and Connie.

"Whatever!" Connie rolled her eyes. "You give in to Ma too easily. It's *your* wedding. She had hers. Do what you want, Vee."

"Well, you're not the one who will have to hear it day in and out for the rest of your life if I don't make the alterations." I shook my head. "Of course with my luck, my fiancé has to walk in on me during my fitting."

"Stop it! You're starting to sound like Ma—bad luck this and that. But yeah, I know what you mean. Who wants their fiancé to see them in their wedding dress months before the wedding?"

Rita was eating a slice of *prosciutto,* without any bread. She was on a carb-free diet to look her best in her maid of honor dress. Both she and Connie were going to be my maids of honor. I didn't want to choose one sister over the other.

Connie, who was standing behind Rita, slapped her in the back of the head. "Some help you are!"

"I'm just empathizing."

Rita went over to one of the fitting room mirrors and patted back down into place her frizz-prone curls.

"I'm sure whatever you decide will be beautiful, Vee. Don't stress out too much over it. And don't let Ma get to you!"

Rita gave me a quick hug. "We have to go. We have a double date with the Broccoli Brothers. Come on, Connie."

My eyes widened. "The Broccoli Brothers? How long has this been going on?"

Rita just smiled and waved as she pushed Connie, who was giggling, toward the door. And here I was thinking they weren't dating at the moment. I could feel a small pang of hurt at being left out of my sisters' lives once again. The moment we'd shared jumping and joking together had been quickly extinguished. Just when I thought I was finally entering their inner sanctum, the door was shut on me once again.

I watched them walking down Ditmars Boulevard, arm in arm, laughing as always—probably about how they'd managed to shock me with their revelation. The Broccoli Brothers were waiting for them outside of the 718 Lounge. I stretched my neck to get a better look outside the window. Both brothers kissed my sisters on the cheeks. I couldn't see any more once they turned around to enter 718.

The Broccoli Brothers were John and Lou Rabe, as in the vegetable broccoli rabe. The Mayor of 35th Street had given them this name when they were in high school. Whenever he'd see the two brothers, who lived on the corner from us, the Mayor would yell out, "Broccoli Brothers! Got any good broccoli for me?" He always erupted into laughter as if it were the first time he was making the joke. John and Lou were good sports about it. Now everyone in the neighborhood referred to them as the Broccoli Brothers.

Well, at least they were nice, respectable guys—and Italian. My mom would be happy about that, of course. But she wouldn't be thrilled that Lou Rabe owned a motorcycle. Of course, Connie was arm in arm with him. Their rebellious natures made them a good fit for each other. Lou was a paramedic and often looked exhausted from both the stressful work and late hours he tended to work.

John Rabe was more subdued than his brother. He was 6'3" and very broad-shouldered. Rita's bigger frame looked smaller next to his. He worked as a paralegal in Manhattan and was studying for his LSATs.

I push my sisters and the Broccoli Brothers out of my mind as I return to my dilemma. Frantically searching my mind for an answer as to how I can make my dress look different without ruining its original design, I sigh deeply when nothing comes to mind. My design is perfect as it is, just as Ma had said. My completed gown has been my ideal vision for months now. From sketching the design to drawing the pattern and cutting it out carefully over the fabric to the meticulous hand stitching and sewing the pearl beads on one by one, I have bonded with my dress, much like the unborn baby you grow to love day by day as it is being formed. I just can't imagine this dress looking any other way than it does now.

I glance back out the window and notice the snowflakes are falling more heavily, mesmerizing me as I stare.

"Snowflakes!" I cry out. "I'll add a few snowflake-shaped embroidered appliqués to the skirt." Right now the skirt has no ornamentation. Then I can place crystals over the appliqués, making them sparkle.

I spin around for joy. If there is ever a time that I am happy it's winter and snowing, this is it! My enthusiasm suddenly freezes just like the icy temperature outside. Winter. It is winter now, but I'm getting married in June and in a Mediterranean country no less. Although Venice has its share of overcast, rainy days, I can't have snowflakes on my dress. What am I thinking? I smack my head and all but collapse onto the plush suede couch we keep outside of the fitting rooms for brides' relatives and friends.

"Think, Valentina, think!" I say aloud.

A *Modern Bride* magazine is on the couch. The glittering diamond necklace the model is wearing catches my attention. A thin strand of round-cut diamonds circles the model's neck.

That's it! It's even better than snowflakes. I can't believe I was actually entertaining the idea of putting snowflakes on a wedding dress! Diamonds. Yes! They're sparkly so I'll still get the same effect that the crystals over the snowflake appliqués would've given me. I can scatter crystal beads throughout the dress's skirt. I can even add a few to the floor-length veil I'm planning on wearing. The dress will be different but I won't have to alter the actual cut or style of my original design. But will it be enough? Michael probably won't remember such a small detail as crystals and whether the dress has them when he sees me in it. Then again, most men don't have good short-term memories. Maybe he doesn't remember most of the dress, and my mother is stressing me out for nothing?

My cell phone rings. 8:20! I am supposed to meet Michael at Antoniella's for coffee at eight!

"Hey, Vee. I'm sorry. I'm running late, but I'm on my way. Were you waiting long?"

"No. No. I actually lost track of time. I'm still at the shop, so don't kill yourself to get to Antoniella's."

"Great. I'll see you in about half an hour. Love you."

"Love you, too."

My heart still skips a beat whenever Michael says he loves me. Will it continue to skip throughout our marriage?

I grab my cashmere camel-colored coat as I switch off the lights throughout the shop. My hand reaches for one of the many umbrellas we keep in a wicker basket by the door, but on second thought, I decide to leave it and enjoy the snow. I'm feeling lucky for a change.

4

Rotten Eggs

The radio in Antoniella's Bakery is broadcasting a blizzard. The meteorologists had gotten it wrong yesterday when they predicted only three to six inches. Since the time I left Sposa Rosa, the snow has been falling at a rate of two inches per hour. I am sitting by the window at Antoniella's, enjoying watching everyone trudge through the snow.

Kids are throwing snowballs at each other. Old ladies pushing their grocery carts are making their way carefully through the slippery pavement. Suddenly, a black poodle stands up against the bakery's window, its nostrils flaring and puffing up the glass, as it takes in the pastries' scent. Taking a closer look, I notice its milky white eyes and realize it is Mitzy, Betsy Offenheimer's blind dog.

Betsy and Mitzy slowly make their way into the shop.

"What will it be today, Mitzy? A black-and-white cookie or a mini *cannoli?*"

Mitzy continues sniffing, waving her head from side to side.

"Hi, Betsy. I see you're still spoiling Mitzy."

I smile as Betsy hobbles over to me. She walks with a black shiny cane that matches her black cat-shaped eyeglasses, circa 1950, of course. Every Tuesday morning, she gets her roller set. Her tightly wound white curls are kept in place all week by a hairnet, which she removes only on the weekends. It's not like the weekends are any different for Betsy from the weekdays. She always stays at home or wanders the neighborhood with Mitzy. Maybe looking extra nice makes the weekends feel different for her? Today, she's wearing her navy blue pea coat that hides her breasts well. Normally, her double D-cup breasts stand out like two cocked pistols in her knit shirts, never bouncing in their ultra-supportive 18 Hour Playtex bra, à la Jane Russell.

The kids on my block teased her mercilessly.

"Hey, Torpedo Tits! Look everybody, she's got Torpedo Tits!"

"Stop that! You stop that right now!"

Poor Betsy's face would turn the shade of the cherry peppers my mother grew in our backyard as she stood toe to toe with the kids. After that first incident, the kids on my block nicknamed her "Torpedo Tits." My mother and the other Italian women dubbed her *"La Vecchia Coi Mini"* or "The Lady with the Tits." Even after knowing her all these years, it's hard not to stare.

"You look so PRETTY today, Valentina. You should always wear violet, it suits your GORGEOUS brown hair." Every adjective that drops out of Betsy's mouth is always pronounced extra loud, especially if she's paying you a compliment.

"Thank you, Betsy. You're so sweet. Sit down and keep me company until Michael gets here."

"No, no, thank you. I have to be home by nine tonight. Masterpiece Theater is playing *Pride and Prejudice*. That's my favorite Jane Austen novel. On that note, I'd better get going. Have a good night. Say hello to your mother for me."

"I will. Be careful in the snow."

I watch as she orders a quarter pound of miniature black-and-white cookies for Mitzy, who's still sniffing and waving her head from side to side like a blind man's walking stick, sensing where it's safe to walk. Betsy bends over and gives Mitzy a cookie.

"Can't make her wait until she gets home to get a taste," Betsy says to Antoniella, who just nods with her trademark tight-lipped grin. Antoniella's eyes meet mine, and she rolls them when Betsy stoops over to feed Mitzy, as if to say, *"Quest' e pazza!"* I can imagine Antoniella pointing to her head with her finger.

I return my attention back to the scene outside. A lot of the shops have closed early, but not Antoniella's. As sturdy as the Abruzzi Mountains from where she comes, Antoniella always keeps her store open. Her only exceptions are Christmas and Easter, when she closes at noon.

"People need their *pasticcerie* to bring to family."

She offers this justification whenever someone asks her why she isn't closed for the two most important Christian holidays of the year. But everyone knows how cheap Antoniella can be.

As the owner of the most popular bakery on Ditmars Boulevard, Antoniella—or the Hunchback, as my mother likes to call her—does well financially. But you'd never know it by her shabby coat that has a trailing hem and is missing one or more buttons . . . or by the many cracks in the sidewalk in front of her house, which is in sore need of a new coat of paint . . . or by the shoes whose soles have been glued on too many times before.

"What does the Hunchback do with her money?" Ma always wonders aloud. She's not the only one. Our neighbors also wonder. Antoniella has never had kids. Her husband died ten years ago. And as far as we know, there are no other relatives here in the United States.

Just barely five feet tall, the Hunchback wears beige wedge-heeled nurses' shoes so she can see over her sales counter. But all the customers can see is her head. Everything from the chin below is invisible. The towers of *panettone* from the Christmas season that line either side of the counter obscure her even more. Soon, Perugina chocolate Easter eggs will take the place of the *panettone* boxes.

Antoniella's shoulders and upper back are slouched forward, hence her nickname. The Hunchback dyes her hair dark blond, giving it the appearance of matted straw, since she colors it as soon as she sees a stray gray hair. I want to introduce her to conditioner so badly. Her brown eyes are always squinted, and her lips seem to remain in a perpetual tight-lipped frown, making her look like she's always mad. Her brusque manners match the scowl on her face.

I often wonder if it weren't for her pastries being so good, would Antoniella even have any customers?

"Are you still waiting for the Carello boy before placing your order, Valentina?"

Antoniella startles me out of my reverie.

"Oh. Yes, Antoniella, I am waiting for Michael, but you know what? I'll just go ahead and order now. You know me. I can't stay in here too long without sampling one of your sweets."

"That's what I thought," Antoniella says in a very matter-of-fact tone. I can see a little twinkle in her eye, appreciating my praise. She never allows herself to fully smile whenever her patrons compliment her baking.

"*Cappuccino* with skim milk as always and what will you have to eat?"

"I really shouldn't, with my wedding coming up, but I've been dying for a slice of your *Pastiera di Grano*. But can you do me a favor and cut the slice in half? I'll take the other half home."

"You're getting too thin, Valentina. You lose any more weight and you'll have to keep taking that dress in. But I'll do as you wish."

"Thank you, Antoniella."

Another simple pleasure of mine in addition to people watching is smelling all the delicious pastries and cookies along with the brewing *espresso* in Antoniella's. I can just stay in here forever.

"So how's business been in these cold winter months?"

Antoniella carefully places the cup of *cappuccino* in front of me. She always fills the cup to the brim, lest any of her customers accuse her of skimping them.

I take a sip before answering.

"Business has never been better, actually. Usually, it slows up a bit in the winter, but this year, we're almost as busy as we were in the fall. Brides don't seem to care anymore if they have more than a year's time until their wedding. The dress is the first purchase they want to make. Of course, that interview *Brides* magazine did has brought in so many clients."

Antoniella nods her head. "It's helped my business, too. I've had so many wedding cake orders since the magazine interviewed Sposa Rosa. Do you need business cards to place in your boutique?"

"We still have them, but you can give me more. This way as

soon as we run out, I can restock them. You know I always personally recommend your bakery to all of my clients for their wedding
cakes?"

"*Si, si.* You and your family have helped me out a lot. I am so
grateful. When I get customers who come in to place an order for
their cakes, I ask them if they have already bought their dresses. If
they haven't bought the wedding dress yet, I make sure to tell them
to go to Sposa Rosa. Usually, though, they've already bought their
dress. So then I ask them if their bridesmaids have ordered their
dresses. Or I tell them if they know of anyone who's just gotten engaged to go to your shop. I always refer them to you with the highest praise."

"*Grazie,* Antoniella."

My mother and Antoniella had agreed upon this promotional
arrangement when Ma first opened the shop. In addition to both
shops displaying the other's business cards, customers get 15 percent off if Antoniella or Sposa Rosa refers them. To thank us for all
the business we've given her, Antoniella has insisted on making my
wedding cake, free of charge. And though she may be thrifty when
it comes to her own possessions, she's been very generous and en-
couraging of me to choose the most elaborate design and not worry
about the costs.

The cake comes in third as the most important element of the
wedding, followed by the venue first, and the dress second. Although I want my cake to look gorgeous, I care more about how it
tastes. So I've decided to stick to a simple whipped cream frosting
with a cheesecake filling. The cheesecake is actually Michael's idea.
Have I mentioned the guy has taste? The cake will have four tiers.
Its whipped cream base will feature a basket weave design. Pale
green and ivory ribbons, my wedding colors, will cascade down the
sides. Cream-colored peonies and roses, my flowers, will be adorning the sides of the cake. The top will be an elegant bow. "So what's
his excuse for being late this time?"

Antoniella interrupts my thoughts.

I smile. "Ahhh . . . You know Michael well. It's always work
these days that's keeping him."

"Hmm."

Antoniella wags her index finger at me and says, "Watch out for him. Make sure the eggs are fresh before you buy them. You can never be too careful."

With that, she walks off. What does she mean by that? Whatever. I take a bite of my cake and let its sweetness soothe me.

"*Ciao,* Antoniella!"

Michael's voice booms loudly. I look at my watch. At least he was just half an hour late this time. After he gives Antoniella his usual order of double *espresso* with a shot of Sambuca, he strides over to me. Instead of Antoniella hurrying over to the *espresso* machine to get Michael's order ready, she makes eye contact with me behind Michael's back and tilts her head in his direction as if to say, "Remember what I told you."

Damn Hunchback! So what if she's making my cake for free! Who does she think she is, criticizing everyone as if she's God? My mother's easily frayed temper is making an appearance in me.

Michael bends over to kiss me. As he's about to pull away, I continue kissing him. I can tell Michael is aroused by my aggressiveness. When he pulls away, his hand lightly, but subtly, brushes against my breast. I don't think the Hunchback sees that, but she definitely hasn't missed the long kiss. Her lips are pursed even tighter than usual before she finally walks off to make Michael's *espresso.*

"Well, that was a reception. I thought I was going to get my usual 'Thanks for keeping me waiting yet again' lecture. You must've missed me."

Michael winks at me as he takes off his Armani cashmere overcoat and sits down. His infamous winks had returned once we started dating.

"You should take charge like that more often. I like it."

"If you start being on time, I'll consider it."

I smile at him to let him know I'm really not mad.

Antoniella comes over and brings Michael's *espresso.* She isn't as careful carrying his cup as she was with mine, and some of the *espresso* spills over onto the saucer.

"Can I also get a slice of *tiramisu?* I wasn't hungry when I walked in, but suddenly I'm famished." Michael grins from ear to ear then very slowly licks his lips in the most suggestive manner. I turn away, feeling my face flush.

"Why don't you go have a real meal then if you're that hungry?"

Antoniella plops his *espresso* cup hard onto the table, spilling more of the *espresso*. She storms off.

Michael and I look at each other and laugh.

"You're terrible!"

"I know. That's why you love me, baby!"

"You know that's not true!"

I swat him playfully on his arm. Even though I hate to admit it, I am also drawn to the bad boy side of him that comes out on occasion. Seeing him making out with Tracy that night certainly has cast him in a bad boy light. But more of him is good, and *that's* the real reason why I love him.

"So what's up with Antoniella? She seems to be acting very weird toward you."

"Toward me and all of Astoria. Haven't you noticed?"

I laugh. "She's not terrible to everyone."

"The only person I've seen her be nice to is you and your family, and that's because you guys have helped promote her business. Something's in it for her."

I think about the validity of his statement. It bothers me a bit that that might be the case with Antoniella. I shrug the thought away.

"So, Vee, I'm really sorry about seeing you in your wedding dress yesterday. I had no idea you'd be trying it on. I hope you're not too disappointed?"

"No, no. It's okay. It's not the end of the world. You know me. I'm not one of your typical Bridezillas who believes in all that superstitious nonsense."

I stroke Michael's hand.

"Thank God! I felt horrible. Oh! And your mother! The way she was carrying on, '*Malocchio! Malocchio!*'"

Michael wipes his eyes with a napkin as we both laugh hysterically. I notice the Hunchback is glowering at Michael from behind the pastry display.

"My sisters were imitating her all day long. They offered to take me to a fortune-teller to remove the curse from me."

"Well, I'm sure your mother must still be cursing me out for walking in on you. I'll have to think of something to get back in her good graces."

"Oh, stop! My mother loves you. She wouldn't want anyone else for me. You know that!" I take a sip of *cappuccino* and clear my throat. "Hmmm . . . so, how much of the dress did you see?"

"I thought you said you didn't believe in that superstitious crap?"

"I don't. But I was just wondering, that's all."

"Honestly, I didn't see much. All I remembered was that the dress was strapless or almost strapless, and that your legs showed, which doesn't make sense to me since I saw plenty of fabric in the back of the dress. Was the dress temporarily pinned up for some alteration reason?"

My heart sinks a little. Okay, a lot. It sounds like he'd seen most of the dress. I've been praying fervently that he'd hardly seen it, especially since Ma had charged as fast as a wild boar to get him out of the shop. I'm not that superstitious. But what bride wants her fiancé to see her dress before the wedding? I've been looking forward to the expression on his face when he would first see me walk down the aisle in the gown that I'd designed. I notice Michael staring at me, trying to read my thoughts, something he does often. I put on my best phony smile.

"No, the dress wasn't temporarily hemmed up in the front. That was intentional. The front hem is shorter than the back. It's actually my favorite part of the dress. Doesn't it look dramatic with the traditional, cathedral-length train?"

Michael shrugs his shoulders. "I guess."

"Some of the best couture designers have designed dresses this way, and I love the combination of the traditional train with the daring shorter hem."

"Really? Your fashion tastes are usually more conservative. If Connie had designed that dress I could see it, since she's more of a risk taker when it comes to fashion."

"Oh, so I'm boring?"

"I didn't say that, Vee. You know what I mean. I love your fashion sensibility. You wear classics. You have a sophisticated sense when it comes to clothes, kind of like an Audrey Hepburn or Jackie O. That's part of what I love about you. This dress just doesn't seem you. Where did this all come from? It's almost like you're trying to be someone you're not."

"Yes, it's true. I do like the classics, but I wanted to spread my wings a bit. I wanted to dazzle you with something you wouldn't expect. A wedding dress is supposed to accentuate a bride's best features. Since you've always said my best trait is my legs, I thought, why not show them off?"

"Without a doubt you have the most beautiful, sexy legs that I've ever seen on any woman. I adore those legs, especially when they're wrapped around me while we're making love."

"Sshhhh . . . She'll hear you." I glance nervously toward Antoniella, who is spraying Windex on her pastry display.

"Don't sweat over the Hunchback."

Michael waves dismissively toward her. I hate it when he does that. He often gives me the same dismissive wave when I say something he doesn't take seriously.

"Look, baby, I appreciate your wanting to show me your magnificent legs on our wedding day, but think about it. Is it really appropriate, especially in church?"

I can't believe what I'm hearing. I am utterly shocked. Since when has Michael shown any sign of being old-fashioned? He doesn't even get jealous when other men on the street are eyeing me. *That* has always bothered me.

"You didn't get a good look at the dress before my mother rushed you out of there. The front hem isn't that short. It rests slightly below my knee. As you said, I have a more conservative, classic style. And I'm not an idiot. I'm aware that my dress needs to be respectable for church. But this is the twenty-first century, not the nineteenth century. We're not traipsing around in gowns every day. People wear shorts to Sunday Mass, for crying out loud."

"In America, people wear shorts to Mass. But you know the churches in Italy won't let you enter unless your knees and shoulders are covered. I remember when I was there the first time so many of the American tourists didn't know this. Maybe they won't appreciate you showing your legs."

I can feel my pulse pounding feverishly. "My knees *will* be covered. It's just my calves that are showing. Women do attend church in Italy with skirts and dresses. You act like I'm wearing a miniskirt."

"Okay, okay. The dress isn't that short, but I still think you should drop the hem and cover your legs completely. After all, aren't wedding dresses supposed to be long? What about that dress I saw in Sposa Rosa with the really long, traditional train and high neckline. Can't you design your dress more like that?"

Suddenly it's as hot as a sauna. Michael is referring to Sposa Rosa's featured dress for February: an Oscar de la Renta Alençon lace ball gown with a cathedral-length train and high neckline. The dress sports long sleeves, which are appropriate for winter weddings, but I'm getting married in June, *not* January! The dress is exquisite, but it's more for brides who have to follow strict religious guidelines about baring skin during the wedding ceremony. A lovely Orthodox Jewish girl had put a deposit on the dress last weekend. And I had noticed the girl was staring longingly at the strapless gowns that were all the rage now. Ugghhhh!!! I want to scream and would if we weren't in the Hunchback's bakery.

I let out a deep sigh. "So, Michael, you want me covered from head to toe like a cloistered nun? That's a first."

"Of course I don't want you to look like a nun! But be reasonable! See it from my eyes. I don't want my future wife to be wearing next to nothing either."

And he hasn't even seen the deep plunging back. He would really be having a fit now if he'd seen it.

"You're being old-fashioned. This isn't you. Where is this coming from?"

"Valentina, just consider it at least."

Hunchback or no Hunchback, I'm not holding back now.

"What do you know about women's fashion, let alone bridal fashion? And how dare you tell me what I should wear on my wedding day, especially after you had the nerve to walk in on me! Do you know how many hours I have been slaving away over that dress? What's the matter with you? Have you suddenly turned into a prude?"

Michael laughed. "You're overreacting, and keep your voice down if you don't want the Hunchback telling all of Astoria that I saw your dress."

"Whatever! I don't care. Look, Michael. I don't appreciate you telling me what I can wear. Pretty soon, you'll pull a Robert DeNiro and go all Raging Bull on me, trying to control every aspect of my life."

"Who's exaggerating now, Vee? I'm just looking out for you."

"You're looking out for me? It sounds like you're looking out for *you!* It sounds like you'd be embarrassed to have me by your side in that dress on our wedding day."

The more I think about it, the more I become convinced that's what this is all about. Michael is worried about his own image.

"You know how people talk, and they *will* talk if you keep that dress the way it is now. I care about you, and I don't want people gossiping about my bride. I'm surprised your mother hasn't said anything to you. I can only imagine what my mother will say."

BINGO! This is about his mother. Although Michael is very independent, he still defers to his mother on a regular basis. This has annoyed me since I'd first noticed how Michael acted around his mother. A few times while I waited for him to finish getting dressed to go to a family member's wedding or other party, his mother would comment on his tie or shirt. She'd be very passive-aggressive and use the "insult disguised as a compliment" tactic to get to him.

"That's an *interesting* choice of tie for a christening."

Or . . . "Those shoes are in style now? Really?"

Michael would immediately second guess himself, and though I would reassure him that he looked great, he would end up changing the criticized article of clothing.

In my case, she once said, "I *love* your hair pulled back. It makes your neck look longer."

I often wonder if Michael will continue to defer to his mother even after we are married. There were plenty of times when Michael asked my opinion, only to then turn to his mother and ask her what she thought. He'd never taken my opinion over his mother's.

"Michael, it's my decision what I'll wear on my wedding day.

I'm not telling you what to wear, am I? Thanks for your input. It's late. I need to get going."

"Okay. Let me pay the bill, and I'll drive you."

I hold up my hand. "No, don't. I'd rather walk and get some fresh air."

Michael stands up and kisses me, but I hardly open my mouth. I can't help but note how different this kiss is from the earlier one we'd shared.

As I walk out of the bakery, Antoniella glances my way. I quickly wave to her. She nods her head but then looks away, almost embarrassed. She must've heard the argument.

After walking only a few feet, I begin to wish I'd let Michael drive me home. With the high winds, the temperature feels like it's in the single digits. But I need to get away from him. His comments on my dress have really infuriated me. Maybe he is right. Maybe I'm being irrational and selfish. Did my mother have the same thoughts when she saw the dress but didn't say anything since she knew how hard I'd been working on it? No. I could tell my mother loved the dress, and though she's a traditional Catholic, she's also fashion forward and can respect the more daring modern designs of today. My mother isn't as old school as Michael's mother. I love my future mother-in-law, but she is just so reserved at times, and she's worse than my mother in worrying about what others think.

I dig my fingernails into my hands. I'm still seething at what Michael has said to me. No wonder he'd looked stunned when he saw me in my gown. I thought it was because of the beauty of my gown, but instead, he was horrified. I try to fight back the tears, but it hurts too much.

Maybe I should drop the hem in the front? After all, Ma believes I should change the dress since Michael had seen it. It's just the hem of the dress. But that's also my favorite detail. My head starts to throb as I feel a headache coming on.

Make sure the eggs are fresh before you buy them.

The Hunchback's words come back to me. I now realize what she meant. If Michael has surprised me with this conservative side of him tonight, what else am I in store for?

❧ 5 ❧

Trashy Trumpet

"**D**id I get the right dress?"

This is the eternal question that brides-to-be ask themselves almost as soon as they've left the bridal shop after purchasing their gowns. And now this is the question I'm grappling with as it swings back and forth in my head, much like a pendulum, hitting each side of my temples and giving me the worst tension headache.

The dilemma started after I had my argument with Michael. Now I'm completely insecure about my dress, which only two weeks ago seemed perfect. Maybe I should just change it completely?

I've taken my tenth order this month for a trumpet- or mermaid-style gown. The trend has picked up steam fast in the past few years. Now there's even a newer twist on the mermaid dress for brides who want a softer, less sexy or body-hugging look than the mermaid offers—the fit-and-flare style. The fit and flare was fitted from the bodice to either the waist or below the waist, but then flared out. It was the right fit for a bride who didn't want to have the fuller skirt of a ball gown or A-line dress, but didn't want the ultra-snug fit that a trumpet or mermaid dress gave her.

I've always preferred the fuller skirt of an A-line. With my petite frame, I don't want an ultra-poofy ball gown that will swallow me up or be hard to move around in. But I have to admit the sleeker version of the fit-and-flare gowns is growing on me. Maybe I should switch?

Stop it! Stop it! Stop it! I have to keep telling myself to just stop obsessing. I've devoted too much time to my dress to start from scratch again, and that's basically what I would have to do if I decide to switch from my A-line to a fit-and-flare or trumpet gown. I can't believe that I'm falling prey to the same insecurities my clients are known for—even though with Michael's concerns, I have good reason.

I've seen it countless times, and my family and I have always assured our clients it's just their anxieties about wanting the perfect dress and wedding that are making them doubt their choice. We've had brides who forfeited their nonrefundable deposit once we started sewing the dress just so they could order another dress. That doesn't happen often though, since my family and I have become experts at persuasiveness. But sometimes even our arguments fall on deaf ears.

And it's just such a client whom I'm working with now. She'd originally chosen a Vera Wang ball gown dress with a cathedral train from our portfolio. She had wanted it replicated exactly and had wanted nothing changed about the designer's original creation. Now, she doesn't want to even look at our books but instead wants a custom-made design.

"My dress must be the only design like it! I don't want anyone else to have it after I wear it. I'll draft up some papers for you to sign to ensure that you don't sell this design you're creating for me to another client."

Amy Porter is an attorney—and a typical Bridezilla client. She refuses to work with anyone else at Sposa Rosa but me. When I tried to reassure her that she'd receive the same expert attention from either my mother or one of my sisters, she replied, "I either work with you alone or I take my business elsewhere. And don't think I'm not getting my deposit back from my first gown. I can find loopholes in that agreement you made me sign."

I definitely don't want to face off with Amy in court. I had Googled her name and learned that she was a litigation lawyer who had won 90 percent of her cases. So I just smile and agree to all of Amy's demands—no matter how over-the-top they are. At the moment, she's telling me that she is getting too old to have a traditional-style ball gown like the one she'd ordered a month ago. Besides, she's just realized that the original gown's design doesn't adequately represent who she is.

"The sleeker silhouette of a trumpet gown doesn't hide anything. And that's me. You see what you get. After all, why have I been killing myself in Bridal Boot Camp at the gym only to hide it underneath all the layers of a ball gown?"

Even though I think Amy is a bit off her rocker, I have to agree her rationale here makes perfect sense.

The pendulum swings fiercely in my head: "A-line or trumpet? A-line or trumpet?"

If I change my dress to a trumpet, that will solve the *malocchio* problem since Michael has seen my dress. My mother can sleep peacefully the rest of her days, and I can just keep the gown long, which would make Michael and his mother happy. Besides, I can't see a shorter front hem working as well on a trumpet gown as it does on an A-line or ball gown, although I've seen that look on some of the couture dresses. That's too avant-garde for my more classical fashion tastes. I have to take some time out tonight when I'm alone to look at my gown's silhouette and see if I have made the right choice.

So I'm finishing up sketching my new design for Amy as she watches over my shoulder, giving me cues as though I were sketching the portrait of a criminal who has just attacked her, when I hear that voice.

Tracy!

My first thought is to flee. I can take my break early. Ugghhhh! I suddenly remember I'm in the shop alone. Rita's taking her break, and Connie is at the dentist with Ma.

What is she doing here? Is she getting married? My stomach is doing somersaults.

As if reading my thoughts, I hear Tracy say, "I'm glad I'm not the one getting married and losing *my* single life. Ha, ha-HAAAAAAA!"

She still has the same annoying laugh she had as a teenager. I've always suspected it's fake and a way for Tracy to add more drama to herself because she always needs to be the center of attention. The way she draws out the "HAAAAA" at the end can't be natural. My thoughts go back to the night of our sophomore dance when I'd caught her making out with Michael in the alleyway. The next day I had called her.

"How could you, Tracy? You knew how much I liked him."

"I'm sorry, Vee. I didn't mean for anything to happen. It just did."

"That's supposed to make me feel better?"

"I really am sorry, Vee, that I made out with Michael. I didn't completely know what I was doing. You have to believe me. Don't tell anyone, but I was buzzed. During the dance, I went outside for a cigarette with Ray and Gary, and they pulled out of their suit pockets those little liquor bottles they give out on planes. I drank two of the vodka bottles. They hit me pretty quickly. I wasn't even sure at first it was you staring at me kissing Michael. When I realized you had seen us, I was horrified. But it was too late. You'd run off. Vee, I would never intentionally hurt you. You've got to believe that."

I didn't know whether she was lying again as usual. I couldn't wipe from my memory the satisfied look she gave me after I caught her kissing Michael. I wasn't going to let her off so easily.

"I don't know, Tracy. You didn't look so hammered to me that you didn't know what you were doing."

"It was nothing, Vee! It's not like we're boyfriend/girlfriend. It was just a little kissing."

"A little kissing? It looked like a lot more to me. His hands were all over you!"

"Vee, you're overreacting. Besides, it's not like the two of you are dating."

This last sentence caused me to see flames with Tracy in the center of them.

"So my not dating him made it okay? You knew how crazy I am about him. You're supposed to be my best friend! Friends don't steal their friends' guys!"

"I'm sorry, Vee. Really, I am. But again, you weren't his girlfriend. If you were, I would've stayed away."

"No, you wouldn't have. And you kept kissing him even after you saw me watching you. You seemed to take some sick pleasure out of it. It was as if you were rubbing my face in it! I don't believe for a second that you were too drunk to recognize me."

"I was hoping we could be mature about this whole thing, and you'd see it was just a little making out on one night between two people who had a little too much to drink. It's not like it's going to happen again. Michael is going back to Cornell this weekend. Probably the next time I'll see him will be years from now. He's not even going to remember we made out. Look, Vee. I didn't want to have to tell you this, but I see I'm going to have to. Michael and I talked about you."

"What? You didn't tell him how I feel about him, did you?"

"No, no! I'd never do that. I'd never betray your secret."

I wasn't too sure about that either. How could I after what she'd done?

"So why were you talking to him about me?"

"He saw me walking home from the dance alone. He was coming out of McGuinn's Pub. He looked like he'd had a few too many drinks himself. He asked me if we were still good friends, and I told him we were. He told me what a sweet person you were and how he'd always looked out for you when you were a kid. He couldn't believe how much you'd grown up. How pretty you'd become."

"He said that?"

"Yes, he did. He said all of his friends had the hots for you, but he told them to steer clear of you or they'd have to deal with him."

"Really?"

"Really. He said he wouldn't trust most of his friends with his little sister if he'd had one as pretty and nice as you. He said he always thought of you as the little sister he didn't have."

My heart sank. Just when I was starting to think that he might have some feelings for me, my suspicions that he only thought of me as his kid sister had been right all along.

"So when he told me that, I knew he'd never let himself feel anything more for you. He cares about you a lot. That was obvious, Vee. But he doesn't care for you in the way you want him to."

Tears sprang into my eyes.

"Then he grabbed my hand and told me how sexy I looked. He was staring at me with that intense gaze of his. That did it for me. I was hooked."

Yes, I knew that gaze. It had undone me on several occasions.

"I tried to let go of his hand, but he kept grabbing it. Then he started running and pulled me into that alleyway. I told him he was just drunk and didn't know what he was doing. He was laughing and said he knew *exactly* what he was doing."

I didn't want to hear these details, but I couldn't bring myself to tell Tracy to stop. Part of me was envisioning myself running with Michael into that alley instead of Tracy. Michael's hands were all over *my* body, *not* Tracy's. I was feeling his tongue thrusting into my mouth, and his hot kisses were lingering down my neck. I was the one making him crazy with desire, *not* my best friend.

"Before I knew it, he was kissing me. I started to pull away, but then I remembered what he said, that he thought of you as a sister. If I had any hint that he had feelings for you, I would've pushed him off. Honestly, Vee."

"I don't know, Tracy. I'm having a hard time believing you even tried to resist him. It sounds like you were very willing, and I can't forget the look you gave me. Why did you do that? It was as if you didn't care and you wanted to hurt me."

Then Tracy started crying.

"Please, Vee! I feel horrible about what happened; you have to forgive me! You've been my best friend since we were kids. I don't know what I'd do without you. I swear I was drunk. It was so easy for me to do what Michael wanted. He wouldn't let me walk away. I was out of it. And I didn't know it was you staring at me. I swear!"

Something about her crying lessened my anger a bit.

"I don't know. I have to think about it."

I hung up the phone. Part of me felt a little better in knowing that at least Michael had thought I was pretty, but the knowledge that he still only saw me as a little sister overshadowed his thoughts about my looks. I wanted to believe Tracy. If it were true that she'd been drunk and hadn't known I was the one staring at them that would make a huge difference. In the end, just like the other times, I forgave her. But forgetting what I'd witnessed that night was much harder to do. And had I realized that every time I forgave Tracy, I was only allowing her next transgression against me to become graver, I would've never forgiven her. For her next betrayal was too horrible to forgive, and the long friendship we'd had could not survive it.

Now after fourteen years of not seeing each other, Tracy is here in my shop. Realizing there's no escape for me, I know I need to get this confrontation over with. I finish up with Amy and walk over to Tracy. She greets me with the biggest smile though her eyes look nervous.

Tracy is with a young girl, who has to be no more than twenty years old.

"Hi, Vee! It's so good to see you! God, it's been so long!"

"Hi, Tracy." I cut straight to the chase. "What can I do for you today?"

Tracy frowns for a moment but quickly reverts to her phony mode.

"This is my sweet, sweet cousin Kathleen. She's so young—and innocent! Can you believe she's getting married at nineteen? You and I could never do that! But I have to say Kathleen is in love, and nothing will keep her from marrying Andrew, not even listening to her older cousin. But who am I to stop her? Kathleen is an adult now."

With all of Tracy's faults, she is blessed with the gift of condescension. On many occasions, I too have been made to feel like Tracy is far superior to me. Poor Kathleen. The color in her cheeks is slowly flaring up, and she gives me a timid smile. Her shyness is in extreme opposition to Tracy's obnoxious personality.

I shake Kathleen's hand. "Hi, I'm Valentina. Congratulations on your engagement! I'm sure you must be so excited."

Kathleen lifts her gaze from the floor, and I detect a glow in her eyes. "Thank you. I am excited but nervous, too."

"It's okay to be nervous. But I don't want you to be nervous about your dress. If you decide to order your dress at Sposa Rosa, you can put away any worries you might have about your gown. That's what you're paying us for. We'll take care of everything. Now, have you thought about what you might want your dress to look like?"

"Well, I . . ."

"Of course, she won't have to worry about getting the perfect dress here. I told Kathleen she had to go to the best bridal shop in Queens. And since you and I were friends in high school, I knew you'd take care of us, Vee."

Naturally, Tracy has to turn the spotlight back on her.

"So you were beginning to say, Kathleen, what you want in a dress before Tracy interrupted you."

I shoot Tracy a look that tells her she'd better let her cousin speak for herself. She gives me one of her own dirty looks and crosses her arms.

"Well, I was thinking of something simple yet elegant?"

Kathleen looks to Tracy for approval. But I quickly jump in before Tracy can take over the reins again.

"Yes, many brides are going for the simple yet elegant look now."

That isn't entirely true. This trend had been hot about a decade ago. I'm disappointed that Kathleen is going for what I've always thought is a bit of a boring look in wedding gowns. But I need to remind myself that this is her wedding, and not everyone has my fashion tastes. I have to fight the urge to tell brides-to-be what I think they should choose in a design. Of course, I can give recommendations. But completely swaying a bride as to what she wants for herself, that's out of the question. I also must ensure the bride is choosing the dress *she* likes. Often, their mothers or whomever else they bring to help them with the dress shopping influence their choices.

"I don't know if you know anything about Sposa Rosa, but we do offer brides knockoff designs of famous designers' dresses. Most brides, however, usually want the dress to be slightly different from the original designer dress, but if you saw a dress you liked on a celebrity bride that you want replicated exactly, we can do that. We also do custom-made designs, so if you want us to create a dress that looks like nothing any celebrity has worn or designer has already created, we can do that, too. Lastly, we have a 'Featured Gown of the Month.' Each month we display a particular gown. And it just so happens that this month's featured gown sports a simple yet elegant design."

I point to the dress on our mannequin in the center window display. The dress is a clean, strapless gown in satin with a modified A-line skirt and a ruched bodice. No embroidery or beading adorns the dress.

Kathleen walks over to the featured gown to get a better look.

"This is very nice, but I'm not sure it's what I want." Kathleen says this with uncertainty, looks down at the floor, almost as if she's afraid she'll be hurting my feelings.

Tracy chimes in, "How about a—"

"Of course, you need to look at several dresses before you decide." I interrupt Tracy again and take Kathleen's arm in mine, leading her to our portfolios.

"We have photographs in these books of all the gowns we've designed. Pick a few you like, and then you can try on the samples. Oh, I forgot to ask you. Did you bring any pictures from magazines that you want to show me?"

"No. I haven't looked at any magazines yet. I only got engaged two nights ago, and Tracy told me we couldn't waste any time in shopping for a dress."

I wonder where Kathleen's mother is. Maybe she passed away? Brides always bring their mothers. I don't ask out of fear of bringing up a sensitive subject on what should be a happy occasion.

"Well, you can take a seat on our couch, and I'll bring you a cup of coffee and pastries while you browse through our books. Take your time."

"Thank you." Kathleen smiles at me.

I bring out a tray with coffee and miniature pastries for both Kathleen and Tracy, although I really don't want to extend the courtesy to Tracy. God knows she'd taken enough from me when we were friends.

Kathleen picks up a mini Napoleon, but Tracy shoots out her

hand, grabbing her cousin's arm. "You can't! You have to be on a strict diet from now until the wedding day or else you'll mess up your figure! I see you eyeing those tighter mermaid dresses. You'll never fit into them if you keep eating junk!"

Kathleen places the Napoleon back onto the tray.

"Oh, come on, Tracy! One tiny Napoleon isn't going to kill her. Besides, I'm sure you have plenty of time until the wedding. That reminds me, I haven't asked you when the date is?"

Tracy's eyes are absolutely shooting daggers into me. She isn't even attempting to keep her trademark frozen smile on her face anymore.

"We haven't decided on the exact date yet, but we were thinking maybe six months from now, so I guess Tracy is right. I should watch my figure, but thank you so much for the pastries, Valentina."

"You have a beautiful figure. Don't be too strict on yourself with your diet. You don't want to lose too much weight."

Okay, I'm acting like Tracy now, telling this girl what to do. This is about Kathleen, I have to remind myself, *not* my battle with Tracy.

"I'll give you some time to look over the books. Just let me know when you need me."

I walk to the front of the store and check a few e-mails. Since it's Monday, our slowest day of the week, the shop is empty except for Kathleen and Tracy.

"So I see congratulations are in order for you, too."

I look up to see Tracy staring at my engagement ring. The expression on her face is equivalent to a dog staring at a juicy hunk of raw meat.

"Yes, thank you."

"So you got him after all."

Of course she must've heard from someone in Astoria that it's Michael whom I'm engaged to. I pretend not to hear her, focusing my attention back on the computer screen, hoping she'd get the message and leave me alone. No such luck. I should've known the inevitable was coming as soon as I saw her drag her bony butt into Sposa Rosa. She's still a very unhealthy-looking size zero.

"I guess I was wrong that he would never see you as more than just a little sister. My bad."

Something in her voice makes me look up. She is wearing that same warped smile she had on the night she was making out with Michael. And her nostrils are flared slightly, just like on that night, giving her the appearance that something smells really bad. Flashing back to that image makes my blood boil. I feel territorial toward Michael, especially now that he is my fiancé.

And then she pushes my fury over the edge by adding, "I'm very happy for you, Vee. You deserve to be happy."

That's it. I can't hold back any longer.

"Thank you, Tracy. You don't know how good that makes me feel to know that you of all people are concerned for my happiness, especially since you never seemed to want anything for me but misery when we were friends."

I didn't have the nerve to stand up to her when I was a teen, but I'm not that helpless kid anymore.

"I don't understand, Vee. I thought we'd put everything behind us. I thought you'd forgiven me. But it's obvious you haven't."

"I'm not getting into this with you at my workplace, Tracy. Besides, this was over fourteen years ago. I did forgive you. But don't expect me to be thrilled whenever I see your face or even think that we're going to pick up our friendship. You know those days are over."

Tracy actually looks like she is going to cry. Crocodile tears. That's all they are. She's a good actress. I know that now.

"It's because you're engaged to Michael, isn't it? You're still mad about that night you saw us?"

"This has nothing to do with Michael, and you know it. Stop trying to shift the blame for your ugly actions onto others."

"Vee, I'm so sorry over how things ended with us in high school. I don't know how many times I have to apologize."

"Let me make this easy for you. Stop apologizing. I told you this all those years ago, and I'll say it again. I can't ever be your friend. I don't hate you. I just don't care about you. You don't exist for me anymore. Being friends with you gave me nothing but grief. All the times you lied to people and told them I said things about them when I hadn't. You always competed with me—my grades, my family life, my friends. I could go on and on. I have no interest in being friends with someone I can't trust. How could I be friends with you again when just the sight of you brings me back to that horrible day when my father died?"

Tracy's tears spill down her face. She grabs a few tissues from the counter.

"I shouldn't have come in here," she whispers, glancing nervously at her cousin, obviously not wanting her to see how upset she is.

"Then why did you?"

"My cousin."

"There are other bridal shops in Queens."

"Okay, I'll admit it. I was hoping things would be different after all this time. I was hoping you'd see I was a kid who made a lot of stupid mistakes."

"See, that's what got to me even after all those other times I forgave you. You never really seemed sorry for what you did. And there was always some excuse. I was a kid, too. I didn't act the way you did. I never hurt you. You don't deserve my forgiveness."

"But that's not like you, Vee. You always forgave me."

"Well, things change. I'm not that naive girl anymore who lets others take advantage of her. Look where my forgiveness got me. You just kept treating me like a doormat. You never changed your ways. No wonder. By constantly forgiving you, I just made you think it was okay to act the way you did. 'Vee will just forgive me if I lie to her again or make out with her crush. It doesn't matter what I do to her. She's a sucker, and she'll always forgive me and be my friend.' Well, not anymore."

"I know I hurt you, and I messed up big time, but you think you're so perfect?"

"No, I don't."

"Yes, you do. You were always lording it over all of us in high school. You were such a Goody Two-shoes. You wouldn't even smoke a cigarette, for crying out loud. You thought you were better than us."

"That's not true, and you know it."

"It was true, and it's still true. You're just as bad as me that you can't even show me some compassion."

"You have a lot of nerve. Where was your compassion when my father was dying, and you sent those little skanks to my house? If it weren't for your cousin, I'd throw you out of here right now." I struggle to keep my voice low, not wanting Kathleen to hear our argument.

The front door swings open. It's Rita. She freezes when she sees Tracy.

"What are you doing here?"

"Her cousin is shopping for a wedding dress."

I tilt my head toward the back of the shop where Kathleen is. I know if Kathleen weren't there Rita would make a scene.

"You okay, Vee?"

Rita scowls at Tracy as she walks over to us.

"Yes, I'm fine. Tracy and I were just clearing the air. Excuse me. I just remembered I have an important phone call to make. I'll check in on you and Kathleen as soon as I'm off the phone."

After I walk past Tracy, I can't help muttering under my breath, "Slut."

Not long after Tracy made out with Michael, she developed her rep as "The Slut of Astoria." Almost every guy in Astoria was dating her. Even though Tracy had transferred to a different high school in her junior year, I still heard about her notorious rep for going through guys like yesterday's dirty laundry. Most of the girls in town both despised and were in awe of her. She wasn't that pretty, so why were all the guys drooling over her? What did she have that the rest of us didn't? Of course, soon the other girls and I figured it out. Tracy was easy with a capital E. Tracy had even confided in me about many of her sexual exploits. I had tried to talk some sense into her, but she'd laughed at me and said, "Oh, Vee! Just lose it already so you can stop preaching to me!"

I hadn't liked hearing the way people talked about her in high school. She was my best friend, after all. Now, I looked at her and couldn't believe what poor judgment I'd had in staying friends with her for so long.

I didn't really have to make a phone call, but I need a few minutes to compose myself before it gets ugly. And I refuse to let Tracy make me lose my professionalism. I go to the restroom and count to ten, making sure I take extra-long, deep breaths. This is a calming technique I learned from Connie. Maybe she is the smartest of us DeLuca women for taking up meditation and yoga. I make my way back out to where Kathleen is pointing to a dress in the portfolio and chatting animatedly with Tracy.

"I see a dress has got your attention, Kathleen?"

"I really like this mermaid gown. But I'm still not sure. All I know is that I don't want anything too poofy, but I am open to trying a couple of fuller A-line gowns."

"No problem. I can give you a few modified A-line gowns, which aren't as full as a traditional A-line, and we'll definitely steer you away from the ball gowns. So let's get you into a few sample gowns. And then we can talk about the specifics of the design. Remember, you can change any elements of the dresses you see in the pictures."

"I don't think an A-line gown would look good on you, Kathleen. It'll make you look shorter than you already are."

"That's why I mentioned the newer modified A-line gowns, which are more fitted." I say this as sternly as I can without giving away to Kathleen that there is animosity between Tracy and myself.

"Whatever. I'm just trying to help you out, Kathleen. Go for a sexy, body-hugging mermaid dress! Have a little fun!"

I leave to pull the samples before I lose my professional demeanor altogether. Tracy is trying to push my buttons in front of her cousin, and I won't let her. As I walk past her, I notice her eyeliner is a bit smudged from the crying she's done. But I feel no sympathy that I am the cause of her tears. Part of me almost relishes the suffering I'm causing her.

As I riffle through the samples, I can't help but wonder what Tracy's choice in a wedding dress would be—the Trashy Trumpet? And with that thought in mind, I suddenly have no doubt as to whether I'll change my gown from an A-line to a trumpet. A-line it will stay.

6

Karma

The oak trees are dancing the mambo, swaying side to side, letting the winds coming off the East River's currents choreograph their movements. Four seagulls circle overhead, squawking to one another. I love watching them whenever I go to the beach. But in this urban setting, they appear menacing and out of place.

Instead of going home directly after work that night, I had decided to walk to Astoria Park. When I need to think and be alone, I often come here. There is something about the landscape of the East River running beneath the Triborough Bridge with the Manhattan skyline off in the distance that calms me. It's also a great place for coming up with new design ideas.

A white limo pulls up, and a bridal party gets out. The bride is wearing an organza overlay mermaid dress. I smile, suddenly remembering how I used to tell my father when I was a little girl that I wanted to be a mermaid. When he'd come home from work, he'd shout out, "Where's my mermaid?" I'd run out and rush into his arms, giggling.

A few boats sail by on the East River. My father, or "Baba" as we called him in our Sicilian dialect, used to take me to Astoria Park when I was a kid and always pointed the boats out to me. One time he drove to the Brooklyn Navy Yard, where we stopped and took pictures of the freight ships. On our way back home, he always bought my favorite ice cream—pistachio on a wafer cone.

He tended to spoil my sisters and me, buying us little gifts on a regular basis.

"Nicola, you're not teaching these girls the value of a penny."

"Relax, Olivia. They're my girls. How can I not treat them like princesses? And I am teaching them something."

"That money falls from trees?" Ma scowled.

"No. I'm teaching them how a man should treat his woman. If they see how well I treat you and them, they will stay away from the, what do the Americans call them? 'Riffraff'?"

Ma sighed. But even she saw the wisdom in his words. And from that day forward, she never complained to Nicola again about him spending money on my sisters and me. She often told me this story after Baba died. She wanted me to know how much he loved us and how he was thinking of our future even when we were little girls.

Baba's cancer seemed to have sprouted overnight, though we all knew that it could take years for cancer to manifest itself. He began coughing uncontrollably one day after mopping the floors.

"Nicola, you're going to kill yourself with all that ammonia you put in the pail. One little cap is all you need. I keep telling you, but you never listen to me."

Ma handed my father a glass of milk to help "coat his lungs," but he spit it all up as his coughing spasms continued. He dismissed Ma with an angry wave of his arm as he bent over the kitchen sink.

About two weeks after the first attack, my father started coughing violently every morning, and sometimes even in the middle of the night. We all could hear him hacking away in the bathroom.

"Nicola, something is wrong. You need to go see a doctor."

"I'm just getting old, is all it is. Haven't you noticed all the old men in the neighborhood coughing and spitting on the streets?"

Italian men are very stubborn, more so than the women. They also like to think of themselves as invincible. It wasn't until a month later that Baba finally made an appointment with Dr. Serafino, our family doctor. Dr. Serafino sent Baba for an X-ray. As soon as he got the results, he called Baba and told him he was referring him to a pulmonary specialist.

To Italians, *specialist* is one of the most dreaded words in the dictionary. It's one thing to go to your family doctor, but when the specialist is brought in, it can be nothing but bad news. And in my father's case, it did turn out to be bad news—*very* bad news.

We were all stunned to learn he had lung cancer. Today, everyone knows someone who has cancer. But when my father was diagnosed, it wasn't as prevalent as it is now. People regularly came up to my family and me, telling us they didn't know anyone who had cancer, which only made us feel more alienated. Of course, in my mother's case, she felt cursed.

Baba began the full round of chemo and radiation treatments. Of course, there were numerous surgeries. In the beginning, Baba tackled the illness head-on, never once showing any fear or doubts that he would beat the cancer—that is, until close to the end.

Often many cancer patients seem to rebound toward the end of their illness, but then have a relapse. Such was the case with Baba. About two months before he died, he woke up in the middle of the night with a nosebleed. Just like the coughing that wouldn't stop at the start of his illness, his nose now bled endlessly.

I remember the sound of the rushing water coming from the kitchen sink, awakening me from my deep slumber. *Why is the kitchen faucet on at three a.m.?* I wondered. My heart started to skip a beat, but I convinced myself it was nothing, even though I knew my father was sleeping in our finished basement because it was cooler. It was one of those sweltering July nights for which New York City is notorious. We didn't own an air conditioner, and our basement was the only place where we could get some relief from the heat in the summer.

Maybe he's just thirsty, I thought. I tried to go back to sleep, but all I could focus on was the sound of the running water. *Why am I worrying?* Ma was sleeping with him on the sofa bed just in case something happened.

I drifted back to sleep but woke up again half an hour later. I could still hear the water. What was he doing? I lay there paralyzed even though a voice inside me was saying, *See what's going on.* But sleep was calling me like the enchanting cries of a siren. *I'm sure it's nothing,* I told myself. Just as soon as my eyes closed, I heard my mother speaking in a low voice to Baba, then suddenly a loud thump.

"Nicola! Nicola!"

I shot out of bed fast and ran down to the basement.

As I came into view of the kitchen, I didn't know what awaited me. My heart had stopped beating. Even my breathing seemed strangled in my throat. I could still hear the faucet running. Splotches of blood dotted the floor. Four blood-soaked handkerchiefs sat crumpled on top of the kitchen counter. Two blood-soaked dish towels lay on the floor. Ma was leaning up against the kitchen sink. Her arms were wrapped around Baba's waist, as she tried to hold him up, but his weight was quickly overpowering her. I ran forward, placing my hands in his armpits to get a good grip to lower him to the ground. But Ma wasn't picking up on my cue. She continued screaming, "Nicola!"

"Ma, help me lower him to the ground!"

"Nicola! Nicola!" My mother didn't seem to hear me. Then, Baba's eyes fluttered open.

"His eyes opened! They opened!" I never heard such relief in her voice as I did in that moment.

"Ma, quick! We have to place him on the floor!" I didn't know how much longer I could support my father's weight, especially since my mother's grip had loosened considerably.

Ma nodded her head as we slowly squatted down, gently lowering him.

"Hold his head while I go get a pillow and call nine-one-one."

"Rita's on the phone with them right now."

Connie was standing behind me with the most terrified look I'd ever seen on her face.

"Stay with Ma. I'm going to get a pillow and blanket for Baba."

Connie's arms were wrapped around her waist. Her face looked as white as the nightgown she wore.

"Don't be scared. He'll be all right."

I tried to reassure Connie, though I really didn't believe Baba was going to be okay. He'd lost so much blood. And I'd heard that water running for what must've been an hour, maybe more. I tried to push my fear aside along with my guilt for not getting out of bed sooner and ran to the sofa bed my parents had been sleeping on. I grabbed one of the pillows and ripped the duvet off the bed. Even though it was the middle of July and quite warm, sometimes Baba would get the chills.

"They're coming!" Rita shouted out as she ran down the basement stairs.

I placed the blanket over Baba, and Rita took the pillow from me, placing it under his head. But Ma still held onto the sides of his head, not wanting to let go.

"Before your father fainted, he told me his nose was bleeding for almost an hour."

"Why didn't you call me?" I asked Ma.

"I didn't know until ten minutes ago. You know what a heavy sleeper I am."

That was true. If it weren't for Ma's cantankerous snoring, we would've thought she was dead since it was near impossible to wake her up.

"When I saw all the bloody handkerchiefs and towels, I knew something was terribly wrong. I told him we needed to go to the emergency room right away. But he kept telling me it was nothing to worry about. The man has cancer and his nose is running like Niagara Falls, and he tells me there's nothing to worry about!"

Leave it to Ma to still make one of her wisecracks during a moment of crisis.

"I'll be okay. Just help me stand."

We all were startled to finally hear Baba speak. His nose had stopped bleeding.

"You stay right where you are, Nicola DeLuca! I'm tired of you not listening to me and then look what happens!"

"Valentina, help me up."

"Baba, you're in no shape to get back up on your feet so soon after collapsing. Sorry, but Ma is right this time."

"What do you mean 'this time'? I am always right!" Ma's eyebrows were knitted furiously together as she gave a sharp nod of her head, indicating she had triumphed.

Sirens wailed outside.

I ran to the front door to let in the paramedics.

"He's in the basement."

I was about to close the door when I heard more sirens. A police car stopped in front of our house. There was no doubt in my mind that most of the neighbors were probably up now and peering out from behind their windows. The thought of having to explain to everyone once again the details of my father's illness made me feel queasy.

I escorted the police officers inside, leading them downstairs. Their gazes took in our finished, but somewhat crude, basement.

Ma must've also noticed their observations since she quickly came over and said, "Our air conditioner broke. My husband was sleeping down here because it's cooler."

The police officers nodded understandingly but continued to look around our basement. I could tell they'd seen through Ma's lies and realized the truth was that we couldn't afford an air conditioner. My sisters and I went to Catholic schools, and the tuition on top of the house's mortgage made it necessary for my parents to cut out whatever they could.

One of the paramedics' voices reached my ears. He reminded me of Sonny Bono. He had the same thick brown mustache and hair color, and even his voice sounded similar to Sonny Bono's. Of the two paramedics, he seemed to be the leader even though the other paramedic looked older. Sonny Bono's voice interrupted my thoughts.

"You have CAN-CERRRR? Yes? You have CAN-CERRRR?"

Why do paramedics seem to have a tendency to talk to people who are ill as if they're deaf? I guess it is protocol, and they probably need to be certain the patient is hearing them correctly. Nevertheless, it was infuriating. They were talking to him as if he had a limited mental capacity. *He's not deaf, you morons!* I wanted to scream.

"Tell me where it HURTS."

I heard Baba murmur something to them.

"You are feeling BETTER? YES? YES?"

Again, my father murmured something, but I couldn't hear. The police had asked us to give the paramedics some space, so we were standing a few feet away. Ma kept straining her neck and looking over, desperate to know what Baba was saying.

"You think you can get up? You want to get up?"

"No!" my mother yelled out.

"It's okay, Mrs. DeLuca. We'll be right by his side."

The older paramedic held up his hands as if Ma were the one with a gun in her possession and not the police officers.

Ma chewed on her lip—a nervous habit of hers.

The paramedics slowly helped Baba come to a seated position first.

"On the count of three, we'll stand together with you, OKAY?"

I couldn't see Sonny Bono being able to lift my father, even with the help of his sidekick. He was all of 5'5" and looked as though he weighed less than 130 pounds.

"Here we go, Mr. DeLuca. ONE."

"I can hear you. You don't need to talk so loud," Baba said. He sounded very weary and frustrated.

"Just making sure, Mr. DELUCAHHH."

The older paramedic who had seemed happy to let his younger partner take the lead finally seemed to be asserting himself. He was also copying Sonny Bono's annoying habit of talking loudly. On the count of three, both of them hoisted up Baba, who had his arms around their shoulders. We all held our breath as he took two steps. Then a third and a fourth.

"I feel better. I think I can walk on my own."

"Are you SURE?" Sonny Bono asked.

"Si, si." Baba gave Sonny his trademark dismissive wave.

Slowly, the paramedics let go of Baba and waited. We all held our breath. Baba took baby steps, and then without warning began careening to the side.

"Help him!" I yelled, but the paramedics had reached him before I was even done crying out.

"I told you!" My mother shook her fist at the paramedics.

Baba's eyes fluttered closed, then opened again. He was fighting to stay conscious. The police officers scrambled and helped the paramedics carry him over to the gurney.

"We're going to take you to the hospital, Mr. DELUCAHHH, OKAY?"

Baba just stared blankly up at the ceiling as the EMTs began rolling the gurney out toward the back entrance that led to the yard. As they passed me, Baba's eyes locked with mine. For the first time in my life, I saw fear in his eyes. The father who had made me feel safe when I was a child was gone, replaced by a very weak and scared man. I fought back tears. It was my turn now to be strong for him, to take away his fear.

As soon as they passed me, I turned around. This time, it was my mother's hollow stare that greeted me. I walked over to her and collapsed into her arms as we held on to each other, sobbing uncontrollably. Rita and Connie were crying silently as they watched Ma and me. We should've held ourselves together for the younger girls, but we couldn't. One of the police officers stared sympathetically at us. I suddenly remembered I wasn't wearing a bra. Had the policemen noticed I was braless when I let them into our house? I knew the police were here to help us, but suddenly their presence felt more like an invasion as they became privy to our secrets and observed us in our worst and most private moment.

Baba had emergency surgery and was in the intensive care unit for two weeks. The cancer cells, which his doctors were hopeful they'd killed, had returned and metastasized. He only had one month left to live. Ma had decided not to tell him. But I sensed that he knew. How could he not?

We had chosen to have him die at home rather than at a hospice. True to the doctors' prognosis, Baba died four weeks after he came home from the hospital. But to us, he died that night when the paramedics came to take him to the emergency room. For the father who came home was not the father we'd known. The night he was rushed to the ER, he looked his fifty-five years of age. But when he returned home, his appearance was that of an eighty-year-old man. I saw Baba distancing himself from us. He hardly spoke to anyone. Part of me wanted to believe it wasn't intentional, and it was a direct result of the pain he was experiencing. But the other part of me sensed he was aware that he was alienating himself. He seemed to have checked out, indifferent to us and the world of living that was going on around him. Mentally, he'd already crossed over to the other side. Sometimes I saw a heavy sadness in his eyes, and sometimes I even saw a fierce anger. Maybe his refusing to talk to us anymore was the only control he had left over an illness that was robbing him of everything.

And then on a Friday afternoon, at 4:15 p.m., the tremors started. Baba's broken body rocked softly, almost as if he was cold and was shivering. A ghostly white pallor slowly draped over his skin. His eyes were staring off into the distance as they took on the appearance of gray, glassy marbles.

My aunts and uncles had been summoned. But only my aunt Mary decided to stay. She insisted we had to eat even though none of us had an appetite, and she sent me to the supermarket to buy her a few groceries she needed. As I walked back from the store, I saw two girls standing in front of my house. Cheryl and Lauren.

Cheryl Anapolis and Lauren Murphy were known for walking around Astoria looking for kids to beat up. When I was in eighth grade, my friend Sara was coming out of school one day when Cheryl and Lauren decided to pick on her for no reason. They had a bunch of their friends—all guys—hold Sara still against the schoolyard fence while Cheryl and Lauren took turns punching her in the gut and face. I hadn't witnessed it since I had called in to school sick, but the next day everyone was talking about it. Poor Sara returned to school only two days after the incident, wearing sunglasses to hide her huge black eyes. I didn't even know how she was able to see the blackboard through those glasses. I was mad that her parents made her go back to school so soon. Couldn't they have waited at least a week for the swelling to go down? I'm sure her teachers and the principal would've understood.

Now Cheryl and Lauren were standing in front of my house, picking by the handful the azaleas my mother had planted. They threw the petals up in the air, laughing the entire time.

"Hey, what you got in those bags?" Lauren yelled out to me.

I ignored her and started making my way up my driveway to

enter my house through the back. I silently prayed they'd leave me alone.

Suddenly, I felt a vise-like grip on my shoulder. Cheryl swung me around so hard I dropped my groceries.

"She was talking to you. Who do you think you are, ignoring us?"

"What do you want? I don't even know you guys."

Lauren laughed. "Stop with the act. *Everyone* knows us. We rule this neighborhood."

"Yeah, just like we know you were talking shit about Miriam and her boyfriend. Telling everyone they're drug addicts. Why would you make up lies like that about your friends?"

"I didn't. It's Tracy. She took what I said and twisted it. All I said was that my neighbors assume Pat must be doing drugs since he hangs out with Brett. It's a fact Brett's been stoned since he was in high school twenty years ago. And since Miriam is dating Pat, naturally my neighbors think she's doing drugs, too. But I know she's not, and I know Pat isn't doing drugs either."

Lauren and Cheryl looked at each other with a sly smile.

"We don't believe you."

Cheryl walked over to me, sticking her face right into mine. Her breath stunk. But I continued to stare right back at her.

"This one's got some nerve," Cheryl said.

"Yeah, I don't know why. It's not like anyone knows who the hell she is. You're a nobody." Now Lauren was by my side, standing with her arms crossed in front of her super-flat chest. Maybe that's where her anger issues stemmed from?

I squatted down to pick up the groceries that had fallen. I'd had it. I wasn't going to stand there while they harassed me.

"What do you think you're doing?" Lauren asked me.

"What does it look like?"

I ignored them while I picked up my groceries, when a moment later I felt a kick in my back that toppled me forward onto my knees. Before I could even attempt to get up, Cheryl's fist came crashing into my eye. I'd never felt such searing pain. Lauren yanked my ponytail back so hard that tears immediately sprang out of my eyes. She then gripped the back of my head and slammed my face down to the sidewalk. I felt the gravel on the concrete scratch my left cheek. Pain radiated throughout my body.

"Bitch! We're going to teach you a lesson. After we're through with you, you'll never spread shit about anyone again."

Cheryl kicked my belly. Lauren joined her, slamming her boot heels into my ribs.

"Hey, bitch, how do you like this?" Cheryl gave me a back-handed slap.

Somehow I managed to get out, "I swear. I didn't say anything. Someone is making this all up."

"You're not only a liar, you're a stupid liar who doesn't even know how to keep her mouth shut when she's getting the shit kicked out of her." Lauren spit at me.

"Please! Stop! Stop! My father's in there . . . Ahhh!"

At the mention of my father, I couldn't stop the tears that were running down my face. He was dying, and I wasn't there. Had he died already?

"So what if your father's in there? You think we care? Let him come out and see what a loser he has for a daughter."

This enraged me. I yelled out, "He can't! He's dying!"

"Man, what a spineless liar we have here. She's even trying to play the sympathy card with us by telling us her father's dying. Now that deserves an extra-special punishment. What do you think, Lauren? I think her face doesn't look ugly enough yet."

"Yeah, you're right. Let me take care of that."

Lauren curled her hand into a fist, getting ready to punch the side of my face that hadn't gotten acquainted yet with her. I shut my eyes tight, tensing my muscles in anticipation of the blow.

"Get the hell off her!"

Cheryl fell on top of me as someone tackled her. Lauren started kicking at whoever had stopped Cheryl.

Thank God, I thought.

"Get the fuck out of here!"

My relief turned to humiliation. It was Michael. I didn't want him seeing me like this, unable to fend for myself.

"Come on, Cheryl. We'll finish this another day."

Michael got up fast and shoved both Cheryl and Lauren up against a parked car on the street. I heard Lauren grimace in pain.

"If I ever catch you guys even within a hundred feet of her, you'll have me to deal with. And don't think I wouldn't hit you because you're girls. In my book, you're not even girls. You're filthy trash."

He kept staring at them until they were forced to look away, their heads hanging to the side. He finally released his grip on them. They walked away.

"Valentina! Stop! Don't get up! You might make one of your injuries worse." Michael ran to me, kneeling down by my side. I had tried to lift myself up, but I was in too much pain. My head felt very heavy and like it was glued to the concrete. Tears streamed down my face.

"Thank you."

"Hey! You're going to be okay."

Michael brushed the tears off my face with his fingers and pushed my blood-stained hair off my face.

"Tell me where it hurts."

"All over, but mostly my side and back. They were getting extreme pleasure out of kicking me repeatedly in my ribs. My face is hurting, too." I reached up to touch my swollen face, which felt like a grapefruit.

"I'm going to gently lift your head up and place my arm underneath it. We'll take this very slowly. If anything hurts too much, just tell me, okay?"

I nodded.

Michael gingerly placed his right arm underneath the base of my skull and propped my head slightly up.

"How does that feel?"

"Fine."

"Okay, just let your head rest there. I'm going to slide my other arm under your back so I can try to lift you up. Okay?"

"Okay."

Michael started to lift my pelvis, but I let out a shriek.

"I'm sorry! I'm sorry!"

"That's the side where they kept kicking me. Maybe if you try the other side."

"Okay. That's a good idea. I should've thought to ask you which was the bad side."

He placed my head back down on the ground very carefully and went over to my other side. Again, he slid one arm beneath my head, and then very slowly nudged my side up, asking me constantly if I was in pain. I was, but I knew he had to get me off the ground, so I gritted my teeth as he got his arm fully underneath my body.

"Michael, wait."

"Are you in too much pain?"

"I just need a moment before you bring me inside."

My voice cracked, and I broke down sobbing.

"Valentina. It's going to be okay. Sshhh . . . sshhh."

Michael bent his head low, close to my face, and whispered into my ear: "I won't let them hurt you again. I won't let anyone ever hurt you again."

"I'm so embarrassed. My family. They don't need this right now."

"I know. I know, sweetie. But there's nothing to be embarrassed about. Those pigs should be embarrassed."

"My father, Michael. It's started."

I tried to talk through my choked sobs.

"What's started?"

But as soon as Michael uttered his question, recognition dawned on his face.

"Oh, Vee. I'm so sorry. I'm so, so sorry."

He held me close to him.

"Hey! What the hell is going on here?"

Leave it to the Mayor of 35th Street to ruin my special moment with Michael.

"What are you doing, for crying out loud?"

Paulie was screaming at the top of his lungs. I'm sure from his vantage point it must've looked like Michael and I were getting it on right on the concrete, no matter how ridiculous that seemed. But Paulie would've believed it.

Michael looked up.

"Oh my God! Valentina, what happened to you?"

All color drained from Paulie's face.

"I've got to get her inside."

"Who did this to her?"

"We'll talk about that later. Paulie, can you please ring her doorbell so I can quickly carry her in?"

"Of course! Of course!"

Paulie ran up the steps of my porch.

"Oh, great. Everyone will know now that I had my ass kicked. Paulie's going to be talking about this forever."

I managed to let out a little laugh, but I regretted it when the pain in my ribs returned.

"I hate to tell you this, Vee, but unless you hide in your house for a month, everyone will know once they see your black eye."

"That's true." I smiled at Michael.

"That's my Valentina. Okay, let's do this. On the count of three, I'm going to slowly get up, okay?"

I nodded my head. "I'm ready."

"One . . . two . . . three."

Michael lifted me up. The movement ricocheted pain from my head down to my back. I sucked in my breath, hoping Michael hadn't noticed. But it was useless.

"I know, sweetie. It hurts."

Now off the ground, I noticed a crowd of people had gathered a few feet away and were staring. At least they had the courtesy to give us some space.

"Michael, is she going to be all right?"

Betsy Offenheimer's voice crackled through the air. She sounded like she was on the verge of crying.

"Yes, Betsy. She'll be fine as soon as I get her inside."

"It was those two good-for-nothing girls who run around Astoria trying to make trouble for nice kids like Valentina. I heard them talking in my bakery about how they beat up poor Valentina. They were showing off. They tried to order Italian ices, but I kicked them out and told them never to show their faces in my bakery again. I then quickly ran over here to see if Valentina was okay."

I heard Betsy gasp as Antoniella told her what had happened to me.

"Valentina, I will come over later and bring you your favorite *biscotti,*" Antoniella yelled out at me.

I tried to lift my head higher to smile at her, but it felt like dead weight on top of Michael's arms. Hearing how my neighbors were so concerned for me brought new tears to my eyes.

My mother opened the door after what seemed like eons of Paulie pressing down on the bell.

"Paulie, I'm sorry. This is not a good ti—Valentina! *Dio mio!* What happened to my daughter?" Ma started crying. "Who did this to her?"

"I'm okay, Ma. It looks worse than it is."

I feebly tried to reassure her, though I knew from the look of my face that she wasn't buying it. Seeing her crying killed me. She didn't need this. Not now. I looked away, knowing I was about to lose all control. I had to be strong for her.

"Signora DeLuca, I need to place her on a bed."

"*Si, si.* This way. Please, be quiet. I don't want Nicola to hear. He can't know what's happened to his little mermaid."

I squeezed my eyes tightly shut, trying to keep a new round of tears from breaking through.

Paulie followed. I was certain he would start recounting what he'd seen outside so loudly that my father would hear even in his semiconscious state. But to my surprise, Paulie just hung his head low as he followed Michael and my mother into my bedroom.

"Should we take her to the emergency room?" Ma asked Michael.

"Probably, but I don't want to put her through that hassle just yet. Let's call Dr. Serafino first and see what he can do."

"I'll call him. You stay with Valentina, Signora DeLuca."

Paulie took charge as he walked over to the phone on my night-stand and dialed Dr. Serafino's number.

My mother left the room and returned with Rita and Connie by her side. They started crying when they saw me.

"It's okay. Stop crying," I told them. Why did my mother even bring them in here? But I think Ma was too preoccupied at the moment. She had a basin of cold water and sat by my bedside as she gently washed the blood off my face. She gathered my hair and twisted it up into a bun and clipped it back. She then applied some ointment to the cuts on my face.

"Connie, get me a glass of cold water. *Fai presto!*"

Connie nodded her head and ran out. My poor little sisters. If it weren't bad enough that they were seeing their father dying, now they had the sight of their older sister, who looked like she was at death's door as well.

Rita had come over to the other side of my bed and was holding my hand, crying silently. I squeezed her hand back in reassurance.

We heard the doorbell ring.

"I'll get it. It must be Dr. Serafino." Michael ran to the door.

Seconds later, Dr. Serafino stepped into my bedroom.

"Signora DeLuca." He nodded his head toward my mother. "Paulie told me what happened. I'll need to examine her in private. You can stay, signora, but everyone else should step out for a few minutes."

Rita seemed reluctant to let go of my hand. I tried reassuring her. "Don't worry. I'll be fine."

Michael put his arm around Rita as he walked out with her. Paulie followed.

After Dr. Serafino examined me, he told me I was lucky. Though I had cuts, I didn't need any stitches, and there was no sign of a concussion even though Lauren had slammed my face with such brutal force to the sidewalk.

"Those girls aren't as strong as they like to think they are." Dr. Serafino winked at me. "You'll be fine. I'm sorry this had to happen to you, Valentina, and at a time like this. What's become of this world?" He shook his head. I heard him mutter, "Disgusting, disgusting." He patted my hand. "Get some rest. I'll come back tomorrow to see how you're doing."

Ma escorted him out. They stopped outside of my bedroom, and I could hear them whispering. Then, I heard Dr. Serafino's footsteps, making their way down the hall to my father's room. My mother must've asked him to look in on my father, not that he could do anything for him at this point. We all knew that.

Michael knocked on my door. "Can I come in?"

"Hi." I smiled when I saw him. He smiled back and sat down on my bed.

"Does it still hurt a lot?"

"A little, but Dr. Serafino gave me codeine and even a Valium. I'm feeling drowsy."

"I won't stay too long."

"No, that's okay. Stay as long as you like."

I looked into Michael's eyes. He looked back for what seemed like an eternity. Suddenly realizing what I'd said, I glanced nervously away. Michael held my hand.

"I was so terrified when I saw you on the ground. I don't think I've ever been that afraid before."

"Really?"

"Really."

"Yeah, I was afraid, too, but mostly I just kept thinking about my family. I was more afraid one of them would come out and witness my getting beat up. My mother would've probably fainted on the spot."

"Oh, knowing your mother, I doubt that! She would've pounced on Cheryl and Lauren like a tiger protecting her cubs. She would've gotten a few of her own punches in there."

I laughed. "That's true. My mother is very emotional, but she's also the toughest woman I know."

"Yeah, I think Cheryl and Lauren had better pray they don't see her on the street—or me, for that matter. I meant what I said to them."

"Would you hit a girl, Michael? I can't see you doing that."

"No, I wouldn't. But I swear I came so close to wanting to when I saw what they did to you. I just wanted to scare them when I threatened them. Besides, I know everyone in this neighborhood, and I could even get some of my female friends who can give a good ass kickin' to take care of them."

"Wow! I didn't know you had such power." I smirked.

"Ha! There's a lot about me you don't know, Valentina."

Again, he stared into my eyes. I could feel myself getting warm and my stomach fluttering. He was still holding my hand, but now he was swirling his index finger around the back of my hand.

"Well, I should let you get some sleep."

"Can you do me a favor, Michael?"

"Sure, anything for you, Valentina."

"Can you just wait until I fall asleep?"

Something changed in Michael's face when I said that. It was as if he were moved that I had made this request.

"Of course."

"Thank you."

"Always so polite. You don't have to keep thanking me."

"I know. But I want to." I shot him a seductive smile. I was feeling more and more courageous around him.

"Why do I get the feeling there's also a lot about you that I don't know, Valentina?"

"Hmmm . . . I don't know. I guess you'll have to try and find out."

I closed my eyes. The drugs Dr. Serafino had given me were making it harder for me to win the battle to stay awake. As I drifted deeper into sleep, I felt someone kiss my forehead. Maybe my mother had come in. When I was a child, she always kissed my forehead after she'd tucked me in.

My deep sleep had only lasted for an hour. Connie and Rita were shaking my shoulder.

"Valentina, wake up! Wake up!"

I woke up. My head was killing me. I'd never had such a pounding headache before. The pain in my ribs and back had returned, too. The drugs must've worn off.

"It's Baba, Vee. He's going." Rita was crying.

"What?"

"Hurry, Vee." Connie was pulling my hand.

I sat up a little too quickly. The room spun for a few seconds. I closed my eyes tightly, willing myself to feel better.

"I need some help standing."

Rita and Connie placed their hands under my armpits as they lifted me with a strength I was surprised they had. We held on to each other as we slowly made our way to my parents' room. I could hear moaning in the distance. It sounded like my mother and my aunt Mary. I'd never heard anyone cry like that before. Was I too late? Had I been sleeping while my father died?

We got to the room.

Ma and Aunt Mary were seated side by side on the bed. They were holding each other as they cried. My father was still lying on his right side. His eyes stared off to a place only he could see. He'd been in this same position when I had left three hours earlier to go to the supermarket. But now his body was trembling at a faster pace, and his eyes seemed more unfocused. Though his heart was still beating, I knew he'd already left us since the first signs of death made their presence known earlier that day.

My sisters and I huddled closely together, crying silently, as we stared at Baba. I could feel their weight supporting my weakened body. They were trying to be strong for me. Guilt instantly washed over me. I was the oldest. I should've been the one consoling them, consoling my mother. With that thought, I shifted my weight so I wasn't leaning so heavily on Connie and Rita. They looked up at me, worried I was going to faint on them. I wrapped my arms around them, and whispered, "I'm okay." They seemed to collapse into me; relieved they could finally drop their heavy burden, they started sobbing loudly. I held them closely even though it hurt to have them pressed up against my sore ribs.

My father suddenly let out one last gasp of breath. Startled, we all stopped crying. His eyes remained looking off to that place only he could see. And then his body stopped shuddering.

"É morto . . . é morto," Ma whispered. And then she held her arms out to my sisters and me. My sisters rushed into her arms, kneeling at her side. I was in too much pain to crouch down and was left standing alone. I just stared at my father as I silently cried. Aunt Mary came over to me and held me. As I stood there hugging my aunt, I couldn't help glancing in my parents' dresser mirror and noticing the scene that was staring back at me.

A seagull flies into my line of vision, startling me out of my reverie and bringing me back to the present. It lands by my feet, pecking at broken pieces of a pizza crust. I inhale deeply. The breeze is picking up at the park, and the tide in the East River looks higher now, too. I begin making my way out of Astoria Park and head home.

Though it has been fourteen years since Baba died, I still feel devastated whenever I think about that day. It still hurts that he's no longer here with us. It still hurts that Tracy had conspired behind my back to have me beat up, knowing my father had just been given one month to live.

On October 18, 1996, I'd gotten my ass kicked, my father had died, and it had been Tracy's seventeenth birthday—a birthday I was sure she'd never forget. From that day forward, I became a believer in karma: What goes around comes around.

But there had also been good karma present on that day. Michael and I had formed a deep bond that was the seed of our growing friendship and romance.

Michael had postponed going back to Cornell for another week so that he could attend my father's funeral. When he heard the news, he came to my house. I was lying in bed, still nursing my wounds.

Neither of us said anything as he came over to me. He sat down at my bedside and pulled me into his arms. I broke down crying. He held me and stroked my hair for what felt like the longest time.

"Just let it out. Let it all out," he whispered.

I'd been strong for my mother and sisters. Again, I felt the weight of my being the oldest and wanting to be their tower of strength. It felt so good to finally have someone console me. When I eventually stopped crying, I looked up into Michael's face. His eyes were red, as if he'd been fighting off tears.

"Shouldn't you be on your way back to school?"

"I couldn't go after I got the news. But I had decided to put off returning to school for a few days even before your father died. I wanted to make sure you were healing okay. I was going to check in on you."

"Thanks, Michael, but you didn't have to do that. Weren't your parents upset that you didn't go back?"

"No, no. They understood. They were horrified when they heard what happened to you. And now that your father has passed away . . . well, I think in a way they're proud of me that I'm looking out for you and your family. They actually came here with me. They're talking to your mother in the living room."

"I should get up and say hello to them."

"Valentina, wait. I want to talk to you."

His face was gravely serious.

"Is everything okay?"

"Yeah. It's just—" He looked away.

"You can tell me anything, Michael. I hope you know that. Whatever it is, I'd never betray your trust. You've done so much for me. If there's something you need help with or just someone to listen, I'm here."

He smiled. Then my heart stopped when he picked up my hand and brought it to his lips and kissed it. "You're always thinking of others. You're so kind. I've never met anyone like you. It seems most girls nowadays just care about themselves and getting what they want or playing some game or other. But not you, Vee. You're not like that."

I blushed. "Well, it seems that being the way I've been doesn't keep the guys around. The few boyfriends I've had always seem to leave me for the girls who are more like what you're describing."

"They're idiots. What do they know?"

Suddenly, I thought about when I saw him kissing Tracy on the night of the sophomore dance. Maybe Aldo had been right that Michael was just thinking with his base urges but didn't want a girl like Tracy for a girlfriend.

"So, what is it? What were you going to tell me?"

"I-I was wondering if it would be all right if I e-mailed you every once in a while to see how you're doing."

"Sure. But I'll be okay, Michael. I'm not that fragile, you know?" I smiled and patted his hand. He looked down at it. I quickly pulled my hand away.

"No, I know. I guess what I'm trying to say is now that you're older I'd like us to be better friends. I'd like to get to know you better."

"Oh." I swallowed hard. I could see he was waiting for my response. "Yeah, that would be nice."

Michael smiled, looking relieved and something else, but I couldn't quite put my finger on it.

"I'm going to let you rest. I'll see you tomorrow night at the funeral home."

The reminder of my father's death sent pain through me again. Michael must've noticed. I'd almost forgotten in the few minutes I'd spent in Michael's company what was ahead for my family and me. Sensing the change in my mood, Michael lifted my chin with his fingers. He then brushed the side of my cheek with the back of his hand and pushed a strand of hair that had fallen out of my clip back behind my ear.

"I promise you, things will get better. It's just going to take some time."

He stood up and kissed my head before he walked out of my room. Suddenly, I remembered yesterday when I was falling asleep after having taken the painkillers and feeling someone kiss my head. It had been Michael! I was positive of it now. In my groggy state I thought it was Ma, but I remembered how he was still sitting on my bed when I fell asleep.

I don't know how long I stayed frozen in place, staring up at the ceiling, after he'd left. Had I been dreaming? Did Michael really kiss me? And not once but twice? Okay, it was just an innocent kiss on my head, not my lips. Had I also dreamed that he wanted to e-mail me while he was away at school and get to know me better?

"Stop it, Valentina!" I muttered aloud to myself. He was just feeling sorry for me. Who wouldn't? First, I get my ass kicked, and then my father dies. Michael was just doing the right thing. But still. It meant the world to me, more than he'd ever know.

True to his word, as soon as Michael returned to Cornell, he e-mailed me a few times a week. Those e-mails were what kept me going while I was grieving for my father. Most of his e-mails were funny. I could see what he was trying to do—take my mind off my father, if only briefly. He answered all of my questions about college life and had a lot of questions for me, too, mostly silly stuff like what was my favorite flavor ice cream (vanilla for soft ice cream, pistachio for hard ice cream), what was my favorite color (violet), who was my favorite band (The Cure, of course), what was my favorite book (*Tess of the d'Urbervilles*), where did I want to travel to some day (Venice and Bali), what were my favorite flowers (peonies and roses).

But the odd thing was I never saw him when he came home for school breaks. I'd ask him what he was doing, and he was always vague. I couldn't help wondering if he was dating someone back home. The e-mails continued for the rest of his four years of college and even when he went on to Germany for business school. Once, he sent me a postcard from Munich with just the words, *Add this to your list of places to see.*

I'd begun feeling like he was playing a game with me. So I set my sights on going out with other guys. But of course, they all fell far short of Michael. There was the wannabe guido James who didn't have an ounce of Italian in him, but kept insisting on reciting love poems to me in the most butchered Italian.

"Too say oo-nuh foh-ray del me caw-rah-sohn." (Translation: "You are the flower of my heart.")

"James, *corazon* is Spanish for 'heart.' It's *cuore* in Italian."

"Really? Are you sure?"

"Yes, very. Remember, I've been speaking Italian since I was born. You've been speaking it for a matter of what, two weeks?"

James blushed. He'd also tried to win me over by playing Italian opera in the car only to have me tell him that I didn't like listening to opera blasting from a Corvette.

Then there was Daniel, whose parents were from Russia. He was in law school and had the most impeccable manners. He insisted on asking Ma for permission to date me, which of course had my mother drooling. He took me to the Russian Tea Room and Le Cirque. He'd also insisted I accept a string of freshwater pearls on our second date. Yes, he was wealthy, or rather his parents were. But I had enough of the "caviar treatment," as he liked to call his pampering of me, on our sixth date, when his true colors surfaced.

We were at the Colonial, a four-star Vietnamese restaurant in midtown Manhattan, which I'd fallen in love with after he'd taken me there on our third date. He'd gone to the restroom, and I had struck up a conversation with our waiter, who was from Sicily. When Daniel returned, he rudely said to the waiter, "We won't be needing you anymore." The poor waiter blushed and excused himself.

"What do you think you're doing?" Daniel grilled me.

"Excuse me?"

"Don't play dumb. You know what you were doing."

"I was talking to the waiter. You saw that. Was that a crime?"

"You were flirting with him. And don't deny it."

"Okay, I won't."

"Ah-ha! I knew it."

"I was not flirting with him, Daniel. You told me not to deny it. I was having an innocent conversation with him because he's from Sicily like my parents."

"Who started the conversation?"

"This is ridiculous. I'm leaving. And don't bother calling me again."

I could go on and on with the horrible dates. I finally decided to just focus on my work at the bridal shop, throwing myself into becoming an excellent seamstress and designer. Whenever Ma would ask me why I didn't have a date on a Saturday night, I'd say, "Because I enjoy my own company more."

"You can't be alone forever." Ma would shake her head.

I was lonely, but I'd also gotten tired of being disappointed so many times—first with Michael, then with the string of other guys who followed. I just didn't want to put forth any more effort in meeting someone. If it happened, it happened. So as I made other brides' wedding dreams come true, I buried my own, refusing to think about the day I had fantasized about since childhood.

Then two years ago, I came to work on a Friday morning in early June. There was a package waiting for me at the front desk that was delivered by messenger. No return address was on the package. I opened it up and found a CD of The Cure's single hit "Friday I'm in Love."

The only person I could think of who would send me this was Aldo, my buddy in our love of New Wave music.

"Ooh!!! Secret admirer and one with good taste, too! Maybe he has a friend for me," Aldo cooed when we met for lunch later that day.

"So, it wasn't you who sent me this?"

"No! Why would I surprise you like that? You know what a sucker I am for any compliment and the lengths I go to make sure I receive the praise coming to me when I give someone a gift."

That was true. You couldn't thank Aldo enough when he did something nice for you.

"This is kind of creepy. I don't like it."

"Oh, come on, Vee! Where's your sense of intrigue?"

"It's nonexistent. I live in New York City in the twenty-first century where there are so many weirdos out there."

Then the following Monday, another package arrived, again without a return address. A DVD of the movie *Tess* was in there. I felt a cold chill run down my spine. Not many people knew I loved that movie and book.

I was looking over my shoulder all week when I was walking alone on the street. My mother and sisters weren't even concerned. Like Aldo, they thought it was cool that I had a secret admirer.

Then, three weeks passed and no packages came. Finally, I could relax. I got home after an especially grueling day at the shop. When I opened the front door, a huge bouquet of the most gorgeous violet peonies was sitting on the table in the foyer. Even though I was ten feet away from the flowers, I could make out my name written large on the gift card. *Not another mysterious gift,* I thought to myself.

I pulled the envelope off the transparent wrapping around the peonies and quickly ripped it open.

"The Cure . . . *Tess of the d'Urbervilles* . . . violet . . . peonies . . . now all that's left is for you to have two scoops of vanilla and pistachio ice cream with me. . . ."

"Oh my God!" I said out loud, covering my mouth with my hands. The note was unsigned, but I immediately knew whom it was from. The e-mail I had sent to Michael when he was in college, in which I'd told him all of my favorite things, flashed before my eyes. How stupid was I that I hadn't figured out the gifts were from him. Out of my peripheral vision, I saw a movement at the top of the stairs. I looked up. Ma, Rita, and Connie were peeking over the banister. But as soon as our eyes met, they pulled back. I heard Connie's giggling.

They knew! No wonder they weren't worried about the gifts being from some deranged stalker.

"Why didn't you tell me those gifts were from Michael? Do you know how afraid I've been these past few weeks?"

I ran up the stairs. They were sitting on Ma's queen-size bed, the same one she'd shared with Baba all the years of their marriage.

Ma spoke up. "He begged us not to tell you. He wanted to surprise you. Isn't it wonderful, Valentina? I know you've waited for this a very long time!"

She knew? I was a bigger fool than I thought. Of course she knew that I'd been harboring a secret crush on Michael all these years. How could she not? I was her daughter, after all, and like I've said before, *nothing* got past those eagle eyes.

"You're my family! You're supposed to be loyal to me, not to some guy you haven't seen in years!"

I was mad, probably madder than I should've been. But I couldn't help it. My emotions were jumbled. Michael! I still couldn't believe he was the one sending me those gifts. What kind of game was he playing with me now? Was he back? Ohhhh! The anger boiled in me. I didn't care. That guy had me running around in circles since he'd come to my rescue at Li's Grocery Store. And I was tired of it.

"Signora DeLuca, since your loyalty is to Mr. Carello, would you please do me the honor of telling him that I don't appreciate having the crap scared out of me?"

"Oh come on, Vee! You're actually mad at him? This is so romantic what he's done! The closest I've come to romance was receiving a bottle of nasty acai juice from that creep Victor." Rita grimaced.

"Yeah, Vee! I know you can be uptight, but come on! Michael's finally into you!"

"Uptight? So that's what you think of me, Connie? Thank you! That's what you all think of me. To hell with all of you!"

I ran down the stairs.

"Valentina! Valentina!" Ma's screams went unheeded.

And just in case I hadn't made my point clear, I slammed the door behind me. I was about to dash across the street but stopped dead in my tracks when I looked up. Beady Eyes were at their usual post behind their tall black gate, holding on to the spires and just staring at me with their huge German shepherd, Gus. Even Gus was looking at me with the same penetrating stare his owners always seemed to possess, hence my family's nickname for them.

Beady Eyes were the sixty-ish couple who lived across the street from us, and whose house I dreamed of living in even though I'd never seen its interior. Something about it had that happy Brady Bunch quality to it. And what kid didn't want to live in the Brady Bunch house? Judging from the exterior with its pale lemon-colored door, shiny black gate, and large driveway that led to a spacious yard, which I was sure had to be bigger than ours, I was convinced their house was nice on the inside, too. Not that our house wasn't nice, but I just had a feeling theirs was nicer. Plus, they had a huge oak tree in front of their house. For this alone, I wished I lived at their house. I'd always wanted a tree to call my own.

It wasn't until I was nine that I learned what their real name was—Tom and Gladys Hoffman. Ma laughed at me when she heard that I'd thought "Beady Eyes" was their name. I *did* feel stupid. "Beady Eyes" was Ma's nickname for them because of their staring problem.

Whenever one of us came out of our house, there was Mr. Beady Eyes's entire 5'6" frame, standing behind his gate with his dark, sallow eyes. He looked like a prisoner on death row, waiting each excruciating hour until his execution.

Mrs. Beady Eyes was almost always in her housecoat, and her honey-blond hair was often set in rollers. When she smiled it was hard to tell since she pursed her lips so tightly together—even tighter than Hunchback Antoniella's lips. Whenever she "smiled," you'd swear those were stitches and not age lines above her mouth, giving her more the appearance of The Bride of Frankenstein.

It took many years to say hi to them. They scared me when I was a kid. One day, Ma scolded me for not saying hello.

"Are they nice people?"

"Yes, Valentina. They are nice people. They just don't know

that it makes others uncomfortable to keep looking at them the way they do. But you should always be respectful and say hello."

The first time I said hi to them, I could tell it shocked them. Mr. Beady Eyes, who never even seemed to attempt a smile like his wife, actually smiled at me and said in a very proper manner, "Hello."

But the staring never stopped.

"Hi, Mr. and Mrs. Hoffman. How are you?"

"We're fine. Thank you. How are you?"

"Good, good. Thanks for asking."

I nodded my head toward them and kept walking. Gus had even turned his head so he could keep staring at me as I walked by.

"Weird," I whispered to myself. I still couldn't get used to them.

Seeing Beady Eyes did manage to slow my racing pulse and make me forget for a couple of minutes the drama that had played out at my house.

I had overreacted. Yes, it was romantic and thoughtful what Michael had done. Then why had it bothered me so much? I guess I was still hurt that I hadn't heard from him except for that post-card since he went to business school in Munich. I couldn't just let him think he could go back to our friendship being exactly the way it was, and I'd be all sweet about that. I wasn't that same kid any-more.

I walked by the bridal shop. This month the featured gown was a Justin Alexander knockoff. It sported a huge tulle ball gown skirt with a basque waist. The bodice was covered in lace embroidery that resembled vines. The vines stretched down to the left side of the mannequin's hip. It was stunning, and an excellent example of keeping a design modest without sacrificing elegance and beauty.

I looked over my shoulder to make sure my family hadn't come running after me. Quickly unlocking the shop, I entered. Keeping the lights off, I made my way to the back, using the light that was streaming in from the street lamps. This was a guilty pleasure of mine no one knew about. Whenever I was feeling down, I snuck in here at night and tried on a few dresses. Of course, Rita, Connie, and I had tried on dresses in the past in each other's presence. What girl working in a bridal dress boutique wouldn't? But this was different. Trying the dresses on alone made me feel even gid-dier than when my sisters and I donned them together. I would even practice how I'd walk down the aisle when it was my turn—if ever—to get married. The walk was very important.

Sometimes, if I were especially mad, like tonight, I'd go through as many as a dozen dresses. I usually tried the gowns I hadn't worn yet.

I first put on the Justin Alexander dress that was in our display window. The dress swallowed my petite frame even with the four-inch stilettos I slipped on. Next, I threw on a super-tight Monique L'huillier mermaid charmeuse gown in champagne. The dress was gathered to the side of the waist, creating dramatic shirring and emphasizing the curves of my hips and derriere. A large sparkly brooch adorned the fabric where it was gathered to the side. An-other brooch was clipped to the bodice, throwing attention to the plunging neckline. I swept my hair to the side and fastened it with one of the jeweled hair combs we kept in our accessories case. I strutted around the boutique with my hands on my hips and sway-ing them in the most exaggerated manner from side to side, emu-lating models I'd seen on catwalks.

Going from princess to siren bride, it was now my turn for something different. I opted to be a super-modern bride, wearing a short, punky-looking taffeta dress that Connie had created. It was one of her designs and not a designer knockoff. Asymmetrical tulle peeked out from the hem, and a corseted lace bodice topped off the flirty dress. I wore a bird's nest on my head, and pulled the net-ting of the fifties retro hairpiece over my face.

I looked at the clock hanging on the wall. It was well past ten. Ma would be worried. I changed into my street clothes and put everything carefully back as I'd found it. For the moment, I paused the video that was still playing in my mind of my one-woman fash-ion show.

As I locked the door of the shop, a shadow neared me. Before I had time to look up, I heard, "Isn't it past your bedtime?"

I jumped. My nerves were still jittery from thinking I'd had a stalker the past few weeks.

"Michael! Geez! You scared me!"

"Sorry! Didn't mean to do that. I know it's been a while. Do I look that bad?"

He gave me his trademark wink, but instead of its usual bone-melting effect on me, it angered me even more.

"When did you get back?"

"This morning. Other than the scare I gave you, you don't look that surprised to see me, Valentina."

"My mind has been preoccupied. And it's late."

"Are you okay? What's on your mind?"

"I've been receiving anonymous packages from someone the past few weeks, and it's been freaking me out a bit."

"Really?" Michael was grinning. I wanted to smack that smug smile off his face. Instead, I decided to continue with my game.

"So, how have you been? How's Munich?"

"I've been well, thank you. Munich is great. You definitely have to go some time."

I nodded my head.

"How are you?"

"I'm good. Like I said, my nerves have been on edge a bit."

"Valentina, I should probably tell you that I just came from your house."

The charade was up. He knew I was on to him. Couldn't my family ever keep quiet about anything? I felt the color rising in my face.

"Thank you for the gifts. That was nice of you. But I wish you had signed your name to them. You really did give me a scare."

"I'm sorry, Vee. I never meant to do that. Honestly, I thought you would've picked up sooner that they were from me. I guess I was wrong."

Michael's attention was diverted by the jingle of the Mister Sof-tee truck, which had just pulled up at the corner. He looked hurt that I hadn't known he was the source of the gifts.

"I've been so busy at the shop. My memory isn't as good as it used to be. And I guess I'm surprised that you even remembered all of my favorite things."

"Of course I remembered. Why wouldn't I?"

I shrugged my shoulders.

"What's the matter, Valentina? I can tell something other than the gifts is bothering you."

"Do you really need me to spell it out for you?"

"What?"

"Why haven't I heard from you in almost a year? You only sent me that postcard from Germany shortly after you got there, and then that was it. I haven't even gotten one e-mail from you. I thought we were *friends*." I drawled out the last word, shocking myself at how sarcastic I sounded.

A shadow passed over Michael's eyes.

"Come on, Michael. Didn't you think I'd be wondering why you dropped off the face of the earth?"

"I'm sorry. You have every right to be mad at me."

"I'm not mad. I'm just . . . I don't know. Disappointed? But maybe I'm overreacting again, the way I overreacted with my family tonight. I know they must've told you about the argument we got into."

"All they said was that you were very upset about the gifts. They didn't tell me you got into an argument with them."

"Well, it was more one-sided. I was doing most of the yelling."

"Sounds like you've inherited the infamous Olivia DeLuca temper." Michael laughed.

"Please don't say that!" I was laughing now, too.

"I was beginning to wonder if I was ever going to see that gorgeous smile again!"

Had I heard him right? He thought my smile was gorgeous?

"I'm sorry, Michael. I know you were busy in Munich with business school. I shouldn't have expected you to be constantly e-mailing and staying in touch with me. But it did seem odd."

"Stop apologizing. I had a feeling you'd be upset. That's probably why I sent those gifts and didn't sign my name to them. Part of me was afraid if you knew they were from me, you might trash them!"

"So what happened? Why did you stop e-mailing? Is business school that demanding?"

"It was tough, but not that tough that I couldn't send you a quick e-mail. I took the easy way out, being so far away. I figured you were busy yourself, graduating from FIT, going to work at Sposa Rosa full time, that you probably wouldn't even notice much if I suddenly stopped e-mailing you."

"You still haven't answered my question. I'm not going to let you off the hook that easy." I gave him a stern look.

"There it is again. Olivia DeLuca is coming through in those eyes!"

I hit him on the arm. I'd never taken such liberties with him before. I was feeling more daring and confident. Even though it was just a swat of his arm, the contact tied my stomach into knots. I still had it bad for this guy.

"The truth is, Valentina, I was getting scared. And I took the cowardly road by not e-mailing you anymore."

"Getting scared of what?"

Michael paused. He stared at the street lamps. I followed his gaze. A fine mist was starting to form and the droplets swirling around the street lamp resembled mosquitoes. We were protected from the mist, which was now a more steady rain from Sposa Rosa's awning.

"I was getting scared of my feelings. My feelings for you."

My heart dropped to my knees—no, make that my feet. I swallowed hard, not knowing what to say, still in too much shock.

"I've liked you for a long time, Valentina. Ever since I saw you at that dance at St. John's Prep. I almost didn't even have the nerve to ask you to dance."

"Really?"

"Yeah, really."

"Then why didn't you ask me out that night? Why did you go off with Tracy and make out with her?"

"You know about that?"

"I saw the two of you going at it. Couldn't you have picked an alley that wasn't on my street?"

"I'm an idiot. That's all I can say. I wasn't thinking straight. I also didn't think you'd say yes that night if I asked you out. Plus, I figured your parents wouldn't be too keen on us dating. I know how strict they were."

"Well, you should've given it a shot."

"I know. I know. I'm giving it a shot now, though. So will you go out with me for ice cream?"

I waited . . . and waited . . . and waited. It was sadistic of me, but I had to play hard to get. I couldn't make it easy for him. And part of me was still ticked off that I'd only heard from him once since he went to Munich.

He looked at me like a puppy that was pleading with his eyes to be petted. Then he sighed and looked away.

"I guess the answer's no."

His face was flushed. Even when he was upset, he was so handsome.

"We can have ice cream. I don't see any harm in that."

The tension that had set in his jaw visibly relaxed. He smiled slightly, not wanting to give away how excited he was that I'd agreed to the date.

"Great. Tomorrow night. I'll pick you—"

"I'm busy tomorrow night. How about next week on Saturday?"

I saw the disappointed look in his face that he'd have to wait a week and a half to go out with me, but he quickly recovered.

"Okay. Next Saturday is good. I'll call you before then. Would that be all right?"

"Sure. I should get going. My mother's probably worried about me, especially after the way I stormed out of there."

"I'll walk you back."

"I'll be fine. But thanks."

"Vee, I insist."

I decided I had punished him enough for one night. I couldn't completely emasculate him. So we walked slowly back to my house, prolonging our time together. When we arrived, he kissed me on the cheek.

"It was really good seeing you again after so long."

"It was good seeing you, too."

I couldn't help myself and smiled.

"I'll see you next Saturday. I'm looking forward to it."

Michael held my gaze.

" 'Bye, Michael."

"I'll wait until you get inside."

I climbed up the stairs to my front door. I looked over my shoulder and waved at him. He winked at me. I froze, not wanting to leave. Michael was fixed in place as well. We just kept staring at each other until finally Michael came up the steps. He picked up my hand and brought it to his lips. My head swirled, making me woozy. I stared at his lips. He must've noticed because when I glanced back up into his eyes I saw him looking at me like he never had before. He wanted me. There was no doubt.

Still holding on to my hand, he drew me closer to him and kissed me. His lips were so soft. First he planted little kisses, but then when I parted my lips slightly, he started tracing the shape of my mouth with his tongue. It was so slow and sensual. God, I'd never been kissed like this. In all the fantasies I'd had of kissing Michael, this was better than anything I could've imagined. Suddenly realizing we were on my porch, I pulled back and looked around. But it was eleven on a Wednesday night. No one was out. The blinds of the neighboring houses were all drawn. I could just hear Ma's voice in my head right now: *What would the neighbors have thought if they saw you kissing Michael?*

"I'm sorry. I probably shouldn't have done that."

"No, it's okay. I just pulled away because I was afraid one of the neighbors would see us. I'd never hear the end of it from my mother!"

"Ha! That's true. I forgot where we were. I couldn't help myself. I've been wanting to kiss you for so long."

The same lust that, moments before, had been in Michael's eyes returned.

"Well, good night."

Before he changed his mind and kissed me again, I quickly turned around and climbed the last two steps of my porch.

"Good night, Vee."

I stepped inside. I wanted to peek through one of the three small windows that adorned my door, but I didn't out of fear that he'd see me. Instead, I quickly tiptoed over to the living room to peek through the blinds. Luckily, none of my family was in sight. Ma had left the blinds slightly ajar as she always did to let the sunlight in, but she must've forgotten to draw them as night fell. Michael was walking slowly away but staring at the windows of my house. There was no way he could see me. I was standing too far back and the lights were off. He had a huge grin on his face while he stared at the windows, then looked away. As he walked down the street, I could hear him whistling.

I let out a big sigh. Now that I was alone, I could drop the tough stance I'd taken with him and just revel in the fact that I would be finally going on a date with the man I had been madly in love with for so long.

And that's how it all started. After that first date, getting ice cream, we went out almost every weekend after that. I still played a little hard to get in the beginning, so that's why we weren't seeing each other every week. But after two months, when Michael asked me if I'd officially become his girlfriend, I said yes.

I'll never forget that year. He sent me peonies at the bridal shop every week. And when they weren't in season, he sent me roses in every color. He took me to some of the best restaurants throughout New York City. And in the summer, he took me out to Central Park, where he rented a boat. We also went to the beach a lot.

Ma, Rita, and Connie were thrilled for me.

Then one year from our first date, he proposed to me. And of course, he made sure the proposal was just as romantic, if not more, than anything he'd done before.

After we had dinner at Tao, one of my favorite restaurants in Manhattan, he said, "Let's take a carriage ride in Central Park."

"I've always wanted to do that!"

"I know." Michael seemed pleased with himself.

"But it's snowing."

"It's not snowing that hard, and they keep blankets in the carriages. I promise you won't regret it!"

"How can I say no when you put it that way?"

We hopped into a cab and got out at the park's entrance by 60th Street and Fifth Avenue. The smell of horse manure was overpowering. Several carriages lined the street, waiting for passengers. Plenty of tourists were getting into the carriages. They weren't going to let the weather stop them. Besides, there was something romantic about taking a carriage ride through Central Park while it was snowing.

Michael helped me into the carriage and we were off. Two stunning white horses pulled the elaborately adorned carriage. The temperature was slightly below the freezing mark. So we huddled closely together and draped the heavy blanket that was provided across our laps. Michael had his arm around me, and I leaned into him.

Central Park has always been one of my favorite places in New York City. Every time I came here, I never ceased to be amazed at the genius of the city's engineers who decided to place this sprawling park in the middle of Manhattan. Although it was cold, the air was invigorating. I took in several deep breaths and just admired the beauty of the winter wonderland before me.

The snow kept falling. About an inch covered the ground now. The bare trees were outlined in the milky dust. There were only a few people walking around the park since it was getting later. I stared up ahead at another carriage and imagined I'd been transported back to nineteenth-century New York City where only horse-drawn carriages dotted the streets instead of hundreds of honking cars. I imagined women in long skirts and mufflers, and men in coattails and top hats walking in the park.

"What are you thinking about?"

"I'm picturing what it must've looked like here a hundred years ago when cars didn't exist. There's something about that era in New York City that I've always been fascinated by."

"Yeah, whenever I look at those old photos of the city it's hard to imagine, especially in comparison to today's Manhattan."

We fell silent again, just taking in the serene landscape before us. We were now approaching Central Park's Bow Bridge, where many couples exchanged their wedding vows. I could see why. The beautiful bridge was made out of cast iron and was designed to resemble the bow of a violinist. Our carriage stopped at the bridge.

"Why are we stopping? Is the ride over already?"

"No, Vee. I just asked the driver to stop so we can enjoy the beautiful view here for a little bit."

"Oh, okay." I thought that was odd, but I didn't question it. Michael sat up, removing his arm from around me. He placed both of his hands in his lap. He looked peculiar.

"Are you feeling all right?"

"Yeah." Michael seemed to jump at my question. "Let's just sit here for a moment quietly and just take it all in."

I nodded my head. He was acting strange, but so be it.

I was looking at the snow, which was now falling more heavily, and how it had completely blanketed the park. It looked like heaps of soft, fluffy cotton candy, without the added food coloring.

"Valentina?"

I turned toward Michael. He was kneeling on the floor of the carriage. I had been so lost in my thoughts that I hadn't even felt him move away from me.

"Did you drop something? Why are you down there?"

Now I was really beginning to worry about his sudden odd behavior.

He reached into his coat pocket and held out a small black velvet box. My heart began racing.

He slowly opened the box. A gorgeous three-carat emerald-cut ring sparkled in the box. I couldn't refrain from gasping.

"Will you marry me, Valentina?"

I started crying and laughing all at once.

"Yes! Oh my God, Michael! Yes!"

I threw my arms around Michael, who was laughing now, too. He finally looked more like his usual self as the color returned to his cheeks. Taking the ring out of the box, he slid it onto my finger.

"It fits perfectly! How did you know my ring size and that I love emerald-cut rings?"

"I had a little help from three women." Michael smiled mischievously. "Oh, and a guy, too."

"Hmmm, let me guess. My mother, sisters, and Aldo?"

Michael laughed. "Who else? Thank God, they know your tastes. I wanted to surprise you. I know we haven't talked at all about getting married so I was taking a huge chance just popping the question to you. But you know how much I love to surprise you."

"And you know how much I love surprises!" I giggled like a schoolgirl.

We stared into each other's eyes then. I leaned into Michael as he kissed me. We didn't care that it felt like the longest kiss we'd ever shared and were keeping the carriage driver waiting. I was sure he understood, and I was sure Michael would be tipping him nicely later for his patience. When we finally stopped kissing, Michael told the driver he could continue.

The driver turned around before resuming the ride. "Congratulations! May you have many years of happiness, like my wife and me."

"Thank you!" Michael and I shouted back to him in unison.

"I can't believe this is really happening. You're going to be my husband."

"And you're going to be my wife."

I snuggled back into Michael's embrace. He wrapped both of his arms around me and placed his cheek against mine.

"I feel like the luckiest man in the world. I love you so much, Valentina."

"I love you, Michael."

"We're going to be so happy together, Valentina."

We rode the rest of the ride in silence, trying to preserve this perfect memory. I couldn't help thinking back to when I was a little girl and Michael had rescued me at Mr. Li's Grocery Store. A part of me always knew Michael would be mine someday, and now that my dream had finally come true, I felt a sense of wholeness like I'd never felt before.

❧ 7 ❧

Noxzema

"What's your secret to having such smooth skin?"
"Noxzema."

Whenever Olivia was asked how she kept her fifty-year-old skin looking so smooth, she always referred to her favorite beauty product since she'd first stepped foot on American soil.

An unattainable prize when she lived in Sicily, Noxzema was also sold in her country. She and her sisters used to watch the Italian TV commercials of beautiful women swearing by it, but since it was imported from the United States, it was too expensive for them to buy it. Many evenings, Olivia and her sisters would go to *la drogheria* and admire the sapphire-blue jars of Noxzema.

"Noxzema will be my first purchase when I get to America," Olivia proudly exclaimed.

"You must send us some jars! You must!" Her sisters pleaded with her.

After Olivia and Nicola became engaged, they had agreed to go to America. She began daydreaming on a daily basis about what her new home would be like. She shared all the plans she'd envisioned with her sisters, whom she kept nothing from.

"First, Nicola and I will get jobs as tailors in a department store like Lord & Taylor or B. Altman's. We will live in one of those fancy apartments we've seen in movies about New York. Everyone in Manhattan wears nothing but the best designer clothes. So I'll go to work wearing Oscar de la Renta suits, and I will get my hair set every week at the beauty parlor like the other stylish American women do."

This last plan brought tears to Olivia's eyes. To think that she would no longer have to struggle taming her own thick, unruly curls brought such a feeling of elation over her.

"And then, of course, every morning and night, I will wash my face with . . ."

"NOXZEMA!" Olivia's five sisters cried out in unison. Their eyes glowed as they imagined this wonderful world that their sister was about to enter.

Olivia smiled and shook her head, remembering her sisters back home. How she missed them even after all these years. She sighed. It was time to go to bed.

She slipped under the covers, fluffed and propped up her pillows, and reached over for her Bible that lay on her nightstand. She removed her rosary beads, which hung on her bed's head post for easy access. First she prayed, fingering over each rosary bead, ensuring she hadn't missed one. Then she opened up her Bible to where she had left off the last time. She was up to the Book of Psalms, one of her favorite books in the Bible. The verses read like music, and sometimes she even sang the words to herself in her head.

After reading a few more psalms, she closed her Bible and placed it back on her night table. Olivia stared at the small framed photo of Nicola that sat adjacent to her Bible. Nicola was standing alone on the shores of the beach in her town in Tindari—at the foot of the cliffs where the cathedral of the Black Madonna of Tindari was perched. In the background of the photo, a tiny image of the cathedral could be made out at the top of the cliff. And the sand formations in the ocean, where the Black Madonna was said to have performed her miracle many years ago, could also be seen.

Since Olivia was a child she had loved the story of the pilgrim who had gone to Tindari to see the statue of the Virgin. The pilgrim's baby fell into the ocean below the craggy cliffs. The Madonna was believed to have performed a miracle by raising the land from beneath the ocean to save the baby, who was found playing on the sand formations, which were in the shape of the Madonna's profile.

Pulling open her night table drawer, Olivia took out a red leather-bound journal. Feeling along the side panel of the drawer, where the contact paper she'd used to line it was becoming loose, Olivia wedged her pinky finger beneath the lining and pulled out a tiny key.

She inserted the key into the diary's lock and unfastened the latch holding the covers together. Olivia had loved keeping a journal when she was young. She wondered why she had stopped doing so. Maybe because as a married woman, she hadn't had many secrets worth recording—although one did come to mind.

Flipping toward the back of the diary, she came to the part where she'd first met Nicola.

Dear Diary,

My sisters and I were at the beach below Tindari this morning, walking along the shore, when we came upon a group of fishermen casting their nets. The sun was still making her ascent in the sky, and the sunlight cast a glow on the shimmering fish that were flipping out of the water and into the nets. A group gathered along the shoreline. Though it was early, the villagers never tire of coming to this spectacle. They often know which days the fishermen will be out.

The sardines are abundant in the waters surrounding Sicily. The sight of so many fish mesmerized me as their graceful bodies leaped into the air before plunging to their deaths. It was beautiful, magical, and terrible all at once. But the magic of that moment penetrated me the most. It wasn't the first time I had seen fishermen at work, but for some reason, I had never really looked before as I did now. The sight was breathtaking.

"Olivia, vieni."

My sister Lucia called to me as she and my other two sisters walked ahead. I tore my gaze away and reluctantly followed.

"Scusa, signorina."

I looked over my shoulder. It was one of the fishermen from the boat. He was one of the younger ones, close to my age.

"Prendi."

He offered a few of the fish to me wrapped in a bundle of newspaper.

"Grazie. Grazie, molto." I smiled at the fisherman.

"My pleasure. Do you like watching the sardines being caught?"

He motioned to the fishermen, who were now putting their nets back into the boat. They were slapping each other on the backs. They were no doubt congratulating themselves over a good day's catch.

"Yes, I liked watching."

"It is beautiful, isn't it?"

"Beautiful and sad."

"Ahhh! You feel sorry for the fish, don't you?"

I smiled. "A little."

"My name is Nicola."

"Olivia."

"Do you come here a lot?"

"A few mornings a week. My sisters and I like to take a quick walk before we begin our chores. This is the only time of the day that we have to ourselves until we go to bed."

"Sometimes I come out with my friends. I love to catch fish, but I wouldn't want to do it every day of my life."

"So you are not a fisherman?"

"No, I'm an apprentice to a tailor."

"Da vero? I love to sew. I make clothes for my mother and sisters—and of course, for myself." I gave Nicola a shy smile. He returned my smile.

"I'm coming out with my friends to fish on Friday. I hope to see you again. Buon giorno, Olivia."

"Buon giorno."

Nicola hurried back to his boat. I watched him as he ran away. He had gentle eyes.

Olivia closed her diary and put it back in her night table's drawer. As she reached over to turn off her lamp, her eyes rested on the photograph of Nicola. She picked up the frame and stared at her deceased husband. She brought the frame to her lips and kissed the picture. This was something she did with the frames that held photos of her parents, who had also died quite some time ago. Olivia felt some comfort when she did this—a gesture that she was still sharing her love for them. She shut off the light and nestled down into bed. But she could not fall asleep. Her thoughts wandered to those early days when she and Nicola had first arrived in America.

Upon arrival at Ellis Island, she and the thousands of other immigrants were forced to wait in excruciatingly long lines. The worst was the medical examinations forced upon them. Olivia was terrified when she was detained after the health inspectors thought she had tuberculosis because of a spot they'd seen on her chest X-ray. Olivia had explained to the Italian translator that the spot was from a bout with pleurisy she'd had when she was fourteen. The doctors looked skeptically at Olivia, their eyes accusing her of lying. But upon further examination, they were able to rule out that she had tuberculosis, and she was allowed entry into the country.

Instead of getting a job as a tailor at a department store, the only work Nicola found was as a dishwasher in Sutton's Restaurant on MacDougal Street in Greenwich Village. Olivia did some tailoring at home after Nicola mentioned to Raquel Sutton, the restaurant owner's wife, that he and his wife were tailors. The owner's wife gave him clothes she and her friends owned that needed to be tailored. One day, Raquel asked Nicola if his wife could make her a dress for a party she was attending.

Olivia went to the restaurant to take Raquel's measurements. She never forgot how kind Raquel was and how she had first offered her a drink and asked if she'd eaten, insisting she have lunch with her before going to work. When Raquel showed Olivia the pattern she wanted, Olivia was not shy to tell her, "This is a beautiful dress design, but I think it can be even better with a few minor adjustments. But if you want this design copied exactly, I'll do that."

Raquel decided to trust Olivia's judgment, and she was very pleased with the dress once it was completed. She continued asking Olivia to make clothes for her, and their friendship grew. In addition to providing her with a steady income and being her friend, Raquel, who was fluent in Italian and French, had also helped Olivia with her English. The daytime soaps Olivia watched also came in handy for learning the language.

Raquel's friends had seen the gorgeous dresses Olivia had sewn. It wasn't long before she was bringing in quite a bit of money from all her seamstress work. She prayed that she and Nicola would be able to soon move into a nicer apartment than the rat-infested slum tenement they now lived in on the Lower East Side. Nicola had even taken a second job as a bricklayer.

"Don't worry. This life we now have won't be for long. Once we have enough money, we'll get a larger apartment, maybe even a small house. And we'll even open our own tailor shop!"

Nicola always seemed to know when Olivia was feeling especially beaten by all the difficult adjustments they'd had to make since they left Sicily.

Her sisters kept writing to her, asking if she'd forgotten about them and her promise to send jars of Noxzema. She couldn't blame them, though. They were like most other Europeans who thought the streets were paved with gold in America and all they had to do was move to her shores. Olivia was too embarrassed to tell them how different her life actually was in New York from the glamorous life she had bragged to her sisters she'd have once she got there. But she did admit to them that they weren't making enough money yet for her to send the Noxzema. She told them she was still waiting to buy her first jar. They probably didn't believe her.

And then with Raquel Sutton's help, Nicola landed a job altering men's suits at Lord & Taylor. Before she met her husband, John, Raquel had worked as a cosmetics sales consultant at Lord & Taylor and had become good friends with the store's president. So when she made a few inquiries and learned they indeed could use another talented tailor in the men's alterations department, Raquel immediately referred Nicola.

Now Olivia and Nicola were able to move into a larger apartment in Astoria, Queens, right by Astoria Park. And it was perfect timing since Olivia was pregnant with Valentina, and she couldn't imagine bringing a baby home to stay in the shabby tenement apartment they lived in. Though she was sad to leave Manhattan, which she'd grown to love, she was happier to have a much nicer apartment where she wouldn't have to worry that the rats had entered her pantry once again. Best of all, they would no longer have to share the communal bathroom in the hallway with the rest of the building, as they had in their former apartment.

The first night in their new home, Olivia had cooked a special dinner for Nicola. She made veal *saltimbocca.* It was a Neapolitan recipe her neighbor from the Lower East Side had given her. She also baked a *crostata de pomme,* knowing how much Nicola loved apple tarts.

Olivia wasn't the only one with a surprise. When Nicola came home, he held a shopping bag he tried to keep out of Olivia's view.

"Nicola, what are you hiding from me?"

"Nothing. I just bought a few things for myself."

Nicola continued walking toward the bedroom.

Olivia decided to let it be. She supposed she'd find out soon enough what he was up to. Nicola wasn't so good at keeping secrets.

They enjoyed a candlelit dinner and talked about how blessed they were to have finally found jobs as tailors and to have good friends like Raquel and John Sutton.

Olivia excused herself to go to the bathroom. Their railroad-style apartment forced her to walk through their bedroom before she could enter the bathroom. She froze when she saw what was on the bed—*ten* boxes of Noxzema! She ran over to pick one up, still not believing she was holding one in her very *own* home and not in a drugstore. She took out one of the jars, removed the lid, and smelled the cream. She then noticed the card that lay on her pillow. She ripped open the envelope.

Cara Olivia. Ti amo con tutto mio cuore. Tuo sposo, Nicola

Olivia turned to run out to the dining room, but Nicola was standing in the doorway smiling.

"You can finally have all the Noxzema you want."

"I can't believe you!" Olivia ran into his arms.

Nicola kissed Olivia. "You can send a few of those boxes to your sisters in Sicily. I know they've been begging you."

"You are the best husband in the world!"

"You are the best wife!"

That night, Olivia generously slathered the cool Noxzema all over her face, spreading it smoothly and making sure to create deep circles around her delicate eye area as she'd seen the TV commercial model do. She kept the Noxzema on for ten minutes, reveling in the tingling sensation and inhaling deeply its minty fragrance, as if its properties could benefit her lungs in addition to her complexion. When she rinsed off the cream, she was convinced that already her skin looked brighter and younger than it had that morning.

So this thirty-year-old Noxzema ritual Olivia still swore by did more than just keep her skin looking young. For it reminded her of her early days in New York, of how far she'd come since she'd left Sicily, and most of all, of her love for Nicola.

Olivia yawned, finally feeling herself surrender to sleep. Though Nicola was the last person in her mind before she drifted off to sleep, she didn't dream of him tonight. Instead, she found herself back in her beloved home in Tindari, Sicily, and dreaming of her first love—Salvatore Corvo.

❧ 8 ❧

Another Time,
Another Place

"*Ave, ave, ave, Maria! Ave, ave, ave, Maria!*"
My friends and I are standing on the cliff where the cathedral of the Black Madonna of Tindari is perched. Wreaths of orange blossoms crown our heads, and we stand in a ring around the statue of the Black Madonna. Every so often a soft breeze blows, carrying the citrus fragrance from the flowers in our hair.

I always feel a magical feeling every year when May, the month of the Madonna, comes around. My love for her and for God fills my lungs. I sing as beautifully as I can, offering my gift to the Madonna.

The buzzing sound of several motorinos *reaches our ears as they make their way up the tortuous road of the mountain that leads to the sanctuary. Soon we hear men's shouting. Entranced by our devotion, we all ignore them. But it becomes harder to stay focused, as the sounds grow louder. From my peripheral vision, I can see they are fast approaching the mountaintop. A few of my friends lower their voices and turn their heads toward the motorists, but I sing even louder, giving everyone a stern glance. But it's no use. My voice is soon drowned out by the raucous laughter of five young men riding their* motorinos. *I, too, am now forced to look. The men's shirts puff out behind them like a boat's sails on a gusty day.*

How dare these crass, stupid boys disrespect us and disturb our

veneration? Closing my eyes, I concentrate on my singing again, rais-
ing my voice as high as it can go. The men have now reached the cliff
and are parking their motorinos. Their boisterous talk and laughter
continues. Suddenly, one of them breaks out in song.

"Lasciate mehhh cantahhh-re . . ."

My eyes flash open. All of my friends are staring at the fool who is
singing this song. They start laughing when he begins marching to-
ward us like a soldier. Lifting his legs high and bending his knees in
an exaggerated manner, he salutes every second or so. He is so en-
tranced with his song that his eyes are closed. Has he been drinking?
The audacity of this buffoon! And he has the nerve to be singing the
words "Let me sing." No doubt he is mocking the Madonna and us.

"Cretino!" *I mutter under my breath.*

His friends are keeping their distance. No doubt they've seen the
furious look on my face. At least they have some sense. But just when
I think this they break down laughing. A couple of them are bent
over holding their crotches, laughing quietly as tears stream down
their faces.

Of course we have ceased our singing amid this spectacle. I glower
at the pagliaccio *before me whose eyes are shut and who now raises*
his voice in an ear-splitting soprano.

I walk over to him with my hands on my waist. The breeze kicks
up from the ocean below, whipping the white scarf that holds my hair
back like a gesture of peace. But I am far from calling an end to the
war that is brewing. Finally, he opens his eyes. We scan each other
from head to toe. His eyes are as black as the lava rocks that spew
from neighboring Mount Etna's volcano when it is erupting. But in-
stead of instilling fear in me, his eyes awe me. Everything about him
is mysterious and dark. I cross my arms in front of my chest.

"Why have you stopped singing? Well? Go on! Canti! You disrupted our worship so that you could be heard, and now that you
have our attention you just stand there mute!"

"Forgive me, signorina. *My friends and I were just carried away*
with the beautiful day. We didn't—"

"Canti! I don't want you to talk!"

"Signorina, *please accept my apology. I'll leave now and let you*
continue with your feast."

He turns to walk away, but I jump in front of him.

"Sing! Now!"

I point to the ground with my index finger, a gesture my father always uses when he commands us to listen. I glance around to see where this clown's friends are, but of course, none of the cowards are in sight. My singing partners have slowly advanced, all of their eyes fixed on this young man I am torturing. We now completely surround him. A few of the women whisper to each other, giggling softly. Even the three nuns in their heavy dark habits have their hands over their mouths.

"Come on, let's hear you sing," *my best friend Gabriella shouts.*

"Yes, that's what you wanted, after all. You were singing 'Lasciate Me Cantare.'"

Sister Pia Maria, who never disagrees with anyone, shouts, startling me. "Canti!"

The statue of our Virgin Mary has been forgotten as everyone joins in, "Canti, canti, canti!" *Instead of the Black Madonna, the brazen young man now is at the center of our circle.*

"Okay, okay. Just please give me some space."

Everyone steps back except for me. I can't resist smirking, but my rigid stance has not relaxed. The man sings, but not the same foolish song he had sung before. Instead he chooses a very sad love song that is popular with the girls. He closes his eyes and sings, in a deep, rich voice, the story of two tragic lovers. We are all mesmerized.

The song is short. When he is finished, I resist the urge to beg him not to stop. Everyone applauds except for me.

"Have I humiliated myself enough for you now, signorina?"

His fierce, dark eyes meet mine. I lower my gaze to the ground.

"Buon giorno, signorine."

"Buon giorno, signore," *the choir echoes in unison.*

He walks away. I take a step forward but stop. My friends watch me, their eyes imploring me. I break into a run, calling after him:

"Ritorni, per favore! Ritorni! *I'm sorry. I know you didn't mean any harm. Please come back.*"

"È niente. *No offense taken,* signorina. *Don't worry.*" *He continues walking toward his* motorino. *My head throbs. What am I doing? Young ladies don't run after men, my father always told my sisters and me, but I continue to follow him.*

"*Please, come join us in our picnic. We all would like you to stay. My name is Olivia Sera Repetti.*"

He stops but does not turn around. "*Sera?* Come la sera?"

"*Si, like the evening.*"

He gazes off into the distance for what feels like an eternity. I'm about to walk away when he says, "*You should go by your middle name.*"

"*Why?*"

"*It suits you better. Your mood is brooding and dark like the evening.*"

My anger flares up again. I'm about to lash at him when I see his smirk. That is exactly what he wants—for me to lose my temper so he will be right.

"*And your name is?*" *I force a smile, hoping to belie my true feelings of wanting to slap him.*

"*Salvatore Corvo.*"

"*Salvatore? What are you the savior of? Fools?*"

I can't resist my sharp retort.

Salvatore frowns and is about to say something, but doesn't. Ha! I got the better of him.

"*Well,* signorina. *I should be on my way and see where my friends are. I'm sorry again that we disrupted you and your prayers. Buon giorno.*"

"*Please. Won't you join us—even just for a little while?*"

"*No, grazie.*" *Salvatore walks away.*

My heart sinks when I realize he is not going to accept my apology. I am such a silly, stupid girl. I turn around and begin walking back to my friends, who are still watching us.

"*You know what? My friends will find me when they're ready. I suppose it wouldn't hurt if I joined you and your friends just for a few minutes. That is, if you are sure I wouldn't be interrupting? I've already created a distraction from your singing and praying.*"

"*No, it would be my . . . our pleasure. We were going to break soon for a picnic. We have more than enough wine and food.*"

"Grazie."

Salvatore walks by my side.

"Aspetta."

I wait for him as he walks over to a jasmine bush. He breaks off a cluster of the sweet flowers.

"For you. I know you are already wearing flowers in your hair, but I wanted to offer a peace gesture after my bad behavior earlier."

I smile as I take the flowers. "Grazie."

"And you know, I was only joking about your name. It's beautiful. Nighttime happens to be my favorite time of the day. Would you mind if I called you Sera instead of Olivia?"

No one has ever called me by my middle name before. The thought of having Salvatore call me Sera intrigues me. It is almost as if I have another identity.

"Yes, you may call me Sera. I was only joking about your name, too."

Salvatore smiles at me. We join my friends and lay out our picnic. Salvatore has not left my side, and instead of staying for only a few minutes, he is with us for the remainder of the afternoon. He asks me where I am from and how long have I been singing. We also talk about our love of music. Salvatore's friends eventually return and join our picnic. They seem nice, but from this moment on, there is only one man who exists for me—Salvatore.

Olivia awoke from her sleep with a start. Sighing deeply, she reached over to turn on her lamp and noticed the time on her alarm clock—five o'clock in the morning. Nicola's photograph caught her attention once again. Olivia picked up the frame and stared at her deceased husband. She remembered her dream, which was really a memory of the first time she'd met Salvatore. Very little was different in her dream from the actual meeting. How odd that she should have a dream that mirrored an event that had taken place in her life. She always dreamed of her youth and spending time with her family and friends in Sicily, but it had never been an actual recording of events as it had been tonight.

Though Olivia never told Nicola about Salvatore, she sensed he knew that she had loved before and had suffered. For he took his time with her, letting their friendship deepen before wooing her.

And when Olivia was finally able to close the chapter on Salvatore, she gave her heart fully to Nicola. So every once in a while when she had a dream about Salvatore, she always felt extremely guilty. Nicola was her husband, after all. Salvatore was just a part of her past.

Perhaps she still dreamed of Salvatore from time to time because she never had—what did the Americans call it? Closure? Salvatore had disappeared from her life as abruptly as he had entered it. But none of that mattered now after all these years. She'd moved on and had met Nicola two years after she'd last heard from Salvatore.

Olivia noticed some light coming in through her curtains. Glancing at her clock, she couldn't believe it was already almost six in the morning. There was no way she'd be able to go back to sleep. She pulled the covers off herself and got out of bed. Walking over to the window, Olivia stared at the sky. Dawn was her favorite time of the day, for it reminded her of those magical mornings on the beach in Tindari and of Nicola.

9

Mussolini Mansion

May 14, 2010—just one month before my wedding. Almost all of the plans are complete. I still can't believe it. The day I've been waiting for is almost here.

"Come on, get out of bed, we're going shopping for your honeymoon!"

Connie opens the blinds to my bedroom, and Rita opens my closet and throws a few of my clothes onto the bed.

"Today? Weren't we going to do that next week? I was going to pack a picnic and surprise Michael at his office, try to lure him to the park."

"What's up with him, anyway? Working on a Saturday? Total workaholic!"

Rita's voice sounds disgusted.

"He's ambitious."

"Well, you'd better get him in line. You don't want to be spending every Saturday without your husband. What's the point in getting married then?"

Rita's words affect me. Even though I've had more time since I finished sewing my dress and the wedding plans are all taken care of, I'm still not seeing Michael much. His hours at the office have only increased, especially after he'd received a promotion. He's managed to keep Saturday nights free for me and has promised he'll be able to come home earlier after we get married. But it still doesn't feel like enough.

"Sorry, Vee. That was harsh. But you know I call it how I see it. Someone's got to look out for you. I know how much he loves you, but he's got to make you his number-one priority, especially after you become his wife."

"I know. I know. I hate to admit it, but it's been bothering me, too. He's just thinking about our future. He wants to make sure he'll be able to provide for me."

"All I'm saying, Vee, is don't be afraid to ask for what you want and need."

"I'll be okay. Don't worry about your big sis. Let's go do some serious shopping!"

For my honeymoon shopping, Rita and Connie want to go all out and decide they want to take me to Manhasset's Miracle Mile on Long Island. We've only window-shopped there before, but since business has been good, we can now afford to splurge at the pricier boutiques and department stores that line this boulevard. As one of their wedding gifts to me, Rita and Connie will be picking up the tab for my honeymoon clothes.

Rita is driving down our street when suddenly she stops.

"Oh, crap! Vee, I just remembered that Signora Tesca told me she wanted you to see her today. She had something important to tell you."

"What? Signora Tesca? What could she have to tell me that's so important? Did you ask her what it was?"

"No, of course not! I mean, I got the feeling it was private. I didn't want to intrude or have her think I was being nosy."

"Since when have you been afraid of being blunt, Rita?"

"You don't want to anger Signora Tesca. Maybe she's left some of her riches to you in her will," Connie chimes in.

"Well, it can wait. I can talk to her when we get back from shopping."

"Oh, it's too late, Vee. Signora Tesca just opened her door. She's waving for you to go over."

Connie nods her head at Signora Tesca as if she's being summoned.

"Okay, okay. This is really weird."

Rita parks the car in a spot that's just opened up one house down from the Mussolini Mansion. That's what my sisters and I call Signora Tesca's home. Designed like an Italian villa, the house also sports a large yard that is seen from the street. Greco-Roman statues are scattered throughout the grassy yard. Remember, this is Astoria, Queens, and not some palatial estate on Long Island's Gold Coast. So this house really stands out among the semidetached row houses that are typical for a Queens neighborhood. Of course, the Mussolini Mansion is not attached to any of its mediocre counterparts.

When my sisters and I were kids, we used to like to walk by the Mussolini Mansion just before dusk. We'd pretend the statues were haunted and were staring and whispering at us. One night, as our parents hung out with our neighbors on our stoop, Rita, Connie, and I walked arm in arm to see if Signora Tesca's statues would come to life. We stood in front of the gate and waited.

"I just saw the statue of the lady holding grapes turn and look at me," Rita whispered excitedly.

"She's eating a grape now!" Connie pointed to the statue.

I was the only one who knew the statues were really not staring at us or eating grapes. But I played along for my younger sisters.

"The statue of the man in the back is waving to us. He wants us to go in. He must have something to tell us," I said with as much terror in my voice as I could muster.

I felt my sisters' grip on my arms tighten.

"We can't go in there. That's stress-passing." Connie looked at me, hoping her argument would persuade me not to go in.

"It's 'trespassing,' Connie, not 'stress-passing.' I don't think Signora Tesca would call the cops on us. She knows us, after all. She might just yell at us if she catches us, but she's probably asleep by now."

Suddenly, out of the corner of my eye, I saw something move in the shadows of the yard. We all screamed as we saw three pairs of bright yellow eyes staring back at us. Rita and Connie broke free of me and ran back toward my parents, screaming, "They're alive! They're alive!"

I was too afraid to move. Two of the creatures moved into the light that was cast from the street lamps. They stared at me with as much fear as I'm sure was written all over my face. I noticed they were raccoons! Opening my eyes wider to make sure I was seeing correctly, I took a step closer to the gate. Yes, they were definitely raccoons, and they were huge. What were raccoons doing in urban Queens? Where did they come from? They stared at me for another second, then turned away and munched on the grass in Signora Tesca's yard.

Signora Tesca added to the macabre nature of her property, since she was often seen staring through her blinds. She had small weasel-like eyes, penny-red wavy hair, which was cut in a pixie style, and she always wore a navy-blue polyester dress. Her shoulders were slightly stooped forward. Signora Tesca liked to walk up and down our street with her hands interlocked behind her back. She kept her gaze lowered to the concrete as if she were contemplating the universe's mysteries.

I was afraid of Signora Tesca until one day she talked to me. I was twelve years old at the time, and I was surprised she was being so nice to me since I thought she'd never forgive me for riding by her house on my bike and pulling the daisies that grew from her front lawn. She caught me once and asked me why I always did that. From that day forward, I never even glanced at the daisies. I was bummed since I loved flowers, and part of me couldn't see what the big deal was in taking a daisy or two once a week or so. There were so many of them. But deep down, I knew they weren't mine to take.

Signora Tesca told me how her home in Rome was across the street from former Italian dictator Mussolini's villa. She smiled as she mentioned this fact. I could never understand why Signora Tesca seemed proud of this since I'd heard from my father about the horrors Mussolini and his regime had committed during World War II. From that day on, my sisters and I called her house the Mussolini Mansion.

I'd never stepped through its doors. I was always curious to see what a rich lady's house looked like. It bothered me that Signora Tesca never invited me since I had done her a couple of favors and she would talk to me when she'd see me alone sitting on my stoop. She even showed me the locket that hung around her neck and the tiny photo of the baby girl inside it. Signora Tesca told me about the baby she'd had for just three months before she became very sick and died. Sometimes her words still haunted me. "Even though forty years have passed since she died, I think about her every day."

I never looked at Signora Tesca the same way again. Instead of seeing a creepy, stingy old lady who didn't even want a kid picking her daisies, I saw a mother whose heart was broken when her baby girl died; a very lonely woman who took my sisters and me to the beach on weekends in the summer and who treated us to pizza afterward; a sad woman whose son only visited once every few months.

"Vieni, Valentina. Vieni."

Signora Tesca motions for me to follow her into her home as I step out of Rita's car.

Oh my God! She's finally going to let me in, I think. I am finally going to see what the Mussolini Mansion looks like on the inside!

"I want to show you something, Valentina. Come in."

My heart races in delight. When I walk in, the first thing I notice is the sitting room to the right with the huge Steinway piano in it. Statues of dogs sit along the foyer. Two *capodimonte* vases stuffed with peacock feathers stand on either side of the foyer before the entrance to what must be the living room. Paintings from the Italian Renaissance era hang on the walls. One painting looks like a Titian that I had written a paper on for my Venetian Renaissance art history class in college. With Signora Tesca's fortune, I know it has to be the real deal.

I follow Signora Tesca into the living room, which is closed off by French doors. I stretch my neck, anxious to see what other riches lie in her house, when I hear, "SURPRISE!"

I barely have enough time to register what's going on before a swarm of people come rushing toward me. My mother is at the front of the crowd and crushes me to her chest, hugging the life force out of me.

Streamers with the words *Showers of Happiness* are strewn across the room. My shower? At Signora Tesca's? Signora Tesca is smiling, a sight I rarely see. I suddenly realize how much she cares about me to have the shower at her home—a home which few people enter. This woman is fiercely protective of her privacy. I look at Signora Tesca, who is staring at me much the way my own mother does—with pride and a glow in her eyes. And I know in that moment she's probably thinking of her baby girl and what might have been.

After I greet everyone and sit down, two of Signora Tesca's housekeepers begin taking everyone's orders for dinner. I take this opportunity to excuse myself and go to the bathroom.

"Valentina?"

I only make it to the foyer when I hear Mrs. Carello's voice. I turn around.

"May I talk to you alone for a moment?"

"Of course, Mrs. Carello."

"Come, let's go in here."

She walks through Signora Tesca's foyer and into a room that's on the opposite side from where the shower is being held. Floor-to-ceiling bookshelves line the walls. A chocolate-brown leather couch and armchairs are situated in the middle of the room. Ever since I was a kid, I'd dreamed about having a house one day with my own library.

We sit down on the couch.

"Is everything all right, Mrs. Carello?"

"Yes, of course. I just wanted to tell you that Michael told me about the argument the two of you had over your wedding dress."

"Oh." I'm taken aback. I can't believe Michael has told her.

"Yes, it's okay, honey. I'm sure you must know how close Michael and I are. He confides in me a lot."

Now I'm wondering what else he's told her about. I can feel the trademark DeLuca temper simmering my blood.

"So you know how he accidentally walked in on my dress fitting?"

"Yes, yes. I'm sorry he saw the dress."

"Well, he didn't see all of it."

"He's probably forgotten what the dress looks like already. Don't worry."

"He hasn't forgotten about the shorter hem of the dress. Since he told you about our fight, I'm sure he mentioned that."

"Yes, he did. He's like his father, worried over what people might think."

Like his father? I think. *More like you!*

"So you're not concerned about it?"

"I've known you, Valentina, since you were a little girl. You have a good head on your shoulders. I'm sure your dress is tasteful. You're not about to become someone you're not."

She pats my hand and smiles. I am shocked. Maybe I've misread her.

"You're not going to try and talk me into a conservative gown that covers every inch of my body?"

Mrs. Carello laughs. "Oh, no! It's not my place."

"What about Mr. Carello? You said he cares about what people think."

"He'll be fine. It's a different time. Joseph does worry about making a good impression. But again, he'll be fine. I don't know why Michael is being so old-fashioned about this. I told him to trust you."

"You did?"

"Of course, honey. I wanted to talk to you and ask you to be patient with him. He's been more stressed than usual lately with all those hours he's been putting in at work and the upcoming wedding, of course. He'll come around. You'll see."

"I hope so. I am going to change the dress slightly since he saw it. You know my mother and how superstitious she can be. She insisted on it, but I have worked so hard on this dress. I can't see myself wearing anything else."

"Yes, Olivia has always been worried about bad luck. I tried to tell her once it's all nonsense, and she got mad at me. You can't change people's beliefs when they're that strong. I think you made the right decision—keeping the dress mostly intact. And I know men, especially my Michael, they have the worst memories."

Mrs. Carello hugs me.

"Thank you. This makes me feel much better."

"Let's go back to your shower before your mother thinks someone abducted you!"

"Knowing her, she *would* think that!"

After cake and coffee are served, it's time to open my gifts.

"Okay, Vee. Come take your throne!" Rita screams out from Signora Tesca's living room, where we all follow her booming voice. In the center of the room is a white wicker chair that people rent for bridal showers. I'm registered at Bloomingdale's and Macy's, and I pray that most of the guests have honored my wishes by purchasing gifts off the registry. There's nothing that annoys a bride more than receiving gifts she doesn't want—or like—just because people are too lazy to go to the store where the bride and groom are registered.

Connie brings over my first gift. I saw Ma hand it to her, so I know it has to be from her.

"Ooh! This is heavy!" I exclaim after taking the gift from Connie.

"Aldo, are you getting what she says down?"

"Of course, Rita. Stop fussing!"

I almost forgot to mention that Aldo is at my shower. He's the only guy present and seems to be enjoying himself the most out of anyone there. I'm happy my family invited him. After all, Aldo is my best friend.

At the moment, Aldo is scribbling everything I say down in a notebook. Personally, I hate this bridal shower game where someone writes down every word coming out of the bride's mouth while she opens her gifts. Then later, the words are read back. They do usually prove to be funny, but I think it's a cheesy practice. But my mother and sisters love adhering to tradition.

I open Ma's gift. The scent of mothballs greets me, and I see why the box weighs so much. Embroidered sheets, towels, and doilies are wrapped in tissue paper. I already knew I'd be getting this trousseau that every Italian-American bride receives. I'd even seen these linens, since my father had brought some of them back from a trip to Sicily, where my aunts gave them to him. My *zia* Concetta, Connie's namesake, still embroiders even though she is in her late seventies. A few of the other pieces my aunt had sent over, and a few Ma had bought on some of her own trips to Sicily.

"Embroidered linens. They're beautiful."

I hold up a few of the linens so the guests can see them and do my best to act surprised.

"Are they from Sicily?" Aldo asks.

"Yes. Most of them my aunt embroidered."

Antoniella and Signora Tesca nod their heads in approval.

"What is Sicily known for?"

I frown. Why is Aldo asking me this?

"Ahhh . . . a lot. Spicier food."

"That's good! Keep going. What else?"

"Mount Etna and their volcanic islands."

"The climate. What about the climate?"

"It's hot."

"That's it! How hot?"

"Very hot!"

"Yes!"

Aldo smiles as he quickly scribbles away.

"Why are you suddenly so interested in Sicily, Aldo?"

He ignores my question. "Would you say it's big compared to the rest of Italy?"

"No, of course not. You know it's the rock that the boot shape of Italy is kicking. It's much smaller."

Aldo now has the biggest grin as he continues writing in his notebook. It then dawns on me what he's trying to do. He is trying to get me to say sexually suggestive words so that when he reads back my dialogue it will sound funnier and more risqué. I mentally roll my eyes. Only Aldo would go through so much trouble to make a bridal shower memorable.

Connie hands me the next gift.

"Open this one."

I read the card aloud. " 'May you have the "time" of your lives in your marriage. Love, Betsy and Mitzy.' "

Gee, let me guess? A clock? I open the box. An exquisite brass mantelpiece clock is carefully wrapped in bubble wrap. It looks like Betsy has added the bubble wrap herself out of fear that the original packaging is not sturdy enough to keep the clock from breaking. It's lovely, but it wasn't on my registry. The clock also doesn't go with how Michael and I have decided we'll decorate our new apartment. We're going with an Asian-inspired theme. Betsy is sweet, though. Maybe I can find a place where the clock won't stand out in stark contrast to our décor.

"Thank you, Betsy! It's gorgeous. And please thank Mitzy for me."

I stretch my neck trying to make eye contact with Betsy, who's sitting at the back of the room. I spot her double Ds poking through the space in between Ma and Signora Tesca. She stands up and waves to me, then turns around, waving to everyone else who has applauded her gift.

I unwrap several more gifts, all of which are not on my registry list and run the gamut from a vibrating massage chair to a dual WaterPik to monogrammed his and hers bath towels. Whatever happened to functional gifts like a toaster? But just when that thought pops into my head, the cheap toasters and electric can openers make their appearance. About half of the gifts aren't from my registry. But as I open the latter half, I finally start seeing items that I had registered for: Waterford crystal glasses, Noritake china, 500-thread Egyptian cotton sheet sets, a Ralph Lauren comforter set.

Michael's parents have been very generous and will buy our living room furniture set. My mother and sisters are chipping in to buy our bedroom furniture. Photos of the furniture are passed around for everyone to see. Mrs. Carello has also bought me a Lavazza coffee maker, which I almost hadn't put on my registry list out of fear that it was too pricey for any of my guests to buy.

I see Rita and Connie whispering to each other and laughing. They must've known which of the guests were less likely to schlep to Bloomie's and Macy's and they'd given me their gifts first to scare me. They notice me staring at them. I shake my index finger at them and mouth the words, "I'll get you."

"Rita, give that box next to Valentina."

Ma points to a box that resembles most of the other boxes with *Showers of Happiness* scrawled over the wrapping paper. But this one has a huge gold bow on top, probably to distinguish it from the rest. Rita begins pushing it toward me.

"Don't push it! Lift it!" Ma yells at Rita, who places her hand over her mouth and says, "I forgot."

Of course, that's my clue that something very fragile is in the box. Connie opens the card and hands it to me. She and Rita are working at lightning speed as they bring the gifts to me, clear the torn wrapping paper, and help me with the boxes that are tougher to open.

After I see whom the card is from and what it says, I can't read it aloud. Tears spring into my eyes. The guests' laughter and talking subside. Everyone's noticed the change in my expression.

I remove the gift wrap. *Lladro* is imprinted on the top of the box. The Spanish company is famous for its exquisite porcelain figurines. I gingerly take the item out of the box.

"Careful, Valentina!"

"I know, Ma."

Connie and Rita grasp the sides of the box, keeping it firmly planted to the ground as I pull out the Styrofoam brackets that hold snugly the figurine of a mermaid. It's useless fighting the tears as they quickly race down my face. Rita pulls from her cleavage a tissue and hands it to me. Even in my distress, I'm amazed that she's thought of everything.

I wipe my eyes. "I'm sorry. This is a gift from my father. It was a private joke we had about a mermaid."

"Ohhh!" The guests exclaim around the room.

Betsy lifts her glasses and rubs her eyes. Even Aldo, who never cries, looks like he's about to bawl. I am embarrassed even though I know I shouldn't be. I've always hated being the center of attention and now everyone pities me. Sensing my feelings, Rita quickly takes the reins.

"Isn't the figurine beautiful? It's Lladro."

"It's gorgeous. Yes, beautiful."

The guests immediately pick up on Rita's cue and are doing their best to move on with an awkward moment.

I look at Ma, who is wiping away her own tears. I mouth the words, "Thank you" to her. I start welling up again after seeing Ma cry.

"Okay, next gift."

Rita begins unwrapping the gift and blocks me from the guests until I have fully composed myself. I look up at her gratefully. She simply nods her head.

When I see the next present, I realize how brilliant Rita is.

"Whoa!!! Look at what we got here."

Rita pulls out a racy, sheer, red teddy followed by a matching thong. The box is full of different-colored teddies and negligees.

The guests instantly applaud and laugh. The sexy lingerie on display now overshadows the sadness that had been in the room a few seconds earlier.

"Michael is going to have a heart attack when he sees me in these!"

More laughter and rounds of applause ensue.

"Vee, what are they?" Aldo asks me. A few of the ladies look at him as if to say, "What's the matter with you? Are you that stupid?" But I know he's playing his game again.

"They're hot! And they'll make me feel sexy!"

"How sexy are they?"

"*Very* sexy!"

Ma is blushing, but she's also smiling.

"Who bought them?" Aldo asks.

"We did!" Connie and Rita sing out in unison.

"You girls are so naughty! I love it!"

Aldo gives my sisters a thumbs-up.

"Well, you have to start off the marriage right or else it'll go downhill even faster!" Connie says, giving Rita a high five.

"Yeah, Vee. You can tell Michael to thank us after the wedding night." Rita laughs.

The lingerie wasn't on my registry list, but I should've known my wacky sisters would think of everything for my wedding. I stand up, hugging both of them, and whisper, "You're the best kid sisters in the world."

"Yeah, we know!" Rita says.

"Okay, that's it for the gifts, folks!" Connie claps her hands, signaling the shower's end.

"Wait! What about that one behind Vee's chair?"

Aldo points to a small box.

"Oh, we must've not seen it."

Connie walks over and picks it up.

"I recognize it. I can't believe I forgot. It was part of my other gift."

Antoniella quickly comes over.

"I should've tied them together with the ribbon."

"Antoniella, you didn't need to get me a second gift. The Mikasa platter you bought me would've been enough."

Of course, the platter was one of the gifts not on my registry list. I would *never* choose Mikasa.

"It's nothing much."

The guests who are getting ready to leave stop to see this one last gift. I tear off the wrapping paper and freeze. I turn around quickly to throw the gift into one of the shopping bags that contains a few of the smaller gifts, hoping Ma hasn't seen it. Too late. Her anguished voice reaches my ears.

"Coltelli? Erano coltelli, vero?"

"No, Ma. They're not knives. They are . . . cooking utensils! Yes, you know those cooking utensils that are safe for nonstick pans?"

I pray my mother's nearsighted vision will lead her to believe she's seen incorrectly. She pushes through the crowd, making her way over to me.

"Rita, Connie, quick. Take this bag out of here."

Rita and Connie have the same frozen look of fear on their faces I'd had when I saw the knife set.

Connie grabs the bag from me and walks the fastest I've ever seen her walk.

"Connie! *Aspetti!* Let me help you. I'll carry that bag for you," Ma calls out, but Rita jumps in front of her and asks for help with a huge box she's carrying, giving Connie enough time to scramble out the door.

I make my way around the guests, thanking them and saying good-bye. When the last guest has left, my mother comes over to me.

"They were knives, weren't they? Tell me now. I'll find out sooner or later. I can always ask the Hunchback if you and the girls hide them from me."

"Ma, just let it go. Antoniella didn't mean any harm by it. She probably doesn't know about that stupid superstition."

"It's not stupid! What is the matter with her? She's Italian! Every Italian, no matter if you are from Roma, Calabria, Abbruzzi, Sicilia, knows it's bad luck to give knives as a wedding gift. It means the marriage will be cut. It will either end or not be a happy one."

"I know, Ma. You've told me about other showers you went to where someone gave knives. And every time, you were outraged and told me what it means when a bride receives knives."

"This is not good. First Michael sees your dress, and now the knives. These are signs." Ma whips out her rosary beads and crosses herself repeatedly, whispering, *"O Dio mio!"*

Though I try to ignore Ma's worries, the knives have struck a chord with me, too.

❧ 10 ☙

The Power

When a woman is going through the worst, she often confides in her best friend first. So it was natural that Olivia had called Raquel on that exceptionally sunny day in April, two months before Valentina's wedding, to say, "I found a cyst in my breast."

After Olivia had made the discovery, she immediately called her primary care doctor, who gave her the name of a breast cancer specialist. The specialist's office wasted no time in fitting Olivia into the schedule for the following afternoon. Dr. Preston was a female breast surgeon in her early thirties, but Olivia's primary care doctor had assured her that Dr. Preston was one of the best doctors in the field, despite her age. Olivia could see that she knew her stuff and was being very thorough. She was impressed that Dr. Preston could perform on the same day a fine needle aspiration. The procedure consisted of a needle that was inserted into the cyst to withdraw fluid. The fluid was then examined under a microscope for cancer cells. Dr. Preston and a pathologist by the name of Dr. Muhammed each studied the cells on a small microscope right in front of Olivia in the examination room. Her heart was pounding so loud that she was convinced the doctors could hear it. She almost fainted when they told her that they could not determine that the cyst was benign. Some of the cells were questionable. The only way they'd know for certain if she had cancer was after the entire cyst was surgically removed, and the cyst was sent for a pathology workup.

Olivia would never forget the irony that she had received such horrible news on a beautiful day. When she'd left the cancer center that Dr. Preston worked out of, she couldn't help but notice the clear blue sky and comfortable, mild temperatures. Everyone was enjoying the day and looking happy while Olivia felt so sad. She wanted to be like the other people she saw on the street—happy and seemingly without worries. And all she could think about was that she would not be around long to enjoy warm days like this anymore.

"Basta!" she muttered aloud.

She was feeling sorry for herself and acting as if the death sentence had been decreed already. After all, Dr. Preston had told her that there was a good chance it was not cancer. But Olivia had learned from Nicola's illness to not put too much of your trust in the words of doctors. She needed to stop. The day Olivia DeLuca pitied herself was the day she might as well die.

When Raquel Sutton heard Olivia so distraught, she immediately asked her to spend the weekend at her apartment in Greenwich Village. Raquel's husband, John, had died of a heart attack a year ago, leaving the responsibility of running Sutton's Restaurant solely to his wife. The Suttons had never had children.

"I don't want to be a burden. You have your own problems."

"Olivia! Don't be silly. What are friends for? And I know you. You haven't told your daughters yet, have you?"

The silence on the other end of the line confirmed Raquel's suspicions.

"Besides, you'll keep me company. This place is getting too quiet with just Mr. Magoo and me."

Olivia heard a bark, as if he was objecting to Raquel dismissing him as an acceptable companion. The Scottish Westie had grown on Olivia. She couldn't resist sneaking some *Palline di Limone biscotti* to Mr. Magoo, who seemed to swallow them whole. Raquel kept him on a strict diet and never gave him food other than dog food. No wonder the poor dog followed Olivia around whenever she visited.

"Ahhhh . . . Okay. I will come over, but first I have to pay someone else a visit."

The steps leading up to the fortune-teller's shop were enough to kill Olivia right on the spot. She had to stop and take a deep breath after reaching the eighth step. She used to be able to climb the fifteen steps all the way to the top before she needed to take a break. She'd been feeling very drained for the past three months. But at first, she wrote it off to all the preparations for Valentina's wedding and the increased clientele at the shop after they were featured in *Brides* magazine. So she'd started sleeping in on Sundays, opting to go to the eleven a.m. Mass instead of the eight a.m. Mass she went to every week. But that didn't seem to help her fatigue. She began going to bed two hours earlier than she normally did, and she even left the shop for lunch, using the excuse that she had to run errands, so she could rush home and take a nap. But the tired feeling would just not go away.

Valentina and Rita had noticed one day.

"Ma, are you getting enough sleep? The bags under your eyes are horrible."

Leave it to Rita's trademark bluntness to cut to the truth.

"I'm okay. We've just been really busy lately."

"Ma, why don't you go home and rest? We can finish up for the day."

"Well, I—okay. A nap is probably just what I need. Don't forget to—"

"Lock up. We know, Ma. When have we ever forgotten to lock up?"

Olivia picked up her purse and walked out of the store.

Making her way very slowly up Ditmars Boulevard, Olivia was certain if she were to stop and retrace her steps, she'd be able to see her daughters staring at her from Sposa Rosa's storefront window as they debated her welfare. She couldn't help smiling to herself as she imagined the conversation her daughters must surely be having right now about her.

"I don't think she's okay. She's not even walking as fast as she normally does."

"Well, Vee, she is getting old."

"She's only sixty, Rita. Sixty today is the new fifty, haven't you heard?"

"Yeah, maybe if you're Christie Brinkley or Diane Sawyer, not a seamstress who doesn't know the meaning of relax and take a vacation."

"Maybe we should take her to the doctor."

"I think you're over-worrying, Vee. Like Ma said, we've been very busy. We're all tired. We're younger, though, and can bounce back quicker than she can."

"Yeah, I guess you're right. Let's get back to work. We have five Bridezillas coming in tonight for fittings."

"All brides are Bridezillas."

"Are you accusing me of being a Bridezilla, too?"

"Of course not, Vee." Rita smirked.

Olivia sighed. How would she go on without them? Ahhhhh!

"I'm doing it again," she muttered aloud to herself.

At the sound of her voice, a young teenage girl opened the door to the fortune-teller's shop.

"I thought I heard someone out here. You didn't ring the bell, did you?"

"I forgot. I'm sorry. I have a lot on my mind."

"Yes, I can see that."

The girl stared into Olivia's eyes.

"Come in. Would you like a glass of water?"

"I don't want to trouble you."

"Trouble? It's just water. I'll be right back."

Olivia sat down on the black sectional that wrapped around half of the shop. She loved coming here. The fortune-teller had done a wonderful job of creating a welcoming, intimate feel to the shop that also served as her apartment. Lush scarlet wall-to-wall carpeting complemented the black sectional and matching loveseat. Mirrors covered two of the walls from floor to ceiling. A sweet fragrance always lingered in the air—a mix of recently burned candles and incense.

"Here you are, ma'am." The girl set the water down on a coaster with a picture of a maple leaf and *Canada* underneath it. The tacky souvenir coaster seemed out of place on the expensive glass coffee table it rested on. In fact, all of the furnishings looked pricey. Olivia had never noticed that before. The drapes were shantung silk. The chandelier looked very much like a Swarovski crystal chandelier Olivia had seen in a copy of *Architectural Digest*. She turned her attention back to the girl, who was staring at her with that same intensity again.

"Where is your mother?"

"She's not here."

"Oh. Is it okay if I wait for her?"

"Sure. But you'd be waiting a long time. She's out of town."

"I see." Olivia's heart sank.

"Well, will she be back this weekend?"

"I doubt it. My grandfather is dying in Romania. My mother flew out right away last night. We have no idea when she'll be back."

"I'm so sorry."

"Thank you."

"Are you here alone?"

"My father, brothers, and cousins are at church, praying for my grandfather."

Olivia knew that the girl's mother, Madame Elena, was married, but Olivia had never known that she had children, which she found odd. When the girl had opened the door, there was no mistaking that she was Madame Elena's daughter. The resemblance was striking.

How had Madame Elena managed to keep from her that she had children? Olivia had been seeing her for over a year now. Why hadn't she ever mentioned them? The only reason she knew the fortune-teller was married is that once she saw Madame Elena's husband walk out from a room in the back and say hello as he was leaving. All Madame Elena said was, "My husband." She hadn't even introduced them. Olivia thought Madame was too focused on her reading to distract herself with introductions. Olivia had always been curious about Madame Elena, but the few questions she had asked about her life were always met with vague responses and sometimes they were ignored altogether.

Olivia took a few sips of water, then got up.

"I shouldn't be here at this difficult time for you and your family. Thank you for the water. I'll come back when your mother is here."

"Why? I can give you a reading."

"How did you know I wanted a reading? I could just be a friend of your mother's."

"Because I saw it."

Olivia frowned. Was this girl playing a joke on her? She might be old and have an accent, but she was no idiot.

"I'll have to get going. Thank you again."

Olivia made her way toward the door.

"You don't believe me."

Olivia froze just as she was about to place her hand on the doorknob.

She turned around. "It's not that. I'm just used to seeing your mother."

She hoped that would be enough, but this girl was even more stubborn than the mule her grandparents had owned on their tiny farm in Sicily.

"I have the power, too. So do my brothers and father."

"The power?"

"The power to read thoughts, see the future."

"Oh."

Olivia frowned. She couldn't help but find it strange that this young girl referred to her psychic ability as a "power." Did she see herself as some sort of superhero like Spider-Man or Wonder Woman?

"It runs in the family?" Olivia asked, her curiosity beginning to win over her doubts.

"Of course. Why wouldn't we inherit it if our parents have the ability to see the past and future? Come back to the couch and we can begin your reading."

"That's okay. I really need to return to work."

"You still don't believe me. I can feel it. Why don't you let me prove it to you?"

Olivia sighed. What did she have to lose? Some money? Lord knows she'd given the girl's mother quite a bit of money over the past year for her readings. But Madame Elena definitely had the gift of foresight. She had predicted several events for Olivia, including Valentina's engagement to Michael.

"All right. You can give me a reading. But first I need to know your name."

"Sonia." She extended her hand. "Pleasure to meet you, ma'am."

"I'm Olivia. Please stop calling me 'ma'am.' I know you're being polite, but I don't like it. It makes me feel like I'm from the last century. I'm old but not that old."

Sonia looked a little taken aback by Olivia's forthrightness.

"Of course. Whatever you like."

This girl was odd. Olivia had never heard a kid talk like this before. *She* sounded old.

"So would you like a palm or tarot card reading?"

"I always do tarot cards."

Sonia nodded her head, approving Olivia's choice.

"Would you like the cross-style reading?"

"Yes."

Olivia didn't mind paying extra for the full cross-style reading, which showed her past, present, and future. The only way she'd know if Sonia were the real deal was by seeing how accurately she read Olivia's past.

Sonia took out a deck of cards and was about to shuffle them when Olivia held up her hand.

"Wait. Before you give me my reading, I have a few questions for you."

Looking slightly miffed, knowing Olivia was testing her, Sonia shrugged her shoulders in resignation.

"All right. Go ahead."

She placed the cards on the table and folded her hands in her lap, calmly staring back at Olivia. Why didn't this girl act like the other teenagers Olivia knew? Certainly, her daughters hadn't acted like this girl when they were her age.

"How old are you?"

"I'm fourteen."

"I don't believe it! You look no more than twelve—even ten years old!"

Sonia knitted her brows and narrowed her eyes, still maintaining her poise, but just barely. "Well, I *am* fourteen."

"I'm sorry. I didn't mean to offend you. It's hard to believe because you . . ."

"Look so young. I know. I get it all the time. It's okay. I'm used to it."

But she wasn't used to it. Clearly, Olivia could see she had ruffled the girl's nerve. Maybe that was why she strived so hard to appear older in both her demeanor and voice. Some girls did develop later than others, like Valentina had. Olivia decided to quickly change the subject.

"So you said everyone in your family has the psychic gift?"

"Yes, we all do. My grandparents on both sides of my family were also blessed with 'the power.' And my maternal great-grandmother and paternal great-grandfather also were psychic."

"If you're all psychic, then why is your family in church praying for your grandfather? Don't they know already if he'll live or die?"

"We're not praying for God to spare my grandfather's life. We don't have the right to ask God that. We're praying for his soul and that his suffering will be minimal as he goes from this life to the next."

"So you do know for certain he's dying then?"

"As psychics, we don't have the ability to predict our own futures. But since my father also has 'the power,' he can predict his father-in-law's death, since he's not a blood relative. My mother begged my father to tell her. My father couldn't bear to. So my mother knew he must've seen that her father was going to die and she rushed to get to Romania in time."

"I see. Okay, you can continue with the reading. Thank you for answering my questions."

Sonia picked up the cards once more from the coffee table and shuffled them expertly. This kid could've gotten a job as a Vegas casino dealer. After shuffling the deck, she placed the pile of cards back down on the table.

Instinctively, Olivia reached for them, knowing from all her previous visits that she must cut the deck into three piles. Sonia then began flipping over the cards from each of the three piles.

"The past," she announced as she began studying the cards.

"Your husband passed away many years ago. Devastating illness. Much suffering. You and your daughters were heartbroken. You were terribly afraid—afraid that you were going to lose everything with his death—your home, your tailor shop, and the money for your daughters' education. But you put your fears aside to survive."

So far, so good. Okay, I guess she *did* have "the power." But then again, Madame Elena might've shared this info with Sonia. As if reading her thoughts, Sonia looked up at Olivia.

"Yes, yes, please go on."

"Wedding dresses, lots of them. Oh, I see. You turned the tailor shop into a bridal store. Your daughters helped you and decided to go to work for you full time once they were done with college." Sonia looked up and smiled. "That's not too different from my family."

Olivia smiled faintly. She was stunned. All the details Sonia was giving her were accurate. Madame Elena had been more vague when reading Olivia's past. Hmmm. She couldn't help wondering now how much of "the power" Sonia's mother really had in comparison to her daughter.

"There was another love in your life. Before your husband, but he went off into the navy. He wrote a few letters to you, but then he stopped. You never heard from him again."

Olivia's heart dropped. Her face felt like it had caught fire. Not even Sonia's mother had been able to see Salvatore. Or maybe she had but knew Olivia would be embarrassed and decided not to mention it?

"We were very young. He was my first love."

"Of course. We never forget our first loves."

Olivia frowned. What did this fourteen-year-old girl know about first love?

"That was a very long time ago. Then I met Nicola, my true

love, the one I was destined to be with. He gave me a good, happy life. We were together for twenty-three years."

Sonia nodded. "Yes, I can see you both loved each other very much. But there were a few difficulties."

"*Every* marriage has a few difficulties," Olivia quickly added. Was this girl playing games with her? If she were, she would have Olivia's *malocchio* to deal with. Fortune-tellers weren't the only ones who could cast curses. And no one wanted to experience the wrath of a Sicilian woman and her evil eye.

Sonia sensed she'd piqued Olivia's nerves and wisely moved on. She talked about Olivia and Nicola immigrating to America and the birth of their daughters. Then she proceeded to the present and future.

"Your business has been doing really well. I see another wedding, someone close to you. Oh, it's your eldest daughter."

Sonia paused, her brows joined together now as she squinted her eyes, staring closely at the card before her.

"What is it?"

"I can't be sure at this time."

"It's about Valentina, isn't it?"

Sonia didn't say anything but continued scrutinizing the card intensely, much the way she had scrutinized Olivia earlier.

"*Dio mio!* What is it? Tell me!"

Olivia pulled out from underneath her blouse the ruby-red-colored rosary made out of rose petals, which she'd bought when she had visited the Vatican a few years back. Making the sign of the cross three times, she kissed the crucifix each time. The blend of the scents coming from the burning candles in the shop and the sweet rose fragrance from Olivia's rosary was making her feel woozy.

"Calm down. I do see a very tough road ahead, but I'm not sure which daughter, or if all of them, will be facing this obstacle."

Olivia knew right away what her daughters' crosses to bear would be. As if picking up immediately on her thoughts, Sonia looked up and said, "No, it's not your health. That's not the only difficulty I see."

"You know? Ahhh! Of course you know."

"I can see there is some problem with health, but I cannot see specifically what the problem is. May I ask what is the matter?"

Olivia told Sonia about the cyst in her breast and how the doctor told her it was questionable and about her imminent surgery. Tears ran down her face. Sonia placed her hand on top of Olivia's.

"That must be very scary. I will pray for you that it is not cancer."

"I haven't even told my daughters yet. How can I tell them I might have cancer and that they'll have to go through again what they went through with my husband? I need to know now if I have cancer, and if I do, will I die? I need to know before I can tell my children."

"I don't have the answer as to whether or not you have cancer, Olivia. I can't see everything. And death. Well, death is very complex—even for psychics. We can't always predict it. I'm sorry."

"But your father was able to see that your grandfather is going to die. So why can't you?"

"I don't see it. I just see that there is something concerning your health, something to be concerned about and that needs to be taken care of. But that doesn't mean it is cancer. The doctor did say it was questionable and for you to avoid jumping to the conclusion that it was cancer. Again, I'm sorry I'm not getting anything else. Sometimes we see death, and sometimes we don't. It's whatever God wants us to see."

"You just don't want to tell me, or is it you really have no idea because you're a fake?"

"Olivia, I know you're mad at me. I know you're probably also mad that you are sick, and you feel helpless. You have to trust God that He is doing what is right for you. I might get more clarity as time goes by. Focus on getting well and living for now rather than the end result."

Olivia sighed. "You sound like one of those, what do they call them? Self-help books?"

"I'm sorry. I didn't mean to make what you're going through sound so general."

"It's okay. I know what you were trying to say. You're a good girl, just trying to help me. What has this world come to? I can't believe I'm taking advice from a teenage girl and a psychic one! Are you sure you're only fourteen years old?"

Sonia laughed. "Yes, I'm sure."

Olivia got up and walked to the door.

"My family and I will pray for you and burn our special candles. I'll tell my mother when she gets back from Romania that you were here."

"I almost forgot to pay you."

"No, no. That's okay. This one is free."

"Are you sure?"

"Yes, please. You've been coming to see my mother for a while now. Your loyalty is my payment for today."

"Thank you."

Olivia carefully made her way down the long flight of steps. She thought she would have walked out of there with answers. Instead, she felt more afraid and desperate. Well, at least the girl hadn't charged her. She didn't need to blow $40 on having someone tell her about her past and present—teen psychic or not. She already knew those chapters of her life. She needed to know about her future. The best the girl could predict was her health problem and the overwhelming obstacle one or all of her daughters would face. Ha! She could've predicted that herself. Life is always filled with roadblocks. The girl was sweet, though.

Olivia's mind drifted back to what Sonia had said about Salvatore. Guilt washed over her. She must remain faithful to Nicola's memory. She shook her head, attempting to physically erase all thoughts of her first love before she'd met her husband.

Before she stepped out of the hallway that led up to the fortune-teller's shop, she strained her neck to peer out the door in either direction, making sure no one she knew was walking by. Though many people in Astoria visited fortune-tellers, no one liked to admit they'd gone to one. And if Valentina, Rita, and Connie found out, they'd be furious with her. They gave her enough grief as it was about her superstitious beliefs. As soon as she was sure none of her nosy neighbors were strolling by, Olivia stepped out onto Ditmars Boulevard and hurriedly made her way back to Sposa Rosa.

❧ 11 ❧

Bridal Blues

Since I had grown up with a mother who was such a believer in superstition, it didn't escape my notice that rain or snow had marked several milestones in my relationship with Michael. It was raining when Michael had finally asked me out on our first date. It was snowing the night he'd proposed to me. It was also snowing the day he told me what he thought of my wedding dress after having walked in on the fitting. And now today has been pouring with a vengeance since early in the morning. There's a nor'easter making its way up the eastern seaboard. It's a horrible day to be out, but Michael had insisted that he needed to see me. So I'm waiting for him to come pick me up at the shop. Of course, he's late as usual.

I don't bother waiting for Michael to get lunch. He won't mind since he knows how early I wake up on the days I have to be at work, and if I wait for him, I'll pass out from hunger. Sighing aloud, I wonder if he will ever get better with his tardiness—probably not.

Since the weather is so miserable, my sisters and I decide to order gyros from Pizza Palace. They make the best gyros on Ditmars, maybe even in all of Astoria. I am so spoiled by the authentic gyros and Greek food in Astoria, which is also known as Little

Greece, that I can't eat Greek food anywhere else in New York—not even in Manhattan!

Multitasker extraordinaire that I am, I'm finishing writing the last of my bridal shower thank-you cards while I eat. Thanks to my family and future in-laws, I'd received most of the gifts I wanted from my bridal shower. With a little less than one month to go until my fairy-tale wedding in the fairy-tale city of Venice, I should be happy that the day is almost here. But for the past two weeks, I just can't shake my low spirits. Have I fallen victim to a case of the "Bridal Blues"?

"Bridal Blues" is what my family and I call it when brides suddenly get depressed before their weddings. We've seen it often when clients come in for their final fitting. Ma always attributes it to nerves and says grooms go through it, too, perhaps even more so than brides. But my sisters and I suspect something else is at play. Though engaged couples complain about the headaches involved in planning a wedding, the truth of the matter is that brides love it. They love every aspect of making the day they dreamed about since they were little girls perfect, no matter how stressful it can be.

"It's kind of like postpartum depression. You're sad because you've had the baby, and now all the attention is on the baby instead of on the pregnant mom-to-be."

Rita's explaining the concept of "Bridal Blues" to Aldo, who is also eating lunch with us. He and my sisters are glued to the TV watching repeats of *Say Yes to the Dress*. Monday mornings are our quietest time in the shop, and with the rain, it's even deader than usual.

Aldo had been laid off last month from his job at Christie's auction house. He's devastated since, as he puts it, "Art is my life. And I'll *never, ever, ever* find a job in a prestigious art gallery like Christie's again. That's a once-in-a-lifetime opportunity."

Art is another passion we have in common. From Impressionism to abstract realism to Renaissance art, I can't get enough. Aldo and I often visit the museums and art galleries around Manhattan. We make a whole day out of it, starting as soon as the museums open. Then we have afternoon tea and finger sandwiches. When the Waldorf Astoria was open, we loved having our tea there. We were so upset when they closed their doors. Now we just go to any café or coffeehouse. After tea or cappuccino, we take a stroll through Chelsea and go to whatever art galleries are open. Then we end the day with dinner.

Ever since I had gotten engaged, we hadn't been having our "art days" anymore. I'm to blame with all the preparations for the wedding and making my dress. Aldo has been a good sport about it. I'll have to make it up to him soon.

Art appreciation is the one area where Michael and I have nothing in common. Michael likes going to museums—as long as they're science or history museums. He's accompanied me a few times to the Met. I think the Met is a safe bet for introducing a newbie to art. There's no way I'm taking him anywhere near the Guggenheim or even MOMA until he's had more time to appreciate the classics. After all, how could he understand the paintings of Pollack or de Kooning or even Picasso before he'd understood the masters before them?

Well, it turned out I didn't have to worry about slowly inducting Michael into the world of art. During our third outing to the Met, Michael blurted to me one day, "I'm so bored."

He must've seen the hurt look in my eyes because he quickly came back with, "I'm sorry, Vee. I tried, but other than the Egyptian exhibit I just can't get into this. I just don't find it as fascinating as you do."

"Don't some of these paintings move you when you look at them?" I asked, incredulous that he wasn't feeling anything. We were standing before Caravaggio's *Death of the Virgin*.

Michael shrugged his shoulders and looked guiltily at me. I decided to drop the subject and the idea that he would become a lover of art.

"That girl is such a bee-otch!" Aldo cries out. "She's knocked every dress her sister has tried on, and they all looked stunning on her. She's just jealous that she doesn't have her drop-dead gorgeous figure!"

Aldo's protests shake me out of my daydreaming.

"No, Aldo. You're not getting it. She's jealous and mad that it's not her trying on the dresses. Trust us, we know. We've seen it thousands of times." Connie frowns. "She had her turn."

Just like on *Say Yes to the Dress,* we've seen clients who had purchased their dresses at Sposa Rosa return with family members or friends whose turn it was to tie the knot, and the former brides would try to take over the session.

"She should just divorce her husband then and marry someone else so she can do it all over again!"

Aldo elbows Connie as the two of them laugh.

"It's not always former brides who get jealous. Sometimes it's a family member or friend who's never been married before. They can get quite opinionated, too."

I give my take on the subject.

"So, it sounds like it's not really about the dress but about themselves? Their own hang-ups and insecurities?"

"Now you've got it!" Rita slaps Aldo on the back as she walks by him.

"See, Aldo, we're not just dressmakers. We're also psychologists."

I place my last thank-you card in the envelope. I stare at the blank envelope. This would be the last time I wrote thank-you cards for a bridal shower. There it is again. The tidal wave of sadness quickly washes over me.

"What's gotten into you? Why are you staring at that blank envelope? Did you forget whose card that is?"

Rita's voice brings me out of my stupor.

"No, no. It's Signora Tesca's card."

"Are you sure, Vee? We know how absentminded you can get. Why don't you just place the steamer over the envelope's seal so you can open it and be sure it's Signora Tesca's card?"

Connie doesn't wait for my answer. She walks over with the steamer.

"I don't need the steamer! I'm positive this is Signora Tesca's card because I intentionally saved her card for last. I wanted to write her a longer note to express how grateful I was for her hosting the shower at her house."

"And what a house it was! You guys pegged it right when you nicknamed it the Mussolini Mansion. Some of the stuff in that place could bring in a fortune when she dies and it's auctioned off. Maybe I'll be able to get a job as an auctioneer again, and I could represent her estate. *That* would seal my career!"

Aldo's eyes look dreamy as he imagines his possible future career path.

Rita's trademark cynicism rears its head. "Are you kidding me? Most of what I saw looked so old and tacky! Who would want to pay a fortune for that?"

Aldo's lips are pursed tightly together as he rolls his eyes and looks at Rita in the most exasperated fashion. "Tons of people! Have you ever heard of collectors, Rita? Tsskk! Trust me. *I'm* the expert on these things. We're looking at a couple of million just based on the collectibles. Then there's her furniture."

"What? That crap that's been covered in plastic for the past five decades?"

"Rita, I'm not going to debate this with you. It would be like you trying to explain to me why a Pnina Tornai dress is really worth twenty-five thousand as opposed to an inferior dress that's only worth five grand."

"He's got you there, Rita!"

Connie and Aldo high-five each other and laugh.

I'm still staring at the blank envelope.

"Oh my God, Valentina! Snap out of it! Something is the matter. 'Fess up!"

Aldo comes to my side.

"It's nothing. You guys know how quickly my thoughts wander. I was just thinking."

"Nuh-duh! We can see that. *What* were you thinking about? You look like you're going to cry."

Rita's now standing opposite me, staring right into my face.

"I don't want to talk about it. Besides, Michael should be getting here soon."

"It's about Michael, isn't it? I knew it!" Connie all but shouts.

"Shhh! Like I said, he'll probably be here any minute."

"Okay, we'll talk low. So what is it? He's having a hard time in the bedroom, and now you're worried you'll have a dud for life after you get married?"

"Aldo! Of course that's not it."

I walk to the back of the shop, hoping to escape them as I begin to get ready to leave. But they trail after me.

"Vee, we're not letting you leave until you tell us what's the matter." Rita stands right behind me with her arms crossed in front of her chest. Aldo and Connie flank her sides, looking just as determined.

I sigh. "Why can't you guys ever respect my privacy?"

"We're worried about you. And you know how it is in Italian families. When one family member has a problem, it becomes the rest of the family's problem," Connie says.

"That's right!" Aldo knows he's as much a part of my family as my sisters are. I've told him countless times how he is like a brother to me.

"Okay, okay. I give up. I didn't want to admit this. I'm embarrassed, but it seems I've fallen victim to the 'Bridal Blues.' "

"Not you, Vee!" Aldo shouts.

"You're not leveling with us. In a million years, I would've never seen you getting the 'Bridal Blues.' "

Rita's eyebrows are knitted together, making the vein on her forehead thrust out. She scrutinizes me, doubting my claim.

"Well, it's true. Like I said, I was embarrassed to admit it. I should know better from working at Sposa Rosa to let myself get down about something so silly. But I guess I'm not immune to it. Even though life has been more hectic since I got engaged and began planning the wedding, I can't believe it'll be over in a month."

"Instead of feeling glum that you won't have a wedding to plan anymore, you should be looking forward to the future with your hot new husband! Besides, soon you'll have a baby on the way and then all the excitement will be on you again!"

Aldo is next to me now and has placed his arm around my shoulders.

"It's silly. I know. I shouldn't be feeling this way." I can feel my cheeks growing warm. I feel stupid.

"No, it's not silly. You're a woman, and these things matter to us."

I'm surprised Rita is the one to say this. She's always making fun of these brides who get so carried away by their weddings.

"And we know how much your wedding means to you. You've been waiting for the right man to come along for so long, or rather I should say you've been waiting for Michael to come around for so long! If anyone deserves to have a perfect wedding, it's you, Valentina. Of course you're going to feel a little down that this excitement will all be over soon. But you'll be with Michael every day for the rest of your lives. Think of that!"

Sometimes Connie's—and even Rita's—wisdom amazes me. They are my little sisters. They aren't supposed to have the answers. I'm supposed to be giving them advice. But they're very smart and perceptive. All those years that I thought no one knew about my secret crush on Michael, I'd been wrong. Of course, my mother and my sisters knew how I'd felt about Michael. No one knows me better. Well, except for Aldo. Suddenly, another disturbing thought enters my mind. Michael hadn't popped into my mind when I thought of the people who know me best. Shouldn't the man I'm about to marry be one of the top three people who know me the best?

"Are you sure there isn't anything else besides the 'Bridal Blues' that's bothering you?"

Sometimes I swear Aldo has mind-reading abilities.

"Yes, I'm sure."

I avert my eyes from Aldo's penetrating gaze as I say this.

The door's buzzer sounds.

"Hello! Hello!"

"It's Michael! Don't breathe a word about any of this to him."

I make my way to the front of the store.

"We're back here."

"Hey, guys."

Michael nods his head in greeting to everyone.

"Hey, Michael," Rita, Connie, and Aldo call out in unison. Then they just stand there without saying another word, just staring at Michael and me. Michael looks a bit uneasy, which is unlike him.

Though he isn't a big talker like my family and Aldo are, he's always managed to say more than just hello.

"So, you ready to go, Valentina?"

"Yes, yes. I'll see you guys at home tonight. I won't be back at the shop. I have a few wedding-related errands to run."

Michael is looking more and more nervous. Maybe he isn't feeling well.

"Don't worry about it, Vee. Connie and I will hold down the fort. Besides, Ma should be here soon."

"Have fun!" Aldo calls to us as we step out into the stormy weather.

"The car's just across the street. Luckily, I found parking close so we won't get completely drenched."

I nod my head as I follow Michael and hold on to my umbrella with a vise-like grip, hoping the gusty winds won't rip it out of my hands.

Inside the car, Michael hands me a few napkins from his glove compartment.

"Thanks."

I dab at the raindrops on my face.

"So where are we going? I guess our options are limited since it's so lousy outside. I doubt you want to drive far or anything."

"Actually, I thought we'd head over to my house in Oyster Bay."

I smile at him. Has he planned something romantic? Mr. and Mrs. Carello own a second home in Oyster Bay, which they use primarily during the summer months. Michael and I go there when we want to be alone, which is often since I'm still living with my family, and Michael has a roommate who rarely leaves their apartment.

Michael and I had found a house on Upper Ditmars Boulevard that we put a down payment on six months ago. We're having a few renovations done, and it won't be ready to move into for another two weeks. Of course with our traditional Italian upbringing, we won't be living together in the house until on our wedding night.

One day, however, Michael surprised me and took me there. We had a picnic on the floor of the house. Since the electricity wasn't turned on yet, Michael had brought lots of candles. He'd said he couldn't wait for the house to be ready for us to spend some time in it.

"Oyster Bay? I didn't think you'd want to drive all the way out there in this weather, but sure. It'll be nice." I lean over and kiss Michael on the lips. But he just quickly kisses me back and starts the ignition.

"We'd better get going."

Again, he seems anxious to be on our way. He's probably just eager to have me to himself. It's been several weeks since we'd made love. With the wedding fast approaching, my responsibilities at Sposa Rosa, and finishing up the last touches on my gown, it has been hard for me to get away even on a weekend night. Michael's new promotion at Smith Barney has meant longer hours, and he's even gone into the office on weekends. Connie's right. It'll be nice to have the wedding over so that I'll see Michael every day. I'm foolish to be sad that all this craziness with the wedding planning will soon be over. It's definitely putting a dent in my quality time with Michael. He assures me things will free up a bit with his job not long after we get married. And as he puts it, he'll have me for the entire night *every* night even when he does have to work late. The thought of that makes me weak in my knees. I feel a warm glow thinking that soon we'll be in his house, cuddling under the blankets together and making love on this stormy day.

I reach over and place my hand on Michael's thigh, something I've always done when he's driving. Michael looks down at my hand and frowns. He returns his attention to the road.

"Are you okay, Michael?"

"Yeah. Just tired from all the long hours I've been putting in at work."

"Are you sure? You just don't seem yourself today."

"Let's just talk when I'm done driving. I need to keep my attention fully on the road. If you haven't noticed, it's treacherous out there."

His words sting me.

"There's no need for the sarcasm. I was just worried about you."

Michael glances at me. His lips are pursed tightly together, and his eyes look pained.

"I'm sorry. I just have a lot on my mind. You didn't deserve that."

I remain quiet. Even though he'd apologized, he hadn't touched me. In the past whenever he'd spoken out of line, he'd always made sure to touch my hand or stroke my hair or even kiss me. Well, I can play that game, too. I take my hand off his thigh. From my peripheral vision, I can see he's looking at me from time to time while keeping his eyes on the road.

I lean over, turning on the radio and scanning through the music stations until I decide to just switch to AM so that I can listen to the weather report on 1010 WINS.

"Do you mind turning the radio off?"

"I can lower the volume." I reach over to do so, but Michael abruptly slams his hand over the power dial, shutting the radio off.

Now I know for certain something's wrong. I'm too nervous to say anything, though. After riding for fifteen minutes in silence, I can't take it anymore. I decide to keep it light.

"So, can you believe we'll be married and in Venice in just a few weeks? I can't wait. We'll finally get to relax. I've started doing some research on some of the sites we should see in Venice."

Michael is still silent.

"I know you've been busy with work, but have you thought at all about what you might be interested in seeing when we're there?"

"Not really. As you said, I've just been completely consumed by work, especially after I got this promotion."

"I'm thinking I'm going to take an additional month off from work after we return from the honeymoon. This way I can get the house settled and all. I've already started browsing through a few home décor magazines to get a few ideas."

Michael is exiting off the Jewel Avenue ramp of the Grand Central Parkway. Why is he getting off in Forest Hills? We still have at least another twenty minutes to go to get to Oyster Bay.

"What are you doing, Michael?"

"I changed my mind. I don't want to go all the way out to Oyster Bay."

"Oh, okay. Yeah, the weather is bad, and I can see the rush hour traffic is starting to pick up."

"That's not why."

He makes a left onto 110th Street and pulls over into an empty parking space in front of a huge McMansion. The past two decades, McMansions have been sprouting up in the suburbs of New York, mostly on Long Island. Though Forest Hills is in Queens, it has more of a residential urban feel to it. And many of the beautiful older Tudor homes are landmarks. But even here, McMansions have taken root. We are parked in front of a McMansion, which is beautiful but still seems out of place on this city street. Personally, I prefer the older Tudor homes in Forest Hills or even the Italianate villa style of Signora Tesca's Mussolini Mansion. Though they are smaller in scale than the McMansions, they are still spacious houses and hold far more appeal for me.

"Michael, what's going on? You've been acting weird since you got to the shop."

Michael is staring at the McMansion we're parked in front of. I wait for a full two minutes, but he's still silent.

"Michael, you're scaring me. What is it?"

"Damn it, Vee! Can't you let me explain in my own good time? You're always in a rush."

Tears fill my eyes. I look out the window at the ugly McMansion, focusing on the tall wrought-iron gate and the ugly rocking chair that stands by the front door.

Michael hits the steering wheel with his fist. I jump at the sound but refuse to turn toward him. His anger is scaring me. What have I done to make him so upset?

"Valentina, I'm sorry. I didn't mean that."

I turn around and look at him.

"I know. That's not like you. It's okay. Just take your time and tell me what's on your mind whenever you're ready."

Michael sighs deeply.

"Why do you have to always be so nice? You're making this even harder."

Our eyes meet, but he quickly looks away, staring at his windshield. The rain is still coming down hard.

Michael runs his hand over his hair and shuts his eyes, squeezing them tightly. He then says, "I can't do it."

My heart begins thumping.

"Do what?" I ask, my voice barely above a whisper. A small twig falls onto the windshield. I stare at it.

"You know. The wedding."

It's my turn to shut my eyes. I'm not hearing this.

"It's the big wedding, isn't it? I know. It can be overwhelming. But if you want it to be just you and me in Venice, we can still do that. I'm sure our families would understand. It's about us, after all. Whatever you want, Michael. I'm sorry. I've been letting this wedding consume us."

I can't believe the words that are coming out of my mouth. I don't recognize the person who's saying them. *What about me?* I hear somewhere deep down. A big wedding is what I've always wanted. And how could our families not be there? Ma would never forgive me, and after losing Baba, I want my family to share my happy moment with me. But I know I'm desperate, reaching out for a lifesaver to keep me afloat.

"Vee, it's not about the big wedding. I don't want to get married anymore."

I don't even try to keep my tears at bay. They're racing down my face as fast as the raindrops coming down the windshield.

"You're just getting cold feet. That happens to everyone. I've even been feeling a bit blue. Getting married can be scary. Let's just talk. We can work anything out."

"It's not cold feet, Valentina. I've been feeling this way for the past two months."

"Two months? And you're only telling me now?"

"I'm sorry, Vee. I was trying to ignore how I felt. That's why I didn't say anything sooner. I thought maybe it was just your typical getting cold feet before the wedding. But it's not. I can't deny how

I feel. I can't go through with this unless I'm one hundred percent certain. It wouldn't be fair to me or you."

"You're being selfish! Don't try to say you're thinking of me. It's always been about you. And I've been too stupid to see it or want to see it. This started much longer than two months ago."

"Valentina, I swear. It's only been recently that I've had doubts."

"Doubts about me."

"No, it's not you. I just don't think I'd be happy married to anyone."

"You're just saying that to spare my feelings. I'm not an idiot. This goes back to when you were in Munich, and I stopped hearing from you. Again, you put yourself first then just like you're doing now. If you really cared about me, you would've kept in touch with me. And if you did love me, you would've come to me two months ago to tell me how you were feeling. But you have always kept me at a distance."

I reach into his glove compartment, pulling out the whole stack of napkins from restaurants we've visited. I can't stop crying.

"That's not true, Valentina. And you know it."

"No, I don't know it. Don't try to tell me what I'm feeling."

"I'm so sorry. I didn't mean to hurt you."

"Then why are you?"

"Vee, it's complicated."

"Why? Why don't you want to get married anymore? And don't say that you think you don't want to get married to anyone at all. That's bullshit. You know it, and I know it. So spit it out. What did I do?"

"You didn't do anything. I'm just not ready for marriage. You've seen how busy I've been at work. I haven't even had enough time for you. I need to devote myself fully to my career so I can get to where I need to be in a few years."

"Is it someone else?"

"No, of course not."

I can't resist laughing and parroting him.

"No, of *course* not. Like *that's* never happened. After all, you made out with my best friend Tracy right after you danced with me at the sophomore dance even though you told me later you really wanted to ask me out. If I was the one you really wanted, then why was it so easy for you to be sucking face with the Slut of Astoria?"

"Come on, Valentina! You're being unfair. I was a kid—and a guy. Most guys do not think with their heads at that age."

"Oh, you were thinking with your head, all right—just the one between your legs."

"Stop it, Vee! That's not you. You're sounding really ugly."

"Why? Because I'm not being my usual sweet, forgiving self for once? I should've known you were no good. After all, you did make out with the likes of Tracy. For all I know, you probably even slept with her. And maybe that night wasn't the only night. You probably met someone else when you were in Munich, and that's why you stopped e-mailing me. And now, there's someone else, and that's the real reason why you can't marry me anymore. Just own up to it, you coward. Own up to the fact that you don't love me anymore, and you never did."

"I do love you, Vee. I'll always love you."

"Stop!" I hold up my hand. "Stop with the lies! I'm tired of them."

"Vee, please! I know you're upset. You have every right to be mad at me. But please. You've got to believe that I do love you and care about you. I can't go through with this wedding, knowing that there's a chance I could hurt you more down the road. Please, I don't want to end things this way."

"But you are ending things this way. You're the one who's doing this. What did you think? It's a month before our wedding. People have given me gifts already. Deposits have been placed. Our house? What are we going to do about that, Michael?"

"I'll handle it all. I'll sell it. I'll give you your portion of the down payment. I'll even give you my portion. I'll take care of it all. I promise."

"What am I supposed to say to people? And my family! Oh God! My mother. This is going to kill her!"

"This is going to kill my parents, too, Vee. They love you and were so happy about us getting married."

"And my dress! My dress! Do you know how long it took me to complete it? All those hours I stayed up late after the shop closed. And then I even altered it after you walked in on my fitting and didn't like it. And for what? For nothing."

"Valentina, I want us to be friends. I know you're mad at me. But we've known each other since we were kids."

"I'll never forgive you, Michael."

"Not now. But maybe in time."

"I don't think so. Michael, I'm just going to ask you one favor."

"Sure, whatever you want, Valentina."

I want to laugh at his words. He knows what I want. I want to marry him, but he doesn't care. It's what he wants, and that's all that matters to Michael.

"I'm going to get out of the car. I'll take the subway back to Astoria. Please don't insist on driving me home. I need to be alone."

"Okay, but let me at least drive you to the subway station so you don't get drenched."

"No, that's fine." The tone in my voice convinces him to not argue with me.

Before I step out of the car, I look at Michael, knowing this will probably be the last time I see him in a long time, if ever. He's staring at me. Tears are forming in his eyes. I hesitate for a moment and then quickly get out before I change my mind. It's still raining but not as heavily as before. Opening my umbrella, I walk away without even a glance back, making my way toward the subway station on 71st and Continental Avenue. As soon as I know I'm out of sight of Michael's car and that he's not following me, I walk over to the front steps of the closest house and sit down. The houses on this street are more modest than the McMansions where Michael had parked. I start sobbing, making sure to shield my face with my umbrella should anyone be walking by.

I feel empty. The man I've loved for so long doesn't want me. I suddenly realize with horror that I never gave Michael back my engagement ring. I stare at it—a reminder of a broken promise. Pulling it off, I throw the ring into my purse. A strip of white skin encircles my finger where the ring sat.

What am I going to say to my family? Noticing a livery cab waiting at the red light, I suddenly realize the last place I want to be is on a crowded subway. Running over to the cab before the light changes, I motion to the driver to roll down his window.

"Need a ride, miss?"

"Yes, I'm going to Astoria."

"Hop in."

The rain is getting heavy again. Staring out the window, I take some comfort in the fact that the weather is as miserable as I'm feeling.

∽ 12 ∽

Guinea Trash

When the cab pulls up in front of Aldo's apartment building, it's five p.m. I pray he's home. Unable to face my family yet, I decide to go first to Aldo's. After college, Aldo had gotten his own place near Astoria Park. I'd been surprised he didn't move into Manhattan, even after his salary had increased at Christie's.

I press down on the buzzer and wait to hear Aldo's voice come through on the intercom. No answer. I should've called him first. I press the buzzer again. Just as I'm about to leave, static comes through over the intercom.

"Yes?"

"Aldo, it's me. Valentina."

"Vee? What are you doing here? Is Michael with you?"

I start choking up.

"Vee? Can you hear me?"

"Yes. Can I please come in? I'm . . . I'm alone."

"Of course. Come up."

Aldo buzzes me in.

I climb the stairs to his third-floor walkup apartment. My body feels so weary with each step I take. Aldo is waiting for me when I reach his floor. His TV is blasting out into the hallway. From the sounds of it, he's watching repeats of that horrible show *The Real*

Housewives of New Jersey. It escapes me how he can watch that show. The way they portray Italian Americans. Guinea trash. That's what my mother calls them. This brings a smile to my face. Aldo loves anything reality-based, and the trashier it is, the more he loves it.

"So you're watching that garbage again?"

"One of these days I'll wean myself off."

Aldo smiles, but he isn't fooled by my banter. His face shows concern when he sees me, which reminds me that I didn't check my makeup in the cab. Gobs of mascara must be pooling under my eyes.

"Come in. I'll get you a drink. And don't try to refuse. From the looks of you, only Jack Daniel's will do."

I step into his apartment. As usual, the place is immaculately clean. Instantly, I start to feel calmer, remembering how much I used to love hanging out in Aldo's apartment. But I haven't been here since I got engaged. Again, the wedding planning had ruled my life. I feel guilty as I realize that I haven't been the best of friends the past year.

The décor is modern. Aldo has decorated the apartment himself in hues of cream and chocolate brown. An ivory microsuede couch sits in the center of his living room. A shaggy chocolate brown rug rests on the floor between the couch and the 70-inch flat screen TV. Have I mentioned how much Aldo loves TV? When DVRs first came out, he'd wasted no time in getting one.

"Now I won't miss all of my favorite daytime talk shows!"

He'd beamed at me when he announced his new purchase.

One of our favorite pastimes is to microwave popcorn and watch awards shows where we can drool or gag over celebrities' gowns.

The living room is split so that a sofa table behind the couch divides the room into an office and dining area. A glass pub table with four barstools stands in the corner. Aldo always keeps fresh flowers in a vase on the pub table. Even his bedroom has fresh flowers. Right now a beautiful cluster of periwinkle hydrangeas stands in a short round vase.

He's added to his art collection since I was last here. Aldo has become more of a serious art collector in the past two years after he received a huge promotion at Christie's. When he got laid off, he exclaimed, "Well, if I don't find a job in a year, at least I can sell some of my art."

As if! Aldo would rather go without food than sell his children, which is how he has referred to his art collection on several occasions.

I walk over to look at a black-and-white ink drawing of a woman lying down. Only the top half of her body shows, and her face is hardly discernible.

"Do you like that one?"

Aldo comes and stands by my side as he hands me a White Russian. He was only joking when he mentioned the Jack Daniel's. He knows I'd be out cold with just one sip of whiskey.

"Yes, very much. Who's the artist?"

"He's an up-and-coming New York City artist who goes just by one name: Niko."

"Sounds intriguing."

"Exactly. And his art conveys the same mysterious element, as I'm sure you can see from that drawing."

"Do you think he'll go far?"

"Yes, I do, but the art world can be very fickle. It doesn't all depend on talent."

"You can say that with any career. In fact, you can say luck is just as much a factor in almost every facet of life."

I can't help thinking how unlucky I've been in love. Maybe I'm not destined for love. Tears start filling my eyes.

"Valentina, what happened? Why aren't you with Michael right now?"

I take a huge gulp of my cocktail.

"It's over."

"What do you mean 'it's over'? What's over?"

"The wedding . . . Michael and me . . . all of it."

I start crying hysterically.

"Oh my God!"

Aldo takes my drink out of my hand because it's shaking so hard. Another second, and his carpet would've been ruined.

"Come here."

I collapse into Aldo, who's still holding my White Russian with one hand as his other hand pats my back.

"It's okay. It's okay," Aldo coos. I'm crying into his shoulder. I can smell his Cool Water cologne. He hasn't strayed from this cologne since it first came out in the early nineties.

"Let's sit down, and you can tell me all about it. That is, if you want. I understand if you're not ready to talk."

I sit down on the couch.

"Here, finish your drink. It'll make you feel better. I'll go make you another."

He rushes to the kitchen. Before I know it, he's returned with my second White Russian and a box of tissues.

"I added a little extra vodka to this one."

I don't even give my usual fight when he makes my drinks too strong. I've never been much of a drinker. But he's right. My nerves are starting to feel less shaky.

"I'm sorry, Aldo. I didn't mean to just completely lose it."

"Vee! Your fiancé just broke things off with you. Did he? Or was it you?"

I give him an exasperated look. "Would I be such a wreck if I was the one who ended it?"

"Sorry! Sorry! I just didn't want to assume anything since I don't know the details yet. Anyway, your engagement is off. You have every right to have a nervous breakdown! I mean, don't have one! But you know what I mean. I'm sorry. I'm not being very helpful right now, am I? I'm just still so shocked myself."

"That makes two of us."

"So you didn't see this coming at all?"

"No."

I stop to blow my nose as the tears come back.

"I thought everything was fine."

"Well, what about earlier today at the shop? I know you said you'd come down with a case of the 'Bridal Blues,' but I sensed there was more."

"I guess I did notice Michael had been distancing himself a bit from me the past month or so. But I thought I was just being paranoid, and I knew how busy he'd been at work since he got that big promotion. And I've been so busy at the shop and planning this stupid big wedding. I was neglecting him. I've even neglected you, and I'm sorry for that, Aldo. We haven't hung out as much since I got engaged. I shouldn't have let my wedding planning swallow me up."

"Vee, I didn't feel neglected by you. Please! This is what happens when people get engaged. Plus, you were making your own dress on top of all the demands from work. And I don't think you were neglecting Michael."

"I should've made more time for him. I should've insisted we see each other during the week in addition to the weekends."

"Stop it! You're playing the blame game. You're not the one who broke the contract. He did."

"Well, there was no contract. We didn't get to the marriage."

"He made a promise to you, Valentina, when he gave you that ring. Where is it, anyway? You didn't give it back to him, did you?"

"I forgot to, but I will. I can't keep it."

"Of course, you can. Think of it as payment for damages rendered. You can sell the ring, not that it's going to cover all of your wedding-related deposits."

I hadn't even thought of the financial repercussions of Michael's decision. But then I remembered how he said he would take care of the house. But still, we both put money into the deposits. He was losing just as much as me.

"I can't keep the ring, Aldo. I won't. It's not the right thing to do."

"And breaking off an engagement one month before the wedding date is the right thing? Screw him! Stupid pig! Now, that's what I call true guinea trash. No class at all. He acts like he's got it, but I always knew he was nothing more than a wannabe."

Though I'm furious with Michael, I can't agree with Aldo's assessment of him as guinea trash.

"So what did he say? Why the sudden cold feet?"

"He just said he couldn't go through with the wedding anymore. He said he doesn't want to get married. I asked him if there was someone else. He swore there isn't, but I don't believe the only reason he ended it with me is because he doesn't want to get married."

"You're probably right, but who knows? Maybe he did realize he's not the marrying kind. But did he ask you how you would feel if you didn't get married but continued to be in a relationship?"

"No. He knows I'm old-fashioned and want the commitment. And how would he face my mother after making an arrangement like that? My mother would just as good as disown me."

"You underestimate your mom, Vee. I know she's from the Old World, but still. She loves you. If it made you happy to just be with Michael and not make it official, she'd be happy for you even if she was a little disappointed that you weren't tying the knot."

"Well, that wouldn't be good enough for me. I've dreamed about this day since I was a kid. What little girl hasn't? I want to have children. I'm not going to have children with a man who can't even commit to marriage."

"True. I didn't think of that."

"He told me he was doing this for me as much as he was doing this for him."

"Uh-huh. And I'm Brad fuckin' Pitt."

"I know. He's full of it. I told him I didn't believe him. I can't believe I forgot to give him the ring back. Now I'm going to have to face him again. It's not like I can mail it."

"I would. But if you insist that he get the ring in person, I can return it."

"Thank you, Aldo."

I start crying again just at the thought of Aldo's gesture. I can't stop crying.

"Just let it all out."

"I can't believe this is happening to me."

"Listen to me, Valentina DeLuca. This hurts like hell and will keep hurting like hell for some time. I'm not going to deny that. But you *will* get over this and that piece of guinea trash. I promise. And unlike that swine, I keep my promises."

"I hope you're right. I just can't see not having Michael in my life anymore. I've known him my whole life. But I can't even imagine ever being civil toward him or friends after the way he broke my heart."

"Don't worry about that. Just think about yourself. Lean on your family and me. We're here for you."

"My family! This is going to kill them, especially my mother. That's why I came here. I couldn't go home just yet and face them like this. I'm so embarrassed."

"What? He's the one who should be embarrassed. You've done nothing wrong. You hear me?"

"I know, but I can't help feeling like that. All those people who gave us gifts at the shower and others who have been sending gifts. And I just can't help but feel like I somehow have let my mother down."

"First of all, the shower gifts you'll return so there won't be any guilt involved there. And your friends will understand. He's the one who is the villain here. If I were Michael, I'd hightail it back to Germany. He's going to get the worst looks from everyone in the neighborhood. You think Beady Eyes have a staring problem now? Wait till they hear what he did to you."

I laugh. Suddenly, I remember how coldly Antoniella acted toward him that night five months ago when we were having dessert at the bakery.

"I think the Hunchback had his number all along. She even subtly tried to warn me."

"I'm not surprised. People think they're getting what they see with that old woman—a crotchety, cheap woman who only cares about her business and money. But I've always known there's more to her than meets the eye. In fact, I think she's just become my hero."

I shake my head and laugh.

"You can always make me laugh even after my world's just come crashing down."

"That's what good friends are for."

"I hate to ask you for another favor, Aldo, after the way I barged in on you tonight. But would it be okay if I spent the night here? I just want one night to myself before I have to tell my family."

"Of course you can stay here. You don't even have to ask. I have an idea. Why don't you let me break the news to your family?"

"Oh, I don't know about that. It's my responsibility to tell them."

"You take on too much, Vee. Please. Let me do this. I *want* to do this for you. Also, it would give your family the night to process the news. You'll all be stronger this way when you see each other tomorrow."

His reasoning on this last point does make sense. It would be better for both my family and me. I can already feel the heavy burden of having to break the news to them lift off my chest.

"Okay, you can tell them."

"It's decided then. You can sleep in my bed."

I'm about to tell Aldo I'll take the couch when he stops me with his hand. I nod my head.

"I think I'll go to bed now."

"Yes, you do that. I'll put out some clean towels in the bathroom for you, and then I'll call Rita. I think it's better if she tells your mother."

"Yes, you're absolutely right. Thank you again, Aldo. Have I ever told you that you're the best friend in the universe?"

"No, actually. I don't think you have."

I walk over to Aldo and kiss him on the cheek.

After washing up and slipping into Aldo's enormous king-size bed, I don't feel as sleepy as I did a few moments ago. I can just barely make out Aldo's voice. He must've gotten through to Rita. I'm grateful he's talking so low because hearing someone else say my engagement is broken will make it all the more real for me. Then again, all I need to do is look at my bare finger to know this isn't a bad dream. As I drift off to sleep, my thoughts return to my perfect wedding dress—a dress that no one will see now.

❧ 13 ❧

Bridezillas Unleashed

A month has passed since Michael broke off our engagement. I've been in a daze, mostly staying home and not doing much of anything. I haven't been to Sposa Rosa since the day Michael ended it. The thought of being surrounded by wedding dresses and happy brides-to-be is just too much to bear. But I can't stay cooped up any longer. This is my life: making wedding gowns and making other women's dreams come true.

On Saturday mornings, the DeLuca custom is to have breakfast together. As I make my way downstairs, I can smell Ma's special cinnamon French toast, as she likes to call it. You won't find better French toast anywhere. Her secret is adding a few drops of pure vanilla extract and adding enough eggs so that the bread has an extra-thick coating of batter.

"Hey, Ma."

"Oh! Valentina, you scared me. I didn't hear you coming down."

Ma is working at her usual frenetic pace. The woman does nothing slowly. She's flipping the French toast with one hand while the other is dunking a slice of challah bread into the egg batter to replace the slice that's just been removed from the skillet.

Rita is at the table, sipping coffee and sketching a new purse design. I fill my own mug with coffee and sit down next to my sister.

No sooner have I sat down than Ma plops a plate of French
toast in front of me. Of course there are too many slices of toast on
the plate.

"You gave me too much, Ma. I'm just having one slice."

"Valentina, you've lost too much weight. You're going to get
sick. Eat at least two slices."

Ma looks at me as if I'm going to break her heart if I don't do as
she says. With the guilt I've been feeling over my failed wedding
plans, I've done whatever she's asked of me lately, which hasn't
been much, but still.

"Okay. I'll try to eat two slices."

"That's my girl!"

Ma smiles. She's been so strong for me this past month. I
haven't seen her cry once since the end of my engagement. But that
doesn't mean she hasn't shed any tears in private.

I woke up one night at three in the morning. I haven't been able
to sleep throughout the night lately. On my way to the bathroom, I
heard Ma's soft cries in her bedroom. Her door was just slightly
ajar, allowing me a peek. She was holding her favorite photo of me.
It was a photo taken on the night of my high school senior prom.
She'd outdone herself with the dress she'd sewn for me. It was a
one-shouldered violet dress made out of taffeta. The shoulder strap
had little rosettes with sparkling crystals at the center of each
rosette. A skinny belt surrounded the waist of the dress. Two glittering combs adorned with crystal rhinestones swept my hair to
one side, allowing the long strands to drape over my bare shoulder.

Michael had agreed to be my prom date. We weren't dating yet,
but our friendship had deepened in the year since my father's
death. He had made good on his promise to e-mail me while he was
away at Cornell, and he even called me a few times. Whenever he
came home for the holidays, we hung out together. Often it was in
a group setting with friends of ours. Though I had secretly wished
we were dating already, his friendship had meant the world to me
in those days and helped me move on after losing my father. I wasn't

dating anyone at the time, and no one had asked me to the prom. So I'd worked up the courage to ask Michael to escort me.

·He was in the photo, too. His pale gray suit complemented my violet dress perfectly. I liked it that he was wearing a suit as opposed to the tuxedoes all the other guys wore to the prom. He stood out amid the sea of tux-clad penguins. He'd given me a wrist corsage of cream-colored and violet roses. I couldn't believe he'd found violet roses. They weren't a common sight at florist shops.

I was surprised Ma still had this photo, because I hadn't seen it displayed on her dresser since Michael broke up with me. I'd assumed she probably tore it up or at least would've cut Michael out of the photo. She was known for cutting out boys my sisters and I had dated.

"I don't want any reminders of those clowns," she'd say when we'd catch her in the act of snipping yet another guy out of a photo. Ma had loved Michael as if he were the son she'd never had. I guess she wasn't ready to cut him out just yet even though he'd hurt her daughter more than any of my other ex-boyfriends or my sisters' exes had.

"That smell of French toast woke me up. I'm famished."

Connie limps into the kitchen in her silky boy shorts and matching camisole. Her hair looks like a tornado has just whipped through it.

"Rough night?" Rita asks.

"Lou and I went dancing. I don't think I've ever danced that much."

It's out of the bag that Connie and Rita are dating the Broccoli Brothers. I don't even know why they were ever keeping it from Ma. Since they're from the neighborhood, it was only a matter of time before one of our nosy neighbors broke the news to Ma. And that's exactly what happened. Of course, it was the Mayor of 35th Street who spilled the beans to my mother as he spotted her outside of Top Tomato while she was picking her weekly produce.

"*Ciao,* Signora DeLuca!"

"*Buon giorno,* Paulie. *Com'é sta?*"

"Eh . . . *mezza mezza.* How are the vegetables looking today?"

"Not bad. Look at these beautiful, shiny eggplants. And they're on sale. I'm getting a few. My daughters love eggplant rollatini."

"Be sure to pick up some extra broccoli rabe. Your daughters like that, too, from what I hear."

Ma frowned. "What are you talking about? Only Valentina likes broccoli rabe. Rita and Connie think it's too bitter even though I know how to cook it to cut down on the bitterness."

"Oh, really? They don't like broccoli rabe? That's funny considering they're dating the Broccoli Brothers." Ma's eyes opened wide, but she quickly disguised her surprise and said, "They're good boys."

She went back to sorting out her eggplants, squeezing each one to test its ripeness.

"Yeah, I suppose. That Lou Rabe has a bit of a wild streak, riding that motorcycle."

Ma shrugged her shoulders, refusing to give Paulie any validation.

"It's no crime to ride a motorcycle. Well, if you will excuse me, Paulie, I'm ready to go in and pay. *Buon giorno*."

"*Buon giorno,* Signora DeLuca."

When Ma got home that night she scolded Rita and Connie for not telling her about the Broccoli Brothers.

"I had to find out from Paulie, of all people! I hope he didn't notice that I had no idea my own daughters were dating the Rabe boys. He takes such pleasure out of knowing other people's business. And then I have to hear his stupid, rude jokes. *Disgraziato!*"

Although Ma was upset that Rita and Connie yet again hadn't confided in her, she didn't give them any grief about dating the Broccoli Brothers. I always thought she'd go through the roof over Connie dating Lou since he's a bit of a rebel. Maybe it was because Ma found out a week after my engagement was called off. She didn't have the energy for the battle.

"When are you going to invite those boys over for dinner? It's about time I get to know them better. You have been seeing them now for several months, correct?"

Rita and Connie exchange glances.

Before they can think of an excuse to get out of bringing their boyfriends home for dinner, Ma quickly adds, "Why don't you ask them if they're free next weekend? They can come over for Sunday dinner."

"Ahhh, sure. I guess so," Rita says. She knows better than to say anything else, as does Connie.

I decide this is a good time to make my announcement.

"I'm going to the shop today."

"What?" Rita and Connie cry out in unison.

"That's okay, Valentina. We have everything under control. Just relax. Why don't you go outside and enjoy the day? It's going to be beautiful. Maybe Aldo is free. The two of you can go to a museum. You haven't done that in a long time."

Ma is talking so fast.

"I'm okay, Ma. It's time for me to get back to work. I've been away for three weeks. I know you guys are swamped. It'll be good for me. I need to keep busy."

"I agree, Vee. You do need to do more than just hang out inside the house like you've been doing. But why don't you go out with Aldo like Ma suggested. Or even go shopping. You can distract yourself with other things besides work."

It's hard to take Connie seriously with her disheveled hair and smudged mascara, which she hadn't even bothered removing the night before. She presses a napkin to her forehead and examines it for grease.

"I know you guys are just trying to protect me. But I'm a grown girl. It's time I get back to work. I'll be okay. For that matter, you can all stop walking on eggshells around me."

"Vee, I'm going to be blunt with you, since Ma and Connie are too afraid to do so. It's too soon for you to be back at the shop—and this week, no less. You were supposed to be in Venice right now making the final arrangements for your wedding next Saturday. How can you even think about going back to work, where you'll be bombarded with wedding reminders?"

"Rita, I'm a lot tougher than you think."

"I know how strong you are. But this isn't a good idea."

"She's right. Please, Vee, reconsider. Why don't you at least wait a couple of more weeks?"

Connie's bloodshot, mascara-rimmed eyes stare at me imploringly.

"Valentina, it's wonderful that you are feeling better and want to get out of the house. But your sisters are right. Please just wait a little longer."

"I appreciate all of your concern. But I've made up my mind. I'm going back to work today."

I get up and walk out of the kitchen, heading straight for the bathroom, where I can lock the door and escape them. But I know that's not enough. They've had arguments with me in the past through the closed door. I turn on the shower even though I'm not ready to jump in. Looking at myself in the mirror, I see my mother has been right that I've lost weight. Dark rims circle my eyes. My pajama pants feel loose. I pull out the scale from underneath the sink and weigh myself.

One hundred and fifteen pounds! I've lost five pounds in just three weeks.

Kicking the scale back into place, I strip off my pjs and step into the steamy shower. I'm ready to face the outside world again. I've had enough of feeling sorry for myself. Today, I will return to doing what I love most: designing and sewing wedding gowns and helping brides look their best.

Rita and Ma leave for the shop right after breakfast. But Connie's lurking around. When I come out of my bedroom, dressed and ready to go to work, she immediately springs to my side.

"Ready?"

"Yes, but I didn't know you were waiting for me."

"Oh, I figured we'd walk to work together."

Connie pauses at the mirror that hangs on the wall in our upstairs corridor and powders her nose. Since her makeup has been applied in the past hour, there isn't so much as a drop of oil.

"I have some errands to run before I go to the shop. You can go ahead without me, Connie."

I run down the stairs, hoping that will be the end of our discussion. Of course, I'm wrong.

"I'll come with you."

Connie grabs her tote and yoga mat and bolts after me. She often takes a yoga class after work.

I heave a huge sigh and turn around.

"Look, Connie. I know what you're doing, and I appreciate your concern, but I'll be fine going to work by myself."

Connie knows she's busted.

"We just thought it might be easier on your first day back if one of us walked in with you."

"I need to do this by myself, Connie, and I need some time alone to run my errands before going to work. Do you understand?"

Connie lowers her gaze and nods.

"Sure. But if you change your mind, just text me, okay?"

"Okay."

"I'm actually going to stick around here for a bit before I leave for work."

"Thanks, Connie. I'll see you later."

I give her a hug before I walk out.

The air feels good. It's a sunny June day, a little cooler than it should be at this time of the year, but still pleasant. Not a cloud is in the sky.

I inhale deeply and begin walking up the street. Beady Eyes are at their usual post. Gus sits obediently by their side. My heart starts to pound as I realize this will be the first time I see my neighbors since my engagement has ended. I swallow hard and force myself to look up at them. Of course, their gazes are glued on me. Mr. Beady Eyes looks even more morose than usual, and Mrs. Beady Eyes' lips are pressed so tightly together that I can't even see them.

I wave and call out, "Good morning!"

They wave back. "Good morning, Valentina. How are you?"

That's a first. I've never received a "How are you?" from them before.

"I'm fine, thank you. Have a nice day."

"You too, Valentina."

They pity me. Their faces say it all. Even Gus's eyes are mournful. I can feel their stares burning holes through my back as I continue walking up the block. Of course, they always stare, but today it's especially intense.

Our house is at the end of the block. I pray I don't run into any of the other neighbors. As I pass the Mussolini Mansion, I notice Signora Tesca peering through her blinds. A moment later, her old door creaks open.

"Valentina."

I stop and turn around.

"How are you, child?"

"I'm well, Signora Tesca. How are you?"

"I was so sad to hear about your engagement."

"Thank you."

"I know it's hard to hear this now, Valentina. But it was for the best. Imagine if you had married Michael, and then he changed his mind."

That is supposed to make me feel better? My anger starts surfacing, but I quell it. Signora Tesca is just trying to comfort me. People always think they are helping when they offer words of solace to someone during a tough time, but they don't realize that often what they say just makes one feel worse.

"Yes, yes. You're right. Thank you, Signora Tesca. I'm actually already late for work. Please excuse me. Have a nice day."

"Oh, of course, Valentina. I didn't mean to hold you up. I'll continue praying for you."

"Thank you. That's very kind of you. Good-bye."

"Good-bye, Valentina."

Had I been a bit abrupt with Signora Tesca? Whatever. I have to stop feeling guilty all the time. Ma has done a good job of instilling guilt in me since I was born. "Please, God. No more neighbors," I murmur aloud to myself.

I walk quickly. I'm just about to turn the corner onto Ditmars Boulevard, thinking that I've managed to escape any other encounters, when I run headlong into Paulie, knocking his bag of groceries onto the sidewalk.

"I'm so sorry, Paulie!"

I bend down to pick up his bag.

"No, no, that's okay. I've got it. It's good to see you, Valentina. How are you doing?"

"I'm fine. How are you?"

"My arthritis in my knee is acting up a bit today. That's probably why you were able to get me by surprise. My reflexes aren't what they used to be."

"I'm sorry again, Paulie. I was walking quite fast."

"Nah. Don't sweat it. Where are you off to?"

"I'm running a few errands, and then I'm heading to the shop."

"So soon? Ahhh, I mean, shouldn't you take more time off?"

"No, Paulie. I'm ready to get back into the swing of things. But thank you for your concern."

"May I speak frankly, Valentina?"

When has Paulie not spoken frankly? At least this time he's asking for permission.

"I guess so."

Before he speaks, he sticks his pinky finger into his ear and wiggles it. I've forgotten to mention that in addition to his tooth-picking habit, he also has an ear-picking one. He pulls his pinky finger out of his ear, examines the wax, and then flicks it off his finger. I look away, completely repulsed.

"I always thought you were too good for that Carello character. He proved his true colors by letting such a wonderful girl like you go. What a fool! These young hotshots nowadays think they have the world at their feet, and they can take whatever they want with no consequences. Trust me, he has his coming to him someday."

I don't know what to say. So I just stand there in silence.

"You'll get over him. It'll take some time, but trust me, there's someone much better out there for you."

I never thought I'd see the day when the Mayor of 35th Street would be giving me advice on love.

"So what happened, Valentina? Why did he change his mind?"

The nerve! Though this doesn't surprise me coming from Paulie. He never shies away from nosiness.

"It's complicated, Paulie. And I'd rather not talk about it."

"It was another woman, wasn't it?"

My face burns up. Everyone else is thinking this, too.

"I have no idea, Paulie. And to tell you the truth, I don't care. It's over. He's not a part of my thoughts anymore. Thank you for your concern, Paulie, but if you'll excuse me, I need to be going. Saturday is our busiest day at the shop. Have a nice day."

"Of course, of course. You take it easy now, you hear me?"

I nod my head and walk away.

Would anyone else have the guts to question me directly as to why Michael had left me? After the scene with Paulie, I don't know if I can stand another encounter like that. But most people aren't as blunt as Paulie. That gives me some comfort. Perhaps it's good that I've run into a few of the neighbors today. I feel stronger now for when I see the others.

I head over to Immaculate Conception. The church's bells are ringing, signaling it's noon. Entering from the side entrance, I walk into the chapel, where various saints' statues are affixed to the walls. When I was a little girl, I read so many books on the saints' lives. The lives of St. Rose of Lima, St. Elizabeth of Hungary, St. Maria Goretti, and St. Theresa were the ones that had fascinated me the most. St. Rose had received the stigmata on her hands and loved to wear a wreath of roses around her head. St. Elizabeth of Hungary had been a princess who cared more about feeding the poor people outside of her castle's gates than material wealth. Sixteen-year-old St. Maria Goretti, the only saint of the four who had lived in the twentieth century, had forgiven her rapist who attacked her because she'd refused to surrender her virginity. St. Theresa, also known as the Little Flower of Jesus, was my favorite. Her story especially had resonated with me because of the miracle she'd performed after she died of sending roses, her favorite flowers, down from heaven. The image of a shower of roses had been a powerful one to the imagination of an eleven-year-old girl who loved romantic stories. And many of the saints' stories were very romantic. That's part of the appeal of Catholicism: all of the religious rituals and symbols; the ceremonial rites in Mass; even the seven sacraments hold a romanticized, mystical element.

As a child, I'd prayed to these saints and others to help me pass my math tests. Math had been my worst subject. I'd even prayed to the Virgin Mary to make my breasts grow. Even then I'd been worried that someone had placed a curse on me, and I wouldn't go through puberty like everyone else. My prayers had always been answered except regarding my father's illness. No prayer had been powerful enough to save him.

Folding up a few dollar bills, I squeeze them through the slit of the donation box. I light five votive candles, two for each of my grandparents on both sides of my family who had passed away when I was in grammar school, and one for my father. I say a prayer for each of their souls and then enter the main church. Choosing the last pew to the back of the church, I kneel down.

I close my eyes to pray, but the words don't come. I want to ask God to make me understand why He's taken Michael away from me. Why is He giving me this cross to bear? It's not the first time I've asked Him this question, for I had asked Him this when my father was sick and again later when he died. But I can't bring myself to have the conversation with God. I'm angry with Him.

Giving up, I sit down on the bench. I've always loved coming to church when there's no Mass in service. Even now that I'm upset with God, I still feel at peace here.

After fifteen minutes have elapsed, I get up and walk slowly to Sposa Rosa. Though I have put up a strong front for my family, I am nervous about going back. When I reach the shop, I notice the Featured Gown of the Month.

I gasp. Instead of a designer knockoff, it's an original design I had sketched a week before Michael broke up with me. My family must've gone ahead and sewn the dress. Tears spring into my eyes. They knew seeing the dress in its completed form would probably ease my return to the shop once I was ready. They're right. It reminds me of how much I love my work and working with my family at Sposa Rosa.

The strapless gown sports an A-line silhouette. It's made of Duchess satin but has a lace overlay with crystal beading throughout. A satin sash wraps around the waist, ending in a small bow on the front of the dress. It isn't a complicated design, but the lace overlay with crystal beading are what make the dress.

Feeling more empowered, I take a deep breath and enter the shop. It's bustling, which is normal for a busy Saturday.

Melanie, our part-time receptionist/cashier, is taking a deposit.

"Hi, Melanie."

"Vee! Hey! It's great to see you. Your mom told me you'd be coming back to work today. That's great news! We've missed you."

"Thanks, Melanie. It's good to be back."

At least Melanie has the sense to not treat me like I'm going to break any second. I walk toward the fitting room area. Rita and Connie are busy with two brides. Rita spots me.

"Hey, Vee! You picked a winner of a day to return. It's insane here. If you want to go back home and come in on a slower day, we wouldn't blame you."

Rita looks at me. Her brows are knitted furiously together, something she does when she's either stressed out or worried.

"I like it busy. You know that. Where's Ma?"

"She's in the back working on some last-minute alterations for a dress that wasn't fitting quite right for one of our clients."

I glance around to see where Ma's client is. She's standing right outside the alterations room with her arms crossed in front of her chest and a sneer on her face. Four girls stand by her side. No doubt her bridal party.

"I'll go help Ma. From the looks of this Bridezilla, she's going to need all the artillery she can get."

I walk over to the irate client.

"Hello. My name is Valentina DeLuca. Can I offer you coffee or water?"

The client shakes her head at me.

"Why don't you take a seat while you wait for the alterations to be done?"

"I'm fine right where I am. If I wanted tea and crumpets I would've gone to the bakery next door."

Her bridesmaids look mortified but don't dare utter a word.

"I can't believe this is taking so long!"

Her voice keeps getting louder with each complaint.

"What is my mother altering for you, if I may ask?"

"She had to let out the dress. She must not have taken my measurements correctly. There's no way I gained all this weight. The dress was so tight that the zipper didn't budge a centimeter. I knew I should've gone to Kleinfeld for my dress."

"I understand you're worried about your gown. But my mother has been making and altering wedding gowns for almost twenty years, and she's been a seamstress since she was a child. She's a master at her craft. Trust me, your dress will come out perfect. It just takes a little longer when a dress needs to be let out. Are you sure you don't want to come back another day instead of waiting here?"

"I'm not leaving until I'm sure that dress is right."

"Okay. Let me go see how much longer it'll be, and I can let you know how it's going."

"Yeah, that would help."

"I'm sorry. I didn't catch your name earlier."

"Ashley."

"I'll be right back, Ashley."

"Yeah, we'll see about that," Ashley scoffs, rolling her eyes. She finally walks away from the alterations room and is examining the headpieces in the display case. Her bridal entourage follows her. I'm surprised she hasn't stormed into the alterations room. The nerve! She has to be one of the rudest Bridezillas I've ever encountered.

Ma's at the sewing machine, pumping the pedal feverishly as she stitches the back of the gown.

"I just met your worst nightmare."

Ma looks up.

"Ahhh, Valentina. You made it. How are you feeling?"

"Fine, but I really wish people would stop asking me that."

Ma resumes pumping the pedal.

"That girl is like a wild dog. Or I should say she's treating me like her dog. I've never had a client insist that they wait until a major alteration like this is done—and on a Saturday, no less. We're going to be so behind. You saw how crazy it is out there."

"Don't worry, Ma. Rita and Connie are doing a great job of juggling between brides. And I'm here. I was able to calm that Bridezilla a bit by telling her I'd find out how much longer you'd be."

"Another fifteen minutes, I hope!"

"Okay, I'll tell her. Don't kill yourself."

"It's too late for that!"

I go back out in search of Ashley but neither she nor her brides-maids are still in the shop.

"Melanie, do you know where Ashley went?"

Melanie rolls her eyes.

"She said they were going to have coffee next door. She asked me to get them when the dress is done, as if I'm her personal maid. These people act like they've become royalty overnight after some-one pops the question to them when the truth is they're still the low man on the totem pole like the rest of us."

"Yeah, it goes to their heads as soon as they're engaged."

"You weren't like that, Valentina. Oh, sorry. I shouldn't have brought that up." Now Melanie is looking at me like everyone else has this morning.

"Don't sweat it, Melanie. I'm fine. Thank you for the compli-ment. I guess dealing with brides for a living puts things in per-spective when it's your turn, and you try hard not to be like the Bridezillas we've worked with. But they're not all like that. Some of them are such a pleasure to work with and make their dreams come true."

My mind starts to wander. I can't help hearing an internal voice in my head. *My dream won't come true. Why couldn't it have worked out for me like it will for the other brides here today? Will I only wear a wedding dress in this shop when I need to test out a gown's fit?*

I suddenly notice Melanie is staring at me with sadness in her eyes. Is my face registering my thoughts?

"Okay, when Ashley returns, just give a holler if I'm in the back. I don't want to make her wait any longer than she already has. I'll go tell Ma she has a little extra time to get those alterations done now that Bridezilla is at the bakery instead of shooting flames into the alterations room."

I only walk three steps when one of the three clients who are waiting to be helped comes up to me.

"Excuse me. I've been waiting for twenty minutes, and it doesn't look like the two salesgirls in the back are going to be done anytime soon. Can you help me?"

"Yes, of course, but I need to look at the guest book to see who signed in first. There are three other brides waiting. I have to take whoever has the first appointment."

"You don't need to look at the book. *I'm* telling you I had the first appointment."

"Okay, if you'll please be patient just one moment longer, and I'll be with you. What is your name?"

"Lea Stavros."

I'm not taking Lea's word. So I head first to the alterations room to let Ma know she has some extra time finishing Ashley's dress, since they've gone to Antoniella's for coffee. Then I walk back to Melanie's desk and pretend I'm asking her a question while I quickly scan the guest book.

"I'm just making sure Bridezilla number two has the first appointment," I whisper to Melanie.

"Unfortunately, she does. But you're right about her being a Bridezilla. She told her mother and sister that they can't be honest with her if she chooses a dress they don't like. She doesn't want any negativity, as she put it."

"Oh, boy! This is going to be one of those days."

Melanie nods her head.

"Oh yeah, you got that right. Good luck."

"Thanks."

"Lea, I can take you now. My name is Valentina, and if you decide to have Sposa Rosa make your dress, I'll be your consultant for all of your fittings. Who do we have here?"

"This is my mother and my twin sister, Laura."

"It's nice to meet you."

"When is the big day, Lea?"

"A month from today."

"Okay. We don't have much time to work with. How long have you been engaged?"

"For six months."

"Why did you wait to buy your dress?"

I choose my words carefully. What I really want to say is, "What were you thinking waiting until a month before your wedding to buy a gown—no less a custom-made gown?" But I bite my tongue.

"I have been shopping around the past month, but I haven't seen anything I liked. Then a friend of mine told me maybe that's because I have a vision. So she convinced me to get a custom-made dress."

"I see. So tell me, what does your dress look like in your vision?"

I have to fight hard to keep the sarcasm out of my voice.

"I'd love a trumpet gown. I want to stand out and look very chic. I like those new crumb bodices. What are they called?"

"A crumb catcher?"

"Yes, a crumb catcher. I'd love one of those. I'm not sure as to the details other than that. I also want to wear a short net over my face. I think that along with the trumpet silhouette of the gown will definitely scream 'This girl is one chic bride!'"

I jot a note on my pad: *Narcissist with grand delusions of herself.* You might think I'm being mean scribbling these personality traits of my clients, but it actually helps me when I'm trying to decide what would be best for them. After all, we are striving to make our clients happy, and the only way we can do that is by catering to their personalities.

"Okay, Lea. I think I have a good idea what you would like. Have you flipped through our portfolios? Did you see any dresses in there that were similar to what you had in mind?"

"No, I didn't see anything in there. But I don't want to be swayed by something that exists already. I want this to be all my own. Something unique."

Yes, don't they all, I think as I scribble another note in caps for emphasis. *UNIQUE . . . UNIQUE . . . UNIQUE.*

"If you step this way, I'll take some measurements. I am going to have you try on a few samples of trumpet gowns just to be sure the silhouette suits your figure the best before I begin sketching your design."

"Oh, it'll suit my figure. I'm sure of it."

I bring out six gowns: two are trumpets, two are mermaids, and the last two are sexy form-fitting sheaths that I actually think will work better on Lea's frame. Lea has a classic pear shape. I'm worried the trumpet would overemphasize her lower body in a very unflattering way. Of course, the mermaids can present this problem, too, but since a mermaid flares out lower, from the knee down, as opposed to the trumpet, which begins flaring out right below the hips, the eye won't be drawn there. With the sheath, she's still getting a body-hugging dress, but it will be more forgiving around her curves.

"Why aren't these all trumpets?" Lea quickly scans the dresses after I hang them in her fitting room.

"I'd like you to try a couple of other silhouettes just so you can get a feel for what they look like as well."

"Are you NOT listening to me? I told you I wanted a TRUMPITTTT!"

Lea's eyes are shooting a thousand needles into me, but I don't back down.

"I hear you perfectly well, Miss Stavros. You're just trying the dresses on. It doesn't mean I'm forcing you to buy a dress in another silhouette."

"Sweetie, it's good to try on dresses in different shapes. This way you'll be all the more sure that the trumpet gown is really right for you."

Mrs. Stavros has come to my rescue.

"I know what I want, and I don't appreciate someone, especially a salesgirl, trying to convince me otherwise. This isn't a used car I'm buying."

That's it. She's just hit a nerve with me. I absolutely hate it when clients refer to my family and I as salesgirls. No doubt it's an easy mistake to make, but it's always bothered me. We work too hard at designing and sewing these dresses not to receive the respect that we deserve. I'm tired of these spoiled, condescending Bridezillas treating us like we're hired help.

"Excuse me, Miss Stavros. First of all, I am not a salesgirl. My family and I design and sew all of these dresses, but even if I were a salesgirl, that doesn't give you the right to treat me the way you are. Secondly, we take our work very seriously here at Sposa Rosa, and for you to liken it to a used car lot is insulting. I am more than happy to help you, but I will not help you if you continue to disrespect my family, me, and our shop."

"She's sorry, Miss DeLuca. She didn't mean anything by her comments. She's just nervous with her wedding being only a month away."

Lea's twin, who seems to only share DNA and looks with her sister, speaks up. She appears very shy and timid.

"Shut up, Laura! I don't need you speaking for me. I am NOT sorry. She's the one who should be apologizing to me. I'm outta here! You guys are making a big mistake buying your dresses from this joke of a shop!" Lea screams out to the other brides in the shop as she storms out.

"I'm so sorry, Miss DeLuca!"

Mrs. Stavros and Laura can't meet my eyes as they walk out after Lea.

"Are you okay? I heard all of that."

Ma holds out a glass of water to me. I take a quick sip.

"Of course. It's not the first time we've had to deal with the likes of her."

"Valentina, I think you should go home. It's too crazy here today. Why don't you come back on Monday when it'll be quieter? You can ease into things again."

"I'm fine, Ma."

I walk away and over to the next bride who's waiting for a consultation. They can't all be Bridezillas today.

Stacey whatever-her-last-name-is can't stop talking. I've made the mistake of asking her how long she's been engaged and that sets into motion her long story of telling me how her fiancé has proposed to her. I feel like I have to be extra polite after she's witnessed my scene with Bridezilla #2. But I'm not listening to Stacey. The moment she starts to tell me how she was at the top of the Empire State Building when her fiancé proposed, my mind wanders to that night when Michael had surprised me with his proposal at Central Park. It was the best night of my life. Fighting back tears, I congratulate Stacey and quickly interrupt her as I take her to the back to try on a few ball gown samples. I don't even bother bringing out samples in different silhouettes this time. I don't have the energy after my last battle to lock horns with another bride-to-be, though Stacey seems worlds apart from the last two Bridezillas I've dealt with today.

Stacey proves to be as easy as I knew she'd be, choosing the second sample I've pulled for her but requesting that I make a few swaps with other gowns she's seen in our portfolio. She wants an unadorned tulle skirt, but instead of the lace strapless bodice the sample she tried on sports, she wants a bodice she's seen on an Amsale knockoff in our portfolio. The bodice is covered in Swarovski crystals and has two spaghetti straps, which are also covered in Swarovski studs. Stacey has a good eye. And she's even taken my one suggestion of adding a very pale pink sash to the dress that ties in the back, giving her a princess ballerina look.

My spirits soar a little when I see how happy I've made her with the sash. But then the jealousy begins seeping its way in again. *Why isn't it me getting married?*

I push my thoughts aside once again as I take the next client. Her name is Donna, and as the minutes tick by, I want to add "prima" before her name, for she acts like a *prima donna,* ordering me around to get her more and more samples. Brides like her get caught up in the pageantry of the dress shopping and never want the experience to end. I've brought out a dozen samples already. Fifteen will be my limit. No excuses. Of course, after dress fifteen, she requests that I bring out not one but *five* more.

"I'm sorry, Donna, but you've been here for three hours and have still not made up your mind as to a silhouette. You've tried on fifteen samples. You're more than welcome to come back and try on more dresses, but our time for today is over. I have a waiting room full of other clients who need to be seen."

"*I* decide when our appointment is over! My appointment was before these other women, and I am entitled to take my time. This is, after all, *my* wedding day we're talking about. I can't just rush through this decision. So I'd like to see a few more mermaid gowns."

Donna turns her back toward me and talks to her best friend, Tina, as if I'm not standing there.

"Excuse me, Miss Foster."

Just like with Bridezilla #2, I now resort to calling Bridezilla #3 by her last name. But she continues to ignore me. I stand in front of her.

"Did you not hear me, Miss DeLuca? I want to try on five more mermaid gowns. Why are you still standing here?"

"*You're* the one who did not hear me, Miss Foster. I said this appointment is finished for today. You can come back another day."

"I'm *not* leaving until I'm ready to."

Donna places her hands on her hips, tilting her head to the side. Her green eyes squint as she stares at me, sizing me up from head to toe. A smirk is on her face. She can't be more than twenty-two years old, but she has the cocky confidence of a woman who's seized the world.

"Fine. You can stand there as long as you like, but I'm attending to my next client."

I start to walk away, but Donna steps down from the pedestal, almost falling as she trips over the cathedral train that's attached to the Justin Alexander knockoff mermaid gown she has on. She stands in front of me, blocking my path.

"I could slander your name and the name of this shop all over the Internet, damaging your business forever."

That's all it takes for me to lose it.

"Who do you think you are? Just because you're getting married doesn't give you the right to treat other people like your slaves! If you don't leave right now, I'm going to—"

Someone grips my arm, pulling me away from Donna.

"Valentina, stop it!" It's Rita.

I don't realize my hands have curled into tightly clenched fists. I've never lost control before. This isn't the first time I've had to deal with a difficult client. I look at Rita.

"Fine. I'm going to the back. You deal with her."

"I can't believe how I've been treated. I'm planning on spending thousands of dollars in here today, and this is the treatment I get?"

I overhear Rita and Ma trying to calm down Ms. Prima Donna, offering her bribe upon bribe.

"Please excuse her. She's going through a very difficult time right now. She's never acted like this before. You can stay here until we close if you'd like to try on more dresses. Please don't leave."

Ma is begging her, which sickens me. I hate this part of the business: kissing up to clients who don't deserve to be treated well at all, especially after they've treated us so poorly. But it is a business, and the client must come first, as Ma always says. Shouldn't there be a line? I've heard of businesses before that refuse service to customers who treat the employees badly. But this is different. I know that. And it's a different time. The girl has threatened to slander us online. That's all it takes today with the power of the Internet. I'd often consulted online reviews as well before deciding on a new hair salon or restaurant to try. And to Ma, reputation means everything.

Suddenly realizing what I might've done by losing control, I regret my actions immediately. I wait just outside our alterations room and eavesdrop on their conversation to see the outcome.

"We'll give you fifteen percent off the dress." Rita is bribing as well.

"Just fifteen after the way she talked to me? Come on, Tina."

"Wait! We'll give you twenty-five percent off the dress, including alterations, *and* fifteen percent off your headpiece." Ma has never bargained that much before.

"Well, I guess I can reconsider."

"You're getting a great deal. Please, why don't you sit down and have a cup of coffee while we bring you your other gowns to try on."

Suddenly, Ms. Prima Donna makes up her mind.

"You know what? That won't be necessary. I love this dress I have on right now. I knew this was the dress, but I just had to be sure. That's why I wanted to try on a few more. But I know it without a doubt now. All I need are my jewels and headpiece."

She walks toward our headpiece displays.

"Tina, don't just stand there! Come help me choose my headpiece and jewelry. Why else did I bring you?"

I close my eyes. Disaster averted. I walk over to the little stove we keep in the shop's kitchen and pour some *espresso* into a pan. I add milk and place the pan on the gas range.

"Hey. Sorry that had to happen on your first day back to work." Connie comes into the kitchen.

"You weren't the bee-otch brides I had to deal with. No need for you to apologize. If anyone should apologize, it should be me. I can't believe I lost it like that out there. That's all we need—to have our name run through the mud all over the Internet. With all the young brides who walk through our doors, our business could be cut in half."

"Oh, you're overreacting, Vee. We'll be fine. No one is going to go by one bad complaint. Haven't you noticed there's always a disgruntled reviewer or two on those online sites? You can tell they're exaggerating and just want to get revenge on the business by posting such nasty comments. They're not always accurate. Besides, look at all the glowing reviews we have on Citysearch. I was on there last week, and we now have two hundred plus reviews! And I can tell that beast out there isn't going to say anything. She's just a bully who needs to feel like she's the center of attention."

Connie's bending over in front of the kitchen counter, checking out her complexion in the stainless steel toaster. I give up on reprimanding her to stop obsessing over her oily skin. It's no use.

"Well, after the discounts Ma and Rita gave her, I know she's not going to post anything bad now. That's probably why she decided to stay after all. She knew she wouldn't get discounts like that anywhere else, especially from a custom-made boutique! I know it's good business, but sometimes it angers me that Ma is always so accommodating to these Bridezillas."

The strong *espresso* is easing up the huge knot that's formed in my right shoulder after the stressful day I've had.

"Vee, I know you want to get back to your life and come to work, and I know you're tired of everyone telling you what you should do, but I think today proves that you still need time away from the shop."

I don't even try to argue this time. My behavior today is evidence enough that I'm not ready to be surrounded by happy brides-to-be and anything remotely wedding related.

"Yeah, I can see that now. I just can't take being cooped up indoors anymore. I need a distraction. I was hoping work would be it, but all day, I just keep thinking about how things didn't work out for me."

"It's understandable, Vee. Go easy on yourself for once! This was the week leading up to your wedding. You couldn't have chosen a worse week to return to Sposa Rosa."

"I guess I have a sadomasochistic side and just wanted to make myself suffer even more." I'm surprised I can still make jokes.

"You need to get away from here. Maybe you and Aldo can go on vacation. He has the time since he's not working."

"Not anymore. He sent a text last night that he got a job at one of the art galleries down in the Meatpacking District. Of course, he had to take a huge pay cut, but he's happy to be back in the art world."

"Oh. Too bad."

We sit there quietly for a few moments. The thought of getting away is starting to tempt me. So what if I'm alone? I actually am not the best company these days with my surly mood swings. Traveling alone to wander among strangers who know nothing about me is feeling more and more enticing. But where would I go?

I think about Venice. That's the one place I'd longed to go to since I was a kid. But that's out of the question now. After all, it was supposed to be the setting for my wedding and honeymoon. How can I go there now—and alone? I'll just keep thinking how Michael is supposed to be with me.

Damn you, Michael! I scream inside my head. *You ruined it all.*

I think forlornly of all the things I had written down that I wanted to see and do in Venice: St. Mark's Basilica, Il Campanile, Il Rialto, the tiny islands of Murano and Burano, the gondola rides, the narrow alleyways that string around the lagoon.

A crazy idea begins stirring in my mind. *Just go to Venice. Don't let Michael take all of your dreams away. You can still have this.*

Aldo had canceled my flight along with the rest of the wedding-related events. He had to pay a small cancellation fee, but I'd received the rest of the credit on my airfare. My heart starts racing in anticipation. The more I think about this, the more it feels right. I'll be thousands of miles away from home, where no one knows me, and there's so much to explore. This is the distraction I need.

"Connie, you gave me a great idea."

"I did? What?"

"You forgot already? The vacation."

"Oh, right! But I thought you said Aldo found a job."

"He did, but that doesn't mean I can't go alone. I am a grown woman."

"Oh, Vee. I'm not so sure that's a good idea, being all by yourself."

"I'm not suicidal, Connie, for crying out loud!"

"I'm sorry, Vee. We're just very worried about you."

"I know. But you can all stop worrying. I'm going to be okay. And this is just what I need."

"Being by yourself?"

"Yes. I need to be able to hear my thoughts. Besides, I've always wanted to take a vacation alone."

"So where will you go?"

"Venice."

"Are you crazy? I said to take a vacation to distract yourself, and you want to go to the place where you were supposed to marry the love of your life?"

"I know it sounds crazy. But you know I've always wanted to go there. Why should I let Michael ruin this for me? He's already destroyed what we had. Venice will always be the place where I was supposed to have my fairy-tale wedding, but I can change that perception by taking this vacation and making it about me rather than about some guy I thought I knew and about a fantasy wedding day."

Connie sighs.

"Ma's not going to like this."

"That's all right. I'm supposed to like the idea, not her."

"Just do me a favor, Vee?"

"What?"

"Think about this for a few days before you make up your mind."

"Okay. I can do that."

"When were you planning on going?"

"I was thinking at the end of the month."

"That's just two weeks away."

"I would leave now if I could, but despite what you think, I haven't gone completely bonkers. I don't want to be in Venice the week I was supposed to get married or the following week that would've been our honeymoon. So the last week in June is when Michael and I would've been flying back to New York."

Connie nods her head. "Well, that's a relief. At least you have enough sense not to go any earlier."

"I'm going to apologize to that Bridezilla and then I'm heading home to start planning my trip."

"You're already forgetting your promise to me to think about this more!"

But Connie's smiling.

"I'll have a couple weeks to change my mind. Don't worry. That's enough time to think about it."

"Ahh! You and I both know you've already made up your mind."

She's right. I have decided. No one, not even Ma, can stop me. I'm headed for Venice.

14

La Serenissima

The five domes of St. Mark's Basilica in the distance grow larger as the Alilaguna nears Venice. The Alilaguna is a boat operated publicly, which takes people from the Marco Polo airport into Venice. I have read this is the most spectacular mode of transportation to arrive into the heart of Venice. My heart races as we approach the city I'd fallen in love with as a child. The anticipation of the other passengers on the Alilaguna is palpable. They, too, are just as eager to set foot in *La Serenissima*—or "the serene Republic," as Venice is also known. And serene she is.

Golden sunlight bathes the lagoon. As we near the dock, countless gondolas dot the canals. *Gondolieri* stand out like peppermint sticks in their candy-cane-striped shirts and straw hats as they effortlessly glide their gondolas through the undulating waters. In one gondola, a middle-aged woman sits statuesquely. Her cobalt-blue dress stands out in stark contrast to the shiny cranberry-colored accordion she plays. Large, dark sunglasses à la Sophia Loren and a wide-brimmed straw hat with a blue ribbon complete her ensemble. A couple in their sixties hold each other as they listen to the melodically sweet sounds emanating from the accordion. In the distance, someone is belting out notes from an opera. I turn my head, straining to see where the singing is coming from. A young man handsomely dressed in a pale gray sports jacket and crisp linen shirt, opened at the neckline to reveal his bronzed skin, sings notes from the opera *La Traviata*. A group of tourists, mostly young women, sit in this gondola, entranced by the singer.

I feel as if I've stepped into the pages of a fairy tale. Every scene seems surreal. Pale green water serves as lawns surrounding Venice's residences. Lavishly ornate palaces dating back to the Byzantine era grace the landscape. Warm pink crumbling walls stand out against the turquoise-colored sky. Marble and Istrian stone churches gleam white. Shiny onyx-colored gondolas contribute to the *chiaroscuro* tones of the city. Perhaps that is why photos of the city come out so well—all the light and dark shades Venice has to offer are a photographer's dream come true. Suddenly, I understand what so many tourists mean when they say, "You can't take a bad photograph in Venice." As I snap away with my cell phone's camera and examine each photo after it's taken, the pictures are stunning. I know they will look just as perfect once I print them.

Happiness fills the air like the church bells that are currently ringing from St. Mark's Basilica. Everywhere I look, people are smiling and laughing. I can't help but smile as well. It doesn't matter that I'm here alone. I'm blessed just to finally be in this magical city. If you ask me for two words to describe Venice, they're: *happiness* and *perfection*.

From the idyllic views to the sweet sounds of music that seem to surround every corner of the city to the balmy breezes that carry the scent of *espresso* being served at the outdoor cafés, all of my senses are engaged. But instead of being overwhelmed, I am energized and very much alive. My adrenaline is soaring, and all I know is that I want more of this natural high. Tears come to my eyes. To think, I almost didn't come.

The Alilaguna has now arrived at the San Marco dock. With my one sensible rolling piece of luggage and a JanSport backpack, I disembark. Having done my research, I know that the city is most easily traversed on foot, so I made sure to bring only what I absolutely need. Even though I'll be staying for three weeks, I just packed one week's worth of clothes. I'll find the nearest *lavanderia* once I'm out of clean clothes. In addition to sightseeing and acquainting myself with the city, I want to get a sense of what life is like for the locals. Doing my own laundry will make me feel in a small way like one of the natives.

Though I need to walk away from the Piazza San Marco to get to my hotel, I can't resist taking a detour and head for the square. Savoring every moment as I freeze the scene in my mind like a camera capturing a photograph, I take in some of Venice's most popular landmarks—St. Mark's Basilica, Il Campanile, Il Palazzo Ducale, Il Rialto . . . Though San Marco is where throngs of tourists flock, there is an unspoiled atmosphere here that is often found in more remote, less-traveled regions. What strikes me the most is the silence from the absence of motor traffic. That alone enhances *La Serenissima*'s tranquil atmosphere. Even the numerous merchants selling cheap Carnevale masks and miniature gondola replicas do not mar the city like they do in other tourist hot spots. Though I am anxious to see the interiors of the landmarks in San Marco, I need to check into my hotel. My stomach is also growling.

With my street map in hand, I walk toward the direction of my hotel, by the famed Riva degli Schiavoni. A long winding quayside, the Riva degli Schiavoni is busy with the water buses, or *vaporetti;* water taxis; *traghetti,* or gondola ferries; and gondolas. A sea of tourists mob the merchants' stalls, buying everything from T-shirts to marionettes and cheap versions of glass-blown vases. Across the water, I can make out the picturesque island of San Giorgio Maggiore. The church and monastery bear the same name as the island and are some of the architectural marvels I have on my must-see list of attractions. I'm especially eager to go to the top of the *campanile,* or bell tower, and see the spectacular view of Venice it affords.

Venice is separated into six *sestieri,* or districts: San Marco, Dorsoduro, Cannaregio, Castello, San Polo, and Santa Croce. My hotel is in the largest of the *sestieri,* Castello. I did not want to stay in San Marco, the most popular district for visitors. Though still a tourist mecca, Castello also offers a quieter side of Venice just behind its waterfront, with peaceful narrow alleyways, gently weathered *palazzi* (palaces), and breathtaking churches such as Santi Giovanni e Paolo. Another reason why I've chosen to stay in Castello is that it is still accessible to San Marco and is along the

Grand Canal, where I can easily hop onto a *vaporetto* when I don't feel like walking to the farther *sestieri* or the Venetian lagoon islands.

Turning onto the Campo Bandiera e Moro, I locate the red banner with the words *La Residenza* hanging from the second-story terrace of my hotel. The hotel's facade looks just like it did in my Venice guidebook. A fourteenth-century *palazzo,* La Residenza was built in the Gothic-Byzantine style Venice's buildings are known for. Made of what looks to be Istrian stone—a more durable stone than marble—the hotel is three stories. The second story sports five portico windows and is most likely where the Gritti, Partecipazio, Morosini, and Badoer, the patrician families who resided at this palace over the years, had their quarters. I had learned from my art and architecture of Venice course in college that the porticoes signaled where the doges resided in their palaces. Many other wealthy or noble families in the city followed this habit of keeping their quarters on the second floor in the center of the building.

La Residenza's lobby is breathtaking. Frescoes hang on ornate marble walls, and lush drapery and beautiful antique furniture complete the reception area. After I check in, I'm anxious to see my room. I've chosen to pay a little extra to have a room with a view. Since I'd selected a two-star hotel instead of the four-star hotel Michael had chosen for our honeymoon in San Marco, I felt like I could splurge by getting a room with a view. Stepping into the room, I'm relieved to see it isn't tiny. European hotels, unlike American ones, are known for their cramped quarters. Though not as extravagant as the lobby, the room is tastefully decorated in exquisite ivory-colored furniture that complements the *palazzo*'s creamy exterior and interior walls. A king-sized bed is cloaked with a modest duvet that has nothing more than brick-colored stripes. The best, and my favorite, feature of the room is the double arched windows. They're Byzantine in style. The windows' draperies are in the same red as the stripes on the duvet and are tied back.

Setting down my backpack on the bed, I walk over to the windows and open one. The vista looks out onto the facade of a church, whose name I'm not sure of. It doesn't look like any I'd seen in my guidebook or the other books on Venice's landmarks that I've read. I inhale deeply the fresh air.

Content with my surroundings, I quickly unpack and take a shower. At this point, I'm completely famished.

Deciding to wear a halter sundress I'd made years ago, I look at myself in the mirror inside the *armadio,* or armoire, that can be found in every Italian home. Built-in closets like the ones in America are not the norm in Italy, so huge armoires are used instead. My dress is white with tiny, black polka dots and has a snug, collared bodice with a full skirt that reaches halfway down my calves. It seems like the perfect dress to wear in Italy. I pull my hair back in a high ponytail and tie a white chiffon scarf over it. I break the fashion rule of never wearing wedge-heeled sandals with a full skirt so that I can be comfortable walking around. I complete the ensemble with wide black Jackie O–style sunglasses. Grabbing my purse, I leave my hotel room.

I decide to forego asking the hotel's front desk clerk for a recommendation and let my nose guide me to the right restaurant for my dinner. *La seconda colazione* is the midday meal in Italy, unlike the lunch that Americans eat at this time. In the evening, a light *cena*, or supper, will suffice, in which a *panino* or even just a few slices of bread with cheese and olives constitute a typical Italian supper. Again, I want to live just as the Italians do, so I'll eat the way the locals eat.

I make my way back toward Piazza San Marco since I want to explore its streets more. The aroma of cooking fish reaches my nose. I follow the scent and soon come upon Castello Rivetto, and notice the dazzling fish on display in its window. All the times I'd had fish when I visited my relatives in Sicily, it had been the best, most fresh fish I'd ever tasted. Without a second thought, I walk into Castello Rivetto.

Several *gondolieri,* still wearing their straw hats, are seated at some of the tables. Of course, plenty of tourists are also present.

"*Buon giorno, signorina.*"

"*Buon giorno.*"

"Will it be just you dining with us today?"

"Sì."

The waiter smiles and gestures for me to follow him. He doesn't seem to take note that I'm alone. I see another woman seated by herself at a table, and a few men are also dining alone, not that I care. I'm reveling in my own company. And in a city like Venice where throngs of tourists, merchants, and even its residents are always milling about the streets, you never truly feel alone.

For *antipasti,* or appetizers, I have a simple tomato-and-fresh-mozzarella salad. But as I discover after taking my first bite of the salad, there's nothing simple about the taste bursting forth from the juicy grape-sized tomatoes and the smooth ribbon-like texture of the mozzarella, which seems to melt as soon as it touches my palate. After dining on the most heavenly *tagliolini a la carbonara,* I'm convinced I will never be satisfied again with the pasta in the U.S.

I choose a broiled swordfish for my second course, even though the pasta has sated my hunger. In Italy, when one visits a restaurant, it is common to order an appetizer, first course (usually pasta), second course (a meat or fish dish), and sometimes dessert. Restaurants hate it when American tourists order only one dish, and forget it if you even suggest sharing a dish. Italians eat this way in their homes as well. When I'd visited my relatives in Sicily on several occasions, I wanted to cry halfway through the meal because of my bloated stomach. My sisters and I would plead that we'd had enough to eat, but my aunts never believed us and just kept piling the food on our plates. After a trip to Sicily, I always gained weight.

But even if you don't eat an appetizer, first and second course, and dessert, it's easy to pack on the pounds. Italy is a culinary paradise, where food is screaming to be tasted. I once told Aldo, who had never been to Italy, "I'd go to Italy for the *gelato* alone." When there are long spans between my family's visits to Sicily, I begin craving the *gelato* in Italy. I have found one place in Williamsburg, Brooklyn, that comes close to making *gelato* much like what you find in Italy, but it's still not the real thing.

"Signorina, desidere qualche dolce?"

Where has the time flown? I've been too consumed by my stupendous meal to notice that an hour has gone by in a flash. Though the desserts on the menu are tempting, I want to give my belly a break and walk off some of the calories I've just consumed. Plus my sweet tooth is really aching for *gelato.*

"No, grazie. Solemente il conto."

After paying my check, I continue heading over to San Marco. It's two p.m., and the canals and streets are much quieter than they'd been when I'd arrived this morning. People are finishing up their dinners and having their *siestas.* I yawn at the thought of everyone napping, but I fight off the fatigue. I haven't come to Venice to sleep, even though that's what the Venetians are doing right now. So much for living like a native! Most of the merchants at the souvenir stalls have already packed up their wares to go home and eat dinner. They'll return around five p.m., the typical time for businesses in Italy to reopen after *siesta.* I make a mental note to come back in the evening to see the *piazza* in full swing at dusk.

Walking around the cobblestone streets, I'm still in awe of the enormous architecture around me. The most striking is St. Mark's Basilica. I decide to enter.

To my surprise, dark, cavernous space greets me. I was expecting to find a brightly lit cathedral with vivid frescoes adorning the ceilings and walls, much like the other cathedrals I'd visited in Sicily and in the pictures of the churches I'd seen in my college art history courses. But instead, gilded mosaics cover the walls and ceilings of the Basilica. There is a blend of Byzantine, Gothic, and even classical elements in the architecture and art. The gilded surfaces give off their own light, almost as if the source is coming from flickering candles. I'm almost certain this had been the intent of the architects, since certain Biblical passages that are represented in the art shine brighter than others. I suddenly realize that I don't know much about Venice's history even though I've longed to visit the city for so many years. The one Venetian art history course I'd taken had covered some of the city's history but focused more on the paintings. I'll definitely have to take a guided tour of the Basilica and even a walking tour of Venice to learn all there is to know of this amazing city on the water.

I step into one of the pews and kneel down. Making the sign of the cross, I bow my head in prayer. But again, no words come to me. I look up at the altar. Suddenly, I imagine myself standing there in my wedding gown with Michael. I quickly shut my eyes, squeezing them tightly, forcing the image out of my mind.

We were supposed to get married in the church of Santa Maria della Salute. Though not as grand as St. Mark's Basilica, the church is a significant historical landmark and dates back hundreds of years. It was built to honor and thank the Madonna for rescuing the city from one of the deathly plagues that had struck. This piece of history I'd learned from the priest I had spoken to over the phone when I was making my wedding arrangements. Hence, the church's name, which means "Madonna of good health."

Of course, I've known it would be inevitable that I'd be assaulted with thoughts of my canceled wedding and honeymoon that were supposed to take place in Venice. That's why Connie had tried to talk me out of taking this trip. But my anger toward Michael refused to let him take away my dream of going to Venice. Maybe I should've waited a year or two to come here when my heart would be more healed. But there's no going back now. And I refuse to ruin this trip with thoughts of what could've been. This trip will be about me and no one else.

Feeling stronger, I stand up. Genuflecting outside of the pew before I turn my back on the altar, I walk outside. My eyes squint fiercely after being in the dimly lit Basilica. A caretaker is sweeping the mosaic tiles on the ground outside. Maybe he knows about guided tours.

"*Scusa, signore.*"

The caretaker glances up at me but continues his sweeping.

"*Dové posso comprare i biglietti per fare il giro della Basilica?*"

"*Al presbiterio, signorina.*"

The caretaker gestures with his broom toward the left facade of the Basilica.

"*Ma é chiuso adesso. Ritornera per le dieci di mattina.*"

"*Va bene. Molto grazie, signore.*"

The caretaker tips his cap toward me.

"*Buona sera, signorina.*"

I'll return early in the morning to buy my ticket for a guided tour of the Basilica. No doubt there will be a line of visitors waiting well before the rectory's opening at ten a.m.

Since there aren't as many people out right now, it's the perfect time to snap more photos. Walking around the immense Basilica, I take photos at every angle. I then turn my attention to Il Palazzo Ducale, which sits behind the Basilica to the far right if one is looking at it from the front. The palace of the dukes, or *doges* as they were known in Venice, is also breathtaking.

Walking over to the canal, a row of docked gondolas catches my attention. Even at rest, they hold an artistic beauty. I step back a few feet, capturing the gondolas as well as a few pigeons that are pecking at bread crumbs on the cobblestones before the canal. In the distance, across the water, Il Campanile, or the Watchtower, stands majestically.

Seeing Il Campanile reminds me to glance at my wristwatch. It's already four p.m. I'm tempted to get *gelato,* but I'm still too full from the huge dinner I'd had. *Gelato* will have to wait until after supper. I'll make sure to eat nothing more than perhaps a piece of bread with some cheese. I can't stop yawning and decide to head back to the hotel to take my own *siesta.* I also need to call my family and let them know I've arrived safely. It's eleven a.m. in New York. Ma, Rita, and Connie will be at the shop. I wonder how busy they are and how the new intern is working out. No doubt they'll tell me all about it even though we'll be on a long-distance call. Suddenly a pang of sorrow stabs my heart. I miss them already.

❧ 15 ❧

The Savior

Olivia was humming to herself as she sewed lace appliqués to the skirt of a tulle ball gown. Not only was sewing her livelihood, but it was also a calming activity for her, especially when she was sewing by hand. There was something soothing about pushing a needle through fabric, creating a perfect tiny stitch, then pulling the needle back up through the garment. Olivia even loved to marvel at the row of stitches marching their way in single or double file, straight through the fabric. Yes, being a seamstress was in her blood, and she took great pride in her craft.

Though she was sad at seeing Valentina leave for Venice by herself when she was supposed to have left with a groom by her side, Olivia's spirits couldn't be dampened, for she'd received good news. Her doctor had called last night to tell Olivia that the cyst they removed from her right breast was benign. She did not have cancer. Olivia had thanked Dr. Preston profusely as if she were a magician who had powers and could transform a malignant cyst into a benign one. Then she'd run up to her room and knelt in front of her night table on which she kept a small porcelain figurine of the Madonna, whom she had prayed feverishly to since she'd detected the mass in her breast.

Now she would not have to frighten her daughters by telling

them she had cancer. It was one thing for them to have lost one parent to the disease. But to have to put her daughters through it a second time would've been unthinkable.

Thank God for Raquel. She had taken Olivia for the ambulatory surgery to remove her cyst. And just as Dr. Preston had promised, Olivia had minimal, if any, pain after the operation. She had scheduled the surgery for Thursday so that she could stay with Raquel over the weekend. She reversed her situation and told the girls Raquel was having minor surgery and needed her help. Olivia couldn't help smiling at her cleverness, though she felt horrible about lying to the girls. But it was necessary. Surely, God would forgive her this small transgression—she hoped!

The bell announcing a new customer rang through the air. Connie was in the fitting room area helping a client with her second fitting. Rita had taken an early lunch so that she could go to the post office to pick up a package she'd been expecting. Melanie had the day off, and the new intern had fallen sick with food poisoning. So it was up to Olivia and her daughters to play double-duty today as front desk receptionist. She stood up and walked to the front of the shop.

A young woman of about twenty-five stood in their reception area, waiting with an older man who looked to be in his sixties. He was probably the girl's father. This was a growing trend that irked Olivia. Brides-to-be were bringing their fathers and even their fiancés to help choose their wedding gown design. The nerve! This generation today had no respect for traditions that had lasted for hundreds of years. All they wanted to do was change everything. And what bride in her right mind would tempt fate by letting the fiancé see the dress before the wedding day? The bad luck that could bring upon the marriage! Olivia mentally shook her head at the horror of it all.

But this girl standing before her had no one else escorting her. The other clients who had brought their fathers or fiancés always had at least one woman along as well. You needed a woman's opinion, after all, someone close to you besides the sales consultants. Maybe the woman's mother had died? Suddenly, Olivia's annoyance at the sight of the man softened as she thought about this young bride who possibly did not have a mother to see her get married.

"Hello. How are you? Welcome to Sposa Rosa. May I help you?"

Olivia extended her hand first to the woman.

"Nice to meet you. My name is Francesca, and this is my uncle."

The man stepped forward and shook Olivia's hand. Something odd happened when she shook his hand. A warm sensation shot through her arm. And the man seemed to be holding her hand a little too long as he stared into Olivia's eyes. When she let go of his hand, a shiver replaced the warm feeling she'd just experienced.

"Nice to meet you, *signora*."

Olivia could tell from his accent that he was Italian.

"Piacere."

Whenever Olivia learned her clients' relatives were Italian, she always talked to them in their mother country's tongue. It was a gesture of respect and to show that she was one of them and could relate to them.

"We came all the way over from Long Island."

Francesca was smiling and definitely had the glow of a recently engaged woman.

"I hope you did not run into traffic?"

"Always *traffico* in New York! Bah!"

Francesca's uncle threw his hands up dismissively toward the window, pointing to the traffic out on Ditmars Boulevard. There was something very familiar about his gesture, but Olivia could not place where she'd seen it before.

"How did you hear about us, Francesca?"

"I read the article in *Brides* magazine. Your shop sounds just like the place to find what I've always dreamed I would have when I got married someday—a custom-made dress that could rival a high-end couture dress."

"Well, then, you came to the right place. Will anyone else be joining you today?"

Though Olivia's daughters often said she had no—what did

they call it? Discreet? No, that was not it. Discretion! That was it. She knew she could be very delicate, particularly when she wanted to find something out.

"No, it'll just be my uncle and me."

Francesca's eyes looked sad. Olivia regretted that her nosiness had caused the young woman pain. She was about to steer the conversation into a more pleasant topic when Francesca's uncle suddenly said, "Francesca's parents died in a car crash fifteen years ago. Her mother was my sister. I have raised Francesca ever since as if she were my own daughter."

"I'm so sorry."

"Don't be. Zio has provided me with so much. I know it might be unusual to come shopping for my wedding dress with a man, but he is the only person I could think to have here with me on this special occasion. I wouldn't want anyone else."

Francesca's uncle put his arm around his niece and smiled at her. His eyes were glistening.

"Actually, Francesca, it is not so unusual as you might think for a bride-to-be to have a man escort her to shop for her wedding dress. We are seeing it a lot now. In fact, it's not just fathers and uncles that brides are bringing with them nowadays, but even their fiancés."

"What?" Francesca and her uncle cried out in unison.

"You're just saying that to make me feel better."

Francesca wagged her index finger playfully at Olivia as a mischievous smile lit up her beautiful brown eyes. Her brown hair was streaked with soft blond highlights that played up her dark eyes. Her warm, easygoing manners were very attractive. Olivia could tell her uncle had done a fine job in raising her.

"No, no. I am very serious. You can ask my two daughters who work here with me, actually three, one of them is in Venice right now."

"*Pazzi! Sono tutti pazzi! Questo mondo sta falliendo!*"

Again, Francesca's uncle threw his hands up in the air, and again, it looked very familiar to Olivia.

"Oh, Zio! Stop being so old-fashioned. If a girl really wants her fiancé to help her pick her wedding gown, then why not? It's all about what she wants, right?"

Francesca looked to Olivia for approval.

"I'm sorry, Francesca, but I am going to have to agree with your uncle. I think it is important to keep some traditions, and where is the surprise if the man you are going to marry sees your dress before your wedding day? Brides should want their future husbands to be dazzled when they see them walk down the aisle. I guess I am old-fashioned like your uncle—and superstitious!"

"*Vero, vero.*"

Francesca's uncle nodded his head with emphatic approval. Olivia couldn't help noting that like his niece he, too, had a very friendly, likable personality.

"Superstition! You Italians are all so alike with your *malocchio!*"

Francesca rolled her eyes but she was also laughing.

"You sound like my daughter Valentina. She is always telling me I am too superstitious."

"*Che bello nome—Valentina!*"

"*Grazie, signore.* She is my daughter who is in Venice right now."

"*Chi va a Venezia, tornera!*"

Olivia laughed.

"What did you say, Zio? You keep forgetting that I don't know Italian very well."

"If you had studied Italian in high school and college like I told you to instead of that useless German, then you would know what I'm saying. Am I right, *signora?*"

Olivia looked at Francesca's uncle. His eyes squinted as he gazed at her intensely, much the way he had when they'd shaken hands earlier. What was it about this man? There was something about him that unnerved her.

"What your uncle said, Francesca, is a famous saying for people who go to Venice. It means 'He who goes to Venice will return.'"

"Oh, I think I've heard that before, but in English, of course."

"So how did you name your daughter, *signora?* It's not a common name, even in Italy."

"Valentina was born one day before Valentine's Day. She's my oldest daughter. When I saw her and remembered that the next day would be Valentine's Day, I thought to myself that I wanted her to be surrounded by love all of her life. And then the name came to me. My husband at first didn't want to name her this, but when he heard what I was thinking about surrounding her with love and why not start with her name, he agreed."

"What a beautiful story. Isn't it, Zio?"

Francesca's uncle was staring at Olivia again.

"Speaking of names, I'm sorry, but I didn't catch your name, *signora,* when you introduced yourself."

"Oh, I'm sorry. I think I might have forgotten to give you my name. Sometimes I am so focused on learning the names of my clients and making an immediate connection with them that I forget to tell them my name. Or maybe I am going senile."

Olivia laughed. Francesca laughed with her. Only her uncle remained silent. Maybe he thought she was being rude in waiting so long to properly introduce herself.

"Please forgive me. My name is Olivia DeLuca."

"Olivia?"

Francesca's uncle's voice whispered Olivia's name as if he'd suddenly been stricken with laryngitis. He looked pale.

"Are you feeling okay, *signore?* Let me get you a glass of water. Please sit down."

Olivia hurried to the back to get a glass of water.

"Zio, did you remember to take your blood pressure medication?"

Francesca sounded worried.

"He keeps forgetting to take his blood pressure medication."

Francesca took her uncle by the arm and led him to the couch in the reception area.

As Olivia was returning with the water, it dawned on her that she also had not learned the man's name. Francesca had introduced him merely as her uncle.

"Drink this slowly."

"Thank you, Mrs. DeLuca."

Francesca held the glass up to her uncle's lips gingerly, but he took the glass from his niece and gulped the water down quickly. He then pulled out a handkerchief and wiped his brow.

"Are you feeling better?"

Francesca's uncle placed his hand on his niece's shoulder and nodded his head.

"Can you do me a favor, and go to that bakery next door and buy me an *espresso* and a few cookies? The caffeine and sugar will probably help my blood sugar."

He pulled out his wallet, but Francesca waved it away.

"I'll be right back. Will you please look after him?"

The poor girl looked terrified. She was probably afraid of losing the only family member she had left.

"Of course, honey. Don't worry. I'm not going anywhere."

"Thank you."

Francesca walked out of the shop.

"*Signore,* I'll get you another glass of water."

Olivia began to stand when she heard the man say in a much higher voice this time, "*Non mi ricordi?*"

"*Scusa, signore. Ma io non ti conosco. Fosse mi hai sbagliato con un'altra donna.*"

Olivia waited for the stranger to say who he was. He seemed very hurt that Olivia did not know him or remember who he was. She stared deeply into his face, looking for something she recognized. His hair was completely gray. Maybe if she imagined him with darker hair. She then remembered the gesture he'd made earlier that seemed so familiar to her. Who had she seen do that?

An image came to her of a young man walking along the cliff of a mountain and waving dismissively toward her as she apologized to him. Just as the face of the man came into view, Francesca's uncle said, "*Sera, son' io.*"

Olivia gasped, placing her hand over her mouth. Only one person had ever called her by her middle name.

"Salvatore?"

And now it was Olivia's turn to look as if she'd seen a ghost. But in her case, she was really seeing a ghost—for she had believed this man had died so many years ago.

❧ 16 ❧

The Lion

I'm having breakfast, or *la prima colazione,* at a bar not too far from St. Mark's Basilica. Unlike in America, bars in Italy are where patrons can get everything from a cup of *espresso* and pastries to cocktails and even *gelato.* I order an espresso-flavored *granita* topped with *panna* (whipped cream) and a French roll known as a brioche. Originated in Sicily but served throughout Italy, *granitas* are a cross between sorbet and Italian ice but with more of a crystallized texture. I'd fallen in love with *granitas* on my first trip to Sicily when I was ten years old. As a child, I'd marveled at the sweet breakfasts Italians had, which often consisted of either *granitas* or *biscotti.* Of course, Italians and Europeans eat such light breakfasts to save room for their heavier midday meals.

Breaking off another piece of brioche and dipping it into the heavenly *granita,* I have to pinch myself to believe I'm really here in Venice. The bar features arched porticos, giving patrons an unfettered view of the canal. A couple in a gondola that is making its way down the Grand Canal catches my attention. The man's arm is around the woman's shoulders. The man whispers into the woman's ear, and she smiles, looking up into his face. That's the invitation he's waiting for as he leans in to kiss her.

I look away as tears sting my eyes. That couple is supposed to be Michael and me. Though I had been in Venice for only a day, Michael keeps entering my thoughts. I try forcing myself to think of anything but Michael, but it's hopeless. What haunts me the most are the recurring nightmares I've had several times a week since we've broken up. In them, that horrible day when Michael ends our engagement replays itself. The dreams always end with me asking him over and over, Why?

I still grapple with his motives even though I try telling myself the "why" isn't important. It's not going to bring him back if I know fully what had made him change his mind. But the curiosity still gnaws at me. My intuition senses something isn't right. I'm convinced he hadn't completely leveled with me when he said he didn't think marriage was for him. In all the years that I've known Michael, even before we'd begun dating, he's repeatedly told me how he can't wait to have his own family and be a father someday. He's an only child and has always wished he had siblings. No, it's more than a case of cold feet. I'd bet my life on it.

Finishing the last of my *espresso,* I sigh deeply. That's enough of Michael. I'm not in Venice to dwell on why the love of my life has broken my heart. I signal to the waiter. If I hope to get ahead of the lines for the guided tours at the Basilica, I need to leave now. I sign my credit card receipt. Wherever I can, I use my credit card instead of euros so I won't have to convert my U.S. dollars as frequently. The waiter takes my receipt.

"Have a nice day, mees. You are from America, correct?"

All of the merchants and restaurant workers in Venice know English and speak it very well.

"How did you know I was American?"

I'm a little disappointed that he can tell. Whenever I've visited Sicily, people often told me that I looked like one of the natives since I didn't wear the trademark tourist clothes—Bermuda shorts and tennis shoes.

"I jus' know."

The waiter looks to be around twenty.

"Dov'é posso comprare i francobolli?"

Now it's the waiter's turn to look surprised.

"*A un chiosco dei giornali, signorina. É impossibile per non trovare uno.*"

"*Molto grazie.*"

"*Spero che non ha presa offesa?*"

"No, no. You did not offend me."

I smile to assure him.

"Where did you learn to speak Italian so well?"

"My parents are from Sicily."

"I go to Sicilia almost every August. *É molta bella.*"

I nod my head in agreement.

"*Buon giorno.*"

I had only walked three feet when the waiter calls out to me.

"*Scusa, signorina.* Can I make any recommendations while you're here in Venice?"

"Are the tours of the Basilica San Marco good?"

"Yes, they're good, but if you can, try to take one of the Giro Artistico tours. They cost a little more, but the guide is one of the best art historians in Venice."

"*Grazie.* I will take you up on your recommendation."

"If you need anything else while you are in Venice, please feel free to come by and ask me. My name is Fausto."

"*Piacere, Fausto. Io mi chiamo Valentina. Arrivederci.*"

"*Arrivederci.*"

I notice Fausto's eyes scanning me from head to toe—or rather undressing me. I guess my being a decade older doesn't faze him. As I leave the bar, I can still feel his eyes on me. I can't resist looking over my shoulder before I step outside. He's still standing where I left him, scrutinizing me intensely. He smiles and waves, unabashed that I've caught him checking me out.

I shake my head. Italian men.

Making a mental note of the name "Giro Artistico," I quickly walk over to St. Mark's Basilica. With my passion for art history, I will have to take this tour and see if it lives up to Fausto's high praise.

Instead of the abundant sunshine I was greeted with upon land-ing in Venice yesterday, clouds keep rolling in as the morning goes by. But the overcast skies do not deter from Venice's beauty. The Basilica's enormous scale overwhelms me once again as I approach it. Looking at a map of the Basilica inside my guidebook, I locate where the presbytery is. Although it is nine a.m., one full hour before guided tours begin, there are already a dozen tourists ahead of me on line. I take my place behind a family of Swedish tourists and wait.

Today and tomorrow, I'll focus on the main landmarks on San Marco: the Basilica, Il Palazzo Ducale, Il Campanile. Depending on how much I cover of San Marco in the next couple of days, I'll then venture to the outlying islands in the lagoon. One island I cannot miss is Burano, known for its long lace-making tradition. I want to purchase lace to bring back home and use in sewing a few of our wedding gowns.

"Ciao, Stefano!"

"Com'é va, Stefano? Un' altra bella donna!"

"Stefano, non ti dimenticare a venire sta sera!"

"Si, si. Ciao! Ciao! Buon giorno."

I strain my head to see who has caught so many people's attention. Perhaps it's an Italian celebrity?

"Stefano, ti bisogna aiuto oggi?"

I follow the voice of the little boy who's standing by the dockside. The boy is dressed shabbily with dirty, tattered jeans and a long-sleeved New York Yankees T-shirt that's two sizes too large on him. He wears a beat-up pair of black Converse sneakers. The Converse logo is blank, obviously a cheap knockoff.

"Ciao, Giuliano. Sempre mi bisogna aiuto. Compra me un giornale e una granita per te."

The little boy's face lights up at the extra euros the celebrity gives him.

"Grazie."

The celebrity helps out of the gondola the stunning redhead he's with. He takes her mahogany leather trench coat and holds it open for her as she eases herself into it. He pulls out her long penny-red hair, smooths it down, and then kisses her on both cheeks. She smiles as she wraps a silk Fendi scarf around her neck and hoists a black alligator-skin handbag over her shoulder. I can make out the large G on the bag's buckle, indicating it's a Gucci.

"*Ci vederemo doppo. Va bene?*"

The woman nods her head and glides away. Her movements are very lithe as if she's walking on water. Perhaps she's a dancer. She is taller than the celebrity by a good foot. Her heavy makeup and glamorous wardrobe also give her the appearance of a model or a television broadcaster on the Italian public TV network RAI. She carries herself as if she's the most beautiful woman in all of Italy. Heck, make that the universe.

The celebrity is making his way toward the Basilica. He's dressed smartly as well in a sand-colored linen suit with a pale blue button-down shirt that's open at the collar to reveal a tan that can rival that of a Bain de Soleil model. His hair is cut in many layers, and he wears it a little long. He carries off the Rick Springfield look—circa 1982—extremely well, though the style is dated. Flecks of gray lightly dust his chestnut-brown hair. Dark aviator sunglasses hide his eyes. His gait is brisk but easy. He exchanges a few words with the guard who stands at the Basilica's entrance. A gleam in the sky diverts my attention. I look up and see it's the gilded statue of the winged lion that stands over the Basilica's center arch. The winged lion has been a symbol of Venice dating back to the Republic's early days and can be seen on buildings everywhere throughout the city. I glance back down at the celebrity. His whole demeanor exudes confidence that demands to be noticed, much like one of the lions in Venice's architecture.

My curiosity has gotten the better of me, and I want to know if he's a famous Italian star. Maybe I can ask the guard who he is. Unlike Aldo, I'm usually not taken with celebrities, but then again, I've never come this close to one.

Turning my attention back toward the line, I'm surprised to discover that there are only four people in front of me. Distracted by the Italian celebrity, I haven't noticed the line moving. Once at the front, I purchase my ticket. As I walk toward the Basilica's entrance, I overhear the ticket seller tell the person behind me that she has just sold the last ticket for the ten a.m. Giro Artistico tour, but there are still plenty of tickets for the other tour that's also being held at this hour. I'm relieved I've managed to snag the last ticket.

There is just a small group of twelve tourists waiting for the tour to commence. I'm surprised that the tour has sold out. Maybe the guide likes to keep the tours small. I knot my cashmere pashmina. In Italy, visitors are not allowed to enter churches in shorts or bare shoulders. I had forgotten this rule when I'd left my hotel the previous day in my halter dress, but luckily, I had a silk scarf in my purse that I was able to use to wrap around my shoulders when I made my impromptu visit to the Basilica. Today, I'm wearing a white, A-line linen skirt that skims slightly above my knees. Underneath my pashmina, I'm wearing a sapphire-blue strapless lace top, which will be perfect for all the outdoor walking I'm planning on doing this afternoon. Already it's quite warm outside, and I can just imagine how hot and humid it'll feel once the afternoon hours arrive. My violet pashmina complements perfectly my white strappy leather sandals that are adorned with purple and blue jewels.

It's quite cool from the air conditioner in the enormous Basilica. A chill suddenly runs down the back of my neck. My hair is up in a loose chignon, but I decide to let it down. Pulling out the pins that hold my chignon in place, I flip my head over and shake out my hair to give it some body. When I flip my head up, sweeping my tousled mane back, I'm greeted by the most gorgeous pair of green eyes.

It's the celebrity!

He's staring at me just as intently, if not more, as the waiter at the restaurant had where I'd had breakfast this morning. I swallow hard and lick my lips. The celebrity's eyes dart right to my lips.

Oh, why did I lick my lips? I can feel my face warming up. But there's also another sensation happening. Little waves flutter through my stomach, and soon the heat I'm feeling in my face is slowly enveloping the rest of my body. The celebrity's emerald eyes seem to read my thoughts as his gaze slowly, very slowly, travels down the length of my body and rests on my bare legs.

I can't take this intense scrutiny anymore. I pretend not to notice him and turn around, feigning interest in one of the gilded frescoes in the domes above me, when it suddenly hits me that I'm giving him a full view of my backside. Oh God, help me! And right here, in church. This man must think I'm a hussy or, as my mother would put it, a *puttana*.

Casually, I turn back around, making certain I avoid his eyes. I cross my arms and ask one of the tourists standing near me, "So, do you think the tour will start soon?"

Hopefully, he'll get turned off hearing that I'm nothing more than a cheesy American tourist.

"We're about to begin. Hello, everyone. My name is Stefano Lambrusca."

To my astonishment the celebrity is not a celebrity but our tour guide. I can't help but look in his direction. He's smiling cordially at our group, but when he notices me looking at him, his smile deepens.

"As you no doubt have noticed, this is a small group, and that's how I like to keep my tours so that everyone can have the opportunity to ask as many questions as he or she likes and to present a more . . . *ehhh . . . Com'é se dice?*" He pauses, searching for the right word. "A more intimate setting."

He looks at me again, smiling furtively this time. The man is absolutely flirting with me! Why am I shocked? This is Italy, after all—land of the playboy extraordinaire. I'd seen it often enough when I visited Sicily. Men on their *motorinos* would whistle at my sisters and me, making suggestive comments. One summer, we were hounded relentlessly whenever we went to the beach.

The notorious DeLuca temper is beginning to flare up inside of me. The nerve! And he has a girlfriend. The redhead I'd seen with him earlier had to be his lover.

"So since we are such a small group, let's start off with introductions. We'll go around and you can give me your name and tell me briefly in a sentence or two what brought you to Venezia. Let's begin with you, *signorina*."

He points at me. I have to give him credit. The man certainly does not waste any time. The other tourists in the group look at me and smile. I clear my throat.

"My name is Valentina. I'm here on vacation, of course, as I'm sure everyone else here is."

Everyone laughs. That's all he's getting out of me. If the celebrity—or Stefano whatever-his-last-name-is—thinks he's going to get to know me, he has no idea who he's dealing with.

Stefano smiles. "Ahhh, you get me, *signorina.*"

Obviously, he meant to say, "You got me." Though he doesn't have a heavy accent, and his English is as good as most of the other Venetians' English, he still seems to struggle at times to find the correct word.

"What I should have said maybe was how did you decide to choose Venice over all of the other beautiful cities in Italy?"

He isn't letting me off the hook.

"I've always wanted to come to Venice. I also took a course in college on the art and architecture of Venice, and I'd like to see the masterpieces that I studied."

Stefano's eyes glow when I say this for some bizarre reason.

"*Brava! Grazie molto,* Valentina. And you, sir, what is your name and why Venice?"

He nods at the gentleman behind me, giving him permission to speak.

"Venice is the city of all cities. This is my third time here."

The man goes into a lengthy description of why he keeps coming back to Venice. But Stefano doesn't seem to mind, especially since his mind is elsewhere. He's blatantly staring at me again. I pretend not to notice, but my peripheral vision definitely can see he hasn't taken his eyes off me since the tourist behind me has begun speaking. I can't help thinking I've wasted the extra money in purchasing this tour since this playboy of a guide isn't curtailing people's comments, and this is a timed tour. But no sooner have I thought this when Stefano announces, "We'll end about ten minutes later to accommodate for the introductions. Can everyone stay an extra ten minutes? If not, you are welcome to leave, and I will do my best to con . . . con . . . condense the tour into the time allotted."

Everyone murmurs that they can spare an extra ten minutes beyond the original duration of the tour.

"Let us begin."

Stefano manages to keep his eyes off me for the rest of the tour.

His knowledge is comprehensive, and in addition to giving us detailed information on the art and architecture of St. Mark's Basilica, he also outlines Venice's history and the history of the Basilica. One fact I find especially fascinating is the story of how St. Mark's body had been stolen from its original resting place in Alexandria, Egypt. The knights who had stolen the body covered the saint's remains with pork to deter the Muslims from searching for it. Disgusted at the sight of the pork, the Arabs did not detect St. Mark's corpse, and the knights brought the saint's relics to Venice. The original church, which would later become St. Mark's Basilica, was initially built in honor of the saint and to house his remains.

"I'm sure many of you might have noticed already the winged lion on the center arch of St. Mark's Basilica and on many other buildings in Venice. You can also find these lions on buildings in Verona, Chioggia, Vicenza, and other parts of the Veneto. The lion indicated that these cities were part of the Venetian empire."

As Stefano talks about Venice's majestic symbol, it's my turn to stare at him. I'm still floored by his beautiful green eyes. His sense of style is impeccable, and his knowledge is beyond impressive. But there's something else that is intriguing about him. Like the dark, gilded interior of the Basilica that offers glimpses of light in its shadows, Stefano appears to be a mysterious enigma I can't help wanting to know more about.

❦ 17 ❧

Land of the Gigolo

As the tour is winding down, I decide to make a discreet exit. The tourists in my group advance to inspect the Pala d'Oro, the magnificent tenth-century altarpiece comprised of precious stones and gilded panels. I remain still until I am well behind the group. Then I tiptoe to the nearest exit and walk out into Piazza San Marco.

Flocks of pigeons line the *piazza*. My stomach is grumbling, but I don't want a heavy midday meal that will slow me down for my afternoon of exploring as much as I can of San Marco. I pull out of my purse a little notebook in which I have a list of recommended restaurants, cafés, and bars that I had looked up on the Internet before I left New York. Following my street map, I make my way toward Calle delle Botteghe, where Trattoria da Fiore is located. Known for its *cicchetti,* or tapas, Trattoria da Fiore is also popular for its *bacaro*—a separate space apart from its main dining room reserved for patrons who wish to just have tapas and a drink. A light snack and a good glass of wine are all I'll need to refuel and continue my sightseeing.

A cozy, inviting space, Trattoria da Fiore is bustling with both tourists and even locals. As the waiter leads me to my table, several men who are seated in the main dining room follow me with their eyes. Even one septuagenarian winks at me. I will have to get used to being ogled during my stay in Venice.

After perusing the menu, I order a glass of white wine from the local Veneto region and for my *cicchetti,* I can't resist the fried zucchini blossoms and a sampling of fried fish that includes prawns, sardines, and squid. When the waiter brings out the *cicchetti,* I am embarrassed since the portions are quite generous even though it's supposed to be just a light snack. How odd must this look that I am here alone with all this food before me?

I thank the waiter, who doesn't seem to notice or care that I am to consume this huge feast alone. Taking a bite out of the flaky fried zucchini blossom, I am taken back to the summer when I'd first visited Sicily with my family, and my aunt had made this same mysterious culinary delight. I watched as Zia Pia dipped each zucchini blossom into an egg-and-bread-crumb batter and then fried the flowers until they turned amber in color. The zucchini blossoms wake up every taste bud in my mouth. I close my eyes, savoring the flavors. Then I take a sip of my wine, which is the perfect complement to my dish.

"They are heavenly, aren't they?"

I open my eyes and almost jump at the sight before me.

The celebrity! Uhhh . . . I mean the tour guide. I have to stop referring to him as "the celebrity" now that I know he's the farthest thing from a celebrity. How had he found me? I'd left the tour a full ten minutes before it was due to end, and that was not allowing for the extra time Stefano said he would offer to make up for the lengthy tourists' introductions.

Speechless, I just nod my head in greeting.

"Do you mind if I join you?"

Somehow I manage to squeak out, "No, of course not."

But how I do mind. My relaxed, blissful state from just a moment ago is far in my memory now as my nerves take over.

"Ciao, Stefano. Che bevi?"

"Un bicchiero di Prosecco, *per favore. Grazie."*

Of course the waiter knows him. It seems everyone knows Stefano in Venice. Maybe he is a celebrity—to the local Venetians, at least.

Stefano returns his gaze to me and smiles. As if reading my mind, he says, "I come here almost every afternoon after my tours."

I can't help wondering if he isn't just explaining the waiter knowing him, but is also attempting to validate finding me in here. Had he perhaps ended the tour earlier and seen me walk in this direction? I dismiss the notion. Stefano is a handsome man, and Venice is filled with gorgeous women. He doesn't need to follow an American tourist just to add another notch to his belt. Then again this *is* Italy, land of the gigolos and playboys.

"Excuse me a moment while I take a look at the menu."

"I have more than enough *cicchetti* for both of us. Please help yourself. I was not expecting the portions to be so large. I could never finish this all by myself."

Stefano seems to hesitate. He shrugs his shoulders. "Okay. But I must order my favorite *cicchetti*. I get them every time I come. And you must try them as well. I insist."

Stefano motions for the waiter and orders fried *polpetti,* or meatballs. I notice the waiter slides his gaze toward me and then back at Stefano as they share some sort of man speak with their eyes. The waiter is smiling furtively. I pretend not to notice as I take a bite of my prawn.

"Valentina, is this your first time to Venice or Italy?"

"It's my first time in Venice, but I've been to Rome, Florence, and Sicily."

"Sicily?"

The waiter brings Stefano's glass of Prosecco. I watch as he greedily drinks the bubbly drink.

"Excuse me. I get so thirsty after giving a tour. All the talking I do."

He smiles again, but this time it's more of a shy smile. Can it be this cocky man is actually a bit flustered?

Whenever I notice people's discomfort, it's always been my tendency to put them at ease.

"I enjoyed your tour very much."

His eyes register surprise, then delight. The embarrassment from a moment ago is completely forgotten as his smile deepens, and his eyes narrow, looking at me in the same intense manner he had when we first met.

"Thank you. It helps to get some . . . ehhh, how do you Americans call it? Feed . . . feed . . ."

"Feedback."

"Yes, thank you! Feedback. I'm sorry. My English isn't the best."

"No, you speak English very well. It's natural to forget a phrase here and there, especially in our language that has so many idioms."

"You are too kind—and beautiful."

My cheeks flush crimson immediately. What is the matter with me, giving this stranger not one but two compliments? Quick mental note: *Restrain yourself, Valentina.*

"I hope you do not mind me saying so."

"No, thank you."

I take several sips of my wine, hoping to hide behind the glass until my cheeks return to their normal color.

"Polpette di carne," the waiter announces as he returns and sets down on the table Stefano's *cicchetti*.

"They smell just like my mother's."

"Your mother makes these?" Stefano sounds surprised.

"Yes. We do have meatballs in America." The sarcasm is evident in my voice.

"Of course."

Stefano sinks his fork into one of the fried meatballs that aren't coated with sauce, and places it on my plate.

"Have you ever had them without sauce and alone, unaccompanied by pasta?"

"That's the best way to have them. When I was little, every Sunday afternoon when my mother made dinner, I always asked her to save a meatball for me before she placed them in the tomato sauce."

"So your mother made pasta every Sunday?"

"Yes, like any other Italian mother."

"So you are of Italian descent? I should have known. Your looks are more exotic than American."

"My parents were born in Sicily and immigrated to America after they were married."

"*Da vero? Siciliana?* That's right. You mentioned you had been to Sicily. *Allora lei capisce Italiano?*"

"*Si, molto bene.*"

"So I do not have to struggle for the right English word when I talk to you."

I smile. "I guess not."

He smiles back.

"So why did you leave the tour early if you were enjoying it?"

Darn! He's got me. How am I going to explain that?

"I didn't leave the tour early because I wasn't enjoying it anymore." As I talk, I search my brain for the right excuse. "It's just that I wasn't feeling well. I needed to eat something."

I pray he can't tell I'm lying. Stefano nods his head, seemingly accepting my excuse.

"Two hours can be a long time for a tour, especially in the morning."

He raises his glass toward our waiter, signaling for him to bring him another drink.

"Would you like another drink as well?"

"No, thank you. I'm fine."

"Valentina, how long is your stay in Venezia?"

I like the way my name sounds on his tongue. He utters each syllable slowly, almost as if he's taking pleasure in reciting my name.

"I'll be here for three weeks. I only arrived yesterday."

Stefano's eyes seem to brighten at this information.

"Are you planning on taking any other tours?"

"Yes, I'm thinking of taking a tour of a few of the churches that house some of the art I studied in college, and I'd also like to take a tour of Il Palazzo Ducale and maybe a walking tour of the city if I can find one."

"Of course, we have walking tours of the city. I offer them. I can give you a generous discount if you take my walking tour."

"That's kind of you, but that's not necessary. You hardly know me. I can't expect you to give me a discount."

"Nonsense! You are a guest in my city. It would be my pleasure.

I have a walking tour this evening, right after *siesta*. Why don't you take that one? We meet in front of Basilica San Marco at five o'clock."

What can be the harm in taking a tour with him? There will be other tourists, and as I'd learned from the tour of the Basilica this morning, he's very knowledgeable. I'll probably learn so much on this tour as well.

"Okay. Where do I purchase the ticket?"

"You can buy them from me. Since this is a walking tour of the city, I operate independently."

I pull my wallet out of my purse, wanting to pay him now for the ticket. But Stefano places his hand on mine. His touch sends a thousand butterflies loose in my stomach.

"Pay me later. No rush to do so now."

"*Grazie.*"

His hand lingers on mine. He gives it a little squeeze before he lets go. My heart is absolutely racing. I've never met a man who is so forward like him.

"Where do you live in America?"

"New York."

"Ahhh . . . New York! I have always wanted to go there."

"It's an amazing city. But not as beautiful as Venice."

"No city is as beautiful as *La Serenissima*. She's in . . . in her own state."

He meant to say, "She's in her own class." I can't help smiling whenever he trips over the English language. There's something cute about it. Maybe because it stands out in stark contrast to the persona of style and confidence he exudes.

"How about you? Are you from Venice?"

"No. You'll find that many people who work in Venice aren't from here. I'm from Calabria."

It's my turn to sound surprised.

"Calabria?"

I can't help hearing my mother's voice right then: "Those Calabresi are so pigheaded." I never understood why my mother had always had it in for people from Calabria.

"You sound surprised. Or should I say disappointed? I know. Calabria does not sound as glamorous as Venice."

He shrugs his shoulders and holds out his palms when he says this as if he's apologizing.

"No, it's not that. I just assumed you were from Venice since you work here. That's all. I'm also familiar with Calabria, but only briefly since I take *il traghetto* from Calabria to Messina whenever I visit my relatives in Sicily. It's beautiful. And the two cities are so close to each other. We're practically neighbors."

"Isn't that ferry ride over to Sicily gorgeous?"

"Yes, I look forward to it every time I go. People have asked me why I don't just fly to Palermo now that Alitalia has a direct flight from New York, but I'd rather fly from Rome to Calabria so I can take that ferry ride."

"I used to work on that *traghetto* when I was a boy. And I never got tired of the beautiful scene."

Scenery, I correct in my head.

He samples some of my fried fish and eats two of the zucchini blossoms. He's right; the meatballs are very good. We talk some more about Calabria and Sicily. When we are finished with our *cicchetti,* he glances at his watch.

"I'm sorry, but I have an appointment." He pulls a wad of euros out of his trousers' pocket and dumps them on the table.

I reach for my wallet. He shoots his hand out and stops me. This time, he holds my arm.

"*Per favore, signorina.* I know in America it's different, but you are in Italy now where a lady is treated like royalty. The day I let a woman pay for her meal is the day Stefano Lambrusca is not a man anymore."

I want to laugh at this sexist comment, but I know he means no offense. It is a different culture, and as such, I need to respect it.

"*Grazie molto, Signor Lambrusca.*"

"Just Stefano. No need for formalness with me."

I know I should correct his English, but I don't want to embarrass him, or in his case he'll probably feel emasculated.

He stands up and pulls my chair out for me. As I walk out of

Trattoria da Fiore, he places his hand on the small of my back, gently prodding me forward. This man exudes sensuality, and he has no reservations about touching a woman whom he's only met a few hours ago. As I exit, I feel the gazes of the men in the restaurant staring at me. None of them seem to have any reservations about checking out another man's woman—not that I'm Stefano's woman, but they don't know that.

When we step outside, a gust of humid air greets us. The sky has darkened, threatening rain at any moment. I'm still wearing my pashmina and am absolutely burning up in it. I unknot it and take it off. Immediately, Stefano's gaze wanders to my bare shoulders and then drops to my cleavage. In my haste to remove the pashmina, I've forgotten to make sure that the strapless spandex tube top I have on beneath my shawl is hiked up high enough so that I'm not flashing too much cleavage. The top has a tendency to slide down whenever I wear it. When he finally looks away, I glance down at my cleavage and am horrified to note that my top has slid down quite a bit. I quickly hike it back up.

"Will you be returning to your hotel room?"

"No, I think I will walk around a bit."

"I am taking the next *vaporetto* to Cannaregio. I will see you then at five o'clock. It was a pleasure meeting you, Valentina."

Stefano takes my hand and kisses it.

"Arrivederci."

All I can mutter is *"Ciao."*

I instantly scold myself for using the less formal greeting with him. I don't want him to think I'm comfortable with him and we're on a friendship level.

As I walk away, I sense his eyes on me. I hold my head high and keep my posture as erect as possible. Then I realize I'm giving my walk an extra bounce. But it's too late for me to change my gait. This man is making me act strangely. I wonder what his next appointment is. Then I remember the diva he'd been with that morning. Of course, before they'd parted, he had told her he would see her later.

I'm such a fool. Once again, I am letting a clever man seduce me and deceive me. If he thinks I will be *"un'altra donna,"* or "another woman," as I heard one of the men who had greeted him say in admiration upon noting the redhead beside him, he's sorely mistaken. With this thought in mind, I resolve that I will not attend the walking tour that evening. I've come to Venice for a respite from men. This trip is supposed to be about me and no one else. Stefano Lambrusca is like most single men in Italy—a player whose hobby is seducing as many women as he can into his bed.

I walk far enough away until I'm confident that I am out of Stefano's view. I then stop and look back, straining to see if I can make out his sandy suit. But where he had stood, a tourist group is now posed, waiting for a photo to be taken. I decide to start shopping for souvenirs for my family and go over to one of the stalls that are selling elaborate Carnevale masks. Sadness suddenly envelops me, and I feel very alone. In that moment, I can't help wondering if maybe I've made a mistake in coming to Venice by myself.

❧ 18 ❧

City of Pleasures

It's my fourth day in Venice, and I am keeping busy, visiting the sites on my list, eating lots of *gelato,* and just strolling the streets aimlessly and seeing what awaits me around every corner or on the other side of one of the many stone bridges that line the city. From the churches housing many of the masterpieces I'd studied in college to the winding cobblestone streets that are works of art in their own right, Venice is not disappointing me.

I keep my promise and don't join Stefano's walking tour. Afraid I'll run into him, I avoid San Marco that night and explore the Castello *sestiere* where my hotel is. A part of me feels bad that I've stood up Stefano, especially since he'd been so gracious in paying for my meal and offering to give me a discounted ticket for the walking tour. But he's trouble. I can feel it, and I don't need that. My wounds are still too fresh to even entertain notions of dating again—least of all an Italian.

"Have some fun, girl!"

I suddenly hear Aldo's voice in my head. If he were here with me, he'd be egging me on to just have a fling with Stefano and not be so serious. My sisters would've probably also told me to go for Stefano.

I can also imagine Connie scolding me: *"Come on, Vee. It's not*

*like you'll see him again once you leave Venice. Why not enjoy every
pleasure Venice has to offer?"*

"Because I'm not you, Connie," I say aloud.

I'm on the *vaporetto* going to Cannaregio, which is the most
northerly of the city's *sestieri*. A third of Venice's population resides
in Cannaregio. Few tourists take time to explore this *sestiere,* and
here I hope to get a better, more authentic sense of how the Venetians live.

I also want to visit the Madonna dell'Orto church, which houses
works by the Venetian painter Tintoretto. As the *vaporetto* approaches Cannaregio, rows of houses with crumbling facades come
into view. Residents' boats are docked in front of their homes,
much the way cars line a driveway or street outside of houses
erected on land. A group of young *gondolieri* can be seen steering
their gondolas a bit unsteadily while an older man gestures with his
arms the right way to navigate. They are probably students learning
on these much-less-traversed canals of Cannaregio rather than on
the busier canals of San Marco or even Castello.

I disembark at the stop closest to the Madonna dell'Orto
church. Here in Cannaregio, the natives outnumber the tourists. I
stop in front of the Gothic church and begin snapping away with
my cell phone camera. After taking a few shots, I walk toward the
church's entrance.

"Excuse me, miss. Would you like a picture of yourself in front
of the church?"

I had yet to have a photograph taken with me in it. Without even
waiting to see who has made the kind offer, I reply, "Yes, please."

I turn around only to find Stefano standing before me with his
arms crossed and smiling.

What is he doing here of all places? He can't be giving tours
since more money is to be made in San Marco. Before he can even
ask me what had happened the other night, I decide to preempt his
question.

"Ciao, Stefano. Com'é sta?"

"Molto bene. Grazie. E lei?"

"Bene. Grazie. I'm sorry I didn't make the walking tour the
other night. I wasn't feeling well."

"I hope it's nothing too serious. That's the second time that day you weren't feeling well."

Stefano is smirking.

"Oh, just some jet lag. I needed to rest. I feel much better now."

"I'm glad to hear that. You can take my walking tour tonight."

"You have one tonight?"

"*Sì.*"

"What are you doing here? Are you giving a tour of the Madonna dell'Orto church?"

"No. I actually live in Cannaregio. I just finished a tour at Il Palazzo Ducale. I don't have any others until tonight."

"It's very peaceful here, much different from San Marco or even Castello, where I am staying."

"Yes, I love it here. The tranquility is why I decided to live in this *sestiere.*"

"Well, I won't keep you. I'm sure you must be tired and would like to go home and relax. *Arrivederci,* him."

I walk away. As I'm about to pull open the church's door, Stefano is behind me opening the door.

"Please, allow me."

"*Grazie,*" I whisper, not wanting to disturb the Mass that is in progress.

I step inside and am about to wave a final good-bye to him, but when I turn around, I bump into him.

"Excuse me. I thought you were leaving."

"I wanted to ask you a question."

"Oh."

An old woman sitting in the last pew glares at us.

"Let's go into the chapel."

Stefano takes my arm and leads me to the chapel of the church, which is empty.

"If you'd like, Valentina, I can give you a personal tour of this church and a walking tour of Cannaregio."

"In addition to the tour tonight?"

Stefano laughs. "No, I wouldn't expect you to do two tours less than a few hours apart, but if you really wanted to, of course, you could still join the tour tonight."

I hesitate. Though I am enjoying the time alone in Venice to re-flect, I'm also getting lonely. And I had enjoyed Stefano's tour of the Basilica immensely. Fausto, the waiter, had been right. Stefano's tours are the best. Of the few I'd taken in the past couple of days, none of the guides' knowledge measured up to Stefano's. What I particularly love about Stefano's tours is that he also makes them interactive so that he isn't just monotonously lecturing.

"If you're sure you're not too tired, that would be nice. But I in-sist on paying you."

"Ahhh . . . you American women. If that's the only way you'll agree, then fine. But instead of paying me for the tour, I'll let you pay for dinner this time."

"Okay, that works."

"Let's start right here with the Chapel of San Mauro. That will give us enough time to move on to the church right about when Mass will be over."

Stefano points to the statue of the Madonna inside the chapel and begins reciting the history of the church, which was founded in the mid-fourteenth century and was dedicated to St. Christopher, patron saint of travelers. The saint was to protect the boatmen who carried passengers to the lagoon islands.

"But when the church was reconstructed in the fifteenth cen-tury, it was dedicated instead to the Madonna after a statue of the Virgin Mary was found in the *orto,* or vegetable garden, not far from the church. Hence, the church's name Madonna dell'Orto. The statue of Mary was believed to have performed miracles. When we go back outside, I will point out to you the statue of St. Christopher, which is on top of the portal."

I listen to Stefano, but I have to work hard to keep my mind from wandering. It's difficult paying attention when your tour guide is as sexy as he is. Today, he's dressed more casually than when I'd first met him. He wears dark-wash denim jeans and a V-neck, silky T-shirt. The clothes give him a younger appearance, but I'm almost certain Stefano is in his forties. A few lines crease around his eyes whenever he smiles, and of course, he has all those flecks of gray hair. I can't help wondering if he'd ever been married, and if so, what had happened? Maybe he still was married. Italian men often do not wear their wedding bands. The image of the striking redhead he was with in San Marco the other morning comes to mind. I start to feel anxious.

"Is something the matter, Valentina?"

"No, I'm fine."

"Are you sure? You look troubled."

"I think I just need some air. The incense and the burning candles in here are affecting me."

"Of course. Let's step outside. I can give you the tour of the exterior until you feel better, and then we'll come back inside."

As we walk out, the few parishioners who are listening to Mass are making their way toward the front of the church to receive communion. The older women's faces are covered with black lace veils. The men are all wearing suits. I feel like I've gone back in time to pre–Vatican II days.

"Let's take a walk around the church and relax for a bit. I can resume the tour later."

"Thank you. I'm sorry. I didn't mean to startle you."

"You didn't startle me. Please. But I am beginning to wonder if it is something about me that is making you feel sick whenever you are in my presence."

My heart freezes, and my eyes must convey how close he is to the truth, for he quickly adds, "I'm just playing." He laughs.

I smile. "The past two months have been tough for me."

Stefano's face grows serious. "I'm sorry to hear that, Valentina. Is that partly what brought you to Venice?"

I nod. I can't believe I'm confiding in him. Something compels me to let him know there's more going on with me than just a case of jet lag.

"Were your troubles brought about by a man?"

"Aren't they usually?"

I manage to give him a wan smile as I joke.

"Love. We can't live without it; we can't live with it. Why does it have to be so complex?"

I shrug my shoulders, not having any philosophical thoughts to offer on the subject.

"I've been beaten up by that siren before."

"Are you married?"

There, I'd blurted it out.

"No, never married, but I came close to proposing to a woman before."

I'm curious to know more, but I dare not ask. I'm not ready to open myself up fully to this stranger—no matter how charismatic or hot he is. The redhead reappears in my thoughts. I can't refrain.

"I thought that woman you were with on Monday was your wife."

Stefano looks at me, surprised.

"You saw me that day by the canal with Angela? Oh, wait. Of course you did. You were in line waiting to buy the tickets for the tour."

"Yes. Angela was hard not to notice. Everyone was looking at her."

"I know. It's given me much trouble. I'm going to get an ulcer."

So he isn't denying how beautiful this Angela is or that he doesn't like the attention she receives from so many men.

I look away from the canal that I'd been staring off into and notice Stefano is watching me.

"Angela is my sister."

Surprise registers on my face.

"I know. She is twenty years younger than me. My mother had her when she was forty-two. Because of the large age difference between us, I have always looked at Angela as if she were my own daughter rather than just my sister. She is twenty-one years old, but looks like she's twenty-five or even twenty-eight. She still lives with my parents in Calabria, but she was here for a long weekend to visit a friend who lives in Venice."

I suddenly remember the tender gesture Stefano had made of pulling Angela's hair out of her coat and kissing her on her cheeks. I feel foolish. If she had been his lover, he wouldn't have kissed her so innocently.

"That's good of you to still look after her. But you know, she is an adult now and can take care of herself."

He groans. "Not when every young man is after her. But you are right. She has to take care of herself, especially since I no longer live close to her. So you thought Angela was my wife? Do I look *that* young to you?"

"Of course not. It's as you said, Angela could pass for an older woman."

I smile mischievously.

"Valentina, you definitely keep me standing on my toes."

"It's just 'on my toes.' "

"Excuse me?"

"The expression is 'You keep me on my toes.' You don't need to say 'standing.' "

"On my toes. You keep me on my toes?"

"That's it."

He doesn't look embarrassed or emasculated, as I had feared he would feel. He just smiles sheepishly at me.

"I have a proposal for you."

"Already? I've only known you for a couple of days!"

Stefano looks confused. "I said something incorrectly again?"

"I think you meant to say, 'I have a proposition for you.' "

"Yes, that's it. Proposition."

"Never tell a woman, Stefano, that you have a proposal for her or she'll think it's a wedding proposal."

"*Dio mio!* Is that what I suggested?"

"Yes. But you know, in America, when you also say to a woman that you have a proposition for her, that's often considered a suggestive comment."

"Really?" Stefano narrows his gaze and is grinning from ear to ear. "What kind of a suggestive comment?"

"I think you know what I mean. I won't elaborate any further. So what was this 'proposition' you have for me?"

"Why don't we trade tours for English lessons? I give you personal guided tours of whatever attraction you want to see in Venice, and in exchange, you help me with my English."

"Your English is quite good, though, Stefano."

"But it's not perfect, as you've noticed. I have made mistakes."

"You just need to learn idioms better."

"So, do we have a deal?"

"I'll have to give it some thought."

"What is there to think about?"

"I don't make decisions hastily."

"Okay, think about it. But I'm only giving you until the end of our tour today for you to decide."

"Whatever." But I'm laughing. "Let's go back inside the church. I'm ready for my tour."

I walk ahead of Stefano, and again, I am giving my hips an extra sway, knowing full well Stefano is observing my every movement. I can't help myself. This man brings out another person in me. And all I know is that I'm having fun, just as Aldo and my sisters would want.

After the tour of Madonna dell'Orto, Stefano and I are famished, so we find the nearest *trattoria.* We share an appetizer plate of *prosciutto, mortadella,* and a sharp *provoletta.* Then we have octopus salad. I decide to quit after the salad, but Stefano orders *zuppa di mare*—a stew of squid, shrimp, cod, octopus, and scallops, which he insists I sample. We wash it all down with a bottle of Chianti.

Though the tour had consisted of just the two of us, Stefano had still treated it in a professional manner. I can tell he loves what he does and has a true appreciation for his country's architecture and art. I can't help feeling he's also trying to impress me with his vast knowledge. He seems more relaxed now that he's eating and having a glass of wine.

"Have you taken a gondola ride yet, Valentina?"

"No."

"How many days have you been here now?"

"Four."

"And you still have not been on a gondola? That's the first thing most tourists do upon reaching Venice."

I shrug my shoulders. "I don't know. I guess I feel a little weird to take a gondola by myself. From what I've seen, they always have at least two passengers."

"I will have to take you. How about tomorrow night?"

I'm torn. Sharing a gondola with Stefano seems too intimate, but I'm dying to ride one. The ambience of traversing the Grand Canal in a gondola will be different than in the *vaporetti* I've been taking.

"Okay. Why not?"

"We'll meet in front of the Basilica at eight o'clock?"

"That's fine."

We spend the rest of our meal getting to know each other better, though Stefano is asking most of the questions. He asks me about my family, how had my father died, what it's like to be a seamstress of wedding dresses, and even my childhood. He leaves no stone unturned. I don't know how I manage to sit calmly under his penetrating gaze while I regale him with my life story. Waves of anxiety roll through my stomach, and I'm amazed I am able to eat the meal. But of course, the food is heavenly and not difficult at all to eat even with the sensations Stefano is setting off in me. When I finally am able to turn the tables and ask him about his childhood, I stare at his lush lips. They're the most exquisite lips I've ever seen on a man. They look full and soft. I imagine what it would be like to kiss them. Suddenly, an image of Stefano and me alone on a gondola flashes through my mind. In my fantasy, he's running his hand up the side of my thigh. I'm wearing a dress with no stockings. Our tongues are tangled together as our bodies throb for each other.

"Valentina?"

Stefano's question brings me out of my reverie.

"I'm sorry. I got distracted."

"I was asking you if you wanted to order another bottle of wine."

"Oh. No. That's fine. Thank you. I think I've had enough wine."

Stefano smiles. He has a way of smiling in the most devilish way, which completely frazzles me. It's as if he can read my thoughts. I look away, knowing he is still staring at me.

We pay our bill and decide to walk around the streets of Cannaregio. Stefano stops when there's a point of interest and tells me about it. He isn't as serious as he'd been during the tour of the church. He makes several jokes. I hate to admit it, but I'm enjoying his company.

At four p.m., I decide to take the *vaporetto* back to my hotel at Castello.

"I'll accompany you."

"That's not necessary, Stefano. Thank you, but I've already

taken up enough of your time. And you tricked me by paying the waiter when I was in the restroom even though we'd agreed that I was going to pay for dinner."

"Don't be mad, Valentina. It's just who I am. I can't help it. The day I let a woman pay anything for me is the day Stefano Lambrusca—"

"Is not a man. I know. You also said that the other day."

I roll my eyes. Stefano laughs. I can't resist laughing, too.

"You know, it's not a torture being with you, Valentina." Stefano's gaze is traveling the length of my body. "Not a torture at all." His eyes travel back up and rest at my cleavage.

I don't know what to say to that. The silence doesn't seem to bother him, however, as he continues staring at me. The *vaporetto* is only a few feet away as it approaches the dock.

"Thank you again for the tours and dinner. I'll see you tomorrow night."

"So you're not going to let me take you home?"

"I'm a big girl, Stefano. Maybe you can take me home after our gondola ride tomorrow night."

Stefano's eyes twinkle. I suddenly realize what I'd said. I'm not going to let him escort me to the hotel now during the day, but I had just told him he could take me back to my room tomorrow night. He probably thinks he's going to get lucky. I mentally kick myself in the head over and over again.

"*Si, si.* It will be late. You will definitely need me to escort you then. *Allora, ci vederemo domani. Ciao, Valentina.*"

"*Ciao.*"

He waits on the dockside until the *vaporetto* is out of sight. I think it's rude to turn my back on him so I lean against the edge of the *vaporetto,* pretending I'm casually taking in the scenery as the vessel departs. He waves a few times to me, and I wave back. When I'm certain I am far enough away, I let myself smile deeply. There's just something about that man that makes me feel so good.

✎ 19 ✎

A Twist of Fate

After Olivia had received the shock of her life when her first love
Salvatore Corvo showed up alive and well in her shop, she'd
been a wreck. Salvatore's niece Francesca had returned to the shop
with the *espresso* to revive her uncle right after Olivia realized who
he was. And Connie had joined them when she noticed the stranger
lying on their couch. Olivia and Salvatore had exchanged knowing
glances, indicating that nothing should be said in front of their relatives about their past relationship. Francesca rescheduled her appointment for the following Saturday so that she could bring her
uncle home. Before they walked out of the shop, Salvatore had
managed to whisper to Olivia, *"Ti chiamo."*

Olivia nodded, anxiously looking toward Connie to make sure
she hadn't heard. But once Connie was satisfied that Salvatore was
going to be fine, she'd returned to her client in the fitting room.

A few days passed before Salvatore called Olivia at the shop.
Olivia felt slightly comforted by the fact that she wasn't the only
one who was eager to get this discussion over with. She had so
many questions for him and hadn't slept the previous night as
memories from her time spent with Salvatore kept flashing through
her mind.

After initially meeting at the Church of the Black Madonna in

Tindari, Olivia and Salvatore had been inseparable. Olivia always considered their first encounter fateful because she had almost not joined her friends and the nuns that day for their weekly prayer group and hymn rehearsal. She'd woken up with a stomachache and just an overall uneasy feeling that she couldn't ascribe to anything. But not wanting to disappoint her friends, she'd pushed herself to join them. Often, Olivia had wondered what would have happened if she'd never gone to Tindari and had never met Salvatore. Would their paths still have crossed at some other time? And then after he mysteriously disappeared, she wondered all the more how her life would have been different had Salvatore Corvo never entered it to begin with. Certainly, she would've been spared the pain of losing her first love and wondering for years what had become of him.

"*Ciao, Sera. Sono io. Salvatore.*"

"*Ciao.*"

"*Senti. Voglio spiegare tutto. Dov'é possiamo parlare.*"

Olivia's mind raced as she tried to think of places where she and Salvatore could talk privately without anyone she knew seeing them. That was all she needed—for her neighbors to think she had a lover.

"Meet me in Manhattan at this address."

Olivia gave him Raquel Sutton's address. She could trust Raquel with anything, and she knew her dear friend would not judge her or grill her with questions about Salvatore until Olivia was ready to offer the information.

As Olivia sat on the N train taking her into the city, she looked at her watch every five minutes. She was meeting Salvatore at one p.m. Raquel told Olivia she would not return until she received Olivia's call that she was done with her appointment. Her stomach cramped painfully. She should have told Salvatore to meet her in a public place. The thought of being alone with him and in Raquel's apartment began to not sit well with her. Her face flushed at the thought of what her daughters would think of her if they knew she was having this secret rendezvous. Nicola popped into her mind. He could probably see from heaven what she was up to.

"Forgive me, Nicola. Please, forgive me. You are the only man I truly loved."

The subway screeched its brakes as it pulled into Lexington Avenue and 59th Street. Olivia got off the subway car and slowly made her way up the stairs. Her body felt more fatigued than usual. With every step she climbed her breathing became more labored, so that by the time she exited on to the street, her chest was heaving and she was gasping for air. Her heart started racing. She closed her eyes and breathed deeply. Fortunately, there was little humidity today, and the temperatures were unseasonably low for early July in New York City. The high temperature was supposed to hit only 73 today. After a few minutes, she felt better and made her way over to 1st Avenue and 62nd Street.

Whenever Olivia went to Raquel's apartment, she liked to imagine that she was the one living on the Upper East Side of Manhattan. Though she had lived in Manhattan when she first came over from Italy, the Lower East Side paled in comparison to Raquel's affluent, exclusive neighborhood. Even the dogs looked rich by the way they carried themselves. Olivia loved watching all the different breeds of dogs traipsing their way through the streets alongside their owners.

Raquel had given Olivia a key to her apartment when she had found the lump in her breast. Olivia was free to use the apartment whenever Raquel was out of town, and she needed to rest before going back to Queens after one of her doctor's appointments. Olivia had never used the key, considering it a privilege she must only take advantage of in dire circumstances. And this meeting with Salvatore was certainly a dire situation.

She sighed as she reached Raquel's pre-war building. A man was exiting the building as Olivia was inserting the key into the front door. She gave him a nervous smile. Surely he'd know she wasn't one of the residents and would question why she had a key. But the man returned her smile and held the door open for her.

Olivia pushed the elevator button and waited for it to descend. She looked through the glass doors of the front entrance, seeing if Salvatore had arrived. The elevator reached the first floor. Olivia opened the door of the elevator and stepped inside, pushing the sixth-floor button. She felt again the constriction that had been in her chest when she exited the subway station. Gripping her black patent-leather purse tightly, she struggled to take a deep breath as she got off the elevator. Rounding the corridor where Raquel's apartment was situated, she almost screamed when she saw Salvatore leaning against the wall.

"*Sei arrivato gia.*"

"*Si, si.* I'm sorry. I was worried about being late and took an earlier train in from Long Island just in case there were problems with the train."

"How long have you been waiting?"

"About fifteen minutes. Not too long. Don't worry."

Olivia nodded her head, suddenly feeling very self-conscious. She looked for the gold key that was for the apartment and inserted it into the top lock of the door. Her hand was shaking. She hoped Salvatore hadn't noticed. After unlocking the top lock, she then unlocked the second lock and pushed the door open. Mr. Magoo, Raquel's dog, was waiting behind the door and gave a bark of delight when he saw Olivia. Raquel had assured Olivia that Mr. Magoo would not harass Salvatore. True to Raquel's word, Mr. Magoo only gave Salvatore a cursory sniff of his pants leg before returning his attention once again to Olivia.

She reached into her purse and took out a Ziploc bag containing Mr. Magoo's favorite *Palline di Limone* cookies. She held one out as Mr. Magoo quickly snatched it with his mouth and seemed to swallow it whole, waiting for the next one.

"Ha, ha! The dog knows good Italian baking."

Olivia smiled. "Yes, my friend Raquel is very strict with Mr. Magoo's diet, but she lets me spoil him whenever I visit."

Olivia put out two more cookies by Mr. Magoo's bowl and saved the rest for later. She didn't want the dog to eat too much at once and then get sick.

"Make yourself comfortable. Can I get you something to drink?"

"Just a glass of water. *Grazie.*"

This was the first time Olivia had been alone in Raquel's apartment. She liked how it felt and again imagined that she owned this apartment. She knew where everything was from all the times she'd visited Raquel or had stayed overnight. Raquel always kept a pitcher of filtered water in her refrigerator. She poured two glasses of water for both Salvatore and herself. She then opened the produce drawer in the fridge and took out a small, sickly-looking lemon. She mentally shook her head. The produce in Manhattan was not of the same quality Olivia was accustomed to getting in the fruit stores of Astoria, but it would have to do. She cut two wedges and squeezed the juice into their water. She began to carry the glasses over when she spotted the Ziploc bag of *Palline di Limone* cookies she'd left on the kitchen counter to give to Mr. Magoo later. She paused and glanced at Salvatore. He was looking at the photos on Raquel's bookshelf. Olivia walked over to the kitchen cupboards and took out a small plate. She took a few of Mr. Magoo's cookies and placed them on the plate. Mr. Magoo looked up at Olivia as if he knew she was stealing from his stash of goodies.

"Don't worry. There are plenty left for you," she whispered to Mr. Magoo.

She placed the plate of cookies on the coffee table.

"Ecco."

Salvatore smiled, looking into Olivia's eyes, but she quickly glanced away. She sat down in the armchair opposite the couch Salvatore was now seating himself on.

He took a bite out of a cookie.

"Ahhh. The burst of lemon in these *biscotti* complements the lemon water. *Perfetto!"*

"Grazie. A shot of *limoncello* would have suited the cookies better."

"Vero, but we must make do with what we have."

Again, Salvatore caught Olivia's glance, and again, she darted her eyes away.

"So, Sera. Tell me about your life since we last saw each other."

Olivia shrugged her shoulders. "I met Nicola, my husband. We got married, came over to America, and I had my three daughters. Nicola got cancer when my daughters were just teenagers. He died about a year after his diagnosis. My daughters and I own the wedding dress boutique."

Salvatore looked grim.

"Mi dispiacio per tuo marito."

"Grazie. It was very hard losing Nicola, especially on the girls, but we have managed through God's grace. He was a good man."

"I'm sure he was. Your daughter, who was at the shop the other day, seemed like a very fine young woman. You and your husband did a wonderful job of raising her, and I'm sure your other daughters are just as wonderful."

"Grazie. Francesca, your niece, seemed like a lovely woman, too. Losing both of her parents must have been so difficult for her. I can see how much she cares about you and respects you."

Salvatore's eyes lit up at the mention of Francesca, and as he talked about her, his whole face became animated.

"She's like the child I never had. I am very blessed that I have her."

Olivia nodded her head and smiled. She noticed Salvatore was lightly tapping his foot against the coffee table's leg. He was doing it softly so that no sound was made. She then realized she was swinging her leg, which was crossed over her other leg. At least she wasn't the only one with the jitters. The silence continued for another minute. Impatient, Olivia decided to just cut to what she'd been longing to know.

"So what happened to you all those years ago? I thought you were dead."

Olivia couldn't resist saying the last sentence with sarcasm. Her notorious temper was beginning to flare.

Salvatore's face turned as white as Mr. Magoo's pristine furry coat. Squinting his eyes as if in pain, he stood up and walked over to the windows in Raquel's living room. He placed his arms behind his back, interlacing his hands. Pacing to and fro, Salvatore looked down at the Persian carpet that cloaked the hardwood floors, but Olivia was certain he wasn't noticing the intricate weave of the carpet.

"The story is very long, Sera."

"We have time. My friend told me I could have her apartment for as long as I needed it. She won't be returning until I call her to tell her we're finished with our discussion."

Salvatore nodded his head.

"The first thing I want you to know, Sera, is that I loved you very much. That summer we spent together was the best of my life. I swear to God, and I never swear to God."

"Then why were you so set on going to Virginia? And don't tell me it was because of the work at the coal mines."

"Sera, you know I was trying to make some money so that we could build a life together. I had nothing to offer you but the failing cotton farm I had inherited from my deceased father. As I told you back then, I just wanted to work a few months in Virginia to save money to buy a *trattoria* and a small house after we got married. You have to believe that."

"It would be easier for me to believe that if you had come back and married me as you had promised to. But instead you disappeared. Since both of your parents were dead, and your sister was already living in America, I had no one to ask if they'd heard from you. Your friend Matteo told me you had an aunt who lived in Palermo, so one day I took the train out there to see if perhaps she knew something. But of course, she didn't. She said the two of you were never close."

"Yes, that is true. She was my father's sister, and there was some bad blood between them, something to do with the inheritance of the cotton farm. I was closer to my mother's family, but as you know, they are all in Siracusa. And after my mother died, eventually the contact between them and my father and me was very little. They knew that I had gone to Virginia, and when they no longer heard from me, they thought that I had decided to stay there and make a life for myself just as my brother, Andrea, had done. I know this because, a few years ago, I traveled to Sicily and went to visit them."

"So they were right. You did decide to stay in Virginia."

"But not because I wanted to, Sera. There was an accident—in the coal mines. One day when I was excavating with the other miners, the mine collapsed."

"Yes, that is one fact about your time in Virginia that I know about. You see, Salvatore, after not receiving any communication from you in over a month, the thought occurred to me that perhaps something had happened to you in the mines. After much investigating, my father learned that the mine where you had been working collapsed. But he told me that there were no survivors."

"He must have learned of the mine collapse within the first few days after the accident when they thought there were no survivors. But after five days, when they were able to reach the area where the mine gave out, they discovered one of the other miners and me alive. I was unconscious when they found me and did not wake up until a week later."

"I'm so sorry, Salvatore. It must have been horrible."

Olivia regretted her earlier stern tone with him.

"Well, it would have been more horrible if I had not lost consciousness, like the other surviving miner. He told me after we were rescued that he wished he were unconscious like me so he wouldn't have to wonder each day if that was the day he was going to die alone in those mines."

"So why didn't you call me after the accident to tell me you were alive, Salvatore?"

"I lost my memory, Sera. All I could remember was my name. I didn't even remember that I was in America. The doctors assured me the memory loss would be temporary. But for six agonizing months, I worked hard to try to puzzle together the lost fragments of my memory."

Olivia was crying. They were both tears of sadness for all that Salvatore had endured, but they were also tears of relief. For all these years, she'd thought that either Salvatore had died or he had abandoned her. Something in her would not believe that he was really dead when her father had given her the news of the coal mine collapse. So she had chosen to believe instead that Salvatore had willingly left her. Perhaps he had met another woman in Virginia, or the thought of returning to Sicily, where there was no assurance of work, was too much for him to bear after having regular work in America.

Salvatore gave his handkerchief to Olivia.

"*Non piangere,* Sera."

"I never believed you were really dead. I had moments when I would try to convince myself it was true, but my heart told me you were still alive. Even though my father told me the mine that had collapsed was the mine where you had been working, I made up a million excuses: you hadn't gone in to work that day; my father was given the wrong information and you worked at a different mine; you'd quit working at the mine and had decided to stay in America and find some other work; you had returned to Sicily but did not choose to find me or were living in another region; you had met another woman. Every day, I thought of a new excuse. My family was so worried about me. I hardly ate or went out with my sisters or my friends. I wouldn't even go to church or to my choir rehearsals."

"Sera, I did come back to Sicily. Once my memory was fully restored, I remembered you. Yours was actually one of the first faces I remembered. I kept seeing your face, but I could not put a name to the face or place where I had seen you. But as my memory slowly came back, your face kept haunting me. And when I knew who you were and remembered that you were waiting for me back home, I immediately returned to Sicily. I went to Matteo's house first. I was nervous about seeing you again, especially since I knew so much time had passed since you'd last heard from me. I wanted to know what to expect when I found you. Matteo told me you'd gotten married and had moved to America."

"You did keep your promise after all, then."

Olivia was still crying but could not look up into Salvatore's face. Guilt washed over her. She had not kept the vigil long enough for him even though she'd sensed he was alive.

Salvatore tipped Olivia's chin up, forcing her to look into his eyes.

"I never forgot you, Sera. Why do you think I never married?"

Olivia didn't know what to say. This poor man had almost lost his life thousands of miles away from home, only to wake up and have no memory of who he was. Then he returned home to his country only to discover the woman he'd loved had married someone else.

"I'm sorry, Salvatore. I'm so sorry."

"For what, Sera?"

"For everything. I had no right to be mad at you before."

"You thought I'd abandoned you. Of course you had every right to be mad."

"So why aren't you mad at me then? I abandoned *you*."

"Sera, *sei pazza!* Stop talking so crazy! You were told I was dead. I would not expect you to wait for a ghost!"

"But I told you. I never really believed you were dead. I should have listened to myself instead of giving in to the pressure of my family and friends telling me that I needed to move forward with my life."

"Sera, listen to me. Everything happened the way it was supposed to happen. I don't know why. Only God knows. For some reason, we were not meant to be together at that time. But we have had good lives in spite of losing each other. You met a wonderful man. Matteo assured me Nicola was a fine man who would do right by you. My other friends who either knew Nicola or knew of him through our townspeople also told me about his loyal, good character. You had three beautiful daughters with him and began a new and, from what I have heard, very prosperous business. Do not be sorry about all the blessings that you have had."

Salvatore patted Olivia's hand.

"Believe me, I have gone over in my mind how my life would have been different had I not gone to Virginia and just stayed with you in Sicily. But now I can't picture my life being any different from the way it is. And that is because of Francesca. I returned to America after discovering that you were married. I rented the upstairs apartment in the two-family house my sister owned on Long Island. If I had stayed in Sicily, I don't know if I would have received custody of Francesca after my sister and her husband died. She might have gone to her father's brother. But he was only twenty-three and not ready to take on the responsibilities of a young child. Besides, Francesca knew me from the moment she was born, and my living in the apartment above them already made me a member of her immediate family. She was accustomed to always having me around."

"So you have been happy even though you never married?"

"Yes. Francesca has given me so much to be grateful for."

"So I can't believe there was never any special woman since me."

Olivia felt her face warming up. She shouldn't have asked such an intimate question.

"There were a few nice women who were my companions. I almost came close to marriage, but none of them was special enough for me to want to marry her. I also had to take into consideration Francesca, and not all of those women were too happy about inheriting a child along with a husband."

Olivia nodded in understanding. She suddenly realized just how much Salvatore had sacrificed for his niece. She wasn't surprised. The young man she had known and fallen in love with in Sicily was very generous. She was glad to hear that he hadn't changed.

"How about you? Is there another man in your life?"

Olivia's face returned to the crimson color it had been a moment ago, only this time it felt like she was going to catch on fire.

"Of course not. How could you ask such a question?"

"I'm sorry, Sera. I did not mean to offend you. You are still an attractive woman."

This time it was Salvatore whose glance quickly shifted in another direction when Olivia looked at him in surprise.

"I'm sorry. I should not have gotten upset. What I meant to say is that I do not intend to get married again. Nicola was my husband. I will remain loyal to him and his memory."

Salvatore nodded his head, but Olivia saw a pained look in his eyes. She mentally chided herself. He was probably thinking that she could remain loyal to the memory of her dead husband, but was not able to remain loyal to the memory of her first love.

"I want you to know, Salvatore, that I met Nicola two years after I'd heard that you were dead. We were married . . ."

"Six months later. I know. Matteo told me."

Salvatore and Olivia looked into each other's eyes, and this time, neither looked away. "Life is strange—and can be cruel."

"Yes, Sera. But it can also be very wonderful. Look, here we are together again after all these years. Who would have ever thought it?"

"But you knew I was alive and well, Salvatore. And you knew I was living in America. Did you know I was living in the same state as you?"

"Yes, Matteo had told me that you were in New York. But New York is such a large city and state. And for all I knew, you and

Nicola might've eventually moved to another state or even gone back to Sicily. So many Italians I met returned to our country."

"So you never tried to look for me here?"

"I thought about it, but then I thought what good would come of it? You were married to a good man, and I did not want to disrupt your life."

"What makes you so sure you would have disrupted it?"

"I don't mean to sound arrogant. But how would that look to your husband? His wife's first lover returns from the dead and has come to find her? I know how much you loved me, Sera."

Olivia had wanted to tell him since she'd arrived at Raquel's home to stop calling her "Sera," but she couldn't. Every time Salvatore said it, a delicious warmth ran throughout her body—the same sensation she experienced all those years ago when she'd been a young girl in Sicily, falling in love for the first time. She hadn't felt that way since she'd married Nicola. "So you let me continue thinking you were dead for all these years?"

"It was for the better. You might not see that now, Sera, but in time, you will."

Olivia glanced at her watch. It was three o'clock. Two hours had elapsed like a stroke of a magic wand. She still could not believe she was sitting here across from her first love. If what Salvatore had said was true, that there was a reason why they'd been separated, then the opposite was true as well. There was a reason why fate had decided to reunite them. But at the moment, she could not imagine why. It was just a coincidence. But as soon as she thought that, Olivia, with her strong superstitious beliefs, knew very well it could not merely be a coincidence. In fact, it was after Salvatore disappeared that she had begun feeling so superstitious. She was convinced it was Maria Occhiogrosso, one of the girls in her church choir, who had placed the *malocchio* on her and Salvatore. Ironically, Maria's last name, "Occhiogrosso," means "fat eye," and her eyes seemed to bulge out of her very wide and large forehead. Olivia called her "Fat Eye" behind her back. She'd also caught Maria staring at Salvatore on several occasions and trying to flirt with him. "Fat Eye" had even told her after Salvatore disappeared that he'd probably found a rich American woman and had forgotten all about Olivia.

Olivia sighed. She hated to admit it, but Salvatore was right. If he'd found her after her marriage to Nicola, it would've been a disruption. And even now, she felt his reappearance in her life creating turmoil. She could never tell her daughters about Salvatore. With that thought, she stood up and carried their empty glasses to Raquel's dishwasher.

"I should be going. It's getting late, and I promised my children I'd be back by dinnertime. We're quite busy at the shop right now."

"Of course."

Salvatore stood up and began pacing the room again just the way he had earlier, with his arms behind him, hands interlaced, head hung down. He stopped and looked up.

"Would it be okay if I walked you back to the subway station?"

"Thank you, Salvatore, but I will be fine."

Salvatore nodded and resumed his pacing of Raquel's living room. He was encircling the Persian rug. Mr. Magoo was staring at him, but he hadn't budged from the kitchen where he knew more *Palline di Limone* awaited him. Olivia took two more cookies and placed them in Mr. Magoo's bowl. She then picked up her purse from the coffee table where she had rested it and gave Raquel's apartment one last glance to make sure everything was in its place.

"Are you ready, Salvatore?"

"Si. Andiamo."

They rode the elevator down in silence. When they stepped outside, the awkward silence continued until Olivia broke it.

"Well, I'm heading back up toward Lexington to catch the subway. Will you be taking a cab down to Penn Station to catch the Long Island Rail Road?"

"Yes, I'll catch a cab on First Avenue. Usually, I like to walk when I'm in Manhattan, no matter how far I'm going, but I'm feeling a bit more tired than usual today. So I'd better just hop into a cab."

Olivia smiled. "I'm the same way. I love Manhattan and walking around her streets forever. We used to live here, you know, but down on the Lower East Side. That neighborhood has changed since I lived there. It's much nicer now, but it still had a certain unique charm, which seems to be disappearing every day."

"I'd like to hear more about your life back then, Sera. Would it be okay if I called you again?"

"I don't know, Salvatore. This has all been a big shock for me. I'm still taking it all in. I just don't know."

"I understand. No worries. I hope you don't mind if Francesca still keeps her appointment at the bridal shop. She really has her heart set on getting a dress at your store. But if you'd rather not, I can find a way to explain to her."

"No, no, that won't be necessary. It would be my pleasure to help her."

"*Grazie*. I won't accompany her."

"That's all right, Salvatore. I could tell she wanted your approval when you first came to the shop. You have to be there. You're her only family. Just because I don't think it's a good idea for us to meet again alone doesn't mean that I can't see you with your niece at the shop. It's business, after all."

"Well, if you're sure about that, then *va bene*. I don't want to make you feel any more uncomfortable than I already have. Thank you, Sera."

"There's just one favor I have to ask of you, Salvatore."

"Of course. Anything."

"Please don't call me 'Sera' when you come to the shop. If my daughters hear, they'll be wondering what's going on."

"As you wish, Mrs. DeLuca."

Salvatore smiled. He picked up her hand and placed a kiss on it. A cab stopped in front of Raquel's building to let out a passenger. Salvatore ran up to the cab and asked the driver to wait. He waved to Olivia and called out "*Arrivederci!* I'll see you on Saturday, Mrs. DeLuca."

Hearing herself referred to as "Mrs. DeLuca" made Olivia feel matronly and all of the fifty years she now was. Before the cab pulled away, Salvatore lowered the window and waved again to Olivia. She waved back. Their eyes locked, and they continued staring at each other until the cab went down the street and was out of sight.

Pulling out her cell phone, Olivia dialed Raquel's number.

"You can come home. I'm on my way to the subway."

"No, you're not. You're having dinner with me and telling me what's going on. You didn't think I'd let you get away so easily, Olivia, did you?"

"I'm drained, Raquel. I promise I will tell you everything, but not tonight. I need some time to myself."

Raquel heaved a long sigh over the phone.

"Okay. But I am dying of suspense here. I'm coming to Astoria tomorrow, and we'll go have coffee somewhere quiet. And you're going to tell me who this man is and what all this mystery is about."

"That's fine. Just please don't breathe a word of it in front of Connie and Rita."

Olivia shut her cell phone. She took her silk scarf out of her purse and knotted it under her chin. Then, she put on her large black sunglasses. In this hot weather, she really didn't need the scarf, but she couldn't be too careful in making sure no one recognized her. The chances of running into her nosy neighbors from Astoria here in Manhattan were slim, but she'd rather be safe than sorry. As Olivia took her time making her way back up to Lexington Avenue, she thought of how she was actually looking forward to confiding in Raquel about Salvatore. She was still feeling the weight of his suddenly dropping into her life and everything he'd told her. And though Olivia was not going to admit this to Raquel, she was terrified. For her gut was telling her that things were far from over between herself and Salvatore.

❧ 20 ❧

The Real Valentina

St. Mark's Square is full of people as usual, but the fact that it's Friday only adds to the crowds. Italians from neighboring regions of Italy often spend their weekends in Venice. I am standing in front of St. Mark's Basilica, right by the front entrance, waiting for Stefano. I've chosen to wear a strapless white dress made of cotton and a touch of spandex, which is enough to accentuate all of my curves. Since it's quite warm, I opt not to throw on the melon-colored cardigan that matches my melon-colored strappy sandals. Holding my sweater is making my palms sweaty, so I drape it over my purse. There isn't a bigger turnoff on a first date than clammy hands. But this *isn't* a date, as I have to keep reminding myself. Yet repeating over and over "This is *not* a date" is useless. For tonight feels just like the other times when I've gotten ready for one.

I glance down at my cleavage and pull the top of my dress up even though this dress doesn't have a tendency to slide down like the strapless top I'd been wearing at lunch the other day. Unlike last time, my breasts are adequately covered now. Why can't I just relax and accept that it's okay to let some skin show? My hair is swept up in a loose chignon. Tendrils of hair frame my face. My eyes look sultry, shadowed in deep shades of plum and outlined with smoky eyeliner. Elongated silver hoops dangle from my ear-lobes.

My heart thumps erratically as I spot Stefano making his way to-ward St. Mark's Basilica. He seems to be engrossed in the conver-sation he's having on his cell phone and is gesturing animatedly with his free hand. Tonight, he wears the palest gray linen pants with a snug white V-neck shirt that shows off his perfect tan. V-neck shirts are his specialty, and I can see why. The shirts seem to be made for him with his bronze complexion and well-defined shoul-ders, pecs, and biceps. Just like the V-neck he'd worn yesterday, this tee has a silky texture to it, tempting me to glide my hand over the smooth fabric and feel the outline of his toned muscles. *Stop it!* I mentally chide myself. What's the matter with me? Or rather what is it about this man that evokes so many sexual fantasies? Last night, I'd even dreamed he was making love to me.

Stefano closes his phone and turns his attention to the front of the Basilica. His walk slows down a bit as he sees me. His eyes travel the full length of my body and rest at my feet. *Please, God, don't make him have a foot fetish!*

There I go again, acting as if I'm considering him boyfriend ma-terial. I take a deep breath and mentally prep myself for what this is: just an innocent outing with a guide who is used to being friendly with tourists. It's *not* a date with a sinfully delicious species of Italian male who makes every nerve in my body sing to the heav-ens and ache to be touched. *Oh no! What is he doing now?* His eyes are traveling slowly, and I mean *slowly,* back up the length of my body until they rest dead center on my eyes.

Instead of looking away, I stare right back into his eyes. Nar-rowing my own gaze as Stefano is so good at doing, I slowly run my tongue over my lower lip, and then I give him a hint of a smile. *Am I out of my mind? Yes, but I can't stop myself.*

I wave and begin walking toward him, strutting my hips as sen-sually as I can. Nothing is going to happen with him later. I'm sure of that. I'm just having a little fun. After all, I am in Venice—city of romance. Why shouldn't I flirt a little? *Because you're playing with fire.* I ignore the warning voices in my head.

"*Buona sera,* Stefano." I kiss him on both cheeks, surprising Stefano with my boldness. The surprise only lasts momentarily. His lips widen into a deep grin, and his eyes are radiant.

"*Ciao,* Valentina. You look stunning. I almost did not recognize you with your hair up. It suits you very well. You should wear it like that more often."

"*Grazie.*"

Stefano is staring at my hair as if gold is piled on top of it, and he's only just discovered this newfound wealth. His gaze then rests on my neck. Is he a vampire, and I don't know it? Hell, if vampires look this hot, they can turn me any time.

Ughhhh!!! There I go again. *Stop thinking of this man as anything other than a friend. You are not attracted to him. He's too old for you. He is just a friend. He is just a friend. I can will my mind to believe anything. He is just a friend. This is* not *a date. I repeat,* not *a date. Then why do I feel like a giddy schoolgirl who is on her first date?*

"Is something the matter, Valentina? You look upset."

"Oh no, I'm just thinking about some things that I need to do tomorrow before I can relax and see more of the city."

"*Meno male.* I was beginning to get worried you were getting sick again." He flashes a sly smile at me. *Damn him!* He's noticed the effect his presence has on me and doesn't believe for a second that I'd truly not felt well the other times I'd run into him.

Determined not to show him that he can fluster me anymore, I casually say, "I'm looking forward to our gondola ride."

Again, the look of surprise registers on Stefano's face.

"I'm happy to hear that. I am looking forward to it, too. I had a long day, so it will be nice to just relax and be in the company of such a beautiful woman."

I lock my arm in his—a common custom of Italians who are strolling about for their *passeggiattas* along the *piazzas*—and lead him away from the Basilica toward the dockside. I pretend to be looking straight ahead at the Grand Canal, but out of my peripheral vision, I can see Stefano is staring at me. He looks amused. I shouldn't be doing this. I'm teasing the man. But I can't stop myself. Some other person has taken hold of my body and is propelling my actions forward.

Stefano stops walking. "Why don't we have an aperitif before taking the gondola?"

Of course, the Italian in him has to be in charge. I won't have it.

"Better yet, why don't we purchase a bottle of wine and drink it on the gondola? You were right. I can't believe I've been in Venice for five days and have not taken a gondola yet! I just can't wait any longer."

He knows I've got him with my last sentence. *Touché!* I mentally pat my back.

Not waiting for Stefano's answer, I lead him toward the nearest shop that I know sells wine. It's common for people to take bottles of wine or Prosecco on their gondola rides.

"Okay. As you wish."

I let Stefano choose the wine. I'm not going to completely emasculate him. He buys two bottles of Prosecco.

We make our way to the dockside, where plenty of gondolas waft gently on the quiet waters. Stefano begins haggling with several *gondolieri,* who know him of course, to get the best rate. After paying, Stefano helps me board the gondola. He sits opposite me and wastes no time in opening the bottle of Prosecco with a miniature corkscrew that is attached to his key ring.

I laugh. "I see you're ready."

"I have to be. My walking tours at night sometimes include a gondola ride, and the tourists like to have a bottle of wine or Prosecco, but most of them forget they'll need a corkscrew opener."

Expertly, he pops the corkscrew and takes paper cups out of the bag that holds the Prosecco.

"I'm sorry I don't have real glasses. It's a sin to drink wine out of paper."

"Tsk . . . tsk . . . you're not as prepared as I thought. That's one point against you."

Stefano smiles. "So we're counting points now, are we? What happens when I get too many points? Or should I ask, what doesn't happen if I get too many points?"

Stefano's devilish smile returns as he pours the Prosecco into my cup.

"It's a surprise."

"Ahhh! A surprise. I like surprises."

Taking the lead once more, I toast Stefano.

"*Salute!* To your health and business. May you give tours forever."

He laughs. "I'm not sure that's such a great toast. I don't want to give tours forever. But thank you for toasting to my health. *Salute!*"

We tap our cups. I watch him. He seems to know that I have now turned the tables and am blatantly staring at him. I can tell he doesn't like to be scrutinized, but he doesn't say anything. He merely acts as if he hasn't noticed that I'm checking him out.

"So what would you like to do forever?"

"*Scusa?* What do you mean?"

"You said you don't want to give tours forever. So what would you like to do forever instead?"

"Ahhh." Stefano gestures with his hands as if to show me they're empty, and he's at a loss. "I don't know." He looks out once more across the canal.

After a few minutes have elapsed, he replies, "I always thought that maybe someday I would go back to school and get my doctorate in art history so that I could teach at university."

"That would be wonderful, Stefano! You should do it. You already are so knowledgeable on the subject, and I can tell you have a real passion for it."

"You think so?"

The usual confidence he exudes is absent. It's refreshing to see him vulnerable.

"Yes, absolutely. I can totally picture you teaching in college. You're a very social person. The students would like you immediately, and you have a way of making your lectures interesting. You don't just recite your tours like a robot. You engage your students and have them participate. Yes, I think being a college professor is your true calling."

"Perhaps."

A shadow casts over Stefano's features as he looks out over the Grand Canal.

"Why are you doubtful?"

"For one thing, I'm much older now. By the time I am finished with school, I'll be in my fifties. I would not be able to work as much while I'm in school. Essentially, I'll be starting over again. It will be difficult."

"Anything worth having in life is difficult."

"*Vero.*" Stefano sighs deeply. "I guess I have to decide how much I want it."

"You'll figure it out. I'm sure of it." I pour more Prosecco into each of our cups and raise mine in toast to him again. "To your future. Whatever you decide, may you prosper and be happy. *Salute!*"

"*Salute!*" Stefano taps my cup and laughs.

"What is it? Was my toast silly?"

"No, it was very nice. I was touched, actually. I'm just laughing because I couldn't help thinking how will my toast come true when we are drinking wine out of paper cups instead of glasses? There must be some superstition to that."

"You sound like my mother. She is the queen of superstition. I should call her and see if she knows if it's bad luck to toast out of paper cups."

Stefano is laughing so hard that he wipes tears from his eyes. "Your mother sounds like my mother. She is always screaming, '*Quella puttana mi ha dato il malocchio!*'"

Now I'm laughing just as hard as Stefano. "Yes, the mighty *malocchio,* and there always seems to be a whore, or *puttana,* attached to it! My mother is obsessed with the *malocchio.* You'd think after forty years in America, she would've forgotten about it, but no. Everything that has gone wrong in our lives is always because of some curse that someone has cast on us."

"We should get them together and listen to them speak. It would be hysterical."

"Yes, I'm sure it would. Speaking of my mother, I must ask you a question."

"Oh no. This doesn't sound too good, from the sound of your voice."

I can't help it and start laughing. I have a hard time getting the question out.

"You are killing me, Valentina!" Stefano is laughing, too.

"I think we're a little drunk already."

"If you don't ask me the question soon, I am going to have to toss you into the canal."

I hold up my hand, imploring him to give me a few seconds. Taking a huge gulp of Prosecco, I let out a deep sigh. "Do all Calabresi . . ." I pause.

"Oh no. You are about to attack my *paesani* and me. No wonder you are having such a hard time getting your question out."

"It's not me. It's something my mother thinks." I fan my hand in front of my flushed face. The wine combined with our laughter and my anxiety over my impending question has made me very warm.

"Do all Calabresi . . . wait, this will translate better in Italian. *Voglio sapere perche i Calabresi hanno le teste dure?*"

Stefano erupts into laughter once more. "I should have known you were going to ask me about the infamous hard heads of the Calabresi."

"I'm sorry. That is all I've ever heard whenever my mother talks about Calabresi. She says they are the most stubborn people she's met."

"She is right, and of course, there is a stereotype that Calabresi have *teste dure*. I don't know where it originated. *Mio padre aveva un capo tosto.* You could not convince him to do anything he didn't want to do. My poor mother! She never learned to stop wasting her time in persuading him to do anything other than what he wanted."

"Well, I think many Italians are stubborn. My mother should talk. She is one of the most stubborn people I know, and she's Sicilian."

"So if we get married, your mother will not approve of her Calabrese son-in-law."

I'm stunned by what he's just said. I smile shyly and glance down.

"I'm just kidding, Valentina!" Stefano laughs, but his laughter doesn't sound very convincing. Instead, I can tell he's using it to mask his faux pas.

"Of course!" I laugh back, reassuring him. "It's so beautiful here. How can you live in such a gorgeous place and not be in wonder every day?"

"Who says I'm not?"

I lean back, enjoying the slow gliding of our gondola as it meanders lazily through the narrow passageways. The sky has turned a dusky, sapphire blue as the city's shadows deepen and envelop us in a cocoon of darkness that feels very comforting. We both remain silent for some time, enjoying the tranquility of the ride and the serenity of the landscape. The chatting and laughter coming from the neighboring gondolas doesn't disturb us.

"Can you please pour more Prosecco for me?"

I turn toward Stefano, who is peering intently at me. His stare remains unbroken for a moment longer before he reaches for the bottle of wine. He shifts his body over so that he is now sitting next to me. The narrow space of my seat forces our hips to rub against each other. The second bottle of Prosecco runs out as Stefano pours its last contents into my cup.

"*Grazie.*"

I try to hide my face behind the cup. He's still staring at me, but now his face is inches away from mine. I can't ignore the heat that is generating from his body being so close to mine.

"I hope this doesn't make you uncomfortable."

"What makes me uncomfortable?" I play dumb.

"My staring at you so much."

"Oh. I hadn't noticed."

I take a sip of my wine and glance at the Bridge of Sighs, which we're now approaching. Of course, he knows I'm lying. But what am I supposed to say, "Yes, I've noticed you undressing me with your eyes, making love to me with your eyes, and it makes me go crazy every time I catch you doing it"?

"I'm sorry. I can't help myself, and I don't always realize I'm staring until my attention is broken. It's just . . ." Stefano pauses. "I know I keep saying this, but you truly are gorgeous."

I blush and manage to murmur a barely audible "Thank you."

"It's true. I'm not just saying that to butter you all over or however that American expression goes."

I gently say, "It's butter you up."

"Yes." He gives a dismissive wave of his hand. "I am sincere when I say you are one of the most attractive women I have ever laid eyes on. When I first saw you in front of the Basilica tonight, you completely took my breath away."

"Thank you, Stefano."

"I am making you uneasy. I'm sorry. I just can't help myself. I can tell you are not comfortable around me sometimes. And I don't want that. I want you to always feel relaxed when you're with me."

"It's okay, Stefano. You're Italian. I know Italians can't help themselves when it comes to women. And I do feel comfortable around you. So stop worrying."

I pat his hand to reassure him. Big mistake. He quickly latches on to my fingers, stroking the back of my hand with his thumb in slow circles, letting the edge of his fingernails lightly graze my skin. The waves that little motion sends throughout my body are like tidal waves, and I am hopelessly drowning. My body temperature has escalated sharply so that I'm absolutely hot now, but I'm not sure if it's from the wine or his caresses. Suddenly, I hear a voice in the back of my head screaming, *"Get away, this is dangerous!"* But I can't move. It feels too good.

I look up at Stefano. He lowers his head and kisses me. I want to die a thousand times. No, make that a million times. My body melts completely as I take in his lingering kisses. His lush lips tug gently on mine. First, he nibbles my lower lip, then my top lip. I part my lips, but he teases me for a little while until he finally covers my mouth fully with his, and our tongues wrap around each other. He then alternates between the soft kisses he started out with and the deeper thrusts of his tongue.

I've lost track of time when we finally stop kissing. Sneaking a peek at my wristwatch, I realize with a tinge of sadness that our gondola ride will be over soon. Stefano resumes stroking my hand. I need more Prosecco, but I remember it's all gone. Panic rises in me. I have to tell him. I can't lead him on anymore. I can't be the coquettish vixen I set out to be tonight. Who am I kidding? I'm Valentina DeLuca—a down-to-earth Queens girl who makes dresses and daydreams a bit too much. I'm a nice girl who doesn't like to break the rules and actually likes hanging out with her mother. *This* is the real Valentina.

And then it suddenly dawns on me. I wasn't glamorous enough for Michael. Mr. Manhattanite . . . Mr. Up-and-Coming Smith Barney Man who never said the wrong thing or was caught looking bad one day of his life. He must've realized it. He must've realized I was his complete opposite and knew there was no way marriage could work out between such opposites. Fighting back the tears my revelation has brought on, I'm only more determined now to dissuade Stefano. I swallow hard.

"Look, Stefano, although I've only known you for a few days, I can tell you're a nice person. And that's why I have to be honest with you. I'm not ready to get involved with anyone right now, not even for the last two weeks that I'll be in Venice. I'm sorry if I gave you the wrong idea."

For once, I can't read Stefano's face. Then he says, "No, I'm the one who should be apologizing. I have come on too strong. I'm sorry."

"Stefano, you have been a gentleman, but I can see where this is going, and I just can't. I'm sorry."

"It's that man you left behind in New York. The reason why you came to Venice."

I nod my head.

"What was the matter with this fool to have hurt you the way he did?"

"It's a long story."

"You don't have to tell me, Valentina."

"I should tell you some of it. Maybe then you'll understand better why it's so hard for me to get involved with anyone so soon."

Stefano leans over and places his index finger on my lips.

"Shhh. Now is not the time. I can tell you're not ready to open up to me yet. It's not important. Americans often feel compelled to let it all out when sometimes silence is better. Let's just agree to be good friends and enjoy each other's company while you're here in Venice. And I promise, I will stop telling you how beautiful you are and stop staring at you."

His tenderness amazes me. There is more to Stefano Lambrusca than his overwhelming magnetism. The air between us is fraught now with heaviness. I want to salvage what we have left of our night together. After all, Venice is a place intended for happiness. So as I always do when a situation gets too awkward, I resort to humor.

"So you're really going to stop staring at me and telling me what a hot goddess I am? You must not know a lot about women, Stefano—or at least American women. We can't hear enough how beautiful we are."

Stefano looks up at me, returning the smile I am giving him. But there is something else in his eyes. He is thanking me without uttering the words . . . thanking me for trying to make him feel comfortable. My heart starts to ache a little. But it's not the cravings of desire that I've been feeling for him. It's much more. I want to protect him from being hurt. It's crazy. I only met this man a few days ago, but I can't help feeling protective suddenly over him.

"You make me laugh a lot. I don't find that often in women. Ahhh!" Stefano slaps his forehead. "There I go again. Let me shut up before I stick my foot in my mouth. I got that right, didn't I?"

I laugh. "Yes, you got that right."

"So have I completely scared you off? I hope you will still take one of my walking tours at night. You won't regret it. And I promise I'll keep my hands—and mouth—to myself."

I laugh. "I wouldn't miss it for the world. I have to admit I am spoiled by your tours. No other tour I've taken has been as interesting as yours. So I guess I will have to suffer a few more stares from you so that I can take more of your tours."

"I guess you will." Stefano winks at me.

I can't help but think of Michael and his trademark winks. My anger starts to swell. Why shouldn't I let myself fall in love again? He was the one who ended our engagement. Why am I being loyal to his memory? Just because Michael broke my heart doesn't mean every man I meet will do the same. Why am I letting Michael make me miserable—again? I have been enjoying myself with Stefano. Why can't I just have fun for once and stop being the good girl? I should give this man a chance, even if it's just for a couple of weeks.

The temptation to revert to the saucy siren of earlier in the night returns, but I quell it by reminding myself once again who the real Valentina DeLuca is.

❧ 21 ❧

The Redeemer

My third and last week in Venice has arrived. The city is abuzz as it prepares for the Feast of the Redentore, or "Redeemer," which is held every year on the third Sunday in July. My plane is scheduled to depart for New York the day after the feast. Stefano keeps telling me how lucky I am that I will be here for the *festa*.

Dating back to the sixteenth century when a church was erected on Giudecca Island in thanks for delivering the city from a devastating epidemic, the Feast of the Redentore has been celebrated every year since. Thousands of lights are hung from the *piazzas* and terraces of homes. Over one thousand boats and gondolas are also elaborately decorated as they congregate on St. Mark's Basin. The feast reaches its pinnacle at midnight when fireworks are launched from pontoons that stretch from St. Mark's Basin and the Giudecca Canal. Venice receives at least thirty thousand visitors to witness the lavish celebration. Every Venetian I talk to assures me it is a breathtaking sight that I will never forget.

Since the night of my gondola ride with Stefano, we have spent every day together. He's tried to keep his distance. And I've tried to keep mine. But our paths keep crossing just as they had on my first few days in Venice. We've finally both given up and just started making plans to see each other every day for the rest of my time here. I look forward to the time we spend together every day, and I feel our friendship deepening. And though Stefano has promised to keep his hands and mouth to himself, neither of us can fight the overwhelming attraction we feel for each other. Before we part ways, we always end up in each other's arms, kissing as madly as we did that night on the gondola.

Tonight, Stefano and I decide to walk around the *sestiere* of Dorsoduro after having our *cena,* or supper. Though I eat a generous salad of tomatoes, onions, and olives with chunky pieces of crusty bread and blocks of salty ricotta cheese, I still have enough room for *gelato.* We're eating *gelato* topped with lots of *panna* and taking one of our long leisurely strolls, which have become a daily custom for us, when we walk by the church of Santa Maria della Salute. Though I have seen the church from San Marco and whenever I take a *vaporetto* down the Grand Canal, it's been easy for me to look away. But now that I'm standing mere feet away from the church where my wedding to Michael was supposed to take place, I can't ignore it.

"Valentina, you must see the interior of this church. If you loved Hadrian's Pantheon in Rome as much as you've told me you did, you will love Santa Maria della Salute even more."

"Maybe some other time, Stefano."

"What? This is your last week in Venice. You might not have a chance to come back. And in the past two weeks that I've known you, when have you passed up an opportunity to see any of the architectural sites I've insisted upon?"

"I'm getting overwhelmed with all the buildings I've seen. I need a break. Let's just keep walking."

Stefano scrutinizes me closely but follows me as I walk away. I keep my gaze looking forward. It's no use. I've seen enough of the church for the images of what could have been to start playing out in my mind: I arrive at the church in a white gondola decorated with ribbons and roses. My sisters carry my dress's train as we walk up the *piazza* to the church's steps. My dress. My perfect dress that I've tried so hard not to think of since my engagement ended. I don't know what I'm sadder at: my not being able to wear the dress or all the work that I put into it. It had been very much a labor of love. Every ounce of energy I had went into the creation of that gown. The design is no doubt in my mind the best I've ever come up with. The dress is perfect. I can find no flaw in it—even the shorter front hem that Michael detested so much is right.

In moments like this when Venice reminds me of my wedding that never happened, I begin to think Connie was right. Maybe I shouldn't have come here.

"Valentina, what is it?"

The tears stream down my face. I break free of Stefano's hold and walk farther away, not wanting him to see me cry.

I finally told him a few days ago about my canceled wedding that was supposed to take place here in Venice. He was amazed by my strength, as he put it, to decide to still come here. After that day, I've felt closer to Stefano. He seems even more affectionate toward me too, hugging me a lot and quietly observing me as if he's trying to understand more fully the hell I've been through.

"Is that where it was supposed to take place?"

Stefano is behind me but is giving me my space. He is whispering even though no one is standing near us.

"Why are you so perceptive?"

I turn around and force a smile, hoping my joking will stop my tears. But they keep swimming down my face.

"Oh, Valentina." He comes over and takes me in his arms. "You are so brave. So very brave."

I sob silently into his chest. Then I realize with horror that I'm probably ruining his silk V-neck shirt with my mascara-stained tears. He doesn't seem to care, and I just can't stop crying. So I let myself lean fully into him. He smells so good. And his arms feel so good. Stefano props his head against mine as he strokes my hair with one hand and rubs the small of my back with the other.

I look up at his face. His eyes hold a hunger like none I've seen before. I part my lips, hoping he'll take the cue, and boy, does he ever. He starts slowly, planting soft kisses all over my mouth as he cradles my face with both of his hands. Then he slips his tongue into my mouth. I slide my arms over his shoulders and around his neck. A very low growl escapes his lips as he entwines his tongue with mine. His hands slide down my back, cupping my bottom tightly against his pelvis. I gasp when I feel his hardness pressing against my abdomen, but the sigh is muffled by our unbreakable kiss. We continue to kiss for what seems like an eternity. Someone whistles at us, reminding us we're standing in a *piazza* with plenty of gawkers staring at us.

"*Forza!*" A *gondolieri* yells out to Stefano, making a lewd gesture with his hand.

"Ignore him." Stefano laughs. I try to laugh with him, but my tendency to easily blush wins over.

"I'm sorry, Valentina. I hope you don't think I was taking advantage of your being upset."

"Stop apologizing so much to me, Stefano. If you hadn't noticed, I was enjoying myself."

Stefano gives me a sheepish smile that lends him an attractive boyish glow. We continue our stroll. We walk with our arms wrapped around each other's backs.

"If it's anyone that should be apologizing it should be me. I'm sorry that I lost it and cried."

"Nonsense! Anytime you need to, just go ahead."

"Thank you. But I'll try not to take you up on your offer."

Stefano snaps his fingers and cries out, "Demmm!" Of course, he means "Damn," but his pronunciation is off.

"You know I'm just hoping to get more kisses like the one we just shared so I will encourage you to cry as much as possible."

"You're terrible." But I'm laughing.

The effects of that mind-blowing kiss are still with me. If our kisses are that explosive, what sparks will be set off when we make love? Suddenly, a dull ache forms at the pit of my abdomen. My head feels woozy. I look at Stefano. He seems to be somewhere else as well. Is he thinking what I'm thinking? I know that if I decide I'm ready, I will have to give him the green light.

But am I really ready? In a week, I will never see this man again. Sadness surrounds me at the thought of not seeing Stefano every day. A voice inside my head urges me on, *Sleep with him. Just do it.* But I can't just sleep with him and then leave as if it never happened. I'm a fool. It's too late. I'm in love with this man. And I'm the fool who fell in love with a man in another country whom I'll never see again. Maybe it's just the romance one can't escape in Venice. When my plane lands at JFK, I'll realize this was all just a fling in one of the most romantic cities in the world. My feelings for Stefano are nothing more than a crush. But it's not a crush. I can't lie to myself. And then I decide to just take the plunge. No more analyzing. Just do as the Italians do—live *la dolce vita*.

"Stefano, I'm feeling a little tired. Can you please escort me back to my hotel room?"

Stefano looks at me with a questioning look.

"Of course. I should head back home, too, and see if I can get some sleep before my tour this evening."

"You can take your *siesta* in my room."

My gaze locks on to Stefano's. Understanding reaches his eyes. He licks his lips and swallows hard, and then glances away.

"That's nice of you, but it's really no trouble for me to go back to Cannaregio."

I stop walking and take hold of Stefano's hands. "Stefano, I want you to stay with me. We don't have to sleep."

I smile and reach over and kiss him lightly on his lips. He's too stunned to return the kiss.

"Let's go before we miss the *vaporetto*." I lead him away.

"You are sure?"

"*Cento percento.*"

Stefano is waiting for me to join him on the terrace of my hotel room. He's seated at the tiny café-style table, enjoying a shot of Sambuca. We bought a bottle before coming up to my room—no doubt to calm our nerves. Why is it that you're always nervous before the first time you make love to someone?

Yesterday I had the whole afternoon to myself since Stefano was busy working. So I decided to finally set out to Burano to buy some lace. Stefano had warned me that since lace makers were now rare in Burano, it would be difficult to find authentic Burano lace. And even if I did find it, the lace would be very expensive. Despite his warnings, I decided to go anyway, and I'm glad I did.

The lagoon island was absolutely charming with its brightly colored houses, rows of stalls selling linen and lace, and open-air *trat-*

torias serving fish caught by Burano's many fishermen. The beautiful lace negligee I bought was worth the trip alone. At first, I resisted buying it, knowing what would happen if I did. For the teddy was too exquisite not to be worn—or seen. I didn't care that it wasn't made out of original Burano lace, and I doubted Stefano would care. I guess a part of me knew that I could not leave Venice without making love to this extraordinary man.

"Are you okay, Valentina?"

Stefano calls out to me from the terrace.

"Yes. I'm sorry it's taking me so long. I will be out in a minute."

I gently pull the negligee over my body, being extra careful not to snag the lace. I just hope Stefano will exert some restraint and not tear it off me. I tiptoe over to the terrace. Stefano is deep in thought and doesn't hear me approach.

"Want to see what I bought at Burano?"

Stefano turns to look at me. His face looks pensive. I'm about to ask him what's the matter, but his expression changes as soon as he sees my negligee.

"So that's what you were after in Burano. Not some boring lace dollies."

"Doilies, honey."

"Come here. Don't waste any time with those nonsense idioms I still can't grasp even though you've been giving me lessons. Why does your language have to be so full of them? Just say things as they are."

"A doily isn't an idiom."

"Stop correcting me, and stop keeping me waiting. Come here."

I walk into his arms.

"That's better."

I can see from his face that it truly is better having me in his arms. His eyes lose the heavy droop they'd had a moment ago, and he is smiling from ear to ear now.

He hugs me and breathes in deeply.

"Ahhh . . . That's jasmine in your perfume, isn't it? I love the scent of jasmines, especially on you."

He lowers me onto his lap and plants kisses down the side of my neck.

"We should go inside. Someone might see us."

"It's dark outside now. Don't worry, Valentina."

I glance across the alleyway. None of the lights are on in the building opposite my hotel, which houses apartments above the street-level shops. I relax against him, enjoying his musky aftershave scent.

"That's it, *mia bella donna.* Just relax."

His voice slithers out this last sentence as he snakes his tongue in and out of my ear, teasing my earlobe, then sliding down the length of my neck and back up again. At the same time, his thumb kneads my nipple through the tight lace negligee. Embroidered daisy appliqués cover my erect nipples, and sheer organza reveals the fullness of my breasts. He then uses his left thumb to play with my other nipple so that both of his fingers are now caressing me. I tilt my head, trying to catch his tongue as it slides again toward my earlobe. But Stefano is intent on tormenting me tonight. Finally, I catch his lips and waste no time in sucking his tongue, which tastes like licorice—the delicious Sambuca still lingers. I can stand the torture no longer.

"Take me, Stefano. Now."

Unlike me, Stefano is painfully patient.

Straddling him, I tug at the waistband of his jeans but freeze when I feel Stefano's teeth nibbling at my teddy's spaghetti-thin straps until he manages to grasp them and pull them off my shoulders. My breasts are completely exposed now as Stefano's tongue works feverishly on my nipples, teasing them until they resemble taut, ripe raisins. Once more I reach for his pants and manage to pull them down low enough to give me access to what I'm searching for. I stroke him slowly at first, encircling my index finger around the fullest part of him. A moan escapes his lips. In one motion, he pulls at the crotch of my teddy, which has three snaps that pop open, giving him full access. Wrapping his large hands fully around my bottom and hips, he squeezes my curves greedily before he positions me above him. Slowly, I lower myself down. We keep our gazes locked, enjoying the myriad expressions of pleasure that play out over our features. When we both can't seem to take it any longer, he is finally completely inside of me. I throw my head back and softly cry out in ecstasy. Goose bumps explode all over my body.

Stefano quickly unfastens the last ties that are holding my negligee in place and tosses it on the ground. Then he removes his shirt. His pants have collapsed in a pool around his feet, but it's too late for him to stand and rid himself completely of them. For we don't dare break our bodies' contact as we press tightly against each other, reveling in the way our skin feels. Holding each other tightly, we rock back and forth. A broken leg on the wrought-iron chair we sit on keeps tempo to our rhythm, clanging against the terrace's terracotta tiles. I reach climax first, moaning deeply into the night, not caring anymore if anyone sees or hears us.

The Feast of the Redentore does not disappoint, as the Venetians had assured me. The hundreds of lavishly adorned gondolas and boats that have descended upon St. Mark's Basin take my breath away. The *piazza* is teeming with throngs of people as we all anxiously wait for the fireworks show to begin.

Stefano has a friend who rented his boat out to us. I can only imagine how much money Stefano bribed him with to let us have the boat. At first, I thought his friend would be joining us, but Stefano surprised me as we boarded the boat by announcing we'd be alone.

"So you're leaving tomorrow."

"Yes, I am."

I've been wondering for the past few days if Stefano is going to bring up the subject of my leaving.

"How do you feel about that?"

Oh, great! He's going to lay it at my feet. Well, two can play at this game, Signor Lambrusca.

"Oh, you know, one dreads flying nowadays with all the security checkpoints and delays. I'm trying not to think about it and hoping for the best. I just can't wait to get it over with."

Stefano stares off into the distance to where the pontoons sit in the canal. Fireworks should be starting soon. He looks sad, and suddenly, I feel horrible for playing my little game with him. But I remain silent. I want to say something to take his pain away. I don't. I'm too afraid.

"Do you think you will come back to Venice someday?"

He's making this hard. Why can't he just be direct and ask me how I feel about leaving him? After all, that's what he wants to know. But what do I expect from a macho Italian god? I'm still starstruck by his good looks.

"Yes, I'm sure I will come back to Venice. I love it here."

His eyes light up.

"So you've had a good time? With me?"

Okay. Now we're getting somewhere.

"Of course I've had a good time with you. I can't thank you enough for the free tours you gave me."

The light that was in his eyes a moment ago has been replaced by the hollow look I saw earlier. What's the matter with me? The guy must think I've used him for his services. He probably thinks I've used him in bed, too. Oh no! I don't want him thinking that. But what do I say? And before I can regret it, I quickly blurt out, "I'm going to miss you."

He turns his head and looks at me. His eyes are red. Is he or was he about to cry? No, this Adonis-like specimen is too tough to cry.

"I think I'm going to miss you more, Valentina."

Now it's my turn to be rendered speechless. I search my brain to say something. A loud bang erupts into the air, causing me to jump. The fireworks have begun.

Stefano places his arms around me and for the next thirty minutes, we remain in awe of the gorgeous spectacle adorning the Venetian sky. I am so enthralled by the magnificent fireworks that I don't even notice that Stefano has left my side until I feel a gentle tug of my hand. I look down and see Stefano kneeling on the boat.

"What are you doing down there? Are you feeling all right?"

I'm shouting as I struggle to keep my voice above the fireworks' din.

Stefano shouts back at me, *"Valentina! Ti voglio bene! Mi senti? Ti voglio bene tanto! Stai con me! Stai con me per sempre."*

The noise of the fireworks is deafening, but I'm pretty sure I caught every word. Does he realize what he's saying? And then he does it. He slides onto my finger an oval-shaped, antique-looking diamond ring that sparkles as bright as the fireworks that are still lighting up the Venetian sky.

"Did you hear me, Valentina? I said I love you very much. Don't leave me. Stay with me in Venice forever."

22

Shoelaces and a Smile

Ithought I knew love when I was with Michael. But now I see how little I truly knew. And though it's just been three weeks since I've met this man, I can't deny what I'm feeling. I won't deny it. I'm tired of fighting an emotion that refuses to go away. My family, and Lord knows my neighbors back home, will think I've gone absolutely crazy. They'll say, "This is what the Carello kid has done to her—sent her into the arms of a much older man, an Italian gigolo no less, and made her think she's in love after only a few weeks." And I won't blame them for thinking that way. I would've thought the same—until now.

The love I feel for Stefano makes me want to go out and save the world. Corny, I know. But that's the only way I can describe it. I want to do more and more for him. Unlike in my relationship with Michael, I have not thought once what Stefano will offer me or do for me. And it's the same way with Stefano. He showers me with love and is always concerned for my needs.

After Stefano proposes to me, the fears that I've had about loving again vanish. Before I give him my answer, I think for a moment what my life will be like without him in New York. And that's when the real fear sets in.

In these short three weeks that I've spent with Stefano, he's become family to me. I feel as if we've always known each other. Now I can't believe he wasn't in my life prior to us meeting in Venice. So when he pops the question, it's easy for me to say yes, or *si* as I answer in Italian.

Needless to say, I don't fly back to New York the next day. How can I accept the marriage proposal of the man I love, and then fly thousands of miles away from him? Again, I just can't bear his absence in my life. Stefano admits to me that my imminent departure is what had weighed so heavily on his mind the night he'd been sitting on my terrace and before he'd proposed. He'd sensed that I felt the same way about him but had wanted to be sure. And he hadn't wanted to pressure me after all that I'd been through with Michael. He acknowledges that we're having a whirlwind romance, or as he calls it a "world romance," but he says it feels so right and he's never felt this sure of anyone before.

I call my mother the morning after my proposal to tell her that I'd missed my flight. Though I feel like I'm betraying Stefano, I'm just not ready to break the news of my sudden proposal to her. I want to enjoy my recent engagement at least for a few days before all hell breaks loose.

"Are you sure everything is okay, Valentina?"

Ma is yelling into the phone, accustomed to talking this way with her relatives in Sicily even if the party on the other line can hear her.

"Yes, everything is fine. I'm having such a good time with my new friends here that I decided to stay for another week—or two."

The truth is Stefano and I haven't decided how long I'm staying in Venice before returning to New York. I can hear his words again in my head when he'd proposed, "Stay with me in Venice forever." Actually, we haven't discussed much since after returning home from the feast. We've stayed up all night, making love and just holding each other. But I know. I'll be the one staying in Venice. My new life will be here now. And of course when I do eventually return to New York to make plans to ship my belongings to Italy, Stefano will be joining me. As I said earlier, we just can't picture being apart at all.

But I need at least a week to decide how to break the news of my engagement to my family. Right now, I just want to enjoy my happiness with Stefano without hearing my mother's warnings.

"Have you met someone?"

Darn! She knows. Why am I surprised? Sometimes I believe my mother possesses some psychic abilities. I decide playing dumb will be my best recourse.

"Of course I met someone. I told you I've met several wonderful friends here."

"Valentina DeLuca, stop acting like I am a fool. I might be getting old, but my mind is as sharp as ever. Something is not right. I can sense it."

I close my eyes and count to ten. *God, please give me strength.*

"Everything is fine, Ma. The truth is I'm not ready to return to the shop. This trip has done wonders for me. I just don't feel rested enough."

Please forgive me, God. I will have to risk Ma's full wrath at discovering her daughter has lied to her—a transgression she can't stand.

There's silence on the other end.

"Are you still there, Ma?"

"*Si, si.* I'm here. Okay, I will leave you alone. When you are ready to tell me what his name is, I will be here waiting. Have a good time. Don't worry about anything here. The intern is working out well in the shop. I'm thinking of offering her a job when she graduates from school in January."

"Really?"

This doesn't sound like my mother. She's always prided herself on keeping the business in the family, especially the seamstress and design work.

"Yes. We've gotten so busy since that article the magazine did on us. I can't be stubborn and just have your sisters and you handle the sewing. I want to cut back a bit myself. I'm getting too old."

Now my curiosity is really piqued. And I suddenly realize why Ma has let me off so easily with my true intentions for staying in Venice. She's hiding something as well.

"What's going on, Ma?"

"*Niente, niente.* Like I said, we are just getting too busy. And after so many years, I need a bit of a break. I want to enjoy life before I die. Surely, you can understand that with what you just told me about wanting to stay in Venice longer."

Hmmm . . . clever woman. She's giving me a dose of my own medicine. But I'm not giving up just yet.

"Ma, this doesn't sound like you. I can *sense* you are not leveling with me."

"*Basta!* Just trust your mother."

"So something *is* up! I knew it!"

"When you are ready to tell me what's really going on in Venice, maybe I'll tell you."

"Maybe? That's not fair!"

"I'm the parent. It *is* fair!"

After we hang up, I wonder if my sisters know what's going on. Stefano kisses me on the cheek while I'm talking to my mother and leaves for work. He's a saint. He understands about my needing time to tell my family about him. I throw a sundress on and pile my hair on top of my head, securing it with a clip, and head over to the closest Internet café to e-mail Rita and Connie.

As I walk to the Internet café, I glance down at my engagement ring from time to time, still in shock that I'm engaged again. But my heart swells every time I glance at my ring and think of Stefano. I'm so in love with him. Though I know I shouldn't, I can't help comparing how different this feels from when I was engaged to Michael. I had loved Michael. There's never been any doubt of that. But something had been missing throughout our relationship. And now I know what it was—passion. My love for Michael had started as a girlhood crush. Then he'd been there for me when Tracy had betrayed me and had me beaten up. And of course, he was there for my father's death and afterward, when I was grieving. Though he'd been the first man whom I'd made love to, I never experienced the strong desire I now feel for Stefano. I finally feel like a woman with Stefano. That's the only way I can explain it. A large part of me had always remained that childhood girl whom Michael had rescued in Mr. Li's grocery store even though my body had matured.

Suddenly, my bitterness for Michael softens a bit. He'd been ahead of me. He'd sensed that we were different in spite of our shared pasts growing up. And he'd realized that I was still the little girl he'd been protecting throughout her childhood. But out of not wanting to hurt me any more than he had, he'd withheld from telling me this. Can I finally forgive him? My mind immediately answers the question. No. I'm just not ready to pardon him for the mountain of grief he's caused me even if he'd been right in canceling our wedding. I guess my mother—or the Calabresi—aren't the only stubborn ones.

Today is a very gray, foggy day with intervals of mist. Normally, I don't mind the overcast days Venice is known for, and I'd been lucky coming here in the middle of summer, when it rains only occasionally. But for some reason today, the cloudy weather is casting a gloom over my joy of being engaged. And as I near the café, my unease grows. My mother's behavior has really bothered me.

In order to get to the Internet café, I have to pass the Parco delle Rimembranze. Stefano and I love to take some of our daily *passeggiattas* through this park, which isn't far from my hotel room in Castello. The Parco delle Rimembranze, or the Park of Remembrance, memorializes the soldiers that died in World War II. Full of immense trees and lush foliage, the park almost makes me forget that I'm in a city surrounded by water.

I arrive at the Internet café and order a double *espresso macchiato,* an *espresso* with just a drop of milk. The café's owner, Frederico, has come to know me. His nickname for me is *L'Americana,* of course.

He walks over to the bin of fresh brioches, takes one out with his tongs, and then pulls a tall glass from the shelf of just washed glasses. I hold up my hand.

"Grazie, Frederico, ma non voglio granita oggi."

"Ma quando mai lei non vuole una granita?"

"Non ho fame. Ma grazie. L'espresso basta per oggi."

"Si, si. Com'é vorrei."

I still find it amusing how Italians take personal insult when you don't want food they're offering you. To ease the pain I've inflicted, I say to Frederico, *"Prepara mi un kilo di biscotti con mandorle per mi portare con me."*

Bingo! That does the trick as Frederico's eyes light up, and he immediately gets to work taking a few *biscotti* out from his display shelf and weighing them on his scale. I overhear him say to one of the locals who is sipping *espresso* at the bar, *"L'Americana non puo resistere i miei dolci."*

He's right. Normally, I can't resist his sweets or any desserts for that matter—one thing I share in common with my sister Rita. But today, I don't have much of an appetite.

I haven't signed on to my e-mail account in over a week. My in-box is showing that I have ten unread e-mails. I'm relieved there aren't more messages than that. Stefano has been distracting me. But I must admit, I haven't wanted many reminders of home while in Venice. I scan through the subject lines of the e-mails. My stomach immediately coils into knots when I notice the first three e-mails all have urgent subject headlines.

The first one is from Aldo: *WE MUST TALK—NOW!!!*

The second e-mail is also from Aldo: *CAN'T GET THROUGH ON YOUR CELL—CALL ME ASAP!*

The third e-mail is from Rita. Though it's more subdued and isn't in bold caps like Aldo's e-mails were, the message is enough to convey urgency: *Some Bad News . . .*

I quickly scan the subject lines of the remaining e-mails and notice there are three other e-mails from both Rita and Connie imploring me to call them. They have the number of my hotel room. If they can't get through on my cell as Aldo hadn't been able to, why didn't they just call my hotel? What the hell is going on? And why didn't Ma tell me when I spoke to her this morning?

It can't be that bad if Ma hadn't mentioned it—unless this is what she's keeping from me. But no, it's not. Her secret seems to have to do with her and no one else. But still, wouldn't she have told me of any bad news that my sisters and Aldo know about? Can she possibly be in the dark about this bad news like me?

I click first on Rita's e-mail titled "Some Bad News," since it seems like I will get the most info from that e-mail, and begin reading. My heart stops. I do not believe what I'm reading even though it's staring back at me in black and white on the computer monitor.

Hey, Vee. How are you? I hope you're having a blast in Venice. I probably should have waited to tell you this when you were back in New York, but something told me I should tell you now even though Ma didn't want me to. Connie and I tried to call you, but as you've probably noticed by now from your earlier e-mails, we haven't been able to get through on your cell in the past two days. I know. You're probably calling us idiots right now for not calling you at your hotel room. But we were torn between even giving you this news now while you're in Venice trying to have a good time. But the more we thought about it, the more we thought you'd want to know in spite of everything that happened between you guys.

Okay, here it is. I hope you're sitting down. You're not going to believe this. And again, I probably shouldn't be telling you over e-mail, but . . . anyway, it's about Tracy. She died. It happened over the weekend—on Saturday. Her family hasn't made funeral arrangements yet. She had a heart attack. I know. We didn't believe it at first when Michael told us. Oh sorry. I probably shouldn't be mentioning him, but Connie and I ran into him at Anthony's Salumeria on Saturday. You know Astoria. Word spread quickly even though she died only that morning. And then yesterday Tracy's cousin Kathleen, you know the one who's buying her wedding dress from us, came by the shop for her final fitting. We were shocked that she still made the appointment. She was a mess. Of course, we convinced her to come back for the fitting when things were calmer. The poor girl. Her wedding is only a month away. She told us she'd have to find another maid of honor now that Tracy is gone. Anyway, when Michael told Connie and me, we didn't believe she'd had a heart attack. She was too young and a workout addict. That's why there aren't any funeral arrangements yet. Her family is waiting for the autopsy results to come in. Her doctor suspects she might've been born with a congenital heart problem.

God. I don't know what to say. I know you haven't—I mean, hadn't—been friends with her in years, but I thought you'd want to know. I'm sorry. Call me if you want.

Rita

My attention has been so fixed on the e-mail that I don't even notice Frederico has brought my *espresso* and left the bag of *biscotti* I asked for by my side. I take a long sip of the *espresso*. It's very strong, which is just what I need.

Rain droplets are beginning to form on the windows of the café. I just sit there for I don't know how long staring at each of the droplets as they get bigger and the rain becomes heavier. Numbness is all I can feel.

The memories come rushing back. Endless phone calls at night . . . trips with her family to Sunken Meadow Beach where she let me ride her bike as much as I wanted . . . reading in secret the book I bravely borrowed from the library on menstruation and sex . . . shopping together for our first training bras . . . double dating on our first dates behind our parents' backs . . . her lies . . . Michael kissing her in that dark alleyway . . . her having me beat up as my father lay dying . . . her coming to Sposa Rosa and asking for my forgiveness . . . my stubborn refusal to give it. And to think, it all began with shoelaces.

"Tracy, please tie Valentina's laces."

I could tell Tracy had taken great pride in being singled out by Sister Irene to tie my shoelaces. Though she's a year younger, she seemed more mature than me.

She bent down and tied my laces quickly, showing off her skill. When she was done, she smiled at me, immediately erasing my humiliation. After all, I should've known how to tie my own shoes in first grade.

"Hi, I'm Tracy."

"I'm Valentina."

"I know. Just let me know if your shoes get unlaced again." Tracy smiled tenderly at me.

And that was all it took—shoelaces and a smile—for us to become the best of friends. Who would have thought all those years ago in first grade that someday we would also become the worst of enemies?

After my father died, Tracy did feel horrible about what happened to me. She called me the morning of Baba's wake. At first, she tried to deny that she was the one who had gotten Cheryl and Lauren to beat me up. But she didn't realize that Cheryl and Lauren had told me they were beating me up because of the rumor I had supposedly started about our mutual friend Miriam and her boyfriend, Pat, being drug addicts. Tracy was the only person I had told that my neighbors all thought Pat was doing drugs because he hung out with Brett, a known drug addict. And because Miriam was dating Pat, my neighbors had also jumped to the wrong conclusion about her abusing drugs. I never thought that Miriam—or even Pat—was doing drugs. And I never told Tracy that I thought they were, but of course, she twisted my words and made it sound like I'd said it. When I told her I knew it was her because I hadn't told anyone else what my neighbors had said, she knew she couldn't deny anymore her involvement in getting my ass kicked. But even if I had told someone else, I would've still found out that it had been Tracy since everyone at school knew she got Cheryl and Lauren to beat me up. Cheryl and Lauren loved to brag after they kicked ass.

Tracy broke down crying and pleaded with me to forgive her. After a week of her calling me repeatedly, I finally caved and told her I forgave her. But they were just words. I didn't feel forgiveness in my heart toward her, and she knew it. Our friendship was never the same again. I couldn't forget what she'd done to me, and she couldn't get over her guilt. I saw it in her eyes whenever we'd run into each other. I was polite when I did see her, but little by little, I distanced myself from her. She still called me from time to time, lamenting over whoever was her current guy at the moment. I could tell, even then, that she missed me and the long phone conversations we'd had since we were in grade school. I listened but never really offered much. Once I started college, I stopped returning her calls. She finally got the hint. Though we lived in the same neighborhood, fortunately for me I never ran into her again until she came to Sposa Rosa with her cousin a few months ago.

Tracy had done more damage to me than just the physical injuries I'd suffered at Cheryl's and Lauren's hands. For she made it hard for me to trust, and though I formed friendships with other women, I never completely let my guard down around them.

Tracy had been my best friend. She'd made me laugh, and we'd had the best time just being girls as we grew up. The old Tracy I'd known was young, innocent, and looking to be loved.

That was it. She was looking to be loved—by her mother, who doled out discipline with a belt . . . by her father, who was emotionally distant . . . by the cool kids whose inner circle she always strove to be in . . . by all the boys she dated . . . even by me. But she'd had my love. Why couldn't she do right by me as I had done by her? Why had she betrayed me so many times? Maybe she'd felt that she didn't deserve my love or friendship so she hurt me before I could hurt her. After all, if the one person who was supposed to share the closest bond with her—her mother—could make her feel unloved, how was she supposed to give and receive love?

And with that last thought, I finally understood Tracy.

❦ 23 ❦

Sleeping Beauty

It's strange being back in New York after being gone for almost a month. A fine mist is coming down as my plane lands at JFK. Every time I fly back from overseas, the weather at home is overcast, matching my sad mood that my trip is over. But now, I'm down for reasons other than vacation being over.

I had decided to fly back home for Tracy's funeral. Stefano couldn't understand why I felt compelled to pay my respects to a former friend who had betrayed me so much. My family and Aldo were also shocked by my decision. But what disturbed them more was when I told them that I needed to finally forgive her. This would be a very small way for me to do so, as I had explained to Stefano.

"It's time I let go of what she did all those years ago. I've never really left it behind."

Stefano hugged me. "*Va bene*. Go. Do what you have to do. I'll be in New York in a week and a half. I can't wait to meet my future mother-in-law who thinks so highly of Calabresi." Stefano smiled at me. He knew just the right moment to make me laugh when I needed it most.

"I can't wait for you to meet them and my best friend, Aldo. I also can't wait to show you my city. Oh—and take you to all the museums!"

Stefano drove me to the airport the following day. We kissed about ten times or more before we parted. Tears were streaming down my face. He looked just as sad but tried to conceal it.

"Stop crying! I'm flying to New York in just ten days!"

"It's going to feel like forever!"

I finally smiled through my tears and blew a kiss to him. He blew one back to me and then crossed his arms over his chest.

"You'll be right here until I see you again."

I copied him and crossed my arms over my chest. "You're in my heart, too."

We kissed one last time, before I finally walked toward the security lines. I kept looking over my shoulder. Stefano stood there waving and smiling until I was out of sight.

Just thinking about my fiancé makes me tingle all over. I catch my smile in the rearview mirror of the taxi that's driving me to Astoria. But instead of going directly home, I decide to visit Tracy's mother first.

The cab pulls up in front of the two-story brick house that is mostly obscured by azalea bushes. Tracy's mother, Mrs. Santana, has a green thumb, but she takes it overboard. The little garden in front of her house is teeming with flowers and foliage. Gargantuan sunflowers tower over the little wrought-iron fence as if they know they don't really belong in such a tiny garden and are trying to escape. A rose trellis stands at the center, vying to be noticed. Tomato and zucchini plants occupy the back of the garden, along with basil, mint, sage, and thyme plants.

Weathered statues of dwarves and gargoyles that Mrs. Santana had first placed alongside the porch steps when Tracy and I were in grade school still sit in their same location. I walk through the enormous gate of Tracy's house, another element that seems out of place and should belong instead in front of a mansion. The rain starts coming down heavier, and a gust of wind blows the numerous wind chimes that hang at random spots in the garden and on the porch.

Lifting my luggage up the steps, I notice the lights are out in the house. Maybe Mrs. Santana isn't home. Maybe this isn't such a good idea. But just as I'm having this thought, the front door opens.

"Valentina! I thought that was you. I was in my sunroom, watering my plants, when I noticed the taxi out front. I didn't recognize you right away. I thought whoever it was had the wrong house, especially when I saw your luggage. It's good to see you. I'm sure you heard?"

"Yes, Mrs. Santana. I'm so sorry. I don't know what to say. I was in Italy when my sisters gave me the news. I just came straight from the airport. If this is a bad time, I can come back."

"No, no. Please come in. My husband needed to get out for a bit. He's been beside himself and so restless since this happened. I'm all alone."

The weight of her last sentence seems to have struck with her. Her eyes get this faraway look. Just when I think Mrs. Santana is handling Tracy's death with amazing calmness, I see she's not.

I follow Mrs. Santana into her kitchen, and although I insist I am fine, she still decides to brew a fresh pot of coffee. I suppose it helps to keep busy. Her kitchen looks as immaculately clean as it always has. Her hands are shaking as she measures the heaping teaspoons of coffee. Adjusting to the time zone difference and now with that strong coffee Mrs. Santana is making, there's no doubt that I'll be up all night. But I don't say anything.

"It's really so kind of you to come here, Valentina. You've always been my favorite of Tracy's friends. I don't know if you ever knew that."

"Actually, yes, I did. Tracy told me that you and Mr. Santana approved of me."

"Oh, we did, especially in high school when she began to hang out with some of those other characters. I guess I can understand why the two of you grew apart. You always had a good head on your shoulders and would never get yourself mixed up with such trash. But not Tracy."

Mrs. Santana gets that faraway look from earlier again.

"Well, she was young, and a lot of young kids rebel."

"But *you* didn't."

"I wasn't like most typical teenagers. You really can't go by me, Mrs. Santana."

"Yes, I can. Why couldn't Tracy be more like you? Maybe if she were, things would've ended differently."

"Mrs. Santana, go easy on Tracy. It's tough figuring out who you are, especially when you're a teen."

"I only ever had one wish for that girl, and she couldn't manage to do that."

Suddenly, I can see why Tracy had so many issues. Her mother is super-critical and tough to please. No wonder it had been so easy for Tracy to abuse our friendship. How could I have expected her to be more compassionate toward me when her own mother showed so little compassion for her, even now after her death? I suddenly remember the numerous beatings Tracy had suffered at her mother's hands.

"Just one wish. God couldn't even give me that. It's not like I ever asked Him for much."

Mrs. Santana's voice is filled with anger and bitterness.

"May I ask what that wish was, Mrs. Santana?"

"I only wanted her to find a decent boy and get married. You think I didn't know about all those boys she ran around with in high school and all through her twenties? She tried to hide it from me, but I'm not blind—or deaf. I was so humiliated hearing all the gossip about her in the neighborhood. People would think they were talking low enough when they'd see me picking my produce at Top Tomato, but I would always hear every one of their ugly words about my daughter. No matter what, she was still *my* daughter."

Tears fill Mrs. Santana's eyes. I guess she does have some compassion after all.

"But you're right, Valentina. I shouldn't be so hard on her. She was finally beginning to get on the right path. About a year ago, the boys disappeared. She was either alone running in Astoria Park or going to the cafés on 30th Avenue with a few of her girlfriends from the hair salon where she worked. I asked her if she was planning on dropping another surprise on me. I thought maybe she had become a lesbian since I only saw her hanging out with girls now. She told me she was taking a long break from guys, but that she hadn't become a lesbian. I was relieved to hear that, and I was also glad that she wasn't dating a string of guys at the same time anymore. But I told her she shouldn't take too long of a break from dating. Her biological clock was ticking, after all. She needed to think about finding a good man to settle down with. And she did. Though at first, I was mad about whom she'd chosen."

Mrs. Santana brings over my mug of coffee and sits down opposite me at her kitchen table. She takes a long sip of her coffee.

I wait, dying to know if it's anyone I know. But Mrs. Santana has gone quiet. The poor woman's brain must be on overload with all that's happening.

"Who was Tracy dating, Mrs. Santana?"

She jumps. "Oh, I'm sorry. My mind seems to be wandering all over the place. It was Snake God."

"Snake God?" I'm shocked.

"Yes, yes. I couldn't believe it either when she told me. But then it seemed to make sense given the rebellious nature Tracy had displayed since she was in high school. I just thought the girl would never change. This is who she was. But Snake God, I mean, Brandon, ended up being a pleasure. He wasn't the same cocky young man carrying around that stupid python anymore."

Everyone in Astoria called Brandon McKenzie Snake God because of his penchant for walking around the neighborhood shirtless and keeping Monty, his six-foot python, coiled around his neck. Instead of minding the nickname, he loved it. And it was no wonder. He actually seemed to think he was God the way he paraded around town with his tanned muscled body. Snake God's best assets were his toned arms, pecs, and washboard abs—and of course Monty, which he used to attract girls. Michael had once told me that Snake God used to say, "Monty's a chick magnet, dude." But I couldn't see it since most girls I knew were terrified of snakes. I always thought Snake God was probably compensating for his lack of, how should I put it? Manly measurements.

"I guess Tracy didn't mind Monty?"

"Oh, I guess you hadn't heard. Monty died about a month before Tracy started dating Brandon. He was so upset. Tracy saw him sitting on a bench in Astoria Park one day and crying. Can you imagine macho Snake God crying?"

"No, I can't."

"Neither could I when Tracy told me the story, but she said he was blubbering like a little boy who'd just discovered Santa wasn't real. Anyway, Brandon was just sitting there crying in public, not caring if anyone saw him or what that would do to his macho image. Tracy was on her daily run through the park and walked over to Brandon when she saw him crying. And from that point on, they were inseparable. Tracy helped him overcome Monty's loss."

"Wow." I can't help noting the sarcasm in my voice even though I hadn't intended to sound sarcastic. This is all just too bizarre, even for Tracy. I still cannot picture her with Snake God.

Mrs. Santana stands up and goes over to the fridge. She takes a picture off the front.

"Here's a picture of the two of them this past summer in the Florida Everglades. It was a dream of Brandon's to go there, and he asked Tracy to go with him."

I look at the photo magnet. Snake God *has* changed. Though still muscular, he isn't sporting the obnoxiously pumped-up muscles I'd remembered. He no longer shaves his head. His hair is now long enough to show its sandy blond color and tousled curls. He has his arm around Tracy, and they're both smiling. Tracy looks different, too. Her hair is still very long, but she's wearing very little makeup, taking about five years off her age and giving her a more innocent look. I don't think I'd ever seen her look this pretty before, even though she's wearing a baseball cap and a tee that says *Snakes Rule*. There's a glow in her face and eyes that I'd never seen. She looks happy. And then it suddenly dawns on me that I'd never really seen her happy.

"What does Brandon do for work?"

"He's a construction worker. Makes really good money, too. Of course, I had hoped Tracy would've married a professional, someone with a fancy desk job, but after what that girl put me through, I was just happy she found a nice boy who she was crazy about. You know she'd never brought any boy home to meet me? Bran-

don was the first one." Mrs. Santana shakes her head. "Tracy was
smart. She might not have had the school grades, but she had common sense smarts." Mrs. Santana points at her head as if I don't
know what she means.

"She knew all those other boys were garbage and weren't good
enough for her to bring home. That's why she waited. And she was
right. I just know they would have gotten married if she hadn't—"

Mrs. Santana breaks down crying. I pat her hand, feeling helpless.

"I'm sorry. I still can't believe she's gone. For all the trouble she
gave me in her younger years, I still would have her that way if it
meant she could be alive. Sure, I was so ecstatic that she seemed to
be finally growing up and calming down. But now, she's gone. It's
as if she wasn't meant to be good or have some good in her life."

"Oh, don't say that, Mrs. Santana. Think of it this way. She was
happy the last few months of her life. I've never seen Tracy look the
way she does in this picture. Isn't it better that she experienced real
love and happiness, even if it was just for a short time? It would
have been worse if she died and didn't get a chance to have some
happiness in her life."

"That's true. That's true. Oh!"

Mrs. Santana sniffles, rubbing her eyes with the backs of her
hands. "I tend to look at the negative too much, I guess. Tracy always told me that. Well, it is what it is. God wanted it this way, and
I can't do anything about it. But it would have been nice if I
could've just seen my only daughter getting married."

Mrs. Santana goes back into a trance again. I don't want to intrude on her thoughts or time any longer. This is harder than I'd
thought it would be.

"I should get going, Mrs. Santana. I just wanted to tell you in
person how sorry I am and to let you know that if you need anything, please just call me." I scribble my cell number down on an
old business card I find in my wallet. As I hand it over to Mrs. Santana, I notice the front of the card. It's Michael's business card from
Smith Barney. I thought I had thrown all those out.

"Thank you, Valentina. Who knows? Maybe if Tracy were still

alive, the two of you would have picked up your friendship again. Ahhh . . ." Mrs. Santana shakes her head.

I've always wondered if she'd known what Tracy had done to me. I assumed she did. After all, several people in the neighborhood had seen my bloodied face, including Paulie Parlatone, who would have wasted no time recounting every detail to whomever he ran into. Maybe she does know but is too embarrassed to bring it up. It's not important now.

Mrs. Santana hugs me for a long time before I let myself out of her house. As I walk out, I notice a framed photograph of Tracy hanging on the wall. Tracy must've been no more than six years old, the same age she was when I'd first met her and she had tied my shoelaces. Though she's smiling in the picture, her eyes seem so sad. Had I misunderstood my childhood best friend all those years? She'd failed me, but I can't help wondering if perhaps I had failed her, too.

Instead of going home that night, I decide to go to Sposa Rosa. I call my family so they won't be worried and tell them I've decided to stop at Aldo's, and if they're too tired, they should just go to bed and not wait up for me. We'll see each other and catch up in the morning. Of course, Ma isn't too happy to hear that I want to see Aldo before her. Then, I text Aldo.

> HEY! NEED A FAVE. MY FAMILY THINKS I'M
> HANGING WITH YOU RIGHT NOW. COVER 4
> ME IF MY SISTERS CALL U.

> WHAT R U UP 2?!!

I ignore his last text. Aldo knows that eventually I'll tell him. Of course, he will find some way to get me back for not immediately replying.

It's almost nine p.m. We close at seven p.m. except on Fridays and Saturdays when we close at eight. Since it's only Wednesday, the store has now been closed for almost two hours. I don't have to worry about Ma or my sisters working late since I know they've been anxious to see me and hear about Venice. Guilt stabs my heart that I've lied to them and am keeping them waiting. But I need to do something first before I can go home.

On the walk over to Sposa Rosa from Tracy's house, I can't get her out of my mind. I had hoped that I would have found some resolution by visiting Mrs. Santana, but instead I feel worse, especially after hearing about the new leaf that Tracy had turned over. I'm glad she had been dating someone seriously and had stopped going from guy to guy. But hearing what Mrs. Santana had said about Tracy never having her chance to get married has really struck a chord with me. Of course, I can relate only too well.

I let myself into the shop, but before I walk in, I look at what's featured in the display. My eyes open wide. All three mannequins are wearing PINK! I'm gone only a month, and my mom takes over. I can see one of the display mannequins wearing pink, which is becoming more popular with brides who don't want to wear the traditional white, but to have three mannequins wearing pink is absurd and cheesy, especially since our shop's name is Pink Bride in Italian. Also, we never display three mannequins. It's always just one mannequin to promote our Featured Bride of the Month. I can't wait to hear how this all came about when I get home.

I enter the shop with some trepidation, fearing what other changes I might find. But from what I can tell everything else seems to be the same. I've missed the shop tremendously since I've been gone even though I've tried not to think about it, hoping to obliterate all reminders of weddings and Michael.

After taking off my coat, I head over to the back of the shop. I'm finally ready to see my wedding dress since my engagement to Michael ended. But the dress isn't where I'd left it. That's right. I now remember that when I returned to the shop for the first time after Michael broke up with me, the dress hadn't been in its usual place in the sewing room. I didn't question it then since I was a zombie and the last thing I wanted to see was the dress. My mother or sisters must've hidden it before I came into Sposa Rosa that day.

After searching for almost fifteen minutes, I start wondering if they've sold the dress. But no, they wouldn't have done that without consulting with me first. Then again, I never thought they would've changed the model we were following for our display window without consulting me first either. If there's anything I've learned about my family, they can be quite unpredictable.

Finally, I find the dress covered in a garment bag and hanging in our supply closet. My heart starts to pound as I zip open the black garment bag. Great choice. Instead of using one of the translucent garment bags we normally keep our dress samples in, my family had even thought to bring a black garment bag from home to completely conceal my dress in case I went into the supply closet.

Tears come into my eyes. The dress is as beautiful as I remember it. Suddenly, a thought begins taking shape in my mind. I think about it a little while longer before I make up my mind.

Tracy's wake is scheduled for Friday evening, and her funeral will be held on Saturday morning. The autopsy has been performed, and the results will be in next week. It seems as if everyone in Astoria is at the wake, which surprises and angers me. I remember all the nasty gossip everyone spread about Tracy when we were in high school. Even though much of it was true, it still bothers me to see so many hypocrites now at her wake.

But wakes are very sacred for Catholics, especially Italians, and whatever ill feelings people might've had for the deceased while he or she was living, that must all be put aside. Paying respect to the dead and their family is above all else.

Who am I to talk? Aren't I a hypocrite, too? I wasn't able to forgive Tracy when she showed up with her cousin at Sposa Rosa, and here I am.

Ma, Rita, and Connie decide to come to the wake with me, but since the shop closes at eight, we don't arrive until an hour after the viewing hours have begun. As soon as we step into the room where Tracy's body is in repose, everyone's eyes turn to me. I can feel my face burning.

"Why is everyone looking at you, Vee? Sure everyone knows what Tracy did to you, but come on? You're not a cold-blooded bitch without feelings," Rita says.

I silently laugh to myself. My family thinks I am this sweet saint incapable of malice when what I really am is a person who held a grudge for fourteen years and couldn't forgive her childhood best friend.

"Silenzio!" The Sicilian Gestapo that is my mother shuts up Rita. "You do *not* speak ill of the dead at a wake! Tracy was just a young girl when that unfortunate thing happened. She was lost and confused. We must remember we are all sinners."

Rita glances at Connie when she knows Ma isn't looking and rolls her eyes. My mother seems to be taking Tracy's death harder than I thought she would. She has been fighting off tears since we walked into the room. The viewing line is long and wraps all the way to the back of the room. We must have at least twenty people ahead of us. Ma pats her eyes with a white lace handkerchief that she told me has been in her family since her grandmother got married.

"Are you okay, Ma? Maybe you should sit down. You can go up after the line gets shorter."

"Sto bene. Don't worry, Valentina." She gives me a brief smile. Then she returns her attention to the front of the viewing room. I follow her gaze, which seems to rest on Tracy's casket. Sometimes I wish I were a tiny fly, such as a gnat, and could fly into my mother's ear and go straight to her thoughts. For one never really knows what Olivia DeLuca is thinking about.

Olivia knows she, too, is a hypocrite, since how many times did she call that girl *puttana* in her head and blame her for giving Valentina the *malocchio?* She even blamed Tracy's *malocchio* for Valentina's broken engagement. Olivia is ashamed. She has not been acting the way Christ would want her to. And what about all that nonsense over the years of going to the psychic so she could burn candles to protect Olivia and her family from the evil eye? Yes, Olivia thought she would never say this, but she is beginning to lose her faith in the *malocchio*.

She can't stop glancing over at Tracy even though she can barely make out the body with all the people waiting to pay their respects to her. All she can see is the girl's long dark hair, and her face—her very pale face. Tears begin forming in Olivia's eyes again. It's not fair. She was so young, and she finally seemed to be straightening her life out by finding love with that Snake Boy. Strange boy, but everyone has his or her soul mate. She'd seen Tracy and the boy a few times walking hand in hand on Ditmars Boulevard. She recognized that look in both of their faces. They were in love. She'd known that feeling with Nicola—and Salvatore. Tracy would probably have gotten married to the Snake Boy if she hadn't died. And who cast the *malocchio* on Tracy? Not her Valentina. She wasn't capable of hurting an ant, or was it a fly? Even after forty years of being in America, she still got confused with all these sayings they had here. Why couldn't Americans just talk plainly? She sighed.

Yes, it was true. Many people had not liked Tracy because of her loose ways, but she doubted people cared that much to place a curse on her. It was just God's will. Olivia also remembered the last time she saw Tracy. She was in her car outside of the shop, waiting for her cousin Kathleen, who was having one of her dress fittings. Olivia had no idea Tracy was double-parked in front of the shop. She'd gone over to spray the windows with Windex when she saw Tracy looking at her. As soon as Tracy noticed that Olivia had seen her, she quickly looked down at her purse and pretended she was looking for something in it. Olivia knew Tracy still carried the weight of what she'd done to Valentina all those years ago. Olivia should have gone out to her and asked her to wait in the shop. That would have been not only the polite thing to do but also the Christian thing to do. Yet her stubbornness refused to let her budge. Like Valentina, she hadn't forgiven the girl and didn't know if she ever could. Her thoughts are broken as she sees they are finally getting closer to Tracy's body.

As Rita, Connie, Ma, and I make our way toward Tracy's casket, we hear the guests whispering how beautiful Tracy looks.

"Rita's right, Vee. People are taking one look at Tracy and then looking right at you."

Mrs. Santana is sitting in the front row with her husband. I still can't imagine how they must feel, losing their only child. Tracy's uncle has his five children present, including Kathleen, who had come into Sposa Rosa to buy her wedding dress with Tracy. She is sobbing uncontrollably. It's obvious they all loved Tracy very much.

When Mrs. Santana sees me, she gets up and takes me in her arms.

"I know I thanked you already, but I have to thank you again. You don't know how much this means to me." I look into Mrs. Santana's eyes and just nod my head.

Ma, Rita, and Connie shoot questioning glances in my direction.

Mrs. Santana embraces my family and thanks them, too. They say, "You're welcome," even though they have no idea what they are being thanked for.

When they take their place in line again, Connie whispers, "*What* is going on, Vee?"

I know she'll get her answer in a moment.

Rita gasps as she comes into view of Tracy. I then hear Ma murmur a *"Dio mio."*

They all look at me, just the way everyone else has after seeing Tracy.

I'm frozen in place, staring at Tracy. The tears I could not shed when I had first learned of Tracy's death flow freely now. The funeral parlor has done an amazing job. I know everyone says that at wakes, but in this case, it really is true. Her long jet-black locks have been lightly curled. Her makeup is not too heavy and gives her a pinkish glow, as if life is still beating within her. Bobby pins with rhinestones in the shape of a flower are placed randomly on the crown of her head. A ruby-red rosary is wrapped around Tracy's clasped hands. Her face looks very peaceful, and her trademark, bow-shaped lips look like they're slightly puckered as if they're waiting to be kissed.

Though her coloring has always lent itself more toward Snow White, the image of Sleeping Beauty waiting for her prince to wake her up with a kiss comes to mind.

But for all the great work that the funeral home makeup artist has done, what really makes Tracy look beautiful is her dress. She is wearing a wedding dress, but not just any wedding dress. It's *my* wedding dress.

That was the revelation I had at Sposa Rosa the other night. I couldn't get Mrs. Santana's words out of my mind about never seeing her daughter get married. Never seeing her dream—or her daughter's—come true.

I had felt her pain and knew it only too well with my first broken engagement, but now I was getting another chance at happiness with Stefano. Tracy would never have that second chance.

I know I could have donated one of the hundreds of dress samples our shop carries, but I felt that wouldn't be enough. I wanted Tracy to have something that had once meant a lot to me, something that I had loved. For after all, Tracy's friendship had once meant a lot to me, and I had loved her before she hurt me. By my giving her my own wedding dress, I hoped she would know wherever her spirit now was that I had finally forgiven her.

So that night at the shop, I worked feverishly to make a few alterations to the dress. First, I dropped the hem and couldn't help thinking of Michael. Maybe he'd had a point after all about making the gown long? I then cut the halter straps of the gown and used some of the sheer lace I'd bought at Burano to cover the neckline of the dress. I also created sleeves out of the same lace so that the dress was no longer strapless. It would be more appropriate for a funeral yet maintain the beauty of a wedding dress. I wasn't worried about the dress fitting Tracy since she was much thinner than me, and the caretakers at the funeral home could clip the dress in the back to take it in. The dress looked as if it had been made for her. It fit perfectly.

I kneel down to say a prayer and look at the gold chain around Tracy's neck. A small charm in the shape of a snake hangs from it. Snake God must've given it to Tracy. I notice him sitting in the front row with Tracy's family. His eyes are bloodshot.

My mother is kneeling next to me and has been whispering my name, but I've been too wrapped up in my thoughts to hear her until she touches my shoulder.

"That was very generous what you did. We know how much that dress meant to you."

"It felt right, Ma. I hope you're not upset."

"How can I be? I have the most amazing woman for a daughter.

Seeing what you did for Tracy and her mother only makes me love you more. Now let's go. We're holding up the viewing line." My mother places her arm in mine as she leads me away. I glance over at Mrs. Santana and can't help but think how much different her relationship with Tracy was compared to my relationship with my mother. I don't doubt that Mrs. Santana had loved Tracy, but the way she loved her might've been the only way she'd known how.

My family and I sit down in the last few remaining seats at the back of the viewing room. People seated around us lean over and tell me, "That was so generous of you giving Tracy's mother one of Sposa Rosa's wedding dresses."

The guests have no idea that the wedding dress was my own. That secret would remain with my family and me—and Tracy.

∽ 24 ∽

A Revelation

Tracy is buried the next day at St. Michael's Cemetery. The throngs of guests that were present at the wake aren't at the funeral Mass or at the burial. Just Tracy's family, Snake God, and a few friends are in attendance. I'm there alone. Ma, Rita, and Connie had to work.

Long-stemmed white roses are handed out to the guests to throw over her casket after it's lowered into the ground. After I throw my rose, I whisper to Tracy, "I'm sorry. Please forgive me wherever you are. And please remember the good times of our friendship."

I walk away and head toward my car. I'm not going to wait until the dirt is thrown over her casket. That's too much to bear.

"Valentina."

I turn around.

"Michael."

We stare awkwardly at each other. Michael finally breaks the silence.

"I wasn't able to make it to the wake."

I nod my head. "I didn't see you at the church."

"I was standing at the back."

"My sisters told me the two of you had become friendly."

I know Michael picks up on what I'm implying. I can't help myself. Of course I've been wondering if at some point Michael and Tracy had resumed where they left off that night when I saw them making out in the alleyway.

"A little bit. I started running a couple of months ago so I would see her at the park. We just talked."

I nod my head again. I'm beginning to feel like one of those bobble-head dolls.

"I heard you still went to Venice."

"You heard correctly."

"I hope it wasn't too hard."

I want to laugh, but I don't. Of course, all the wrong things are coming out of Michael's mouth. I feel my engagement ring resting against my breastbone. Knowing it's there gives me some added strength in talking to Michael. I had slipped the ring off my finger on the plane back to New York and transferred it to the chain around my neck so that I could keep it concealed under my shirt. Once I tell my family the news of my engagement to Stefano, I can wear the ring on my finger again.

"Venice was all I expected it to be and more. I actually extended my trip to another week, but then I heard about Tracy and decided to fly back for the funeral."

It's Michael's turn to nod his head.

"You know, Valentina, no one would've blamed you if you stayed in Venice and didn't attend Tracy's wake. Everyone was quite shocked that you went. I heard about the dress you donated. That was very kind of you."

"It wasn't just *any* wedding dress, Michael. It was my wedding dress."

Michael's eyes widen in shock.

"Are you crazy?"

I laugh. "I wouldn't expect you to understand, Michael, plus I don't owe you any explanations over what I decided to do with my wedding dress. I suppose I can't call it my wedding dress, though, since the wedding never happened."

A flash of pain shoots through Michael's eyes. I turn around and walk to my car.

"Wait, Vee! I'm sorry. I was just thrown by that news."

I ignore him as I insert my key into my car's door.

"Please, Valentina. Just another minute."

Michael places his hand on my shoulder. I look down at it, and he quickly withdraws it.

"I'm sorry, Michael. I really need to be going. Just please do me a favor."

"Of course, Vee. You know I would do anything for you."

Anything—except marry me, that is.

"Don't tell anyone that it was my wedding dress Tracy was wearing. Except for you and my family, no one else knows. I don't need the gossip mill revolving around me—*again.*"

Once more Michael's face looks hurt. Naturally, he knows I'm referring to the gossip mill of our broken engagement.

Hanging his head low, he softly says, "You got it."

"Thanks."

I get into my car and quickly back out of the lot. I can't resist glancing in my rearview mirror before I exit the cemetery's gates. Michael has turned around and is walking away, still looking down at the ground. He's changed since I last saw him. His confidence seems to have vanished. And he's even aged a bit. There are lines around his eyes that didn't used to be there.

I chide myself for telling him about the dress. But in that moment, I just wanted to hurt him. And from his reaction, I can tell I succeeded. Who would ever think I had it in me? But I don't feel good about it like I'd always envisioned I would. Since the broken engagement, I've had fantasies of getting him back and hurting him just as much as he'd hurt me.

Haven't I learned anything from Tracy's death? How can I truly move forward in my new life with Stefano if I'm still holding on to this baggage with Michael? Maybe Michael is right. Maybe I should've stayed in Venice.

I let out a long sigh and wonder what Stefano is doing at this moment. I glance at my watch. Eleven a.m., which means it's five p.m. Italian time. He's probably waking up from his *siesta.* I feel an ache in my heart and wish I were lying next to him in bed right now. I drive back home and take my own *siesta.*

* * *

A week has passed since Tracy's funeral. Stefano is scheduled to arrive in New York on Wednesday, just two days away. And I still haven't told my family about him or our engagement. I can't wait any longer. I need to give them at least a couple of days to digest the news. I suddenly feel like a big coward and selfish. I should've told them last week. Two days is hardly enough time to get them used to the idea that I have not only fallen in love with a man—a much older man—from overseas but that I am also engaged.

I suppose I've been waiting because I know there is something I must do before I can make my announcement. Since running into Michael at the cemetery, I haven't been able to stop thinking about our meeting.

Instead of going home after work that night, I walk over to Michael's parents' house. Connie mentioned to me that Paulie Parlatone told her Michael had moved back in with his parents this past weekend. I didn't believe it when I heard it, but Connie said she drove by Michael's street yesterday and saw him carrying luggage into the house. Strange. Did he lose his high-powered Smith Barney job? Maybe that was why he looked so dejected walking away in the cemetery's parking lot that day.

Of course, I have no assurances that Michael will be home, and I haven't called ahead of my visit. I'll just take my chances. The larger part of me knows, however, that if I don't do this now, I might chicken out and never do it.

I ring the bell. My heart is pounding.

The door opens. I'm expecting it to be Michael, as if he's the only one who lives here, but instead Mrs. Carello opens the door.

"Valentina? Hello. How are you?"

Mrs. Carello looks embarrassed and nervous.

"Hello, Mrs. Carello. I'm sorry for dropping by like this. I should've called, but I was walking by and just thought I'd stop by quickly."

"You don't need to call ahead of time. You are always welcome here, Valentina."

Mrs. Carello smiles but again she looks very nervous. I see her glance over her shoulder.

"Actually, Mrs. Carello, I'd heard that Michael was staying here. He wouldn't be around, by any chance? I wanted to talk to him."

Surprise registers in Mrs. Carello's face and then something else. Is it hope?

"Yes, he's here. Come in."

I walk in and smell garlic and oregano. Mr. Carello is walking out of the kitchen with a platter of London broil. He stops short when he sees me.

"Valentina."

"Hello, Mr. Carello. How are you? I'm so sorry. I'm disturbing your dinner."

"That's okay. Ahhh . . . would you like to join us?"

He exchanges glances with Mrs. Carello, and now he's the one who looks nervous.

"Valentina wants to speak to Michael."

"Oh. I'll go get him. Please have a seat, Valentina."

Mr. Carello places the platter of London broil on the dining room table and turns to leave, but just as he does so, a little boy of about six or seven years old runs out from the back, giggling.

I turn to Mrs. Carello. "I'm sorry. I didn't realize you had company."

But before Mrs. Carello, whose face looks absolutely ashen now, can respond, Michael comes running out and screaming, "I'm going to get you." He freezes in his tracks when he sees me.

"Valentina."

"She's here to see you, Michael."

Mrs. Carello looks like she's going to cry. What is going on? Obviously, I have not come at a good time.

"I'm sorry. I should have called. I can come back another time."

I turn to leave, but Michael is by my side in a split second.

"No, that's okay. We can talk."

The little boy is staring at me shyly and smiling. I smile back. Michael had loads of cousins, most of whom had married in their early twenties. Maybe the Carellos were babysitting for one of them?

Mr. Carello says, "We'll go for a walk with Ivan so the two of you can have some time alone to talk. Let me just place the London broil back in the oven to stay warm."

"Ivan?" What Italians would call their kid Ivan?

After the Carellos leave, Michael asks me, "Do you want a soda or some wine?"

"Actually, just a glass of water is fine."

"I hope you don't mind if I have something a little stronger."

I wave dismissively to Michael, letting him know I don't care what he drinks.

I sit down on the plush couch in the living room.

Michael comes out with what looks like Scotch in his glass, and offers me a tall glass of water, filled to the brim with ice. Only three months apart, and he's already forgotten that I don't like a lot of ice in my drinks. But I merely thank him and take a sip.

"Who's the little boy?"

"That's Ivan."

"So I heard. Is he one of your cousins' kids? I know I didn't meet all of your cousins, but I think I would've remembered an Ivan. That's an unusual name for Italians to call their kids."

"No, he's not any of my cousins' kids. Look, Valentina. There's no easy way to say this so I'm just going to say it. Ivan is my son."

I feel the blood drain from my face. His son?

"What? You're joking, right?"

Michael shakes his head.

"This is what I wanted to talk to you about that day at the cemetery. I wanted to tell you. I knew it would only be a matter of time before you and everyone else in the neighborhood found out, especially since Ivan and I are staying at my parents' for the remainder of the summer."

"Oh, how noble of you to want to tell me right before all of Astoria found out! How about telling me when you first found out you had a son? How about telling me when you broke off our engagement?" I let out a disgusted sigh and turn my back to him. I feel the tears welling up in my eyes.

"I'm sorry, Valentina. That's all I can say. I wish I had acted differently. I wish I could take it all back and do it right."

"Who is the mother?" I still have my back turned to him.

"It's this girl I was seeing when I was in business school in Germany."

"Oh."

It's silent once more. So he was dating someone while he was in Munich. No wonder he'd stopped e-mailing me. I can tell Michael knows I'm adding two and two.

"Germany. Hence the name Ivan," is all I can say.

"Yes."

"How long have you known about him? Did you know when we were together?" I turn around. I want to see the look in his eyes when he answers.

Michael stares at his Scotch. He takes a quick gulp.

"I found out a couple of weeks before we broke up."

So that's how he chooses to see it. "We broke up." I laugh out loud. It's a cruel laugh, one I've never heard escape from my throat before. "You're still choosing to think our breakup was a mutual decision. When are you going to own up to your responsibility, Michael? You walked out on me!" The rage I've been trying to quell finally bursts, and I'm shouting now at full force.

"You were right that day, Valentina. There was more than my just getting cold feet and not being ready for marriage. Finding out about Ivan was the real reason why I ended our engagement."

"Why didn't you tell me?"

"I thought about it. I swear. I did. But I didn't know how to drop this bomb on the woman I was about to marry. It would be unfair for me to do that to you."

"Unfair? You don't think it was unfair keeping the truth from me? You think it was fair that I didn't know the real reason why the man I'd known, or thought I'd known, since I was a kid was breaking my heart so badly? I blamed myself! Do you know that? I thought I wasn't sophisticated enough for you and that you had realized that and couldn't be with me forever, knowing the vast differences between us."

"It wasn't you, Valentina. I'm sorry. It was all me. I tried to tell you that, but you didn't believe me, and rightly so since there was more to my ending our relationship."

"This girl in Germany. Ivan's mother. So that's why you stopped e-mailing me when I was in college. It wasn't just that you'd gotten too busy with business school as you said when you came back to New York."

"I didn't know how to tell you I was seeing someone else, and since we weren't officially dating yet, I didn't think I was compelled to tell you."

"You led me on, Michael."

" I know now I was wrong for not leveling with you and telling you that I was dating someone, but I was afraid of losing you. I was afraid if you knew that I was dating someone, even though it was casual, you wouldn't wait for me and would meet someone else. Yes, that was selfish of me."

"Very."

"I've made a mess of things."

"All those years, Michael. All those years that we knew each other from the time we were kids, and you didn't trust me enough to tell me that you had a son. I guess you didn't know me that well either, huh?"

"In my heart, I sensed you would accept Ivan, but I was also aware it would be a different life than what you had envisioned for us when you accepted my marriage proposal. I also couldn't deal with the news that I was suddenly a father. And I had no idea how my life would change. I just knew it definitely would and that I needed to take responsibility for my son."

"You pushed me away, Michael. You pushed me away when you should've been turning to me for support and love. You chose to distance yourself from me—even before you found out about Ivan. You're still lying to me and to yourself! God, you can't even be honest with yourself! Don't make it sound like Ivan is the only reason why you ended our engagement. I noticed you were alienating yourself well before you knew about your son. Ivan was just a convenient excuse. You don't want to be the bad guy. You think by telling me that you didn't want to shock me and that it would be unfair of you to expect me to accept your son that will make you less guilty. Just admit it, Michael! You had mixed feelings about getting married. You had doubts about me! Just say it!"

The pain is back. The pain I haven't felt since that day when

Michael broke up with me. I think this hurts more—knowing he kept such a huge secret from me and felt like he couldn't depend on me during the difficult time he was going through. And now, his refusing to still level with me completely hurts like hell.

"I'm sorry, Valentina. I know I have hurt you so much."

"You have no idea how much you hurt me. But I think more than anything else is the disappointment I feel in you. I expected so much more from you." I look into Michael's eyes as I say this.

Tears quickly fill his eyes, and I can see the muscles in his jaw lock tightly. I don't think I've ever seen him close to tears before. It's sad that it's taken a moment like this for me to see some valid emotion coming from him.

Taking a deep breath, I try to calm down. "Why did Ivan's mother wait so long to tell you?"

Michael walks a few steps away from me, looking out his parents' living room window. "Helena—Ivan's mother—and I had lost touch before I left Germany so she didn't have my address or phone number in the States. I got a new cell number, too, when I returned home. She found out she was pregnant about a month and a half after I left Germany. She got married about two years later and forgot all about me until she joined Facebook. She saw my picture on a mutual classmate's page and friended me. We e-mailed for a week or so, and then she told me she wanted to talk to me on the phone. She had to tell me something. So when we talked, Helena told me about Ivan. She said the guilt she felt over the years that I didn't know I had a son always bothered her. She also felt guilty that Ivan would never know who his real father was. Helena told me that if I didn't want to be a part of the boy's life that would be my decision. But she knew she couldn't live with herself if she'd never given me the chance."

"She sounds like a good person. Not many women would see it that way."

"Yes. She's done a wonderful job of raising Ivan. And from what she's told me about Ivan's stepfather, he's treated him as if he were his own son. That's a huge relief to me." He turns back around and finishes off the last of his Scotch. "So I went to Germany after we broke up to meet Ivan."

"That's where you were. People in town thought you were in hiding from the shame of what you'd done."

Michael laughs. "Well, if I had stayed in New York, they would have been right. I probably wouldn't have stepped out until late at night or very early in the morning.

"I was in Germany for a month. Things went very well while I was visiting, so Helena decided Ivan could come stay with me for the rest of the summer. Her husband had a business trip in Manhattan so he flew with Ivan to New York last week. I'll take Ivan back to Germany at the end of August."

It's quiet for what seems like an eternity. Neither of us is looking at the other. My mind is still trying to come to terms with the shock of learning Michael has a son. I struggle to think of what to say next. Part of me wants to unleash more fury on him while another part of me is just spent. I give in to the latter feeling. "Well, I'm happy for you that you found out after all these years that you have a son. I hope everything works out for you and Ivan. I should get going. Your parents will probably be back soon."

I stand up to leave, but Michael reaches for my hand.

"Wait, Vee. I can tell you're still mad at me, and you have every right to be. I can't defend my actions. I know I acted abominably and selfishly. But I have changed in the past few months. Ivan has touched off something in me. I know. That sounds corny, but it's true. He's helped me to see the world through his eyes and not just through my own. I know this is a lot to ask of you, Vee. But maybe someday we can be friends again."

I know Michael is not just asking me to be friends. I can see the look of hope; it's the same expression Mrs. Carello had earlier in the night. They're both hoping I will forgive him and have a change of heart and return to him. Seeing this in his eyes just saddens me more. Although I am still so mad that he couldn't trust me with the news of his son and that he couldn't admit that he'd had doubts about me, I can't help but pity him as well in this moment. But unlike Michael, I will be honest.

"Too much has happened between us, Michael. I don't know if we can ever be friends again. I don't hate you, and I suppose a part of me will always care about you. I'll never forget how you were there for me when my father was dying and after he died. You're a special part of my childhood and past. And I can't hate that or regret it. But you're not the only one who has changed, Michael. You see, I've met someone else."

I wait a few seconds, letting the enormity of this news sink in with Michael. He looks very sad and older than his thirty-four years. In the course of a week, I've managed to hurt him yet again. But this time, I hadn't intended to hurt him. I just needed to be fully honest with him, something he couldn't do for me when he broke off our engagement.

"I'm sorry, Michael. Good luck with everything. Ivan is a beautiful boy."

I pull my arm from his grip. As I'm about to walk out the door, Michael asks in a hoarse whisper, "Are you happy, Valentina?"

I pause. Without turning around, I say, "Yes, I am."

I step outside and quietly close the door behind me. Walking away from Michael's house, the burden that I've been carrying since we broke up finally lifts. I take off my necklace, sliding my engagement ring off the chain and restoring it to its proper resting place—my ring finger on my left hand.

✧ 25 ✧

Past Lives

Olivia was taking a stroll in Astoria Park. The last time she had allowed herself this simple pleasure was probably more than a year ago. The past year had been Sposa Rosa's busiest yet, and though she was happy at how much the business was prospering, she was also the most fatigued she'd ever been. The scare she'd had with finding that cyst in her breast had made her take a hard look at what she wanted out of her life now that she was getting older. Olivia knew she could not keep going at this frenetic pace without her health being affected down the road.

Though Olivia had loved being a seamstress, her aching bones every morning when she got out of bed were a reminder of how physically demanding the work was. And forget about her eyes. She was now wearing bifocals and couldn't go anywhere without her eyeglasses. Her vanity still prevented her from wearing the lenses when out in public. Even at Sposa Rosa, she took them off when she was greeting clients. Olivia did love having her own business and working with her daughters. She was blessed to have had each of her children take an interest in the shop. But she also knew the time would come when they would want to spread their wings and venture on to their own enterprise, whatever that might be. This

young generation was not like hers. They got easily bored and always wanted more. Olivia shook her head. She'd never fully understand them. Then again, she supposed her children would never
completely understand her either.

All Olivia knew was that she wanted the business to remain in
the DeLuca family. She supposed she could take a less active role in
the actual seamstress work involved and assume more of a supervi-
sory role. That way, she'd still be involved in the day-to-day opera-
tions of the shop and could ensure that the same high level of
attention was paid to the design and sewing of the gowns when she
hired other seamstresses. As she'd told Valentina, their intern,
Melanie, had proved to be a fast learner, and Olivia could tell the
girl had a genuine passion for the work. She'd made up her mind
that upon Melanie's graduation she would offer her a full-time job.
Last week, Melanie had brought to the shop two friends of hers
from school who had expressed an interest in interning at Sposa
Rosa. They had beautiful names—Samantha and Megan. Olivia
talked to them for a little while and could tell the girls would be serious about their work as Melanie had been. They also both expressed an interest in becoming dress designers. Samantha was
interested in evening wear and hoped someday to be able to take
her skill to Hollywood, where she could design glamorous gowns
for the actors attending the Oscars. Megan was interested in designing wedding gowns.

So tonight, Olivia would talk to Rita, Connie, and Valentina,
and tell them that she was interested in bringing on Samantha and
Megan as interns in hopes that she could hire them as full-time
seamstresses when they were done with school. She knew that
when she would break the news to her daughters that she needed
to start working less, they would become worried and ask her if
everything was okay with her health. Olivia was nervous, but she
decided she would tell them about the benign cyst that she'd had.
Of course, they would be furious with her for having kept it a secret for so long, but it was time to come clean with her daughters
and make them understand that she needed to slow down.

"*Buon giorno,* Olivia."

Olivia looked up and saw Salvatore walking toward her, waving excitedly. He was holding a copy of *La Corriere della Sera* under his arm, and a Styrofoam cup of coffee.

"*Buon giorno,* Salvatore. What are you doing here?"

"Ha! The same thing you probably are doing—enjoying this beautiful day."

Olivia blushed. "*Scusa.* I just meant you are far from your home. I'm sure there are parks in Long Island that are much closer for you to travel to than Astoria Park."

"I'm just teasing you. I drove Francesca to Sposa Rosa for her dress fitting. She had to wait because we got there much earlier than her appointment, and Francesca knows how fidgety I can get when I have to wait anywhere for longer than ten minutes so she suggested I go for a walk."

"That's right. I almost forgot that Francesca had her last dress fitting today. I'm sorry I was not there. I should go so I can help her."

Salvatore placed his hand on Olivia's shoulder. "*Non c'è bisogno. Tutt' è bene.* Connie told Francesca she already knew all the alterations that you were making on her dress, and she could help her. Stay. Talk to me for a little bit." Salvatore walked over to one of the park benches that overlooked the East River and Triborough Bridge.

Olivia hesitated. Even though she'd become accustomed to seeing Salvatore escort Francesca to the shop for her fittings, she was still a little uncomfortable around him. She slowly followed him to the bench and sat down, making sure to keep a good amount of space between them.

"I'll stay for a little bit. I have a lot of work to do."

Salvatore smiled. "I see you are one hundred percent American now."

Olivia's anger flared. "What do you mean by that?"

Salvatore held up his hand. "It's okay, Sera. *Scusa,* I mean Olivia. All I'm saying is that you are a hard worker."

"And that's a bad thing?"

"Of course not. I am impressed with all you have done with your business. Without your hard work, you would not have had the success you have with your shop. But you seem to have the same illness the Americans have—you work too much and leave little time to relax. That's all." Salvatore shrugged his shoulders. For some reason this action irritated Olivia more. It was as if he was belittling her. She wanted to give him a piece of her mind, but he'd managed to leave her speechless.

"I can see I have upset you. That was not my wish." Salvatore removed the lid from his cup and took a sip, then offered the cup to Olivia.

"No, *grazie*." Olivia felt her face flush once more. She could not believe the nerve of this man, offering her a sip of his coffee—an intimate gesture, as if they were married. They were in love once before, but that gave him no right to think he could take such liberties with her. Again, she struggled to search for the appropriate response that would put him in his place, but she was at a loss for words. So she merely clasped her hands in her lap and stared at a freight liner ship that was slowly making its way across the river.

"Olivia, I know how difficult this all must be for you. I wish it was not like that. I know we can no longer return to what we had so many years ago. We are both different people. But I had hoped that maybe we could become friends."

Olivia glanced sideways at Salvatore. He, too, was following the movements of the freight liner ship.

"We are friends."

"No, we're not, Olivia. You are polite toward me when I come to the shop. Francesca and I are just your clients. If we were friends, you would have introduced me to your daughters. You—"

"I have introduced you to my daughters!" Olivia snapped.

Salvatore shook his head. "You did not let me finish. You would have introduced me to your daughters as an old friend of yours from Sicily."

"I told you that day in Manhattan, Salvatore, that I was not ready to explain all of this to my daughters."

"I know. And I understood. I am not saying that you need to tell them that we were romantically involved."

Olivia pursed her lips tightly, trying to repress her anger. Her heart was racing now. "Then what would I have said? Ah? 'This is

Salvatore, an old friend of mine from Sicily who I thought was dead but showed up alive and well one day in my own shop'? You do not know my daughters. They ask lots of questions."

"Ha! Don't all women? Francesca has asked me a million questions since she was a child. I thought she would outgrow it, but no!"

Olivia couldn't help but laugh, picturing a tiny Francesca grilling her uncle and still doing it now. She took a deep breath. "I'm sorry, Salvatore. I never meant to make you feel bad. I just am afraid of what my daughters would think of me."

"Why? You did nothing wrong. Do you really think they expect you not to have had a life before you met your husband?"

"Yes! That's how it was in our time. Most women, even all of my sisters, married the first man they met."

"But it was not like that for everyone. It is not like you were seeing me and Nicola at the same time."

Olivia's cheeks stung. This man had a way of always embarrassing her.

"I suppose you are right. I am being foolish."

"It is up to you, Olivia. I am not going to force you to be my friend if you don't want to. It's just that there's something comforting about having people in your life who knew you when you were young. I no longer have that. All of my relatives, even the few who I left behind in Sicily, have passed away. And my childhood friends are all in Sicily."

Olivia thought of her sisters and the friends she'd left behind in Sicily. While she had grown to love America and considered it more her home now, there were times she, too, missed having people in her life who had known her when she was young.

"I can understand that. I still miss my sisters sometimes terribly, and I don't get to visit them too often with the demands of my shop. Sometimes, I have to think really hard to remember the girl I once was. It's as if that was a different person, a different life. My daughter, Connie, is very spiritual. She is a good Catholic girl, but she has such a big, open heart and has taken an interest in learning about religions from around the world. She does yoga and rarely lets herself get too upset—unlike me or my other daughters who are known for our quick tempers! She takes after her father a lot.

Nicola was very quiet, and it took a lot to anger him. Don't get me wrong. He was not a saint! And when he did get mad, watch out! But he was better than me at remaining calm. He took the time to think before reacting. Anyway, I overheard Connie talking to her sisters one day at the shop, and she was saying how the Cherokee Indians believe that each stage of our lives—childhood, adolescence, adulthood, and old age—is a different life, almost like a reincarnation. I couldn't help thinking how true that was, and it made me think of how different my life is now compared to when I was a young girl singing at the top of a cliff in Tindari." Olivia fought back the tears in her eyes. She missed that young girl. Salvatore was right. She worked too hard. That was why she'd gotten mad at him earlier. He'd touched on the truth, and she knew it. Olivia looked at Salvatore, who also looked sad.

"You know, Salvatore, it's funny that we are having this conversation. I was thinking as I was walking through the park that I'm tired, and I need to start working less. I am going to tell my daughters tonight. I have already made plans to hire a full-time seamstress and bring on two new interns. I think I need to find that girl who wasn't so serious all the time. Will you help me? After all, you knew that girl."

Salvatore remained silent for a few seconds, leaving Olivia hanging. "So I guess you are saying that we *will* become friends?"

Olivia arched her right eyebrow before answering, "Let's take it one step at a time. Olivia DeLuca does not make quick decisions." But a small smile danced along her lips.

❦ 26 ❦

Bella Fortuna

Four months have passed. It is the first weekend in November—and the morning of my wedding to Stefano. Though I had set my alarm clock to seven o'clock, a rooster from one of the neighbors' houses in Castello wakes me up an hour earlier.

Yes, I am back in *La Serenissima*. And here in this magical, fairytale city, I will marry Stefano. Though I was supposed to marry Michael in Venice, I don't care. For I no longer think of my failed engagement when I think of this magical city. Instead, Venice evokes memories of Stefano and the special times we shared here as we fell in love. Stefano asked me if I was sure and told me we could get married anywhere—even in New York. But *La Serenissima* is where I want to take my vows.

Naturally, my family was stunned when they learned that I had not only fallen in love with an older Italian man, but had also become engaged to him. Their fears were put to rest when Stefano arrived in New York. Charmer that he is, he came to my house with huge bouquets of flowers for my mother and sisters. All Rita could whisper to me when we were alone in the kitchen getting dinner ready was, "He's so sexy. And the way his eyes keep following you. He is completely head over heels in love with you."

Connie thought he looked like an Italian version of Richard Gere. "Does he have any brothers or a son, given his older age?"

Ma had taken me aside after Stefano left that first night and asked me, "Are you sure you're over Michael, Valentina? It's only been a few months since the two of you broke up."

"Yes, Ma. I loved Michael. But the love I feel for Stefano overwhelms what I felt for Michael. I had a few doubts before Michael broke up with me. I thought it was just normal pre-wedding jitters. But I see now it wasn't. Stefano is the man I want to spend the rest of my life with. I'm certain of it. You would think I'd be nervous since this is all happening so fast. But I feel like I've known him my entire life. It's hard for me to imagine he was never a part of my past. He feels like family already. When I left him behind in Italy to attend Tracy's funeral, I felt like I was leaving behind half of my heart. Now that we're reunited again, I no longer feel incomplete. I don't know if any of this makes sense to you, Ma."

"It does. I felt this way for a man once, long before I met your father."

I was stunned to hear this confession from my mother.

"It's a long, complicated story. Please don't ask me to go into it, Valentina. All I will say is that he disappeared from my life suddenly. I didn't feel right. Like you just described, I felt like a part of me had gone with him. It wasn't until I met your father that I felt whole again and like I could move on with my life. And just like you, my love for your father was greater than for that other man."

I was dying to know more about this first love of my mother's, but out of respect for her wishes and privacy, I refrained from asking her questions.

"So you do understand."

Ma nodded her head and placed her hand over mine. "I'm so happy for you, Valentina. When we talked on the phone before you came to New York for Tracy's funeral, I knew you'd met a man and were not just hanging out with 'friends,' as you kept saying. I heard the happiness in your voice. And then when you came home, the glow of being in love was all over your face. He seems like a good man—even though he's from Calabria." But Ma winked at me.

So with my family's blessing, we immediately began planning my wedding. I was surprised that a few of my neighbors in Astoria had decided to come since most of them weren't going to attend my first-planned wedding to Michael. It touched me and showed me how much they cared about me. Connie told me that so many of the neighbors were heartbroken for me when Michael had ended our engagement.

I didn't even mind this time around that Paulie Parlatone has flown to Venice for the wedding. Italy seems to be doing wonders for him since he is behaving like the utmost gentleman, and last night, after our rehearsal dinner, he hadn't reached over once for the toothpicks.

Of course, Antoniella is among the guests. Since she was making my cake for the first wedding, she was one of the few neighbors who had planned to attend originally. Naturally, Antoniella assumed she'd also be making my cake for this wedding. I never asked her. She called me one day and told me she had a few new ideas for this cake. Clever woman that she is, she knew I'd want a different design from the one I had originally chosen. I had given a lot of input on the design of my first cake. To show my gratitude to Antoniella, I'm letting her fully design this second cake, which has pleased her immensely. She won't unveil the design until I see it at my reception. I still can't believe that I have surrendered complete control to Antoniella. And I can't help reflecting on how much I've changed. Stefano has altered my perceptions and has helped me to see what truly matters.

Signora Tesca has decided to attend as well. During the rehearsal dinner, she took me aside and gave me a stunning brooch that featured an aquamarine gemstone.

"I asked your mother and sisters if it would be all right if I gave you your 'something blue' piece to wear on your wedding day. You don't have to wear this if it does not go with your gown, but I thought maybe you could keep it in your purse or pin it to your undergarments for good luck."

Tears filled my eyes, and once again, I was amazed at Signora Tesca's generosity, just as I'd been when she threw my bridal shower at the Mussolini Mansion. Suddenly, I was saddened that I would be leaving Astoria and would not be able to continue my friendship with her, especially now that it seemed we were getting closer. There was so much about this reclusive woman that I'd always longed to know more about. Finally, I was seeing cracks in her sturdy exterior that were giving me glimpses into her personality and showing me what a kind woman she was.

"I'd be honored to wear the brooch, and it's too beautiful to wear under my dress. I'm going to pin it to the sash that wraps around my bouquet."

Signora Tesca's eyes lit up, pleased no doubt that I would be prominently displaying her brooch. "That would be lovely, Valentina."

"May I ask where you got the brooch?"

Signora Tesca glanced down. I started to regret asking the question, although my curiosity was now piqued.

"My sister gave it to me when I got married."

I didn't know Signora Tesca had a sister. Then again, there was little I, or anyone else in Astoria, knew about her. All we'd known was that she was a wealthy widow and had a grown son who visited her occasionally. No one even knew how her husband had died. She was already widowed when she moved to my block when I was a child. Oh, and of course, I knew about her baby girl whom she'd told me had died in infancy.

"Thank you, Signora Tesca. I'll be sure to have my mother return it to you after the wedding."

"You can keep it."

"Oh no, I couldn't! This must mean a lot to you."

"It did once, but I have my memories." Signora Tesca smiled, but it was a sad smile.

"I wouldn't feel right keeping it, Signora Tesca. You've already been so generous to me."

Signora Tesca patted my cheek. "If your mother or sisters don't give you something borrowed, then you can return it to me. This will count as something blue and something borrowed."

"Well, that sounds fair enough." I hugged Signora Tesca.

Betsy Offenheimer wanted to come, but she didn't trust leaving Mitzy with anyone. "She has special needs, you know. I'm afraid she'll get hurt. You have to be very careful walking a blind dog," Betsy explained when telling me why she wouldn't be able to attend. I assured her I understood.

We all were staying at La Residenza, the same hotel I had stayed in over the summer. Stefano's parents and sister, Angela, had arrived from Calabria a week before the wedding. They were staying with Stefano at his apartment in Cannaregio. A few members of his extended family would also be attending the wedding.

Stefano's mother got along instantly with my mother. Signore Lambrusca was as charming as his son, and I could tell he'd been a looker when he was young. And Angela immediately set about making me feel like the older sister she never had. I felt truly blessed to be getting such a wonderful set of in-laws.

Since I had much less time to plan this wedding, I'd decided I wasn't going to make myself crazy designing this dress as I had with my first one. I've come to realize that though the wedding dress is still very important, what really counts is my love for Stefano. I had placed too much emphasis on creating the perfect gown for my wedding to Michael. No wonder I had begun doubting my first dress's silhouette. Looking back now, I see so many of my insecurities over my dress and the wedding were signs telling me I wasn't sure about Michael.

Michael hadn't truly known or trusted me to realize that I would've taken the news of his son much better than he thought I would've. Without a doubt, I would have accepted his son, and my feelings for Michael wouldn't have changed. But he had known me enough to know that my first wedding dress was not me. I had gone against my preference for classic and elegant styles and instead designed a dress that was daring and fashion forward. Even my family had been surprised when they first saw the gown. Had Connie designed the dress with her love for trends and always striving to be one step ahead of the fashion world, it would've seemed natural to everyone.

So for my wedding to Stefano, I've decided to stay true to myself. Using the lace I had purchased at Burano, I covered my dress from top to bottom in it. The silhouette I chose for this gown is a modified mermaid, which isn't as body hugging as a traditional mermaid gown. It shows just enough of my curves without screaming over-the-top sexy. While I love the fuller skirt of a ball gown or an A-line silhouette, and it complements my more classic fashion tastes, I didn't think it would be practical to have a huge dress to come across the canal in a gondola. Also, my first gown had been a ball gown, and I wanted this dress to be different. Though a mermaid dress, the skirt flares out below my hips and stays flared out with four rows of tiered lace. A thin band of jewels wraps around the bodice, right below my chest, and in the center of the band, an elongated cluster of jewels sits. The bodice is strapless with a slight scoop in the center, and its top is slightly pointed over each breast. I had enough lace to make a bolero jacket to cover my shoulders for the ceremony inside the church. The dress is a blend of classic, romantic, and modern. It's definitely me.

My hair is styled in a sideswept chignon. I place a crystal-studded comb just above the chignon, and a fingertip-length veil is tucked underneath my updo. I'd sewn the same lace from the dress around the edges of the veil. Except for diamond-studded earrings and my engagement ring, I wear no other jewelry.

Rita, Connie, Angela, and Ma help me get ready. Surprisingly, Ma hasn't shed a tear, but Rita and Connie can't stop weeping.

"Come on, guys! Enough already!"

"You just look so gorgeous, Valentina. I didn't think you could outdo your first gown. You look so elegant. I can't find anything to criticize."

"Well, that's a first, Rita!"

I smile at Rita. She and Connie look beautiful in their deep plum maid-of-honor dresses. Rita, Connie, and I had co-designed the dresses, which feature a mermaid silhouette to go with my gown. But their dresses fit the lines of their bodies more than mine does. The bodice of their gowns is shirred at the waist and hips, and the fabric is gathered to the side where a crystal brooch is displayed. The neckline is a sweetheart and is covered in lace. But unlike my strapless gown, their dresses sport cap sleeves that are also covered in the same lace as the neckline.

"*Stai ferma, Valentina.*"

Angela is applying my makeup, and at the moment, she's carefully brushing mascara on to my upper lashes. Her makeup is always impeccable so I know I can trust her skills. She'd been touched when I had asked her to do my makeup for the wedding.

Angela is also my bridesmaid. Her dress is a paler shade of purple than my sisters'. Instead of the sweetheart neckline, her dress covers her chest and is shirred from the waist through to her collarbone. Only the upper back of the dress features lace, and it's scooped out to reveal her beautiful bronzed skin. I'm not worried about her showing too much skin in church since her hair is so long. She wears it pulled back in a ponytail so that her back isn't exposed during the ceremony. At the reception, she can adjust the ponytail so that it hangs to the side and will be draped over her left shoulder, revealing the sexy back of her dress.

"Pose for me, Valentina. I'm going to blow up one of these photos to an eleven by fourteen and display it in the shop." Connie is pointing her iPhone at me.

"I'll pose for you, but I'm not so sure I want my photo in the shop."

"*Perche no?* It will be good advertising. I am sure when customers see one of the owners in her own wedding dress, and one as exquisite as this one, they'll want to buy this dress."

"That's exactly why, Ma! I don't want anyone else to have my wedding gown design."

"Bridezilla comes out!" Rita laughs.

Connie quickly comes to my defense. "She's right, Ma. Come on! We're the DeLuca girls, masters of the fine art of designing and creating wedding dresses. No one can have our dresses."

"Yeah, it's like we're royalty." Rita curtsies toward me. I break out laughing.

"*Va bene.* I see what you girls mean. But I think it's a shame not to display this dress. We can tell people it's a design we no longer create."

"Ma, how long have you been in this business, yet you still don't know that the word no is impossible to say to a Bridezilla? They'll just ask you to replicate a dress that is as similar as possible or insist on making this dress."

Ma throws up her hands in resignation. "Okay, okay, Valentina. You have me beat. I give up."

There's a knock at the door. We all call out, "Come in!"

"Buon giorno, Signorina DeLuca. I tuoi fiore."

"Ahh, si. Entra, per favore."

I quickly walk over to examine my flowers. My bouquet contains all white cymbidium orchids. I had purchased crystal bobby pins that matched the crystals in my hair comb and asked the florist to scatter them throughout my bouquet. The stems are wrapped with a deep plum sash to go with the color of my bridal party's dresses. I walk over to the night table in my hotel room and take out Signora Tesca's brooch and fasten it to my bouquet. Rita, Connie, and Angela's bouquets are much smaller than mine and also feature white cymbidium orchids, but theirs do not contain the crystal bobby pins.

Ma wears an exquisite pale green gown, and her corsage holds two cymbidium orchids and two of the same crystal bobby pins that are in my bouquet.

"Hey, why didn't we get the crystal pins?" Rita balks.

"Because you are not her mother. That's why."

Ma nods her head once emphatically and looks at herself in the armoire's mirrors, admiring her sparkly corsage.

"Hello? Is the bride ready?" Aldo holds my hotel suite's door slightly ajar. "Why are you getting ready with your door open?"

"The florist must've left it open on his way out, and we were too busy admiring our beautiful flowers to notice."

"Oh my God, Vee!"

Aldo stops in his tracks when he sees me.

"I swear you guys are a bunch of saps! I thought Ma would've been the one crying nonstop, but it's the rest of you!"

I walk over to Aldo, offering my cheek for him to kiss, but he simply air kisses me.

"I can't smudge your makeup. I'm sorry. I just can't help myself."

Tears stream down Aldo's face while he fans himself with his hand. Connie hands him a bunch of tissues.

"Well, you'd better get yourself together before we walk down the aisle."

"Don't worry. I take my duties very seriously. You can count on me."

Ma and Aldo are giving me away. Aldo had cried when I asked him. He'd also been surprised since I hadn't asked him to give me away when I was supposed to marry Michael. Only Ma was going to give me away, but I'd asked her if she would mind sharing the duties with Aldo. He'd helped me so much after Michael and I broke up. My mother had told me Aldo was family so of course she wouldn't mind.

Aldo is dressed in a charcoal gray tuxedo, which matches Stefano's tux except that it's a little paler in color.

"Oh, before I forget, here's your corsage."

I pin onto his chest his corsage, which contains just one of the cymbidium orchids.

We spend the next hour and a half with my photographer, and before I know it, the time has arrived for me to make my procession in my gondola down the Grand Canal to St. Mark's Basilica, where Stefano and I will exchange our vows. The Basilica is the only ostentatious part of the wedding. We've decided to get married there because it's where our love affair began. And while I adore so many of the other churches in Venice, none of them hold the same allure for me as St. Mark's Basilica. The dim, gilded interior creates an intimate and sacred atmosphere that none of the other churches manage to capture.

The day is overcast, and there is a slight chill in the air. But I don't mind. To me, it's the most perfect day. As my gondola glides down the Grand Canal, I can't help thinking how lucky I am to be here in my favorite city in the world, but more importantly, to be marrying the man I'm crazy in love with. Finally, the tears come into my eyes, but I fight them off. Too late. Aldo's noticed.

"I was beginning to wonder when you'd crack!"

He pulls out of his trousers pocket a plain white handkerchief. He notices me staring at it in shock.

"Can't ruin the Fendi silk one that's in my breast pocket."

I laugh. Aldo lightly dabs the corners of my eyes.

"No damage. So were those tears of joy or sadness?"

"Joy! What would I be sad about?"

Aldo's face clouds over, but he says nothing.

"Forget I even mentioned it."

It still amazes me sometimes how much Aldo and I are psychically linked. I suddenly realize the one thought that could've made me sad today. My father. Of course, he's been in my mind, and I wish he could be here to give me away. But I know his spirit is present. For some reason today, I feel him more than I ever have since he died.

"You were referring to my father."

Aldo smiles. "You're a witch, you know that? How do you know my thoughts so much of the time?"

"If I'm a witch, you're a warlock, since you often know my thoughts as well. I wasn't crying because of my father. I was thinking how lucky and blessed I am."

"Good. I'm glad to hear they were tears of joy."

Aldo looks off into the distance. I see tears forming in his eyes. He quickly puts his sunglasses on.

"I'm really going to miss you."

"Oh, Aldo. I'm going to miss you, too."

He pulls his cheap handkerchief out of his trousers again and dabs at his eyes.

I squeeze his hand gently.

"You have an excuse now to come to Venice whenever you feel like it. And you can always stay with us."

Aldo shakes his finger at me. "Watch what you promise. I might take you up on it more times than you and your Rick Springfield lookalike of a husband will appreciate."

I laugh. "You noticed that too about him, huh?"

"How could I not, being the eighties child that I am?"

"You and me both. I noticed it the first time I laid eyes on him."

"I bet. Stefano told me how you played a little hard to get in the beginning. It's too bad I wasn't here. I would've knocked some sense into your head and made you see what you were missing in bed."

"And how are you so sure he's great in bed?"

"Remember, I'm a warlock. I can sense these things."

I give Aldo a mischievous smile, which is testimony enough that what he's guessed at is true.

I glance at the gondola behind me that's carrying my mother, sisters, and Angela. They're talking and laughing. I'm so happy we're all here together.

We arrive at St. Mark's Square. I wait in the gondola with Aldo until my family and Angela have disembarked. Aldo helps me out of the gondola. He quickly fluffs out my dress, patting it down with his palms to make sure there are no wrinkles. My photographer, who rode in my gondola so that he could snap photos of me on the ride over, takes a few shots of us in front of the Basilica. Passersby and tourists stop to stare at me.

We make our way into the Basilica and down to the crypt where wedding ceremonies are held and where St. Mark's body is entombed. The space is dark and very intimate.

The quartet we've hired begins playing Bach's "Jesu, Joy of Man's Desiring." Signore Lambrusca escorts his wife down the aisle. Then Angela followed by Connie and then Rita make their way down the aisle. There is a brief pause before the notes of Handel's "Largo" fill the air. I look at Ma and Aldo. Ma finally looks like she's about to cry. I loop my arms in theirs as we begin marching slowly down the aisle. My eyes immediately seek out Stefano. He smiles as soon as he sees me. Our gazes lock on to each other's, never breaking until I reach the altar. Aldo and Ma kiss me before taking their places in the front pew. I turn around and give my bouquet to Rita. Stefano and I hold hands, smiling at each other.

Our priest, Padre Domenico, recites the entire ceremony in Italian. I feel bad for a few of my out-of-town guests who do not know the language. My heart races erratically. Stefano lightly strokes my hand with his thumb.

Padre Domenico announces that it's time for us to exchange our vows. I go first. I swallow hard. First, I say my vows in Italian, then I say them in English. Padre Domenico allowed us to do this—a small gesture to make our guests who don't speak Italian and who came all the way here feel as if they're a part of our special day.

Stefano's grip on my hand tightens before he says his vows in

English. I'm wondering if he's forgotten the small sheet of paper he wrote the English vows on. But he hasn't checked his jacket pocket. Instead, he fastens his eyes on mine and recites his vows, speaking slowly and clearly. I'm touched that he memorized the vows in English. And he hasn't mistaken any words!

At the end of the traditional wedding vows, Stefano adds, "I will always love you forever." Our wedding guests are delighted and applaud, receiving a stern glance from Padre Domenico, who without a doubt is not thrilled at Stefano's minor deviation from the traditional Catholic wedding rites. My eyes fill with tears as I silently mouth the same words to Stefano.

The Mass portion of our wedding ceremony continues. Stefano and I receive communion. After all of our guest have received communion and are kneeling in prayer, suddenly Paulie's voice rings out, "Christ!"

Stefano and I look in horror at him. I don't even want to look at Padre Domenico. Everyone is staring at Paulie as if he's transformed into a hideous beast before our eyes. I knew the chivalrous Renaissance man I'd seen the night before at our rehearsal dinner was too good to be true.

"I'm sorry! I'm sorry, Father. *Ahhh . . . mi dispiacio, Padre. Scusa!* Is that how you say it, Signora DeLuca?"

My mother shoots him the dirtiest look I have ever seen her give anyone. Her face is flaming red, and her signature knitted eyebrows are arched as if they're ready to fence. Her fists are coiled around the rosary she's holding, no doubt praying to God to finally rid me of the *malocchio* she believes has plagued me throughout life. Aldo places his hand on Ma's shoulder as if he's afraid she's going to charge Paulie.

"It's just that my video camera's battery is about to die."

I hadn't been able to book a videographer in Venice. They were all booked for my wedding day. Since Paulie was attending, I asked him if he could do it and lent him my mini camcorder. Of course, he agreed and spoke of nothing else in the days leading to my wedding. He had assured me he was practicing every day so he would get the hang of using my camcorder. How could he have forgotten to recharge the battery before the wedding?

"Non ti preoccupare. Lo faccio io." Fortunately, Giovanni, one of Stefano's cousins, comes to the rescue and says he's been recording the entire ceremony with his own camcorder, and he can continue doing so.

I breathe a sigh of relief.

Padre Domenico continues with the rest of Mass. No other disturbances occur, and soon Padre Domenico pronounces us husband and wife. Stefano and I both look at Padre Domenico for permission to kiss. We don't want to upset him any more than he has been today. Finally, his stern face breaks into a smile, and he surprises us by saying in English, "What you wait for? Kiss. Kiss."

Stefano and I kiss, and in that moment, I already feel different. I am now Valentina Lambrusca. Everyone applauds, including Padre Domenico. Stefano and I laugh. Rita returns my bouquet to me. We proceed up the aisle, and I try to make eye contact with my family and friends. Everyone looks truly happy for me. I'll never forget this feeling or this day. Even with Paulie's faux pas, the wedding ceremony was perfect.

After taking photos inside and outside the Basilica, we make our way toward our gondola, which is waiting to take us to the restaurant where we'll be having our reception. Before our gondolier begins steering us away from the dockside, our guests throw rice at us and continue throwing until we're much farther down the canal. Once they're certain they've thrown every last grain of rice, they begin loading two *vaporetti* to follow us to the reception.

"Ahhh! Alone at last!" Stefano looks into my eyes. We kiss, but much longer than the kiss that sealed our union. The gondolier begins singing. The only word that reaches my ears is *amore*.

"I can't believe you're mine." Stefano hugs me even tighter.

"I can't believe *you're* mine." I smile and push back a wisp of Stefano's hair that has blown out of place. We laugh. I place my forehead against Stefano's, and we close our eyes, reveling in this moment.

"We're going to have a very good life, Valentina."

"Yes, we are." I kiss Stefano lightly on the lips before I nestle further down into the gondola seat and wrap his arms around my waist.

We remain silent as our gondola glides down the Grand Canal. Dusk drapes this magical city that never ceases to amaze. Calmness, like none other I've felt before, washes over me as I take in Venice's beauty at twilight. The excitement of the day is making me drowsy. As I drift off to sleep, I hear my father's voice whispering something he always said to me when I was a little girl: *"Che bella fortuna. Bella fortuna."*

Recipes for *Bella Fortuna*

Palline di Limone (Glazed Lemon Cookies)

Makes 80

4 cups all-purpose flour	¾ cup sugar
1 tablespoon baking powder	3 large eggs, at room temperature
½ teaspoon salt	1 tablespoon lemon extract
8 tablespoons (1 stick) unsalted butter, at room temperature	2 teaspoons grated lemon zest
	⅓ cup milk

ICING

1½ cups confectioners' sugar
3 tablespoons fresh lemon juice

Combine the flour, baking powder, and salt.

In the large bowl of an electric mixer, beat the butter and sugar at medium speed until light and fluffy. Beat in the eggs one at a time, scraping the sides of the bowl as necessary, and beat until well blended. Beat in the lemon extract and lemon zest.

Stir in half of the flour mixture and then the milk. Add the remaining flour and stir until thoroughly incorporated. Cover and chill for at least 1 hour, or overnight.

Preheat the oven to 350° F.

Pinch off 1-inch pieces of the dough and shape them into balls. Place the balls 2 inches apart on ungreased baking sheets. Bake for 15 to 18 minutes, or until puffed but not browned. Transfer to wire racks to cool.

To make the icing: In a bowl, combine all of the confectioners' sugar and lemon juice. Stir in a few drops of water, or just enough to make the icing easy to spread. Brush the cookies generously with the icing. Let dry on wire racks.

Torta della Nonna (Grandmother's Cake)

Serves 8

FILLING

3 large egg yolks   2 tablespoons all-purpose flour
⅓ cup sugar   1 cup milk
1½ teaspoons vanilla extract   2 tablespoons orange liqueur

CAKE

1⅔ cups all-purpose flour   1 large egg, lightly beaten
½ cup sugar   1 teaspoon vanilla extract
1 teaspoon baking powder   1 egg yolk beaten with
¼ teaspoon salt   1 teaspoon water, for egg wash
8 tablespoons (1 stick)   Confectioners' sugar
    unsalted butter, cut into
    bits and softened

To make the filling: In a medium saucepan, heat the milk until bubbles form around the edges. Remove from heat.

In a medium bowl, whisk the egg yolks, sugar, and vanilla until pale yellow. Whisk in the flour. Gradually add the hot milk, whisking constantly. Transfer the mixture to the saucepan and cook over low heat, stirring constantly, until it comes to a boil. Reduce the heat and simmer for 1 minute. Scrape the custard into a bowl. Stir in the orange liqueur. Place a piece of plastic wrap directly on the surface of the custard to prevent a skin from forming, and refrigerate until chilled, 1 hour or overnight.

Preheat the oven to 350° F. Butter a 9-inch round cake pan.

To make the cake: In a large bowl, combine the flour, sugar, baking powder, and salt. With a pastry blender, cut in the butter until the mixture resembles coarse crumbs. Add the egg and vanilla and stir until a dough forms. Divide the dough in half.

Press one half of the dough evenly into the bottom of the prepared pan and ½ inch up the sides. Spread the chilled custard cream over the center of the dough, leaving a 1-inch border around the edges.

On a lightly floured surface, roll out the remaining dough into a 9½-inch circle. Drape the dough over the rolling pin and place it over the filling. Pinch the edges of the dough together to seal. Brush the egg wash over the top of the cake. With a small knife, make several slits in the top to allow steam to escape.

Bake for 30 to 35 minutes, or until golden brown on top. Let cool on a wire rack for 10 minutes. Invert the cake onto a wire rack, then invert onto another rack to cool completely. Sprinkle with confectioners' sugar before serving. Store in the refrigerator.

Lemon Wedges in Olive Oil and Vinegar

Serves 4

2–3 large lemons (the larger the better)
Salt to taste

¼ cup extra virgin olive oil
¼ cup red wine vinegar
Loaf of crusty Italian bread

Peel the lemons. Cut them into bite-size wedges. Sprinkle salt generously over lemon wedges. Drizzle the extra virgin olive oil and then the red wine vinegar over the lemon wedges. With salad tongs, toss the lemon wedges until they're coated evenly in the oil-and-vinegar dressing. (Depending on personal taste and how high your tolerance for sour foods is, you might want to add more salt or vinegar after tasting the lemon wedges.)

Break off pieces of bread and eat with the lemon wedges or dip the bread into the oil-and-vinegar dressing.

Saltimbocca (Sautéed Veal with Prosciutto and Sage)

Serves 4

Fresh sage leaves
1 pound thinly sliced veal
   cutlets

¼ pound thinly sliced prosciutto
5 tablespoons olive oil
½ cup dry white wine

Place 1 or 2 sage leaves on each veal cutlet. Place pieces of prosciutto over the sage leaves; secure the layers with toothpicks.

Heat the oil in a skillet over medium-high heat. Add the meat
packets, veal side down, and cook until nicely browned, a minute
or so, then turn and cook until the prosciutto is golden brown; take
care not to overcook the meat.

Pour the wine into the skillet and scrape up any browned bits
stuck to the bottom; cook until the wine is evaporated.

Place the meat on a platter, drizzle the pan juices over, and serve
immediately.

Cinnamon Vanilla French Toast

Serves 2–3

5 eggs
2 tablespoons milk
1 tablespoon vanilla extract
1 teaspoon ground cinnamon
   (or a little more according
   to taste preference)

Butter or canola cooking spray
10 slices challah or potato bread
   (or 2 slices of bread for every
   egg)
Maple syrup
Confectioners' sugar

Beat the eggs in a large bowl. Add the milk, vanilla, and cinnamon, and stir until thoroughly combined.

Place a tablespoon of butter in a griddle or cast-iron skillet and
simmer until butter melts (if using canola cooking spray, spray the
bottom of pan evenly).

Dip each slice of bread into the egg/milk batter and coat each side evenly. Immediately place the coated slices of bread into the griddle.

Cook about 3 minutes, or until batter seems to be absorbed from the side of bread that's facedown on the griddle, and flip over with a spatula. Cook the opposite side for again 3 minutes or until batter seems to be absorbed.

Transfer cooked slices of French toast into an oven-proof dish to keep warm until all of the slices of bread have been cooked.

Drizzle with maple syrup. Sprinkle with confectioners' sugar.

Fried Meatballs

Serves 8–10

1½ pounds of ground beef (or whatever meat you prefer: turkey, veal, etc.)	2 cloves of garlic, finely chopped
	2 tablespoons of pecorino romano cheese
1 tablespoon of chopped parsley	1 tablespoon of red cooking wine
2 eggs, lightly beaten	Canola oil
1 cup of seasoned bread crumbs	Ground black pepper to taste

Place the ground meat in a large bowl. Add the remaining ingredients.

Using your hands, incorporate the ingredients into the meat. Keep kneading the meat until all of the ingredients are thoroughly blended into the meat.

Shape the meat into a large ball. If it seems too dry, add a teaspoon of water, then knead the meat again. (Be careful not to add too much water.)

Pinch off pieces of meat and shape into 2-inch balls.

Heat canola oil in a skillet over medium heat (about 1 minute).

Carefully lower meatballs into skillet. Cook until meat is firm and a deep golden brown (about 2 minutes). Turn meatballs over to cook other side.

Drain cooked meatballs on paper towels in a plate.

Some of these recipes were adapted from the following cookbooks: *La Dolce Vita* and *Sophia Loren's Recipes and Memories*. For more recipes, special reading group features, or to invite Rosanna to visit your book club in person or via phone/Skype, check out www.RosannaChiofalo.com.

**Please turn the page for a very special
Q&A with Rosanna Chiofalo.**

How do you pronounce your last name?

KEY-OH-FAH-LO.

What inspired you to write a novel?

Since I was a child, I always wanted to write a novel someday. I began to seriously write in college. Like many other aspiring writers, I had writer's block and attempted several novels but then abandoned them as I got stuck. It's ironic because a few years ago, I consciously decided to give myself a break from writing or even thinking about my writing. I just needed to stop pressuring myself so much and just walk away from it for a little while to get a better perspective. Deep down, I knew I would return to writing someday. Four years ago, I relocated to Austin, Texas, and I was doing lots of freelance copywriting for several book publishing houses. It was different from when I was an in-house copywriter and copy director since I was writing so many assignments at once as opposed to revising mostly what my freelance copywriters were doing for me. I think being forced to complete so many freelance writing assignments under deadline made me accustomed to writing and not overthinking it, which is what I was doing when I was working on my short stories and novels. It was quite liberating. So when I wrote the outline and first four chapters of *Bella Fortuna* to be considered for publication, the writing just flowed out of me (thank God!).

How did you get the idea for this story?

I became interested in weddings when I was planning my own six years ago. I thought it would be interesting to have a strong female character who finally finds love and becomes engaged after having to make her clients' dreams come true for so many years. I wanted to explore how so many brides-to-be fall victim to becoming obsessed with having the perfect wedding dress . . . the perfect wedding . . . even the perfect man! Valentina, who's seen the crazy behavior of her Bridezilla clients, should know better, but she, too, falls prey to wanting perfection.

Valentina and her mother, Olivia, both believe they've had bad luck or been cursed in their lives. Did you draw on your own experiences with good versus bad luck?

Superstition is very common in the Italian culture. As the daughter of Sicilian immigrants, I did often hear my relatives refer to the powerful *malocchio.* What I often heard was that a curse had been cast on someone when that person suffered a misfortune in their lives. It's funny. Just being jealous of someone could cause a curse to then be placed on the person you're envious of. I never put much stock in curses or bad and good luck, but I am a believer of fate and karma. Ever since I read *Tess of the d'Urbervilles* by Thomas Hardy for a paper I had to write in school, I became intrigued with the notion of fate versus the concept of exercising control over your own life. I do feel that ultimately everyone has the power to alter and control their destiny, but I also believe some things happen because they were meant to occur that particular way.

The secondary characters you created in *Bella Fortuna* are just as memorable as the main characters, especially with their peculiar traits and flaws. What was your intention in including these characters in the novel?

Again, I have to refer to another Victorian master of literature and inspiration to me—Charles Dickens. I always loved how Dickens created a host of characters who had idiosyncrasies. Perhaps I could relate to these characters so much since I grew up in a city as large as New York and encountered so many different types of people with various personalities and quirks. I was also trying to demonstrate how, as a society, we often judge someone based on appearances. And if someone acts in a weird way or exhibits any behavior that deviates from what society considers to be "normal," we're even quicker to condemn without making an attempt to understand their motives. Even Valentina is guilty of this, as we see several times in the novel.

Was it difficult for you to write in the more mature voice of Valentina's mother, Olivia DeLuca?

Though Olivia is quite a bit older than me, I did not have a difficult time writing in her voice. I very much enjoyed writing the chapters that focused on Olivia. Originally, when I came up with the idea for *Bella Fortuna*, I wasn't planning on Olivia having as strong of a role in the novel as she did. But when it came time to describe Olivia, I felt the only way I could do justice to her was to have the reader get to know her through her point of view. And the deeper I got into the novel the more I realized Olivia also had a compelling story to tell. I feel that once the reader learns about her history they can understand why she is so hung up on superstition and believing that fate controls our lives.

Any advice for aspiring writers?

Read, read, READ! Reading has helped me tremendously in my own writing. You can't get better at writing without reading voraciously. And don't be afraid to surrender yourself completely to your writing. Let your imagination take you where it wants to take you as you're writing.

BELLA FORTUNA

Rosanna Chiofalo

About This Guide

The suggested questions are included to enhance
your group's reading of Rosanna Chiofalo's
Bella Fortuna!

DISCUSSION QUESTIONS

1. Do you feel that Valentina has truly been "cursed in love" as she proclaims in the opening chapter of *Bella Fortuna*? Do you feel that she's been unlucky in general in life?

2. How is Valentina different from her mother in her beliefs of the mighty *malocchio* or evil eye? How are they alike in their beliefs of good versus bad luck?

3. How does Michael fit the knight-in-shining-armor stereotype where Valentina is concerned? Do you think that is a large reason why Valentina falls in love with him?

4. Do you agree with Aldo's assessment that Valentina has put Michael on such a high pedestal and that no one can live up to such high expectations? Does that make it easier to forgive Michael's transgressions later? Do you feel that Valentina's expectations of Michael are unrealistic?

5. Discuss the concept of "forgive and forget" and the pros and cons of either forgiving and forgetting or not forgiving and holding on to a grudge. Do you feel that Valentina is justified in her refusal to forgive Tracy when she sees her at her shop? Do you feel that Valentina was harsh? How might Valentina have handled the situation with Tracy in her shop differently?

6. Valentina is close to her family. But we also see she has a special relationship with her neighbors and the people in her neighborhood. Which is your favorite neighbor and why? Which is your least favorite neighbor and why? Do you feel that the neighbors are an extended family for Valentina?

7. What are Valentina's views on friendship with women? Do you feel that her views were shaped by Tracy's betrayal when they were in high school?

8. Valentina and Aldo share a very close friendship and bond. How are they alike and/or different?

9. For most women, weddings are a milestone, and they want their big day to be perfect. Do you feel that Valentina has placed too much importance on having the perfect wedding with Michael? Do you think Valentina is guilty of falling more in love with the notion of getting married than falling in love with Michael?

10. What does Valentina's wedding dress symbolize for her? What does the dress symbolize for her mother? Do you agree with Michael after he has walked in on her gown fitting that she should drop the shorter front hem of her dress? What do you think are his real motives in wanting a more traditional dress for Valentina?

11. Do you believe that Sonia, the teenage fortune-teller Olivia goes to see, truly has "the power"?

12. Do you think it was wise for Valentina to go to Venice after her engagement to Michael is broken? How does the trip hinder her initially from moving on with her life? How does it help her come to terms with what she's lost?

13. How is Stefano different from Michael? Why do you think Valentina falls for him?

14. After Valentina returns to New York and visits Tracy's mother, she learns that Tracy seems to have changed her ways. Did you feel compassion for Tracy? Was it easier to understand her actions toward Valentina when they were in high school?

15. What did you think of Valentina's enormous gesture of giving Tracy's mother her wedding dress? Do you feel that her action has truly brought her peace?

16. Valentina regrets not having forgiven Tracy. Do you think she should have been more understanding toward Michael when he reveals the secret he'd been keeping from her? Why do you think she is not ready to forgive him? Do you think she ever will? Do you think they can ever be friends?

17. How are Valentina's wedding plans to Stefano different from her plans for her first wedding? Do you feel that she's grown?

18. What did you think of her choice in wedding gown for her wedding to Stefano? Did you like it more than the dress she was supposed to wear to her wedding with Michael? Which gown do you feel represented accurately who she was?

19. How do Valentina's relationships with Michael and Stefano mirror her mother's relationships with her first love, Salvatore, and her husband, Nicola? How much did fate play a role in whom they fell in love with?

20. Olivia shares with Salvatore what Connie has told her about the Cherokee Indians' belief that each stage of our lives—childhood, adolescence, adulthood, and old age—is a different life, almost like a reincarnation. Do you agree with this Cherokee belief? How has Olivia reinvented herself in every stage of her life? How has Valentina?

21. How have Olivia's views on bad luck changed toward the end of the novel? How have Valentina's changed?